CHRIS WILLRICH

THE SCROLL OF YEARS

A GAUNT AND BONE NOVEL

an imprint of **Prometheus Books**
Amherst, NY

Published 2013 by Pyr®, an imprint of Prometheus Books

"The Thief with Two Deaths" originally appeared in *The Magazine of Fantasy & Science Fiction*, June 2000.

Cover illustration © Kerem Beyit
Cover design by Nicole Sommer-Lecht

Inquiries should be addressed to

Pyr
59 John Glenn Drive
Amherst, New York 14228–2119
VOICE: 716–691–0133
FAX: 716–691–0137
WWW.PYRSF.COM

17 16 15 14 13   5 4 3 2 1

Library of Congress Cataloging-in-Publication Data

Willrich, Chris, 1967–
    The scroll of years : a gaunt and bone novel / by Chris Willrich.
        pages cm
    ISBN 978–1–61614–813–3 (pbk.)
    ISBN 978–1–61614–814–0 (ebook)
    I. Title.

PS3623.I57775S37 2013
813'.6—dc23

2013022378

Printed in the United States of America

For Becky

CONTENTS

ACKNOWLEDGMENTS

Gaunt and Bone would not exist at all without Gordon Van Gelder, editor of *The Magazine of Fantasy & Science Fiction*. Some supporting characters in their adventures were suggested by Andrew McCool, Becky Willrich, and Mike Wolfson. I'm grateful to many others who've helped keep the rogues on the road with advice, encouragement, or support, including John Joseph Adams, Scott H. Andrews, Carla Campbell, Crystalwizard, Jim Frenkel, Phoebe Harris, Matthew Hughes, Nik Hawkins, Howard Andrew Jones, Jade Lee, Susan McAlexander, John Morressy, John O'Neill, Bev Olson, Robert Rhodes, Anne Rohweder, Scott Stanton, Scott Taylor, and Carl and Mavis Willrich.

In making the patchwork quilt called "Qiangguo" I am indebted to many people. My late mother-in-law Jane Eades would sometimes tell stories she heard as a girl in China, and a couple of those tales are in this book. Ann Hsu, Larry Hsu, Paul T. S. Lee, and Shu-Hua Liu helped with language questions. Paul also contributed the name Meteor-Plum. The poems of the "sage painter" are variations on the Cold Mountain poems of Hanshan, which I am fortunate to have encountered in translations by Red Pine and Gary Snyder. Several nonfiction works served as inspiration, particularly *God's Chinese Son* and *The Search for Modern China* by Jonathan Spence, *The Arts of China* by Michael Sullivan, and the James Legge translation of the *Tao Te Ching*. However, any foolishness in how I have used this material is wholly my own.

I am particularly grateful to my agent, Joe Monti, to my editor at Pyr, Lou Anders, and to my sharp-eyed copyeditor Gabrielle Harbowy. And most especially to my wife Becky, whose reaction to my writing ambitions was never "Are you kidding?" but always "Go for it."

PROLOGUE

The howls of trained springfangs fluted through the gorge. Someone in the temple had seen him, or they'd been loosed for someone else. Imago Bone froze. Springfangs could hear a rabbit scratch itself a mile off.

But the Door of Penitence was not going to come to him.

He shifted until he sat, there on the track he'd just stumbled upon amid the boulders flanking this desert ravine, and with the silence due him from long years of thieving, Bone removed his boots. His bare feet greeted the cooling desert air. He'd never walked this particular track, but he knew the Brothers and Sisters of the Swan, surely with love and mercy in their hearts, had set pit traps here. Nevertheless, it was his best chance. In the ebbing sunset, casting jagged red-edged shadows everywhere like a promise of future blood, he had to trust to his feet.

For speed Bone had buried his pack half a day back, and thus as he stood he laced the boots together and tied them to his belt, so that their jostling could deliver a metaphorical kick in the behind. He could use all the motivation he could get.

He picked his way along the path, his progress slowing as the sun departed. Overhead the Sanctuary glowed pink, a granite promontory painted and sculpted to resemble a titanic, ravaged white feather that had crashed to earth. By now there should be a light high in the upper sanctum, but that window was dark. Below too, shadows pooled everywhere. Lighting like a grasshopper from rock to rock, Bone squinted for thief-worthy landing spots. Increasingly he relied on the skin of his feet to test those stones, and soon he less resembled a locust than a water-strider as he stretched out one leg, then the other.

More howls, closer now. With the gorge's echoes he could not determine the direction. Time for the boots? No.

Nothing we do is direct. The words of Master Sidewinder came to Bone, borne on memory's winds from Bone's first night amid the thousand towers of Palmary. *Our work is too delicate for that. We do not fight, save by ambush. We pass the paucity of doors, where a wealth of windows awaits. Why stalk an Everlux amid its score of guards, when a gawking noblewoman's necklace will do as nicely?*

Why run races with springfangs? Imago Bone wished he could answer his long-dead teacher. Success would have to do for his reply.

If he could continue slow and silent, he might have a chance. Already he could discern a white wall beyond the oranges, browns, and shrub-covered greens of the narrow path, with an iron door set into it. Peace and security, that contrast promised, though not for him. He thought of his lover awaiting him, days away in the desert. It was hard to maintain this deliberate pace. He wanted to demolish the distance between himself and his answers.

But even penitents on their way to and from ordeals in the Sandboil took this path slowly, avoiding the sharpest rocks. And the pits.

His right foot was just brushing upon an unusually large and inviting flat slab of a stone, when he had a vision of this bend in the path as seen from above, on the day when Brother Clement had, perhaps unwisely, shown Bone the bell loft. Looking down, Bone had observed this track snaking amid the rugged scree on the north side of the gorge, and a line of little figures just reaching this bend. Not for the first time, the city thief had wondered at the religious fervor that brought this order out into the desert, twenty miles from the shady spires of Palmary. The believers of the Swan (his lover included, depending upon her mood) even admitted their goddess was dead. Yet as if by some principle of sympathy, they displayed great talent for ushering others to the same state. Bone had noted then, how the penitents' leader had them detour well around the flat stone. He'd thought it peculiar at the time . . .

He paused, precarious, foot extended.

It was at that moment that the springfangs growled.

Bone looked up and saw that the beasts had not caught up with him after all.

They had instead been waiting for him, hiding behind the rocks on either side of the path.

The two lithe creatures scrambled atop boulders, regarding their prey. Heart hammering, he regarded them back. They had the bulk of bears and the grace of leopards. Their coats were a swirl of oranges, reds, yellows, and browns, and by day they were well camouflaged for the desert. In the moonless dusk they appeared scabrous, save for the slitted eyes that glimmered in the last rays of the sun, and the long, tapered ears that jabbed backward like daggers poised to throw.

Bone wanted to throw one of his own daggers, but at best that would slow one of the twain. The springfangs made rattling sounds in their throats and bared their teeth.

It was the teeth of springfangs that made them the stuff of scholarly feuds and campfire legends. Each boasted an asymmetrical set, so that one of the pair bore an oversized saber-like canine upon the left side, and the other brandished a matching tooth upon the right. The skin on the opposing side of the mouth was thin and readily pulled back to reveal a phalanx of grinders. Some scholars and campfire wags had it that ancient wizards bred matched pairs to drag their chariots and rend their enemies. Whatever their origins, today a mated duo would hunt side-by-side, their synchronized attacks simulating one voracious maw.

Bone wished for his own mate about now. In his mind's eye he saw Persimmon Gaunt beside him, her red tresses an answer to the sunset, the rose-and-spiderweb tattoo upon her cheek a symbol of her passion and intellect, the daggers in her hands twin promises that someone watched his back.

But it was Persimmon, pregnant in their hideaway, who was depending upon him.

He edged backward . . . backward . . . wanting every bit of running start he could manage, keeping his eyes on the springfangs, hoping their instincts would overcome any training regarding this path, avoiding their predators' gazes and watching their haunches, awaiting the telltale quiver that presaged their leaps—

Now. He took a running jump, aiming well beyond the wide, flat stone.

The springfangs leapt half a heartbeat later, converging upon the dust he'd left behind. But one took a wild swipe mid-air and buffeted Bone.

He stumbled hard onto the path, the wind knocked from him. He scrambled to his feet, getting a glimpse of the beasts coiling into crouches and launching themselves into a run.

Their charge led them over the area he'd found suspicious.

With a crack of wicker, a clatter of sand and stones, and twin yowls of outrage, the springfangs fell into the trap. A scream confirmed there was something pointy down below.

But Bone was barely conscious of this, for he was lurching down the path as fast as he could manage. No time for finesse. With feet bleeding, but no worse, he fairly collided with the iron door.

We do not celebrate our victories, came Master Sidewinder's voice, *until we are safely in our dens.* Bone was a long way from celebrating. Panting, he eyed the lock. He was familiar with the work of all Palmary's locksmiths and many in Amberhorn to the north. Breaking into their workshops was once a favorite pastime of his. He carried a dozen customized picks.

But to identify the maker, and choose the right pick, in this light . . . The lock appeared to be a Hookworm Special. No, a Dodder Number Nine. . . . The half-diamond pick was called for . . . But the Xenocrates Conundrum greatly resembled the mid-series Dodders and required the snake-rake . . .

With a screech one of the springfangs clawed its way out of the pit. It lost no time sighting Bone and seeking vengeance for its howling mate.

Bone snatched the half-diamond pick, rattled the lock, and swung the iron door open. He barely registered his triumph and the alcove beyond as he slipped inside and flung the door shut.

As he clutched the bolt the springfang slammed the door back open, hurling Bone against the wall.

Luck was with Bone in two respects. First, the alcove was small and opened directly onto a wide stairway heading down; the springfang's momentum carried it into a tumbling plummet. Second, there were also two narrow stairways up, and one was close beside him.

He scrambled upward without another thought. Growls (and perhaps human screams) echoed through the Sanctuary of the Fallen Feather, but he had no time for them. His objective was in the tower in any case. That he might reach it rather more noisily than planned could not be helped.

The room he reached held desert survival gear—robes, dried meat and fruit, packs, tents and the like—and as there were many wicker boxes, Bone shoved several of them into the stairway, plugging that access point. Angry growls confirmed he was followed. He ducked through a beaded curtain, recalling with annoyance that the Sanctuary interior contained few actual doors.

He entered a hallway and realized at once something was wrong here. Something other than the bloody-footed thief and the bloody-minded springfang, that is.

There were no Brothers or Sisters, and the tapestries depicting the Swan Goddess lofting an ocean in her feathers and quenching the scorching primeval sun lay torn and strewn. Here and there lay a bloodstain upon the wall or floor.

Bone had no time to wonder about it. He ripped strips from a holy tapestry to bind his oozing soles before, wincing, he reunited his boots with his feet. Even so, the blood he'd left already would lead the springfang here before long. He got his bearings and found a spiral stairway ascending toward the upper sanctum. He estimated his footpads at the level of two *mouses* in his personal scale of sound, but his taxed lungs were forcing his labored breaths toward three.

Alas, Master Sidewinder once said, *we must keep breathing. Occupational hazard.*

Bone gasped his way out into a window-lined hallway lit with the last rays of the sun and the dying flickers of neglected torches. There a young monk, draped in an oversized robe, stood regarding the desert.

"Brother Tadros," Bone said, recognizing him, "you must run!"

The gangly youth, whose garments always either smothered him or revealed his ankles, simply kept gazing out at the dimming red-orange land. Tower-fires in Palmary glowed upon the horizon. Far to the east, Persimmon's canyon home betrayed no light.

"Tadros, it's Imago Bone. You remember. Gaunt and I came here a few months ago. No one trusted us, but we're used to that. You were always kindly, at least . . ."

Brother Tadros slowly turned to stare at Bone. There was no hint of recognition. Bone, a lean-faced man with dark hair gone sandy-colored from long exposure to the sun, and bearing distinctive scars upon each cheek, one the gift of a blade, the other of a flame, was used to being remembered. Tadros' lack of reaction was more unnerving than any scream.

"You thought we'd left," Bone went on, searching for a glimmer of a response, "but your elders have been hiding us. I sneak in once a month to see Brother Clement for news and supplies. I usually take my time and climb the tower at night, but now . . . I thought something was amiss. Last night I saw the Sanctuary light swinging like a pendulum."

"In fire and glass," Brother Tadros murmured, as though from as far away as Qiangguo, "we are purged."

"That doesn't sound like Swan talk," Bone muttered. "Come on."

He got an arm around Tadros, and while the youth did not resist, it took some effort to steer him to the upper sanctum.

This was a small chapel reserved for the use of the Sanctuary's elders, for those times when their administrative duties permitted only brief observances. The true glory of the Sanctuary of the Fallen Feather was in the public sanctum, which could hold scores of visitors. This one possessed but three pews, a modest stone altar in the likeness of a swan, an earthenware bowl for sacramental rainwater, and a candleholder of red glass hanging from a steel chain. Four open-air windows allowed the shining glass to be seen from miles off.

Pews were overturned, and there were red stains near the altar. The bowl was smashed and the Sanctuary light was dark. The wind from the windows raised a chill.

"Imago Bone," rasped a voice from beneath a pew. "Such remarkable timing."

An old monk, with tufts of white hair cut to resemble wings, stared out at Bone. Tonight his eyes even had the wide round look of a swan's.

"Clement," Bone began.

"You and your lover have ravaged this place," Brother Clement said, crawling out from his hiding place with a bitter scowl, "as surely as if you had set fire to it. How fitting that you are here a day early, but still only just after your enemies have left."

"Clement, later you can curse me from here to the Starborn Sea, but now we have to—"

The springfang leapt into the room.

It crashed into an overturned pew and smashed it away with the saber-toothed side of its mouth. Clement whirled with a speed that belied his age. "The sun is quenched!" he hissed. "Be at peace!"

At his ritualized words the springfang halted and lay down, though it kept its eyes focused upon Imago Bone.

Clement said, "I see the master thief was not so masterful on this occasion."

Retrieving his breath from whatever distant star it had fled to, and shifting away from Tadros to where he'd have the best options for flight of his own, Bone managed to say, "What has happened?"

"As I said, you have happened."

"We did not do this, Persimmon and I." Bone nodded to Tadros. "What has been done to *him*?"

"Purged," Tadros whispered.

Clement placed a shaking hand upon his own temple. "He has been robbed of mind. As were Sister Una and Brother Fion. Perhaps others, I do not know. All is chaos. Many were robbed of life, and perhaps they are better off. Your enemies departed only recently. We are fortunate most of our number were in Palmary to receive a ship from Mother Church in Swanisle, although perhaps it was our weakness that brought *them* upon us—"

"Who, Clement! Damn it, who did this?"

"The assassins of mind. They who are known as Night's Auditors."

Bone steadied himself with the altar. As he did so, the springfang looked as though it might relieve Bone of his throat, command or no command. "I have heard of them . . . They leave no mark . . . They hunt kings at the behest of kings . . ."

"They were hunting *you*. You and the mad poet you call your lover. You told us you were adventurers once, but no more. That you had decided to call it quits to savagery and sorcery and settle down. You hinted you had enemies, and of course we grant sanctuary to any who ask, with no questions. But you never said how powerful your enemies were!"

"I did not know the kleptomancers would send *them*," Bone said. "I did not know we mattered so much . . ."

Brother Clement raised his quivering hands. "Tell me no more! Lest they return and claim more souls!"

"You . . . you talked."

"Of course I talked! I told them everything about you. Persimmon Gaunt and Imago Bone, poet and thief, defying law and sensibility and nature itself, weaving drunkenly about the West until daring to grasp at a mundane life. Daring to start a *family*." Clement nearly spat the word. "As if you were normal human beings, and not lost souls."

"Did you tell them where?"

"I pointed from that very window."

Bone's dagger was out and at Clement's throat. The springfang rose, a rattle in its gullet.

"Blood," Tadros whispered.

"What would you have me do?" Clement said, sweat beading upon his forehead. "You brought this upon us. I saw good folk robbed forever of their wits, made into human cattle. I saw others slaughtered. Including some who'd sought sanctuary of their own. What good would I be to anyone if they sucked the brains from me? They would have had the knowledge they wished either way. And this way . . . Perhaps. Perhaps I can help."

Bone wanted the word *help* to end with a screeching gasp, and let the Brother's treacherous blood spurt hot upon his blade. But then the springfang would be upon him, and there would be no hope for Persimmon Gaunt.

Bone lowered the dagger, which remained as dry as his voice. "When did they leave?"

"Perhaps twenty minutes ago, on horseback, down the gorge."

Bone looked to Tadros, and back again to Clement. "And you lay cowering here? While your people suffered?"

"I blew the silent whistle for the springfangs," Brother Clement said. "In hopes they would secure our vengeance. If they failed, I wished to stay hidden."

"They found me instead."

"That does not altogether displease me."

"I have no hope of outrunning riders."

"You will not be running." Brother Clement turned and whispered into the springfang's tapered ears. He nodded to Bone. "You will be riding Smoke."

Bone regarded his recent opponent. "That animal is not meant for riding."

"Then your lover is doomed."

"I will ride."

"I take it," Brother Clement said, "her mate is dead."

"He is in your pit."

Clement lowered his head. "They were trained to avoid the traps."

"I made him forget his training."

Clement's stare was as sharp as Bone's dagger. "Take me to him."

They left Brother Tadros in the sanctum, his words "death and dust" drifting in the air behind them.

The moon was up as they reached the pit upon the penitents' path. Brother Clement slid into the trap and put his hand upon the springfang that lay there unmoving, with a spike driven through its neck.

"Mirage," Clement said, "is dead." Smoke moaned. Cool air ruffled Bone's desert robe. That, surely, was why he shivered.

"Gaunt yet lives," Bone said. *And the life growing within her.*

"Then save her if you can," said Clement, returning to the path. "But I charge you with one task, one thing only in return for all we have sacrificed. Kill Smoke, once she has borne you to Persimmon Gaunt."

"What?"

"Springfangs mate more completely than any other beings. Next to that union, human love is as a tidepool beside the ocean. Smoke will always be a fragment now, in pain. If you truly bear love within you, thief, do not rob her of her release."

Bone nodded. Smoke crouched and he climbed upon her back, wrapping his arms and legs as best he could about her powerful form. Feeling her breath and pulse and warmth, it was as if he hugged a compact volcano. "Clement—"

"Do not thank me, or apologize, or do anything but leave this place, Imago Bone, and go as far away as the land of the stars' rising."

"Then I take my leave."

"Smoke—" commanded Clement, and the shout was also a farewell. "Now!"

And there came a rush that made the landscape a blur of moonlit boulders, and which left Imago Bone clutching the beast with all his strength, as if the force of gravity was now a phenomenon that originated with the Sanctuary of the Fallen Feather and its grief. He could imagine Master Sidewinder wincing at the insane careening charge of his former student across the desert, but he could not honor the memory of his mentor's subtlety any longer. His work was too urgent for that.

The day of the assassins dawned with a hint of rain amid the coiling clouds threading the gold-and-turquoise sky. The poet Persimmon Gaunt emerged from a cave, stretched, noted the blazing beauty of the morning, and threw up over the cliff.

That business done, she arranged a set of buckets and pots and bowls here and there on the canyon terrace. Rainwater wasn't to be wasted, especially when one battled nausea every morning. She knew there was some risk of discovery (she could imagine Bone chiding her), for a bucket open to the rain was also open to sight. But an enemy would have to hunt deep within this rocky maze to glimpse the containers. And for Gaunt to trek down to the stream bore its own risks.

For all that she was not yet showing, her body reminded her of its condition every day, and she had to be more careful in everything now. Her mother and sisters in distant, misty Swanisle would be aghast to see her facing pregnancy in her desert, in the company of her thief. With an unexpected pang she imagined the care they would now be giving her, and the ample amounts of water on hand, and the eggs and milk and pork, and the green expanse of County Gaunt all around.

Then she imagined the chiding, the nagging, the scorn.

There were ballads about women like her, women who ran off into the wide world, sometimes hooking up with similarly rootless men. Indeed, she'd written a few. Audiences liked it if the protagonists perished weeping, pining for small farms and cramped rooms and respectability. She'd given them what they wanted, for the coin that had bought her—so far—her real ending, of freedom and marvels beheld.

And one more marvel still to come.

She patted her still-flat belly and returned to her empire, a collection of cool caves set halfway up the wall of a side gorge of the great canyon, filled with simple furniture and mementos, and festooned with ropes to trigger traps. For a time she'd feared this outlaw haven would seem an imprisonment after adventures down many roads, among mountains and forests and seas and tundra.

In fact, staying in one spot had opened a door for her, of sorts.

One of her "rooms," well-lit by the rising sun, was her treasure house. While Bone's own dark vault contained a clutch of jewels, coins, and three magical prizes, her bright domain was piled with books, and paper, and quills, and ink. When her various tasks were done, she could contemplate the intricate rockscape and the wide clear sky, or delve into the realms of history and fancy; and when her mind was filled, she could record her own impressions until evening. It was in this place that she'd already completed her *Greylight Idylls*, a feat impossible under the hardships of the road.

And now that her characters were reconciled to the death of the sun and the doom of everything, Gaunt had to accept that destroying the world twice would be repetitive. Memories swirled around her like dust devils. She wondered if the stuff of her recent life could inspire her.

Gaunt snapped a stick from a nearby bush. She did not want to waste paper and ink. Her wax tablet was at the far end of the cave, and in any event she associated it with travel. She swished one title after another into the sand, the thin shadows raised by the furrows offering a kind of insubstantial ink. One by one she swept all away. As time passed, clouds greyed the sky and raindrops fell, plinking inside the buckets and spattering the sand. Still she scribbled. Her eyes lingered on the words *The Book of Tattered Days*.

The sun tore briefly through the gloom.

The thin shadow of the tracing was consumed by the thick shadow of a man.

A man who had just now managed to silently scale the cliff.

Persimmon Gaunt did not think—not until she did three things. She sprang to her feet, threw her dagger, and sprinted into the caves. As she departed her treasure house for the deeper chambers, she paused only to snatch up her wax tablet and to yank upon the cord that collapsed her bookshelves over the opening. The same trigger toppled kitchenware to block the main cave.

An image of the intruder only now entered her mind: a man in black leather who could not possibly be Imago Bone.

Indeed, he could not possibly be alive, for he had a vast, jagged shard of mirrored glass embedded in his skull.

But perhaps worse, within that glass she thought she'd glimpsed herself, and not as a reflection. She had been standing at a barred tower window, alone.

"You cannot escape."

The man's curiously gentle voice followed her like the pattering of the rain into the sitting room. It was punctuated with the sounds of shattering wood and crumbling stone.

"The climb may have wearied me, Persimmon of County Gaunt. But as my strength returns, the shard's futures grow clearer."

She passed many mementos, lit by shafts of light from fissures in the ceiling—a bit of sailcloth from a pirate ship, a river stone from Swanisle, a ptarmigan feather from the tundra, a seashell from the drowned mountains of the South, a chip of peculiarly hovering stone from a wizard's tower—and ascended a rocky slope, ducking through the low entrance to Bone's haven and tugging another cord.

A kingwood portcullis, hauled here with great difficulty weeks ago, whacked down in front of the treasure room.

She took back all the curses she'd flung at Bone for that particular plan. As she sought the three magical souvenirs from the wizard's tower, she heard the man knocking aside her precious books from his path.

"You will compose no more poems, Persimmon. You shall have but one more journey. Be at peace! Life's conundrums will be for others to fathom. Life's wonders will be for other eyes. Accept this like a human being. Do not wriggle like a fish within a net."

She opened a teak box and grabbed the vial of ur-glue, the flask of luck-draught, and the jar of horomire. These were alchemical treasures of a lifetime which she and Bone might never possess again.

She shoved the ur-glue into a pocket, chugged the luckdraught in one burning gulp, and raised the horomire to the light. The oozy substance was the color of yesterday's sunset and it responded but sluggishly to her tipping and turning, as if it acknowledged gravity's pleadings only after a contemplative sip of tea.

A new voice spoke, rasping as with a throat full of dust. "That will not save you, Persimmon of County Gaunt." The second intruder had either bypassed the kitchen's barrier, or had already slipped inside.

The man who now crouched before the portcullis also wore black, and he bore a family resemblance to the man with the shard in his brain. But this one was old, not young, pocked and hulking rather than smooth and slim. He bore an iron lantern upon a thick chain around one hand, and the hissing flame inside sometimes careened outside and skittered to catch up with the lantern's movements, as though the connection of vessel and fire was more a partner-ship gone sour than a matter of cause and effect. Traceries of light, invisible to all but a close observer, coiled outward from the flame and snapped at the portcullis, like a clutch of incandescent baby snakes.

"It is simply 'Persimmon Gaunt,'" she said, meeting the man's bloodshot eyes. "I refused to be 'Persimmon Oakdaughter.' But a surname is useful now and then." She backed away, found amid shadows the thick rope that dangled from a fissure in the ceiling. She looped it around her free hand.

"Persimmon Gaunt," said the older man, "it is our business to understand potentialities. And we have perceived that nothing within your pile of trea-sures, or in your collection of meager skills, can defeat us."

"Then you needn't be worried." She was getting a sense of the horomire's weight. She pulled at the rope, throwing her full weight into it.

All the while the luckdraught flamed through her veins and pores. She felt alight with optimism. Even if she died she knew she would look astounding while doing so. She wanted to write an epic about a former farm girl who battled assassins. She wanted to live it.

New strength burst through her and she pulled, and pulled, and was rewarded with a distant sound of rumbling stones. The rope slackened.

"Whatever that may have accomplished," the lantern bearer said, "it is too remote to affect us."

She was ready to hurl the jar, but she waited, waited . . . "Truly? Then I am but a foolish woman."

She remembered arguing with Bone. *What kind of home has a self-destruct mechanism?*

It would not be the strangest thing I've seen in the houses of the rich, he had replied. *We are not rich!*

That depends greatly on perspective.

The assassin frowned at her from beyond the portcullis. "You cannot bait me in this fashion. And Imago Bone cannot help you either. We've foreseen that only if someone who despises Bone grants him a boon can he intervene. And even were he to appear, we would deal with him."

"You have everything calculated."

"That is our business," said the younger man, who had finally broken her barricade. Gaunt winced to think of him stepping on her books.

Her first impression had been correct; he should not be alive. His face was nearly bisected by a ragged shard of magic mirror that protruded from the tip of his skull and sliced down to his nose. At times one eye or another looked askance at its shifting images. Gaunt again saw herself in the tower, which she recognized as the stronghold of the rulers of Palmary. She also perceived that within this vision she appeared slack-jawed and vacant of gaze.

"We are Night's Auditors," said the younger man. "We sift the stuff of human life, both within and without, both things dreamed and things made manifest, both past and future. It is our calling to reduce the irrational to dust, in honor of a future when all things are gridded, accounted, controlled."

"Really?" Gaunt said, and though she should have been terrified, the luckdraught still burned and perhaps more. *Closer, closer . . .* "I thought you murdered people's minds."

"That is another way we reduce the irrational."

"For gold."

"And amusement. One must earn a living. And your mind, poet, is surely a fascinating one."

"Enough," snapped the older man. "The lantern quivers with sudden new potentialities. Make this quick—"

He did not finish his command, for at that moment a mass of desert-colored fur and muscle slammed into him.

The old man was thrown across the sitting room and landed face-first upon an atlas open to a mostly hypothetical map, swirling with dragons, of the mysterious East.

The arrival of the springfang also toppled Imago Bone from its back. It seemed a wonder he had clung there at all. The face of Gaunt's lover, even with all its old scars and new discomforts, was a welcome sight. That, along with the luckdraught, made Gaunt feel flushed with triumph.

"Fool," said the young man with the shard in his head, and while his choices of fool seemed ample, Gaunt felt sure he addressed her. The springfang advanced upon him. But each nip and swipe it took, the man in black anticipated. Within the shard fluttered images of the springfang lunging and clawing—and missing.

Bone was already on his feet and giving Gaunt a tired wink. He had two daggers out and threw both in turn at the glass-maimed assassin.

Visions of blades flashed through the shard, as the man sidestepped one and ducked beneath the other.

"That's hardly fair," Bone said.

The old man had risen. An atlas burned on the floor beside him. "There is no 'fair.'" He raised the lantern, and the blob of fiery light began to burst forth from its innards. "There is only skill."

Enough. Gaunt hurled the horomire through the kingwood bars.

The shard showed the vessel smashing against the stones. The younger assassin lunged to catch it—

Blazing tendrils whipped from the older assassin's lantern to snare it—

Both were too late. The jar exploded in a burst of light that recalled the colors of dying fires, fading sunsets, scabbing blood, ancient amber. Night's Auditors, and the springfang they battled, all froze in place. As the glow died they remained in a static tableau. Glass from the jar hung mid-air. Tongues of fire from the atlas stood like ruddy ice.

Persimmon Gaunt shuddered and flushed and was drenched in sweat, as the last of the luckdraught fled her system. She felt as though she'd won a footrace or wrestled a bear or passed a full night lovemaking.

"You were correct," she told the assassins. "I could not *hurt* you . . ."

Imago Bone was not quite as lucky. He was not caught in the horomire but the tip of his boot just connected with the effect, and he could not shift his foot. "Hm. Well. Good morning, Mistress Gaunt! Well done! Care to bring me a dagger from the treasure room?"

The caves were full of such things, tucked here and there in the crevices. Gaunt found one and pulled on the portcullis' rope.

It would not budge.

"My dear, I would love to oblige," Gaunt said, "but the horomire effect appears to intersect the barrier." She tossed Bone the dagger and he caught it in mid-air. He began slicing at the boot.

"Bless and curse the work of wizards," he said. "This also suggests I will not be able to slit these fine gentlemen's throats." He rubbed his eyes, looked at her anew, expression shifting from murderous intent to almost motherly concern. "Are you well? Did they harm you?"

"Not at all, thanks to the portcullis. And the horomire. They are trapped in someone else's web for a change."

Bone paused to regard the springfang. "Good. Although that very ensnarement means I cannot honor a promise."

"How so?"

Bone studied the cave shadows. "One more thing on my conscience. I will explain later. I am sorry, Persimmon, but we must be free of this place."

She followed Bone's glance to the blazing lantern and the shining shard. Both were in their own fashion glowing yet. Furthermore, these lights were flickering in defiance of the horomire.

This place, she thought. *My home. Or so I imagined.*

In the silence that followed, the sound of pounding rain filled the cave.

"Bone," Gaunt said quickly, "it is worse than that. I have set off the rockslide mechanism." She nodded at the dangling rope.

He stared at her. "The intended result was to seal away our treasures if we needed to abandon them. I did not think you would be trapped in the treasure room."

"Am I not your greatest treasure?"

"That was not funny," he said.

She nodded. "Then get the axe."

"We chose this wood precisely for its great density—"

"Get the axe," she repeated, and there was no arguing with her voice.

He departed, swiftly returning with their heaviest weapon, thus far used exclusively against firewood. It cut into the portcullis, but with great diffidence. Bone's efforts were accompanied first by grunts and then snarls. The rain fell ever more heavily. The lights within the horomire flickered more rapidly, as if mocking Bone's work.

On Bone's next swing, the axe-head came loose from the handle. It flew into the upper reaches of the horomire and stuck there, suspended over the assassins' heads.

"Try it," Bone said.

Together they shook the portcullis. It splintered some more, but did not break.

"I do not think there is time," Gaunt conceded.

"The luckdraught," Bone said. "Drink it."

"Already done. Well, I am not drinking the ur-glue . . . Wait! Perhaps by tugging—"

"They had horses! Wait here!"

"That was not the brightest thing you have ever said, Bone," she teased, but he was already gone. Gaunt clutched the ur-glue, as this was all she could do. No, not all. She pocketed several large gems and a thick assortment of coins. She made sure her wax tablet was in easy reach.

One had to plan for survival, even if one was anticipating instead the arrival of a diverted flash flood.

Or the awakening of assassins. Already she thought she perceived a twitch of a finger, a wrinkle of an eyebrow, a drop in the level of the axe-head. Alas, it looked as though it would fall between them.

Bone returned with a rope. Together they wove it into the damaged bars of the portcullis, Gaunt dabbing the connections with the alchemical goop. The substance shimmered in an oily way, telling her she was using too much.

But Bone would be needing her more than the ur-glue. Ur-glue could not watch his back or hold his hand. Ur-glue could not sing him to sleep or kindle his body to passion. Ur-glue could not bind anything as tightly as she was bound to him.

"What are you thinking about?" he asked, looking at her face.

"The baby-to-be," she said, not exactly truthful, not entirely false.

"You will be leaving here. I'll pack your tablet. I go to the horses now."

And he was gone again.

Persimmon Gaunt prided herself on her equanimity in the face of inevitable death. Even as a child she'd perceived how her elders were terrified of the thing, and how that terror robbed them of so much living. And so she had danced in graveyards, and sketched skeletons, and composed morbid poetry, earning early the label fey.

She whispered one of her first. Not her best. But it had stayed with her.

> *Laugh in rain*
> *As water soaks*
> *Your every pore.*
> *Scoff at pain*
> *And smiling note*
> *Your every sore.*
> *Life is brief—*
> *The light will fade,*
> *The bell will ring.*
> *Grin at grief.*
> *In death's own shade*
> *The birds will sing.*

Yet the girl Persimmon had not understood everything, the woman Gaunt reflected. This instance was different. This was not mere death. This was loss.

Fool. Her thoughts echoed the word of the assassin. *Even if your hopes are slim, fight for them!*

She gathered the three remaining daggers hidden in the treasure cave, realizing here was an exceptional chance for target practice. She threw one at each assassin, and as they stuck suspended within the horomire, she reckoned that in any fair fight they would strike true. She held the last blade and hesitated. She did not know why, but she intuited that Bone's unspoken promise was to slay the springfang. Something about its eyes . . .

She might try, in this manner, to honor his pledge. But that might remove one more factor in favor of her survival.

Her family's survival.

She kept that last blade and commenced slicing at the kingwood. It was slow work. But it was work.

The springfang's tail coiled a bit, the daggers advanced, and the assassins' feet shifted by quarter-inches, when the rope stretched taut and the portcullis groaned. A distant whinny could be heard over the pounding rain.

The rope itself began to fray.

She thought of hiding at the farthest reach of the cave with her dagger ready. Instead she cut at the wood once more.

The wood gave.

A gap tore free, and the rope whipped out of sight, dragging splintered spears behind. The opening was rough and narrow and full of sharp points, but it was an opening. She wormed her way through, willing herself to move slowly enough to stay unperforated, even though she saw the man with the glass in his skull begin to smile.

She was free. She ran.

Behind her a growl erupted through the caves, an axe-blade clattered, and two men groaned in pain.

She reached the terrace and scrambled down toward the canyon floor in a fashion that under other circumstances would have been madness. At the bottom Bone waited. He waved her toward a pair of black horses snorting beside a dropped rope. One was covered in sweat. Bone pointed her toward the other, fresher-looking steed, and she did not argue.

As they mounted, behind them and high overhead two men in black stepped onto the terrace. Both were covered in blood. Gaunt saw no springfang.

"Ride!" Bone said, spurring his horse with his open-toed boot. "Do not look back!"

She rode. But look back she did, even knowing several legends citing the foolishness of such an act.

As such she was rewarded by the anticipated flash flood's arrival, bursting forth from its diversion through the ceiling-fissures of Gaunt and Bone's lower caves, filling their former home with debris and slapping the invaders aside like a giant, frothy fist.

"Do you think the flood will kill them?" she shouted over the sound of galloping hooves and the roar of waters.

"I don't think that's the key question here!"

Together they fled up a steep-sloping side canyon as they'd long-ago agreed should such a contingency arise. And just in time, for the water surged down the main path and lapped hungrily at the edges of their own. With luck they and their stolen mounts would live. But they would have to abandon the horses soon, as they had abandoned treasure, and books, and security. Perhaps there was no constancy anywhere in this world, only the road, and saying goodbye.

Goodbye to everything but each other.

As their pace slowed with the higher, rougher ground, Bone said something she could not make out. "What?"

"I promised you I would give you a home!" he shouted this time. "I am a breaker of promises!"

Lightning flashed. She thought of the springfang. She thought of the wax writing tablet he had thought to bring along, even now.

"I will go anywhere with you," she said, "through all my tattered days and as far away as the land of the stars' rising." And at first she feared he could not hear her with the rush of rock walls and the rumble of hooves and water and the roar of the sky in answer to its jagged lights.

"Good," came his reply. "Because that is where I think we must go."

PART ONE

FLYBAIT AND NEXT-ONE-A-BOY

CHAPTER I.

The six-masted junk that lurched and heaved in the spray of the Starborn Sea was called *Passport to Heaven*, or something like that. Gaunt's language skills had failed her many months ago and many ports westward, and she now relied on the translations of a well-traveled ship's cook from jungle-shrouded Kpalamaa. "Or perhaps the name translates best to *Capital Punishment*," the cook added cheerfully, leaning on the bow-rail as she waited for her assistants to heat her oven amidships. "For all their legalism, the people of Qiangguo love ambiguities."

Gaunt grunted. Her calligraphic skills were unimpaired, at least, and when she and Imago Bone had boarded this dubious vessel in Serendip she'd noted the somewhat hasty manner in which the wavy logograms had been painted upon the stern. She suspected at some point the ship had swiftly changed hands. A criminal herself, she spoke nothing of it. They could not be choosy.

By now Eshe of Kpalamaa had learned to expect a certain volubility from Gaunt and Bone. So she cocked an eyebrow at the other woman's grunt, her black hair twisting and coiling in the wind, dark freckles covering Eshe's face like strange shadows of stars. The tall cook, muscled like a fighter, given to grins, seemed at once serious and girlish, like one who has given and taken much hurt, yet refuses to surrender anything, even laughter. It was perhaps for that reason that Gaunt tolerated her company—that, and the experience the older woman had with Gaunt's condition.

"Is the baby tiring you?" Eshe asked.

"Is there tea in Qiangguo?" Gaunt snapped.

Now at eight months' pregnant, Gaunt was grateful for her rugged farm girl's body, honed by years of travel. While the bump of her belly was pronounced, and she grew weary quickly, for short stretches she was almost as sturdy as she'd been before her sojourn in the desert. She refused to stay confined to her cabin. She could imagine running the length of this ship (as she did regularly in search of a place to pee) or swimming off it and scaling the cliffs of this coast.

Well, perhaps she wouldn't go that far. Best to conserve energy. Even standing still, her body was busy. She felt the wriggling life within her kick in response to the lurch and heave of the *Passport/Punishment*, and felt pride in her unsprung offspring's vitality.

She watched the wind spill droplets from the waves' foamy peaks into the waves' dark troughs—like little cheese shavings tumbling into a baker's bowl. Her stomach groaned. (Hunger was an ongoing annoyance of pregnancy.) But Gaunt smiled a trifle, thinking of the little ocean inside her, the little one bobbing within it.

Someday I will show this to you, she promised, *or something like it. This Starborn Sea, or the Sandkiss Sea of our journey, or the Spiral Sea of home. I will teach you to love the roiling jewelscape of the water, the blinding fishnet of the light upon it, the sting of salt in the eyes, the coarse delight of brine on the tongue.*

Someday, when we are sure we're safe.

It was as if her lover detected her worries from his perch upon the mainmast, for Eshe reported, "Bone is coming."

Gaunt turned to see him scrambling down the flag-tipped bamboo pinnacle at the heart of the vast junk. In the process Bone clipped his nose upon one of the horizontal battens supporting the thin bamboo sails, slid to a hard landing upon the dark teakwood deck, where he rallied and rolled and danced his way through the crew, hard-looking men who were mostly of Qiangguo origin, though some hailed from spired Mirabad, torrid Serendip, or the mighty city-state of Harimaupura. (All of little relevance now, for their true nationality was the sea, and they now gave Bone looks suggesting he might become an honorary citizen at its bottom.) Bearded sailors, smooth-faced sailors with their hair in ponytails, bald sailors, sailors with peaked hats, sailors with eyepatches and one with a bronze nose, sailors of yellow hue, brown, or black, sailors wearing head scarves and sashed robes, sailors bearing armor and capes, sailors clad only in trousers, with rain-dragons tattooed upon their backs—all glared at the prancing Western rogue who threaded between them as nonchalantly as a sea-wind.

Eshe shot him a somewhat different look, an appraising one that, did Gaunt not know Bone so well, might have raised concern. "Is he always so . . . frenetic?" the cook asked.

"Bone's body," Gaunt said (only in private did she call him Imago, and sometimes not even then) "is perhaps best understood as the dogged manser-vant that trails his spirit."

Bone strode up to the bow, which now lay nearly in the shadow of the three ascending poop decks aft. He leapt into the triangle of ruby light from the setting sun as though it existed solely to accentuate the thief, and alighted beside Gaunt and Eshe.

He seemed to think such acrobatics would amuse Gaunt in her current condition. They did not.

Well, not enough to show, at least.

"Did you see the city?" she demanded. Ahead, across mist and the dark-ening sea, the land was like a vast green eyebrow, edged with spindly hills like grey hairs. Dark mountain spires rose beyond like tassels hung from the hat of the sky.

"I did not," he conceded. "The mists are thick upon the sea." Cockiness faded to awkwardness. With a stiff bow he returned to Eshe the spyglass he'd borrowed, a Kpalamaa artifact of teak and brass, studded with ivory cheetahs depicted running from objective to focus. He moved nearer Gaunt and rubbed her shoulder. Eshe nodded to the pair and discreetly moved amidships, where the galley puffed chimney smoke.

Bone added, "I, ah, did however glimpse the Heavenwalls."

"I suppose," she said, "you'll tell me they are really little more than cattle walls."

Eagerness lit Bone's eyes. "Far more. They are immense. They run from coast to horizon, and back again, snakily."

"Be wary of adverbs," the poet said, shifting into the circle of his arms.

Bone sighed. "They snake from coast to horizon," he said, "and back again."

"Better. Go on."

"I'd mistaken them for rock formations, until through the spyglass I regarded their regularity, the torchlit windows in their sides, the battlements upon their backs, the carved claws that jut at intervals, big as mansions. The nearer Wall's stone has a reddish hue. Peasants tend rice paddies beneath, little dark dots in shallow, gleaming water. Some miles beyond the nearer Wall, the second Wall, this of a blue-grey stone, peeks occasionally above the first. It veers close to its ruddy comrade, before lashing away to a great distance, as if to assert its independence."

Gaunt closed her eyes. "Thank you."

"I hope I am improving." As time had passed, and Gaunt had grudgingly conceded the limitations imposed by pregnancy, she'd recruited Bone as retrieval dog, handhold, and scout. His descriptions in that last role had been porridge-dull at first, but by slow degrees he'd spiced them. "We'll be around that rocky cape soon," he added, "and according to the crew you'll then see the Walls for yourself, and the capital of Riverclaw besides." The city's name, and indeed the Heavenwalls', were of course quite differently pronounced. (*Jiang Zhua* and *Tianqiang*, respectively, as best as she could tell.) But each time Gaunt and Bone tried to speak them, they earned guffaws from the crew.

Gaunt swore she would learn better. Her child might after all be growing up in the Empire of Walls (*Qiangguo*) and would need every advantage it could get. Bone coughed, and said, "That means we'll be disembarking tomorrow."

"I should hope."

He tapped nervous, clever fingers on the railing. "Um. Ships' captains, back home, sometimes perform weddings. Perhaps here . . ."

She studied his lean, scarred face, embroidered with a few recent cuts, testament to their last days in the desert and his determination to keep shaving aboard ship. A hard face. Yet it was a beloved one, one she hoped to see every day for many years. "We do not even know his language, Bone."

"Eshe can translate."

"It is too soon, Bone."

"Of course, of course. It is only the eighth month . . ."

"Imago . . ."

He smirked. "I had never expected, Persimmon, to be the wild-eyed romantic of any couple."

In truth, Gaunt had not expected that either. It was not a thing that reduced easily to words, and at times that worried the poet. She trusted sentences the way sailors trusted lines, but on this topic she felt unmoored.

"Imago, it is simply . . ."

That particular word hung like a dour-eyed seagull in the wind. *Simply* was simply said, but was often harbinger for a flock of paragraphs. *Be wary of adverbs indeed.*

But then events precluded Gaunt giving that speech, and she never learned quite what it would have been.

Without warning the ship lurched hard toward the coast.

The great vessel dwarfed any Amberhornish dromond or Eldshoren caravel, carrying over a hundred sailors. It had such a boxlike configuration Gaunt still had trouble believing it could sail, yet until now it had commanded the waves more regally than its Western counterparts. Bone had said it recalled the Treasure Fleet of the Eunuch Admiral who visited the West in Bone's youth, so long ago there were two moons in the sky. Perhaps it had been a support ship on that expedition.

Despite its size, *Passport/Punishment* had rather less rigging than a Western vessel, and from the bow it was easy to get a sense of activity topside.

Or lack of activity, rather. "No battle," Gaunt said. "No other ships in sight—though with these mists, that means little. Everyone still at their posts . . ."

"*Still* is the operative word," Bone said. "Why do they not react?"

He was right. Instead of the usual ripple of banter or laughter or song there came to her ears only the flapping of the mast-flags with their cheery red calligraphy—that, and the scampering and shouting of the dozen nearest sailors, who alone responded to the danger. But the captain in his silks? The navigator with his book? The cargo-master with his scroll? All those from amidships to the triple-tiered poop decks at the stern stood listlessly, as if transfixed by music only they could hear.

As the ship heaved toward the jagged coast these sternward sailors shifted with unconscious grace to keep their balance but otherwise stood oblivious, staring straight ahead through the ocean mists at oncoming cliffs dancing with crashing foam.

"Their minds . . ." Bone growled, drawing a dagger.

"Night's Auditors," Gaunt agreed, duplicating his action.

Bone raised his hand to the nearer crewmen, displayed his dagger, jabbed it at the stern. He pretended to draw the blade across his throat. *Danger*, he meant to say.

Gaunt waved her fingers dramatically while silently mouthing incantations. *Magic*. The sailors took the hint. They narrowed their eyes, crouched, and drew weapons.

"Where are they, Bone?" Gaunt said, squinting ahead. "Where are those monsters?"

"For that matter," Bone said as the still-lively forward crew cautiously advanced beside them, "how did they reach us? We have seen no ship. Oh . . ."

A taloned shadow crossed the deck.

Gaunt jerked her head, saw a dark cloud mass to southeast—and a winged reptilian form flying beside its cover.

"They've suborned a *dragon*?" Gaunt said. The crewmen beside her, for all the dragon-tattoos upon their bodies, muttered in dismay. This was no kindly, water-aspected dragon of the East. This fire-breather had somehow tracked Gaunt and Bone thousands of miles.

"A big one," Bone said, his greed clearly aroused despite himself. "Watch it glint." Metals glowed upon the dragon's red hide, like deposits of iron, bronze, silver, and gold embedded in a sandstone hill. "An arkendrake, or nearly so. Ready to mate or settle down and begin transmogrifying fully into mineral. The most dangerous, mercurial kind."

"Can even the auditors have such power?" Gaunt said. "And such range, to subdue the crew from there?"

"We've still our wits," Bone said, "so let's assume no to the second. Allow me a deep breath, and a good tremble . . . Now: the auditors are two in number. If one is riding the dragon at this moment, that leaves one other. Perhaps he was brought close at hand amidst the sea-mist and sunset's shadows. Swimming aboard, murdering minds from hiding. Perhaps hiding belowdecks, creeping forward . . ."

Bone jabbed his dagger toward an air-grill in the teak deck. Unusually bright lantern-light swirled and flickered in the darkness below and aft. The glow was not the natural yellow-orange of flame, but an all-too-familiar, eerie illumination that recalled bright gushes of blood. The shadows crawled, as if recoiling from the sorcerous light.

"I'll have to go down there," Bone said, grimacing. "At least there is darkness."

"Wait," said Gaunt, for steam yet rose from the kitchen, and now she saw Eshe of Kpalamaa stalk from the galley, cleaver in hand, searching for danger all around. The cook was not disappointed. For, quite apart from the dragon, the *Passport/Punishment* was now aimed at a stone arch curving over the waves like a giant's petrified hand. Erosion had mimicked finger-gaps in the vine-covered, bird-spattered stone, and the ocean splashed and sucked its way through these gaps and the grand tunnel formed by the arch—a tunnel fractionally too small for the ship to pass through. The vessel was doomed, and soon all aboard must become either landlubbers or chum, unless Night's Auditors should find them *interesting*.

The baby kicked. *Yes, little one*, Gaunt thought. *I must act.* She waved Eshe over.

"Eshe, can you ask the crew to guard the hatches?"

"Enemies below?" This was a direction for danger Eshe had not initially considered, and she looked dubiously at the teak decking.

"One enemy," Bone said.

"If a strange Westerner emerges," Gaunt said, "the men should shut their eyes, babble nonsense, and fight."

"Eccentric tactical advice," Eshe noted. "I'll relay it." She bellowed to the men, who growled their assent. They were more eager to follow her lead than the Western rogues'. Eshe echoed their suspicion when she turned back to Gaunt and Bone. "They are after *you*, aren't they? What are they?"

"The firm of Hackwroth and Lampblack," Bone said. "Known as Night's Auditors. Wizards shunned by most of their ilk, for carving minds like turkeys at harvest time."

"Apparently," Gaunt added, "even magic-workers who commit human sacrifice, annihilate villages, and connive with nameless horrors will balk at having their thoughts so smoothly sifted. So Hackwroth and Lampblack find their employment with rulers. They make exquisite assassins, often leaving the husks of their targets alive."

"I've heard of them," Eshe said quietly, surprising Gaunt. "You make interesting friends. Have you a plan?"

Gaunt nodded at the galley. "Have you hot water?"

Soon poet, thief, and cook crouched around an air-grill, bearing steaming buckets. Armed crew ringed them.

"Now," Bone whispered, "eyes shut." Gaunt did so. Out the corner of her eye she had glimpsed strange flickers of flame belowdecks, writhing like burning worms.

She heard the creaking of a lantern, the tread of footsteps upon planks, a pause, a dry cough that seemed to carry all the dust of a barren life . . .

"Pour!" Bone said.

Three buckets of searing water hissed down the grate.

Below, someone screamed. Gaunt opened her eyes.

The peculiar twisting blood-fire of the lantern-light flared below, framing a hulking shadow that spun and shook.

"We—" Gaunt began, but was interrupted by fiery tendrils hissing straight up through the gaps in the grill.

The fire coalesced in mid-air, like a miniature sun gone mad. Its gyrations reminded Gaunt of wasps caught within a water-trap.

The flame spiraled though the air. As it neared Gaunt, she swung her bucket.

There was an impact as of hitting a jellyfish; the metal of the bucket seared her hand. She dropped it with a clang, nursing her palm while glimpsing the deflected fire-ball intersecting the head of a sailor. That man gasped as the blob burned through one ear and roared out the other, a trifle brighter now.

He stood still, his shocked expression frozen forever in place. He toppled backward into the water.

The lantern-fire orbited at a distance, as if uncertain of its next move.

Gaunt was somewhat estranged from the goddess of her native Swanisle, but she nonetheless made the sign of hooked thumbs and flared fingers upon her chest. She noticed Eshe doing the same.

Bone had noticed something else. "Dragon," he said, a bit giddily, just before its shadow clawed out the sun.

The beast was indeed plunging from the sky. Even from a distance it was hard to take in completely: a body like a snake's but also like a rocky ridge, wings like a bat's but also like thunderclouds, claws like an eagle's but also like shards of obsidian, a head apt for an alligator or a volcanic cinder-cone, smile made of rubies, no simile required.

Gaunt waved everyone with a will toward the bow. Eshe joined her. Bone hesitated, knife drawn, eye upon the wandering flame. He cut at a deck line, thus retrieving a length of rope. He pulled out a vial that glittered a little.

"The ur-glue?" Gaunt said, crouching beside him. He nodded, glaring at the oncoming rocks, applying some to the rope tip.

"Take the rope," he said, before pouring three more drops of the alchemical substance into his empty bucket.

She complied, saying, "But why . . ."

The *Passport/Punishment* heaved again as it shot toward the rocks, and

Gaunt had to stop speaking to avoid retching. She looked skyward so as not to watch the ship lurch, but this did not help much, as the dragon roared toward them. She flicked her gaze aft, and at that moment a man emerged from the gangway near the galley: a pocked, hulking fellow in black leather armor, bearing a lantern upon a thick chain.

The face of Lampblack (for by now she knew him by name) bore the red welts of scalding.

The lantern was empty of light, but the man bellowed, "Flick! Take the thief's mind!" and swung the lantern in Imago Bone's direction.

The blob of flame hissed toward him.

"Gaunt!" Bone cried, raising the bucket in defiance. "Go!"

Gaunt did not take orders from Bone, but she understood his plan. They had to proceed with thread and thimble and hope.

Hers was the thread. She staggered upon the bucking deck to the bow-rail, and waited for the moment to cast the rope.

A whoosh of air and a crack of wings aft, and now the dragon was there, flapping, hovering preternaturally, nearly as large as the junk. It seized a mast, flung it upon the waters like a child playing with a tree-branch.

Between pregnancy and imminent death, Gaunt felt ready to wet herself.

Bone dueled with the fire-blob with his bucket, making the conflict seem some peculiar new martial art. He danced closer and closer to the bow, the thing named Flick following like a mad dog.

A second man in black leapt off the dragon to stand beside the first. Hackwroth, the assassin with the jagged fragment of glass flaring from his skull, was here. (Gaunt saw with satisfaction what might be a dagger-scar on his neck.)

Hackwroth nodded to Lampblack and scowled at the group near the bow.

At once, one of the sailors beside Gaunt screamed and fell.

The sailor's image appeared within Hackwroth's glass fragment, silently wailing. The body still breathed, eyes staring skyward like those of a dead fish.

"Swan be with us," Gaunt muttered.

"Agreed," Eshe said.

The ship grounded. The deck pitched, and sailors tumbled.

Gaunt somehow kept her footing, and threw the rope tipped in enchanted glue.

It hit true, adhering to a rock face just off the port bow. Eshe immediately tied off the line, bellowing commands in the language of Qiangguo. If the ship only held this position, the survivors could escape . . .

Gaunt looked to Bone. He tumbled, seemingly unbalanced, unprepared for the impact. Flick blazed in triumph and hissed toward his head—

—and Bone, successful in his feint, leapt and clamped the bucket over the flame. He drop-kicked it overboard. Flick struggled to escape but was bound for now by the ur-glue. It hissed in evident rage before disappearing into the depths like a falling star.

Its master Lampblack collapsed in seizures into the arms of his snarling colleague Hackwroth.

Bone bowed to the Night's Auditors, and fled.

Somehow in the scramble that ensued, Bone and Eshe were able to help Gaunt over the edge and the three of them alighted upon the tumble of boulders. The junk shifted and plunged further into the echoing, groaning rock tunnel, neatly trapped there. The easy escape was now gone, but more sailors were jumping into the sea. Gaunt hoped they would not be crushed.

She turned her attention to the cliff. Luckily this portion was not entirely sheer, but more a rugged slope where granite outcroppings alternated with inroads of soil and bushes and boulders. They began ascending the gentlest looking such track, but it was still rough going, with pebbles racing seaward at each step.

Hackwroth and Lampblack now rode the dragon, and it nosed toward the cliffs. There was something negligent in its wingbeats, as though mere muscles were but a perfunctory component to its magical flight. Gaunt's bad habit of looking back plagued her anew. She imagined she saw rue in that vast onyx gaze coursing with internal fires. Perhaps gnats saw such weary disgust in human eyes in the moment before swatting.

"Climb!" Bone called. But his voice faded like a stone dropping into the well of that stare. She would never move fast enough. Perhaps when she was just Persimmon Gaunt, but not as almost-a-mother. The miracle of life ensured her death.

She put one hand over her stomach, lifted her eyes to her doom. She would defy the dragon that much.

The dragon had not previously singled her out (reviewing rather the ascending sailors like a cat contemplating a line of ants) but now it fixed its vision upon her. She felt exposed by its regard, as though the furnace of the dragon's sight burned away cover, clothes, skin, dignity, grace, illusion.

It sized her up in a moment, and its expression twisted with the last emotion Gaunt expected.

Fear.

At that moment Hackwroth and Lampblack too stared at the cliff-face. "The child . . ." Hackwroth said, a cascade of images forming in the shard of glass embedded in his skull. The scenes possessed an unnatural clarity, like mountains observed through the thin air of high altitudes, and even across the gulf Gaunt was entranced. This time there was no image of Gaunt trapped alone in a tower in Palmary. She saw herself, Bone, Eshe, people of Qiangguo she did not recognize. She saw battles upon rooftops and inside caves. She saw a mighty Eastern palace and a pagoda upon a mountain. She saw a baby— wrinkled, red, and bawling its health to the world. And she saw, too, eagerness upon the face of Hackwroth, but fear as well.

The assassin was about to speak again, but the dragon prevented him. Snarling like a thunderclap, it whirled and shot out to sea.

Gaunt glimpsed its riders struggling to maintain their grip, before the dragon became a dark spot on the horizon, receding like a thrown stone.

"You . . . brandish an intimidating cleaver, Eshe," Bone remarked.

"I'll take credit in all future tellings," Eshe said.

"Enough," Gaunt said, freed of dragon-gaze and vertigo, but not of the vision of the baby. "Climb!"

The rocky, pebbly ascent gave way to a crumbly, bush-studded ascent— not as perilous, but arduous, and deadly enough if Gaunt's concentration slipped and her with it. Thus she resolutely ignored the wind-whispering trees and shrubs that dazzled in the midmorning light, and which shivered their leaves like an orchestra of tiny tambourines. She disregarded the groan of the junk settling into its rocky prison, and the stinging hint of saltwater in her eyes. Eshe led on, and Bone followed just below Gaunt's shadow, as if he considered all his remaining fortune bounded by a Gaunt-sized package.

"We will be on safe ground shortly, if we're lucky," Bone called.

Gaunt, breathing hard, could only nod.

"I do not believe in luck," Eshe said. "But because we are in Qiangguo, I'll whisper praise to my ancestors, a custom these people and mine share."

"It's said the East retains its many gods," Bone said, "while the West's are dead. I'd implore them if I could, but I don't know their names." He chuckled. "Fortunately, I do believe in luck."

"Those gods are not all dead," Eshe said, a bit archly. "Some will remember us, if we remember them."

"Perhaps!" Gaunt broke in, between hard breaths. "But while we Westerners are trapped in the East perhaps we should stick together."

"I am not exactly a Westerner," the dark Kpalamaa woman said, with a trace of amusement.

"We barbarians then! We will need a translator, Eshe. If you are seeking new employment."

Eshe narrowed her gaze, as though hearing a threat in those words. Intimations of the future seemed to swirl around Gaunt, like images in a broken mirror, like autumn leaves, like whispers.

"I could hear an offer," Eshe said.

They reached the top, and safety, and a green expanse with spindly hills peeking above a distant and enormous rosy barrier. Gaunt's small human worries seemed lost in this land, like tiny black birds against a stormy sky.

The Empire of Walls was at hand.

CHAPTER 2.

Deeper into the Empire, at the farthest point of the Red Heavenwall that the travelers could possibly have seen, a grimy girl crept toward the place where the New Year slept.

The girl, a compact sixteen-year-old with an inkspill of dark hair and a stare that made bandits blink, was named Next-One-A-Boy. She did not really believe the Nian, the monster of the New Year, dwelled in the great shadowy crack in the Heavenwall that loomed ahead, wide as a manor door at the bottom and slicing up till its narrowest crack was high as the junipers. Nor did she believe in flying-carpet fairies, goldfish people, love and justice, and other stories for babies.

She did believe in magic, however, just as she believed in corruption and unfairness and all the other things that could have you eating mud or becoming it. That was why she was here.

"This is it," said the idiot boy the Cloud and Soil Society had sent to test her. At least he was cute for a gangster. "They say an Emperor died here. He didn't die like ordinary people would." Here the boy Flybait mimed a man's death-throes, shuddering and rolling his eyes back into his head. He claimed to be fifteen, but acted twelve. Or eight. "No, he exploded in a burst of chi." To make sure she got the idea, he spread his hands while emitting a whooshing sound that delivered flecks of spittle to her face. Flybait resembled an explosion himself, a bamboo stick of a boy with tangly black hair shooting everywhere like spilled soup. Sometimes he amused her.

"I know that chi means 'breath,'" Next-One-A-Boy said, waving the air. "No need to blow yours in my face. No need to wake the Nian either."

"So you believe in it?" Flybait's eyes widened. He had never attempted this challenge.

"I believe in what I can see . . . and hear and *smell*, dog-breath." She crept forward and stared through the evening twilight at the great fissure in the wall. The moon rose, and permitted her to study the pond at the crack's base. It was big enough for a few fishing boats to work without entanglement, should any fishermen have defied the local legends. But its silver-fringed waters were empty and still. Even the Imperial soldiers perched on the Wall's nearby watchtower never ventured here, rushing past most efficiently when their business took them across the span overhead.

Her heart pounded, but she kept her voice steady. "Earthquakes happen. Emperors die. People confuse things tangled in time with things tangled in cause."

"What about the monster stories?" Flybait said. "The great shadow-beast that rises at the start of spring, that eats cats, cattle, constables?" He made a fanged mouth of his hands, began chomping the air.

The hand-monster came too close to her face and she slapped it into two contritely folded halves. She could not help but smile. "You should have been a shadow puppeteer, not a gangster," she said. "You would know, then, that shadows can trick people into seeing monsters."

"I will be a great gangster," he announced. "Five Finger Chang trusts me. I will be his right-hand man."

"His right hand has no fingers."

"I will finger many a treasure for him! So may you, if you survive your chosen initiation. No one has chosen such a feat before, not even Feng Axe-Big-As-Himself or Muttering Chung."

"I don't need your advice on crime," Next-One-A-Boy scoffed.

"Are you sure?" Flybait said with a bow, before raising something to the moonlight. "Because I think I need this snack I just stole from your pack." He started unwrapping something glistening from its lotus leaf garment.

"Give me that!" Next-One-A-Boy snatched at the rice ball, but Flybait wriggled backward like a snake.

"Sticky rice!" he said in glee. He nibbled and smiled. "Sugary sticky rice!"

"You idiot," she said. "For all you knew it was poisoned."

He stopped eating, but his voice was suspicious. "Explain what it's for, or my stomach takes over."

"It hasn't already?" She considered the eleven other rice balls in her pack. While these might be enough for her purposes, she believed in precision of effort. Moreover, twelve was an apt number. "It is bait for the Nian," she said.

"You don't really believe in the Nian," Flybait said, looking as though he did not really believe either, but did believe in food.

"I believe there's a source to the stories. There are strange creatures in the world, monsters and spirits—but humans may overcome them with cleverness and a bit of luck from Heaven. Do you want me to return to Five Finger Chang and Exceedingly Accurate Wu and tell them you ruined my plan?"

He hesitated, before slowly stretching out his hand. She snatched back the rice ball. She'd bought it from a lady of means in one of the nearby villages, named Lightning Bug, who'd taken pity on a runaway over the last month. Next-One-A-Boy had become a ghost of a servant in Lightning Bug's house, learning something of cookery (mostly how to make a meal from scraps) and even martial arts (mostly how to survive the other kind of scraps). But she could not bow and scrape and scrub forever; for all that Lightning Bug's family was kindly, submission was still submission, and reminded her too much of home. Next-One-A-Boy had made contact with the bandits hereabouts and set out upon a new career. Fear was still with her, but what she feared most was being sucked back into servitude.

She crept downward toward the dark pond and the crack beyond. By now only a suggestion of ebbing sunlight cradled the moon and stars. She was well-concealed from the nearest watchtower and suspected no one would care to arrest her anyway, if the soldiers' beliefs matched Flybait's. Flybait himself was observing from atop a rise, honoring his pledge to verify the dare, but expecting some horrible and un-choosy doom.

She waited. Stars spun.

"I'm bored," Flybait called.

"You could come down here."

"No, thank you."

"Then tell yourself a story."

"At a time like this!" Flybait scoffed.

"Best time for stories," she said. "Especially spooky stories. I'll tell you one. If you come sit beside me."

Slowly he did so, though he stared out at the dark water and the looming crack beyond. Handling males, Lightning Bug once said, was a combination of affection, discipline, and bribery. (Lightning Bug was not exactly a model of the three womanly devotions and four virtues.) Next-One-A-Boy aimed for the bribe, and told Flybait a story of another male, long ago but not so far away, using the words Lightning Bug had taught her.

THE TALE OF THE GIRL IN THE WINDOW

Centuries ago, when the Walls still grew from their tails in the desert, the son of the emperor's master architect caught the eye of the emperor's daughter.

The boy was of course destined for scholarship and was, naturally, sequestered in a country house by the sea. No girl or woman was allowed near, as he'd already shown distraction near the feminine form. Least of all would his father countenance a princess coming near the lad, for such were far beyond his station. A dalliance might upset all the master architect had worked for.

So the boy studied by the wan light of the hovel's window, memorizing the classics, gazing at the turbulent sea. There were in none of these texts the deeper feng shui secrets of his father's craft, the manipulation of the land's chi for the benefit of humankind. Rather the boy learned of literature and history and wise sayings by old masters.

To know these classics was to learn more than dusty old tales. To the elite of the Empire they were like a second language. For the naming of a classic might stand for ten thousand ordinary things.

Thus alluding to the divinatory *Book of Jagged Lines* might convey the full gamut of triumph and reversal. *The Classic of Excruciating Etiquette*, if invoked, might convey that sense of proper behavior to which all of Qiangguo aspired but none quite attained (for to fully engage the mind, the panoply of ritual must surpass the mind). The *Nine-Times-Nine Ruses* may be quoted individually, but referencing the whole work implies a universe of guile. And *The Classic of the Cardinal Directions*, with its monsters of every clime—hungry ghosts yearning for human warmth, treacherous shapeshifting foxfolk, the man-eating Nian driven away by firecrackers every New Year—is synonymous with horror and mystery, but also with childhood. Most classics are not, however, as engrossing to the young as *The Classic of the Cardinal Directions*. And so the boy's tutors had saved it for last.

Wearily he studied, plodding his way toward that treasure at the end of his bookshelf, and felt as though his youth were seeping hour by hour through a small, unscabbed wound.

Thus the boy was thoroughly distracted when a teenaged girl appeared at his window. She was pleasingly slender, and yet rich roundness was visible through clothing sewn a trifle tight. She caught his eye, and as if these two youths shared a secret joke, she giggled, running one hand in a two-second, seemingly eternal journey along the curve of her hip. She moved on, and he saw no more of her the rest of the day. Yet she was there the following day, and the day after that, again passing wordlessly by the window, again miming the caresses he himself longed to give. This was an enchanting mystery, because few people, let alone flirtatious teenage girls, were allowed to intrude upon the boy's solitude. Wrenched with desire, he at last confided with his father, hoping to learn she was a daughter of his household staff or else a village maid with friends at the manor.

The master architect was concerned. He had no idea who the girl could be. He kept watch, but when the boy was accompanied, the girl was always absent.

One night a storm arose while the boy slept in the hovel, his face planted in the *Summer and Winter Annals*. He woke with a start, and his foot brushed something covered in fur.

Terrified, he gave the thing a savage kick.

At that moment lightning split the air and the hovel as well.

The boy fell, dazzle and thunder filling his mind.

When he recovered, he searched the hovel's ruin for his classics, but none was left but *The Classic of Cardinal Directions*. He found as well the corpse of a huge fox. Thereafter his love was never seen.

His father was pleased on two counts. Not only was his son safe, but he knew of a saying, "Monsters are safest under the feet of the worthy." If one of the diabolical foxfolk would seek shelter from the heavens beside the boy, it might mean that Heaven found him particularly favored.

And the Master Architect recalled how the boy's mother had possessed in late pregnancy auspicious stretch marks upon her belly—marks that resembled two coiling dragons.

"Um, so you think the monster is one of the foxfolk?" Flybait said, looking awkward at talk of bellies and curvaceous young women. Next-One-A-Boy had no idea why her own presence might amplify his discomfort. She was plain as a rag, after all. If the boy stared at her, it just proved he was an idiot.

"I think," she said, "that this crack diverts the land's chi from whatever purpose the master architect had in mind. I am guessing chi flows into the

Walls all along their length. But here the chi leaks, and all that leftover energy takes form from the people's fears."

"I think," he said, "you should not be called Next-One-A-Boy. I think you should be called Spooky Girl."

"I am as my parents named me," she snapped.

"Crazy . . . what's that?"

Something was stirring out on the water. Moonlight and shadow and echoes and whispers converged within the great crack in the Wall, and a thing took shape from them, swirling and rippling. Cold wind blew in their faces, and with it came a rasp of vast laughter, ripe with the odor of decay.

"The Nian!" Flybait called, leaping to his feet.

"Maybe," Next-One-A-Boy said, rising and shaking. "Focus now, and help me."

"I am too busy wetting myself."

The thing was a beast of darkness and moonbeams and curdled cloud, crackling with blue lightning, in the shape of a storm-grey lion with flashing eyes and floating hair. It would have been charming at bedroll size, intimidating at man size, terrifying at horse size. It was big as a house. It pawed the water, standing eerily atop it, snorting smoke like the bonfires of all forbidden history books. It roared, and in its roar were the cries of generations of the uprooted and slaughtered. It narrowed its burning gaze at the two bandits.

Flybait surprised Next-One-A-Boy. He splashed into the water ahead of her, saying, "Run! Run away!"

This act of gallant idiocy broke her own hesitation.

She grabbed the rice ball Flybait had nibbled and threw it into the pool. The monster claimed it. Lightning flashed and rice sizzled.

"Come on!" she called to Flybait.

"So! You believe?"

"I believe you are a fool!" She grabbed his arm, dragged him uphill. Some bit of sense trickled through his feeble boy-brain and he followed.

So did the monster. Next-One-A-Boy tossed another rice ball downslope and the beast pounced upon it. She would have to tell Lightning Bug the recipe was a success.

"You have a plan, right?" Flybait babbled. "You have it all figured out. You have worked out a proper exorcism."

"I don't know! Not exactly! I do think it's a manifestation of concentrated chi. This place must be thick with it."

"What do you do with a manifestation of concentrated chi?"

"I don't know!" She threw another rice ball. "But it likes sticky rice. Everyone likes sticky rice." She rummaged in her pack and found the special rice ball with a long string sticking out. "You have a tinder box. Can you use it?"

"I am the best!" said Flybait, tapping a small bamboo tube on his belt. It was filled with paper, a piece of flint and a piece of steel attached to it by twine. "Why, once, when Five Fingers needed a distraction . . ."

"Light the fuse! I will distract!"

"Fuse?"

She did not answer, but dashed toward the Wall, tossing sticky rice balls as she went. The Nian devoured each treat in turn. Each lotus leaf wrapping bore a character representing one of the twelve animals of the zodiac. She had begun with Tiger and by now was on Pig. She hadn't thought the decorations would matter, but if the chi-beast did in fact echo the legendary New Year monster, the ordering might help.

"How are you doing?" she called out to Flybait.

"I have vast hopes! You?"

"I am losing my meal."

"I am preparing a dazzling feast!"

"The guest is coming!" She ran to the Wall and scrambled up it, for in this place the stones were splintered and rough, an earthquake-cracked tumble held in place by the surrounding structure. She tossed another rice ball (Dog) and climbed above the height of the monster, though surely not out of range. The thing made quick work of the rice ball, so she tossed the ones marked with the Rooster, the Monkey, and the Sheep. The beast that resembled the Nian raced around like an overexcited lapdog. It was taking longer to chew each ball, for it was to some degree material, and the sticky rice was gumming up its gullet. It was also paying less and less attention to its surroundings.

She had two rice balls left. She saw Flybait still struggling to light the fuse. The beast snuffled up to the Wall, and she had to throw the ball marked with the Horse. "Hurry," she murmured.

The chi-thing gulped down the morsel and took a long thoughtful look at the antics of the boy on the rise. The girl whistled and threw the last rice ball, the one marked with the sign for Snake.

Her throw was off. Like a wily serpent the rice ball landed in the grass, too near to Flybait. The monster leapt upon the ball, just inches from Flybait. The boy somehow kept working with his flint and steel.

As the thing chomped and swallowed the rice ball, Next-One-A-Boy shouted, "Here! Here! Happy New Year! May you be rich! Congratulations and good fortune, now give me a red envelope!" and anything else that crackled into her mind. It worked. The would-be Nian bounded toward her, and Next-One-A-Boy felt almost as if she too were wrapped in a lotus leaf, smelling of starch and sugar.

Behind it, Flybait struck a light. The paper in his bamboo tube burned.

He would not be in time.

Lightning Bug had told her, *You struggle too much, girl.*

With what? Next-One-A-Boy had answered.

With everything. Be like water. Let go.

Everything good I got by struggling! she had responded. *The only ones who never struggle are the dead!*

Now she was about to be dead. She had just one good way to avoid the oncoming lightning-jaws.

She let go.

Plunging toward the ground, expecting to break bones on impact, she was startled to find herself whisked aside in mid-fall by a leaping figure dressed all in black. Even the face was wreathed; only two stony eyes were revealed in the moonlight.

The leap that carried Next-One-A-Boy to safety was in its own way as astonishing as the lion of storm and shadow. They landed beside the pond, and the figure set the girl gently down.

"Who are you?" she asked.

"Someone who worries when children play with fire," said a woman's muted voice. "But it is too late now. Look."

Flybait was rushing forward, bellowing, "Rice! Yummy tasty sticky rice! Now with extra firepowder!"

For the fuse on the rice ball was lit, and the precious explosive Next-One-A-Boy had purchased and stuffed into the rice was about to go off.

The beast was still searching the Wall for its prize. It turned toward Flybait, but hesitated. Next-One-A-Boy could not let the brave fool perish for her sake. She ran toward Flybait shouting, "Yummy rice! It will be so warm in your stomach!"

Astonished, Flybait saw her and grinned with all the joy of a boy blessed with both a girl's company and an excuse to destroy things.

The beast charged them. Flybait threw.

It gulped the rice ball mid-flight, chewed, gagged, and let out a belch of lightning punctuated with firecracker farts. Colorful flashes burst inside its head. It ran this way and that as though chasing its tail. It covered its ears.

Next-One-A-Boy and Flybait had not so long ago been small children. They knew the procedure for frightening away the New Year. They stomped and clapped and whooped and screeched and bellowed *Out with the old, in with the new! Gimme red envelopes! Happy Year of the Dragon! See ya next time!*

And the Nian-thing acted as a Nian-thing should, and raced into the hills and the night, dispersing into fog as it went.

The girl and boy laughed and slapped each other on the back and hugged. "It is like they say," said Flybait. "A few smelly tanners can beat a champion."

"You may be smelly," said Next-One-A-Boy, disentangling herself. "I am not."

"You smell good," Flybait murmured.

"What?"

"I thought you were dead," he said quickly. "How did you get away?"

"I—the woman! Where is she?"

"What woman?"

"The woman in black! She helped me." Next-One-A-Boy looked back and forth, up and down, but could not spy her rescuer.

"I see no woman in black. I also see no man in black, no ox in black, no bear on stilts in black. Actually, I don't see much at all right now. Those fireworks were bright." He rubbed his eyes. "Those aren't easy to get. Where did you find them?"

"A friend." She grunted. "The soldiers may not be able to ignore the explosion," she said, and indeed there was a doubling of lights in the nearest of the Wall's watchtowers. It would take time for them to lower ladders and investigate, however.

"We'd better get going."

"You are right." She pointed at the crack in the Wall. "This is our only chance to investigate."

"What? Your parents should have named you Crazy Girl!"

"If there is any treasure to be had this night, it is through the crack."

"Huh. Lead on, Crazy Girl."

They walked along the edge of the Wall, where a sure-footed person might reach the crack and stay dry. They only slipped into the pool once. With cold ankles, Next-One-A-Boy led Flybait into the strange cave in the Wall.

The moonlight revealed hulking humanoid shadows.

"We need a torch—" she said.

"We need to run!"

"No, they're not moving. Get your fire-starter."

The absence of a rampaging monster improved Flybait's concentration, and soon his bamboo stick shone with the light of its ignited roll of paper.

"They're statues," Flybait said in awe.

The figures were of eight soldiers, standing at attention with swords drawn. They had lifelike color to their skin, hair, and gear. "That's lamellar lacquer armor," Flybait said. "These figures are old."

"Lamellar?"

"That's armor made of plates laced together. They still use it now, but the plates are metal or leather. The lacquer kind hasn't been used for centuries."

She looked at him with a bit of respect. "How do you know so much?"

"Oh, I love weapons and armor! They show up in all the best stories. These swords are dual-edged bronze, ancient style." He looked at the base of a blade. "Yes! The mark of the Bellows Falls workshop. You know, these would be valuable to collectors . . ."

She had no qualms stealing works of art, but for a moment she wondered about stealing *from* works of art. Yet deeper in she saw another, solitary statue sculpted so as to show billowing robes upon a thick, powerful-seeming bearded man, with a wide, sad face. In his hand he held not a bronze sword, but a tattered scroll.

"I think this is the Emperor who died," she whispered. She tugged on the scroll and was surprised to find that it was not only quite real, it slid easily from the hollow grasp. She pulled it out and concealed it under her tunic.

"Does he have treasure?" Flybait tore himself away from the swords and strolled over to kick the statue. He jumped on it. It did not break. He continued trying.

"That's not respectful."

"It's not a real Emperor. And he's dead. And we're bandits."

"Well, I think the statues are the treasure," she said. "I have heard that the first Emperor had an army of statues such as these, buried somewhere, lost to time. Now this later Emperor must have been honored with something similar, but on a smaller scale. The chi-beast made sure no one came here."

And that no one read the scroll, she thought, heart pounding anew.

A change in the wind brought the sounds of soldiers lowering ladders, far down the Wall. "Let's get out of here. Take as many weapons as you can, Flybait. Five Finger Chang and Exceedingly Accurate Wu will be pleased."

"You sound so confident."

It was not confidence, she thought, as they left the old Emperor face down in the hollow. It was that, scroll hidden against her chest, she now possessed the first treasure, beyond her own body's breath, that was hers alone.

As they slipped beyond the pond into the moonlight, she felt the scroll rustle a bit, as though buffeted by an unseen breeze, but that was surely her imagination.

CHAPTER 3.

Autumn fogs concealed the foreigners. While the weary crew of the *Passport/ Punishment* had staggered up the serrated coast toward the capital of Riverclaw, Gaunt, Bone, and Eshe struck north into rugged misty hills, toward the inland villages of the Ochre River.

"Better the crew not have you to blame," Eshe had told them. "I have a contact north, another Westerner, who came to preach the glories of the Swan Goddess and ended up admiring the glories of the local women. One in particular."

After a chilly night on the heights, the morning mist cleared from the valleys at either hand and they beheld downslope of their aching feet a green landscape of rivers and canals threading between the tall hills and bordered by forests. Over the land a pattern of cultivation lay like glistening lace, torn only by the higher hillcrests. Rice paddies glimmered under the sun, fringed by gardens, orchards of mulberry trees and tea bushes, and ponds adorned with fishermen in long boats. The frame of this setting was the nearer Heavenwall. It paralleled the travelers' course on their right, then many miles ahead bent across their path, underlining the far horizon. A wide, yellow-brown river emerged from the western highlands, converged with the Wall to the north, and paralleled that faux dragon into the hazy east.

"Where the river first touches the Wall," Eshe said, "there is the village of my friend."

"How much should we fear the authorities?" Bone asked.

"In the cities and big towns—much. In the countryside—little, so long as you are nondescript. The Heavenwalls, with the aid of rivers and mountains, slice the Empire into administrative regions. But the provinces can be so large, they have wild stretches that can accommodate bandit hordes."

"What, then, is the point of the Walls?" Gaunt asked, her gaze traveling to the blue-stoned Wall beyond the reddish one, meandering near and far like a basking snake. "If they do not defend the people?"

"Many reasons are given," Eshe said, "which causes one to wonder if none are true. The Blue Heavenwall's northern reaches do indeed guard against barbarians, and the Red Wall's southwestern fringe does deter the kings of the Mangrove Coast. Likewise, both Walls' inner twistings restrict the movements of bandits or rebels. They provide highways for those with the Imperial blessing. They also, to my mind, keep the provinces provincial." Eshe spread her hands to take in the vastness of the Red Heavenwall. Gaunt thought the gesture a trifle theatrical, and wondered, not for the first time, if Eshe were a trained storyteller.

"Yet all this," Eshe said, "could be accomplished with less grandiose means. And the Heavenwalls meander in ways that make little military or administrative sense. Why? Well, there are geomancers at work in the Empire, akin to those who fashioned the Western city of Palmary in the shape of a hand. Perhaps the Empire gains in some mystical fashion by marking itself with twin dragons." Eshe shook her head, smiled. In her more typical voice she said, "You will need local clothing."

"Show me a farmhouse," Bone said, "and the deed is done."

"Of course. You are a thief. This does not greatly bother me, but it might concern the authorities. I presume a thief might always carry a little gold? Then allow me to bargain with the locals."

"We are greatly relying upon her," Bone observed, lighter in pocket, when the Kpalamaa wanderer had left.

Gaunt shrugged. "There is much more to her than she claims. I suspect she does not want us to realize what a good heart she has. At any rate, we took our chances when we fled east." She ran a hand across her belly. "We do have limits, Imago. Even childless in the heart of Archaeopolis we would sometimes depend on others."

Bone silently watched Eshe's receding back.

Her venture was successful and the trio became a huddle of shy peasants, hooded against the autumn chill. The journey proved unexpectedly pleasant, as they meandered their way through rice paddies on winding stone paths. Gaunt noted the Qiangguo farmers followed the natural contours of the land, where Westerners more often created grids. The trio took care to slip around villages, or pass them in interludes of fog or rain. Gaunt wished she could spy the settlements more closely—through mist or out the corner of her eye she spotted wooden buildings with peaked roofs, sometimes embellished by a pagoda or two, walled, gated, packed tight. Oddly, it was in the villages that a predilection for grids did appear; most Western towns she knew sprawled chaotically, as if the wind had scattered the seeds of houses. The well-ordered buildings hid their secrets, and she had better glimpses of the villagers themselves in the fields or rice paddies, where families bent at their labor.

Gaunt had traveled for years now (though never so far) and knew the peril of snap judgments. But what she recalled from the West were both happier peasants and more desperate peasants. She wondered if Qiangguo endeavored to avoid extremes in favor of serenity.

Footsore and pregnant, it was an attitude she could respect.

By nightfall they still had not reached the Wall. They slept against a rocky hillside, starting no fire for fear of bandits. But the moon rose wide and crickets trilled, and Bone told stories of his thieving days in Palmary, that city shaped like a hand, his own hands moving like bats. There was the haunted furniture store at the end of Lifeline Road, which echoed with family arguments in five languages, whose every nook seemed to open out on some different place and time. Down a long alley from there was the Medusa Gallery of Headline Street, its atrium stuffed with sculpture and with sculptors late with their payments, the realistic and fanciful intertwined. And across a fountain-tickled square hung Bone's lodgings in the Webbing, strung between the towers of the Middle and Ring Districts, where tenements twitched upon ropes above an influx of desert sand dotted with the lairs of patient spring-fangs. Ears full of desert horrors, Gaunt slept soundly among the mists.

The next night the Wall was larger but still distant, and they found a wayside shrine, with benches for travelers and an idol of a plump god with a mock-fierce expression, wielding a ladle like a sword. At its feet Eshe told magical tales of Qiangguo, of Living Calligraphy that slithered off its rice paper to guard treasuries or mop floors . . . of the immortal warrior with one shoe who was patron of lost causes . . . of the Windwater Garden representing the Empire in miniature, where dropping a lit pipe on a bush could burn down a thousand-acre forest . . . and of Meteor-Plum Long, sage author of *Record of Brush Methods and Transspatial Dislocation*, into whose paintings an observer could literally lose oneself, becoming but a new paint-stroke upon a fir-clad mountain.

The third night, with the Wall looming a mile away, they might have welcomed such an escape. At first all was calm. They made camp upon a wooded hilltop, beside an open shrine to a large, porous, irregularly shaped boulder, where a chill breeze ruffled bushes made silvery by the full moon. After convincing herself the sacred stone was not in fact some mineral monster, Gaunt told ghost stories that made their hearts pump warm blood. She told them of the phantom wheelbarrow that chased terrified children to offer them rides, and of the spectral courier who conveyed neatly sealed, beautifully scribed, indecipherable messages from the dead. After, she spoke of the haunted rocking chair, and how Doctor Karnak saw no spirit through his enchanted helmet's eyes and knelt in defeat, only then to spy the spectral baby pumping the runner, awaiting a last goodnight kiss—after that, the life inside her kicked, and despite the cold she insisted Bone and Eshe feel her belly until they divined kicks of their own.

Afterward Eshe's gaze lingered, and it seemed to Gaunt a look of cool appraisal passed over her face. Gaunt could not discern the meaning of it, but elected to cover herself.

"Pardon me," Eshe said, the warmth in her voice belying what Gaunt had glimpsed in her eyes. "The lines on your belly, they . . . it is foolish."

"What is it?"

Bone said, "They do resemble dragons, don't they? I had noticed that myself, but thought myself silly."

Eshe nodded.

Gaunt looked down, seeing the swirl of tan discolorations that had emerged as her middle expanded, and noted what she had not quite allowed herself to perceive. Yes, she thought, you might interpret the swirls as two coiling, willowy dragons, meeting at tail and snout. Odd.

"If you two are quite finished studying my stretch marks," Gaunt said, "the expectant woman is tired."

"Of course," Bone said.

"If you are willing to stay awake a time, Bone," Eshe said, the wondering tone still hovering in the air, "I would welcome talk."

Gaunt found it advisable to sleep, desirable to sleep, but impossible to sleep. Bone had surrendered his cloak to her, claiming to be warm enough, and she tried to sleep sidelong, clutching the cloth like lover or nemesis. Between baby-kicks and voices, however, the veil of sleep was ever pierced.

"So," Eshe said to Bone, "the Night's Auditors pursue."

"So," Bone said to Eshe, "you know of them."

"No need to be crafty. I would like to help you."

"I am coming to think that's true, but I am also coming to think the Eshe we know is but the crown of an iceberg. I don't trust icebergs."

"In that case you and Gaunt are in a cold sea without a boat."

Bone chuckled. "The Starborn Lands do seem a sea of sorts, in which we're but droplets. A strange sea, with peculiar currents. So: you wonder whose hand dropped us here? Well then: the kleptomancers of Palmary. You have heard of them, too?"

"The sorcerer-cabal empowered by theft? Who has not?"

"You may also have heard that two of their number were slain, some few years back."

"I might have. That was you?" To Gaunt's ears Eshe sounded a bit horrified, but more than a trifle impressed.

"Gaunt is blameless," Bone replied.

Rarely have I heard myself described so, Gaunt thought.

"It was I," Bone said, "who facilitated their perusal of the damnable tome that claimed their lives. It was self-defense of a sort, but I do bear responsibility . . ."

Gaunt heard him struggle between braggadocio and evasion. She might have kicked him a little, if she could.

"So," Eshe said, "you have been running from their colleagues ever since?"

"Oddly, no," Bone said. "We wandered the West for many moons without pursuit. We were somewhat preoccupied with this or that. It was not until we settled near Palmary, with an eye to raising a family, that the mark was placed." A sour tone spilled over his words. "Foolish of me. I thought myself wise about the area, and about them. I'd assumed they'd shrugged off their loss."

Gaunt thought, *So, behind your protectiveness lies guilt.*

Eshe was silent a moment. An owl hooted. She said, "Perhaps they had . . . for it seems to me there may be other reasons for this assassination, and these assassins in particular."

"You have my full attention."

"What if you are not simply a threat, but an opportunity?"

An owl cried out again, closer. The other night-noises dimmed. Bone said, "I have a notion . . ."

"Yes?"

"That we are being ambushed."

Gaunt rose without preamble, nodded to the others, and prepared to fight. She again heard an owl, this time somewhere in the mists of the forest floor. She doubted this owl was winged, or that its prey were mice.

CHAPTER 4.

After she claimed her scroll, events at first proceeded auspiciously for Next-One-A-Boy. Flybait gave a good account of her (complete with interjected growling, clawing, and leaping) and Five Finger Chang was impressed by the array of ancient weapons they piled at his feet.

"They are magical," he murmured, rubbing his mustaches. "They must be. They will help the gallant fraternity rob from the filthy rich and give one percent to the noble poor." His good hand rubbed his maimed hand, the one studded with bloodstained jade shards, and he bowed to the stone shoe in the alcove nearby, symbol of his patron immortal.

Next-One-A-Boy disagreed with him, and almost dared say so aloud. Her status had already improved considerably among the Cloud and Soil Society. She would be allowed a bedroll away from the lower part of the bandits' caves, where the spray from the underground waterfall chilled the river guards and the hangers-on, and where she'd stayed since the day she'd first arrived, bearing a rich scholar's purse and a defiant grin.

The caves' higher sections lay beside the upper plunge of the waterfall, but it possessed overhead fissures admitting shafts of sunlight. There the bandits proper schemed the fleecing of towns and travelers. Five Finger Chang sat there upon a dragon-crossed carpet between spears of sun, surveying his new toys.

"Um," Flybait said. "I'm not sure . . ."

She elbowed him, and he went silent. He clearly needed someone to watch out for him. There was no point disagreeing with the chief, and they hadn't actually misled. Well, Flybait hadn't. Next-One-A-Boy felt the presence of the scroll beneath her tunic like the rustling of her own heart. Would Five Finger Chang discover her betrayal? Perhaps he'd throw her out. Perhaps he'd kill her. Perhaps he'd claim her for his bed.

But no—Chang was a smelly, ugly, cold-hearted extortionist and highway robber, but like the one-shoed Lord of Lost Causes, he treated his few female comrades with honor. Chang's second in command, Exceedingly Accurate Wu, was even a woman. Albeit one who terrified her. "All men are brothers here in Shadow Margin," Chang would say, "even the women." Men who defied this rule, even those who mistreated the camp followers, were flogged. Next-One-A-Boy had chosen a good entry into the wild outlaw mirror of decent society, that outcast realm which folk called the Rivers-and-Lakes.

"We cannot tell if they are magical," Exceedingly Accurate Wu said, "until they are tested in battle." She studied Next-One-A-Boy and Flybait as though assessing grimy old coins.

That evening Next-One-A-Boy contrived to wash without revealing the scroll hidden in her pile of clothes. The cold touch of the waterfall made her feel born anew, like an immortal with an ethereal body rising through rainbow clouds, attended by a phoenix. She curled up with her bedroll and scroll (well away from Flybait, who should not get any ideas) and in the moonlight shafts of the caves she dared unroll the scroll a little.

The scroll was not a text but a painting, a monochrome landscape of dark ink upon white, formed of intricate brushwork testifying to endless hours of squinting labor. She caught a glimpse of mountains rising rugged and tree-crowned from a wash of clouds, the peaks growing more indistinct with distance. The one hint of color was a signature-chop hovering above all like a faded red sun. The scene blurred and swam as Next-One-A-Boy's fatigue caught up with her, and she slid into a peculiar dream.

THE DREAM OF THE COLD MOUNTAIN

A dreamer once found herself drifting through the sky like a windblown leaf, looking down upon mountains rising like islands from fog. Although snow had not yet come to the waking world, here it lay thick upon the rocks. She meandered among the falling flakes and settled at last upon a winding path, as gently as a lighting songbird.

Solidity came to her, and she hugged herself for warmth, wreaths of breath rising from her pursed lips. How cold it was on the mountain! All around her rugged peaks lay engulfed in silent white, while dark forests rose thick within a breath of mist. Clouds swirled around a wind-tossed moon that ascended like a lonely white bird.

Fear closed its icicle fingers around her heart. She could not remember her name, nor where she belonged.

She ran upslope, seeking illumination. Chased by confusion, the traveler craned her head but caught only snatches of dark blue sky. Snowflakes made tiny cold kisses upon her face. Alpine mist soaked her clothes. She shivered.

"Hello?" she cried out. "Is anyone there? How did I get here?"

The words themselves seemed formless, like something spoken in a distant valley and carried here in an unpredictable flurry of winds, their meaning blurred, their context unknown. Who was the speaker, and who the listener?

No, said something deep and stubborn within her. *No, I cannot lose myself in fog and snow and the dissolution of self. All things may seem unreal, but this fathomless cold will kill me sure as steel.* Although she could not recall her name, the girl's hard thought steadied her. Yes, such bluntness was the natural tenor of her mind. She was returning to herself.

But how to find shelter? She was no hermit, for they had not yet taught her woodcraft. (They? She let the question drop like snow.) Her only clue as to destination was the path underfoot, well worn despite her solitude. Up or down?

She feared this single choice could save or doom her. Looking out at the bright abyss between the neighboring mountains she felt dizzy, and lost her sense of gravity, white clouds and pale sunlight twisting in their slow dance. She faced her mountainside. Something in her heart longed for the sunlit heights, where she might have a view of the other peaks and the void in which they appeared to drift. Yet the mysteries of the lower shadows beckoned also, with the promise of strange grottoes and glades. *I am a poor village girl*, she thought, *unsuited for such rambles*. She reached for a coin-string hanging low around her neck and removed one of the three coppers threaded there. Upon one side coiled twin dragons, on the other side the name of a previous emperor. "Dragons for up," she called, and tossed the coin into the air.

It landed on its side and rolled down the path before disappearing into a tangle of snow and fallen leaves.

"Hey!" she called, for even in this mysterious place she was not about to lose good money. She chased the runaway coin. As she searched amid the detritus of the path, she glimpsed a firelight in the gloomy depths below. It occurred to her then that frozen corpses have little use for money. Her teeth chattered a similar message. She approached the fire.

Orange light seeped into tree-shroud and snow-veil, like a candle seen from behind a sheet, its fire-glow tickling its way into the shadows. Crackles and pops murmured across the snowy silence. Next-One-A-Boy saw a cave, the fire dancing near its mouth. A hulking shadow blotted one wall. As she crept closer the shadow moved, as if slowly breathing.

She approached warily, until she could see a large man sitting cross-legged beside the fire. He appeared to be staring directly at her.

"Uh, hello," she said.

There was no reply but the fire's chatter. Her teeth responded. They kept up this conversation for a time.

"I am cold," she said. "This is a cold mountain. May I come to your fire?"

"Words," said the man, in a deep voice like stones grumbling free of thick mud. "I have not heard words for a time." He wore a hat made of bark. His clothes, once fine, bore tears and patches and stains. "I forget words, just as I forget my path hither."

"I don't know how I got here either. I just know I'm freezing."

"It does not bother me if you use the fire."

She sat, not beside him, and not opposite him, but keeping him to her right, wilderness to her left, good rock at her back. She would never find the money. But a fire was better. They sat as though the burning branches were sharing village news.

It was good to sit. It seemed to her that she'd been traveling much longer than she remembered. A story occurred to her, as though it had happened to someone else: that once upon a time a girl was close to suicide, and yet at the selfsame time her family believed her prideful and in need of beating down. She vowed that whatever she decided about living, she would decide it far away from their shadow. She ran, and ran, and somehow the question of killing herself never came up again. But she was tired. Now, at last, there was nothing to do but breathe and study the fire. Contemplation, respiration, combustion.

"How long have I been running?" she wondered aloud.

"Time is like sparks," the man said. "Who knows when its source will spit up a new moment?"

"You are different from other men."

"Well, I am an illustration."

"What?"

He smiled, as if recalling something. "Are you not within my painting?"

The dreamer woke.

Next-One-A-Boy sat up. Shafts of moonlight stabbed the cave all around her. There was no sign her fellow bandits had noticed anything, nor that the sentry had even looked her way. It seemed she had not moved.

Her clothes were damp. She closed the scroll and lay awake the rest of the night.

The next day was not good. She stumbled through the training regimen Chang demanded of his bandits. There were occasional mutterings about how the Wind and Rain Society upriver had it easier. But instead of punishing the carpers, Exceedingly Accurate Wu kept upbraiding Next-One-A-Boy, as if the girl had volunteered for the job of camp scapegoat. Finally, after Next-One-A-Boy shifted left when Wu called for right, Wu interrupted the drills for a lecture. There was a dim groan from the bandits.

"It is said," Wu addressed all thirty of them, leaning on a bamboo cane, "that in the Summer and Winter period, long before the Empire of Walls, when the land was in chaos, the Sage General went to a job interview with the Lord of Long River."

Wu commanded their attention as simply as gravity commands a stone. She was a thin, spare woman who seemed to possess exactly the minimum bulk for her duties, as though to bear any less flesh would be slacking, and any more ostentatious. Her hair she kept shorter than any other's in the gallant fraternity, just the modicum useful for warmth. Her cloak was an unadorned storm-grey, and her weapon was a single knife, for as a commander, she said, she should not waste time or muscle with superfluous gear.

Exceedingly Accurate Wu was known for her conversational style, or rather her complete lack of it. To speak was to waste perfectly good air that might be serving bandit bodies or feeding bandit fires. So she used this great power of humankind sparingly, and only for the most vital of reasons: to scold, to command, and to lecture. Other uses of speech were beneath contempt. ("Good morning, Wu!" somebody other than Five Finger Chang might say,

"It's a beautiful day." "It is a vast world," Wu might reply, "and thus certainly a horrible day for somebody. Why not make it you?") To hear so many words from her at once was shocking, almost as if the Rabbit of the Moon had hopped into the caves bearing peaches of immortality.

Wu said, "The Lord of Long River enjoyed the Sage General's maxims but desired a field test. He commanded the General to take charge of his hundred giggling concubines, and make of them a fighting force. The General appointed squad leaders and began formation drills. The squad leaders tittered and laughed and their squads maneuvered like drunk puppies. The Sage General had the squad leaders beheaded."

Exceedingly Accurate Wu paused, bamboo cane extended. That, plus the ice in her gaze, were all the theatrics needed to conceptualize the axe.

"Imagine the horror of the Lord of Long River as his beauties' heads rolled in their own blood, their painted eyelids fluttering for the final time. Almost the Lord had the visitor decapitated as well, but the Sage General bade him wait, for the Sage General was still executing the Lord's own command. The Sage General appointed new squad leaders, and this time the concubine army was silent. It performed to near perfection."

Wu smiled. "The Lord said, 'Your methods are monstrous,' and the General replied, 'The Lord of Long River plays at rulership but does not truly want to protect his people.' At these words the Lord recognized the General's wisdom, and appointed him commander of the armies. Never while the Sage General lived did Long River suffer defeat."

Wu paused again, still smiling. The effect of a smile on Wu's face was not unlike that of a daffodil set atop a coiled viper. "What can we learn from this story?"

Feet shuffled. Gazes met toes. Feng Axe-Big-As-Himself cracked his knuckles. Muttering Chung said, ". . ."

Next-One-A-Boy's hand went up.

"Yes."

"We learn," Next-One-A-Boy said in a rush, not sure what drove her to speak, "that if women have no place in the hierarchy of a kingdom, they cannot expect even the wise to protect them. They will become as meat, fit only for consumption in the bedchamber or as sacrifices to settle an argument. For the Sage General spoke of security for the people of Long River. But where was the security for the dead concubines?"

Wu's smile was gone. "We are done drilling for the day. Next-One-A-Boy, meet me beside the waterfall."

Where the waterfall plunged into the caves was where Chang or Wu could confer—or reprimand—with some privacy, as voices were drowned by the roar.

Cold spray hitting her like a slap, Next-One-A-Boy said, "I merely thought, Wu, as a woman, you must be making a point about women . . ."

The bamboo cane connected with her shin. She knelt with a whimper.

"I was instructing a band of bandits, you idiot, not a gaggle of rich daughters. Women with power over men do not speak of it, lest it evaporate like morning mist." Wu shook her head. "There are times I curse my scholar father for educating me, I who could never take the Examinations for civil service."

"That is the fault of men!" The same anger that fueled her words earlier was now redoubled, and brought Next-One-A-Boy back to her feet. "And they get most women to go along! They fear our strength, so they forbid us real work, tell us to yield to others, even bind our feet. I only escaped that fate because we were poor and my parents could not afford to have me shuffling about. I had hard labor in the fields and household chores and a Little Emperor to mind, he who would get all the education the family could muster. We must stick together, we women. You and I are alike."

"You are whining," Wu told her, eyebrows rising. "I do not whine."

"I do not whine either," Next-One-A-Boy objected. "I curse and spit. I bite and kick. I learn and advance."

Wu shook her head. "You whine. You whine when you complain of your past. You whine when you seek allies in other women. You whine when you emphasize your femaleness."

"I wear exactly what the men wear! My hair is no more clean or elaborated than any bandit's. I wear no jewelry or token."

"You walk so as to emphasize the sway of your hips. You lay your hands upon the curves of your body. You stand in an unbalanced way so as to extend a leg. Do not pretend."

Next-One-A-Boy's cheeks burned. Did she truly do these things? She had not thought about it. "I am as nature made me," she said.

"Indeed. And you have not advanced beyond that state. You spend your time daydreaming, not honing your body and mind. You pine for male approval, else you would not complain so much about them. You stare at your reflection in the pools of the cave, revealing your vanity. You waste your obvious intellect—do not smile, it is not a compliment—on catty witticisms, not on researching the many texts we have here in Shadow Margin. Until you apply yourself as a human being, do not cry to me about the unfairness of being a woman."

Next-One-A-Boy was angry now. "Must I pretend to be a man? It would be a lie!"

"You need not pretend to be a man. You must cease to be a child."

Next-One-A-Boy had stalked off then, a parting bamboo rap against her bottom demonstrating that every possible action would mark her as a "child," and therefore she might as well do what would bring her relief. She fled to the surface, stomped past the sentry, and cried beneath a tree. Sobs surged like a flooding river, and just as beyond control. Wu would have disdained her weakness now. Her parents would have claimed she was seeking pity. Her brother, the Little Emperor, would have mocked her. There was no one who accepted her. She was a monster . . . no, not even that, for a monster, like the chi-beast at the Wall, had its grandeur. She was simply a waste of flesh.

At last the sobs came more slowly, like aftershocks of an earthquake. She could breathe now, and think. The world had its freshness again, fog twisting around pines and junipers. A bird flitted from one cloud of branches to the next, watching her sidelong. She watched it back.

A voice said, "This is the moment to stay within. Not the weeping. Nor the thing that brought the weeping. The moment after. When your mind is open to what is really there."

"Who is this?" Next-One-A-Boy demanded, looking this way and that.

"Someone closer than you suppose."

She looked up.

Crouched in the branches of the tree was the Woman in Black, from the Heavenwall.

"I could summon the sentries," Next-One-A-Boy said.

"How interesting!" said the Woman in Black. "I too could summon the sentries. There might be a fight. There might be a chase. There might be a card game. So many possibilities."

"You are crazy. Are you drunk?"

"Yes! Drink is helpful when dressing up in black and approaching monsters or bandits."

Next-One-A-Boy giggled. Just a little. She covered her mouth.

"A girl!" crowed the Woman in Black. "There is a girl in there."

Remembering Wu's words, Next-One-A-Boy shed her smile. "What do you want?"

"Want? I want to experience light and dark, good and bad, turbulence and serenity, and recognize them as counterparts in the eternal dance, so I may turn an open face to nature and its changes. Also, I am fond of children and was wondering how you were."

"I am fine!" Next-One-A-Boy sat up tall. "You can go be mysterious somewhere else." In a gentler voice she added, "Thank you. And thank you for your help at the Wall." She paused. "Who are you?"

"I am of the wulin. I have dedicated myself to esoteric arts so as to be occasionally meddlesome in the world."

Among the gallant fraternity she had heard talk of the wulin. They were of the Rivers-and-Lakes, like bandits and peddlers and rogues and others who could never fit in. But the wulin were remote even from these, for they knew secrets of fighting that set them apart. Wulin warriors could pop up anywhere, and often took up lost causes. The bandits didn't like them much.

"So you like to tell everyone what to do," Next-One-A-Boy said.

"No! If I wished to command I would not skulk about in black. I would lecture people instead of fighting monsters and rogue warriors. But in the end words are as transitory as clouds in the sky. My deeds may be worth more, though they too will fade like a weed-threaded road."

Next-One-A-Boy tried to follow the path of the Woman in Black's speech, but it seemed to meander through strange forests. "Woman in Black," she said. "What do you think? How is a woman to live in the world, and not just exist? How am I to be me, and not just a spirit shackled to the name 'woman'?"

There was a hint of gentle regret in the wulin woman's voice. "Let go of names for a time. 'Woman.' 'Girl.' 'World.' 'Spirit.' Live in the place you reached when you had sobbed your last, and had no thought for *then* or *later,* but only saw what you saw. That is the start of it. The Way. Where it leads is up to you. But you cannot find the Way when you are confounded by chatter. Speaking of chatter . . . someone comes. Therefore, I go—"

CHRIS WILLRICH   69

"Hey," called Flybait, oblivious to the Woman in Black concealed in the leaves overhead. Next-One-A-Boy glanced at his approach only for a blink, but by then the wulin woman had vanished. Flybait seemed the woman's conceptual opposite, stumbling up and flopping himself down beside Next-One-A-Boy as if invited. Almost she would have snarled at him, but then he said something unexpected.

"I wanted to see if you were okay."

"Oh . . ."

"Wu seems to have it in for you. I don't know why. You know, I don't like her. She shouldn't treat you like that."

She sat closer to him, drew her knees up into the embrace of her arms. "Thanks."

"Thanks? I didn't *do* anything . . ."

"Thanks for saying something. Thanks for saying you care, without trying to make me *into* something, or make me *do* something, or make me *perceive* something. Just being there."

"Oh . . ."

They sat that way until lunch call. Flybait seemed gratified to receive approval for doing not much of anything, and he did it with enthusiasm. Next-One-A-Boy thought about moments un-mired by the past and the future, but it was hard. She thought about the dream of just sitting and breathing beside a fire (or had it been more?) but angry thoughts fell upon the image like snow, masking the days behind and the days ahead.

That night there was action. "Just a small foray," Five Finger Chang said to the gathered Society at sunset, leaping down from a cypress tree and patting his spyglass. "I see three travelers approaching the Ochre River and the Wall. They are trying to look like peasants, but I discern they are foreigners! Having come so far, so secretively, they must be carrying wealth. I will take a handful of helpers. This will be a good chance for Flybait and Next-One-A-Boy to learn."

"They were absent their duties today," Exceedingly Accurate Wu objected, her stare indicating she knew exactly why any adolescent boy and girl would go missing together. Next-One-A-Boy stared back, swearing silently to remember Wu's false assumption the next time the older woman pretended to know everything. Wu said, "Should we reward them?"

Chang shared Wu's assumptions but not her disapproval. He chuckled. "They are young and need their exercise . . . And a raid will toughen them up. Unless the Lord of Lost Causes drops his shoe on us, we can afford to indulge the kids. They can watch the horses." He frowned at Next-One-A-Boy. "But girl, you need a new name. A bandit name."

"I will think about it," she said. She could tell Chang wished her well, and she felt guilty for not correcting him about the new swords, which he still believed to be magical, making him overconfident. Should she tell? But there were only three opponents . . .

Flybait was meanwhile entranced with the problem of her name, and as they tromped through the sunset forest, he said, "Your name could be Moon Spider, because you climbed the Wall. Or Firecracker because you know your way around firepowder. Or Auspicious Tiger because you're so fierce. Or Shining Pearl because—"

"Why are you so interested in my name?" she snarled. "And why do you not change the name 'Flybait'?"

"Flybait is a good name!" he said. "It is the kind of name that makes evil spirits pass over you. My family was most thoughtful to bestow it."

"You are a boy." She shook her head. "My family saw another girl as just another mouth. Or at best someone to haul coal and weave silk and watch babies. When Chang says the poor are noble it shows he does not tarry often among them. For the poor can be as cruel as the wealthy. They simply have the power to hurt few, while the rich can hurt many."

"Surely then the cruel rich are worse than the cruel poor?"

"If you're a victim, you're a victim. You don't need to see anyone's purse to know it."

"Well, as long as you rob from the wealthy," Flybait said, "Chang won't mind your attitude."

She spat. "I hope these foreigners really are rich. We needn't kill them, do we?"

"That is up to them," Flybait said, but there was something uneasy beneath his pose of gruffness, like a puppy playing at hunting raptors.

CHAPTER 5.

In his long career, Imago Bone had often been chased by dogs. There had been herd dogs, war dogs, and astonishingly vicious perfumed lap dogs. While many of his canine acquaintances had roamed free, hunting him down cobblestones, piers, corridors, and sewers, many others had been roped or chained, growling their frustration at the intruder who balanced upon the fence, climbed the tree, hung from the rooftop, and dangled suspended from the mad inventor's hot-air balloon. Lately Bone felt a kinship with them, for he too was tethered, unable to venture far from his pregnant lover no matter the danger.

Still, he thought, a pair of daggers in hand, the chain was not real, and would not prevent him from goring any single foe that appeared. He prepared to spring ahead.

Ten shapes emerged from the mists. Bone edged back.

There were six bearded cutthroats, smiling beneath wide-brimmed cone hats, clad in ragged coats with a haphazard assortment of armor pieces distributed among them, motley-looking silks and shifts and gowns shining underneath. They appeared to Bone like incognito clowns. Their swords and knives, however, seemed of decent quality, predictive more of screams than laughter.

There were also two youths trailing, a boy and a girl, leading horses. The boy, maybe fifteen, had a gangly look to him, and a glint of exaggerated bravado beneath his moss-like tangle of hair. The girl, a trifle older, looked to be the boy's temperamental opposite, compact body proudly erect, hard brown eyes staring between locks of hair straight as a dagger and dark as the deepest sea.

The lead bandit, whose extravagant beard and mustaches seemed to dare Bone to tug them, raised a right hand completely devoid of fingers, stubs adorned with pieces of jade. It certainly had a dramatic effect, for all gazes were upon it. The leader barked a command at the youths, who held off, staying close beside each other. The girl patted something within her garment, a hidden weapon perhaps.

The commander sauntered up and conversationally drawled something at the foreigners.

Eshe made crisp reply, and the bandit shook his head. The six elder robbers advanced.

"What did you say to them?" Gaunt asked.

"Take it back," Bone suggested.

Eshe said, "I gave the wrong reply to the question, 'Where are you going?' This must be a criminal pass-phrase hereabouts. For future reference, 'north' is incorrect."

The lead bandit removed a sword from a sheath that seemed a trifle large for it. The weapon had an air of antiquity. He made a menacing statement, which Eshe translated as, "This is a sword of ancient rulers. Its magic is great. Surrender all your possessions and you may live."

At once the fierce-eyed girl beside the horses began interjecting something. The bandit leader snarled her into silence.

"What was that about?" Bone asked.

"The girl warned her leader the sword might be mundane," Eshe said. "She said she would know the difference."

The boy beside the girl spoke now. There was another exchange, in much the tone of the first.

"The boy says the metallurgy of centuries past was inferior to that of today," Eshe continued. "The value of the blade is in sale to collectors. The bandit leader replies children should be silent, and they should consider themselves lucky not to be expelled from the Cloud and Soil Society."

"There is a reason," Bone said, "I was never an organization man."

Having settled their debate for now, the bandits began advancing, ancient blades drawn.

"I think the odds are poor," Gaunt noted.

Bone nodded. "Set aside thinking for now."

In one motion Bone threw two daggers. The lead bandit dropped, with a blade in his throat. A second snarled at the new wound in his arm.

Gaunt felled that one with a dagger to the eye. She passed her remaining blade to Bone, snatched up a fallen tree branch, and climbed the gnarled sacred boulder.

Eshe, her eyes wide, now raised a silver-fringed statuette representing the Swan Goddess. She pressed a switch upon it, and blades sprouted from wingtips and beak. She crouched, her knife shifting from target to target.

The surviving bandits shared a look of mixed fear, calculation, and anger that would make the coldest Western businessman pale. Their leader and one other had fallen. Their prey had proven most expensive.

The young accomplices had reached the same conclusion. With a flurry of hoofbeats, the pair disappeared with the bandits' horses. Those who remained snarled in outrage. Bone smiled in respect.

His smirk soon faded. It seemed the remaining bandits' cost/benefit/rage calculation went against the travelers, for the four rushed the three, swords in hand.

These were no amateurs, and in between dodging and lunging, Bone grew concerned. He and Eshe bloodied an attacker apiece, and Gaunt's branch-swings kept the pair from being engulfed. But a single error would doom them all.

Then came two errors. Bone's nearest opponent saw through his feint, and the Western thief was obliged to roll past the Eastern bandit. Meanwhile Eshe took a blow to the ribs and dropped.

Bone leapt up and tackled his own foe, knocking over Eshe's as well. Bone pierced the throat of the first man and rose again, his foot stomping the windpipe of the second.

A distant, watchful part of his mind noted in amazement he'd never fought so well.

But it was not enough.

The last two bandits had slipped around the stone and were ascending to attack Gaunt. She waved her branch, but they approached with mirthless grins.

She must submit or else jump, risking harm to her child-to-be.

Bone threw the last dagger, cutting one bandit across the back of the neck. The man shrugged off the pain and continued climbing. His comrade turned away from Gaunt, leapt from the boulder, and ran for Bone.

Then a length of wood, seemingly out of nowhere, cracked against Gaunt's opponent's skull. The man toppled down the boulder and lay still.

Bone and the final bandit turned to see a white, four-hoofed blur pass by, with a staff-bearing black-and-red blur on top. Both returned their attention to each other, but Bone a fraction of a second sooner. Diving, he tripped his foe.

When Bone rolled to his feet, the enemy remained prone, his eyes rolled up into his head, the butt of a staff pressing disturbingly deep into his skull.

The staff belonged to a black-clothed man of Qiangguo with a thick mustache recalling that of the bandit chief (Bone would not dream of pulling it) and a red cap with a long tassel fluttering behind. His silk clothes were adorned with white images of a spindly insect, save for one tiny spot, over his heart, marked with a red firefly. His horse, snorting beneath him, was pale and possessed of more ribs than the norm. The nostrils steamed.

Bone locked gazes with the newcomer, decided he faced no immediate threat, and bowed. The staff-wielder nodded. Bone's gaze met Gaunt's, and she nodded yes to his unspoken *Are you all right?*

Gaunt and Bone moved to Eshe's side.

The Kpalamaa woman bled heavily, but was alive. Bone took a bandit's bright cloak and tied strips of it around the wound. Before long, Gaunt and their mysterious savior were helping him.

Bone noted the fallen swan-dagger. "You fought well," Bone said, "Swan priestess."

She smiled weakly, many drops of blood and one secret lighter.

They propped Eshe up against the sacred stone, and she gasped her thanks.

Their rescuer now mounted his horse and galloped off in the direction the two youths had fled. Oddly, Bone hoped they would escape. He had, he thought, glimpsed something familiar about them.

He put his hand upon Gaunt's shoulder, let out a long breath of relief. He hoped Gaunt would say he'd been magnificent.

"My back hurts," she murmured.

He rubbed it. "You were magnificent," he hinted.

"Lower," she said.

His breathing eased, as normality of a sort returned. The reality of carnage touched his mind, his nose, his shaking hands. All at once Bone crouched, stomach nearly heaving.

And now it was Gaunt's turn to caress him, stroking his neck, cradling his head. "I know," she said. "I know."

"Foolishness," he croaked. "I've seen death before."

"Rarely by your own hand, Bone. Ever you avoid battle, as you would a viper."

After several minutes the horseman returned, reined up, and snapped a quick question, words stiff and blunt. Bone stirred himself to rise, but it was Eshe who answered, with words whispery and gentle. After a few more exchanges, she said, "The name he gives might be rendered as 'Walking Stick.' He is a government official from the very Purple Forbidden City in Riverclaw, on a mission of some urgency." Eshe coughed, but held up a hand before Bone or Gaunt could interrupt. "As such, he will overlook the presence of mysterious foreigners who so enthusiastically dispose of bandits . . . so long as he accompanies us where you are going. I have told him."

"This time 'north' was the correct answer?" Bone asked.

Eshe said, "More or less. You go to the town of Abundant Bamboo."

"You are most free with information," Gaunt murmured.

Walking Stick stared at Gaunt, eyes taking in the shape of her middle. Bone wondered if he should pull that mustache after all.

Walking Stick exchanged more words with Eshe, who said, "I am free in no other sense. The rope is tangled, as we say in Kpalamaa. This man could kill us all. I speak not merely of his skill, but of his station. Let him reach any provincial garrison and he could set a small army upon us . . . He merely wishes to help us to the town—a small kindness for him, and a minor delay."

Gaunt nodded. "So be it. He saved our lives." Bone grunted acceptance.

Walking Stick bowed and remounted. With gestures he enlisted Bone's aid in getting Eshe upon his horse, whom he led through the trees and moonlight, the Westerners trailing. From time to time the priestess and official exchanged murmurs in the tongue of Qiangguo.

"*He* does not seem so bothered by death," Bone muttered. He was not sure he wanted to know the young bandits' fate.

"Let us not forget that," Gaunt replied.

CHAPTER 6.

Next-One-A-Boy and Flybait fled through the forest, casting looks backward through moon-spattered shadow and fear-scented sweat for bandits or foreign devils. They saw neither. They kept riding anyway.

"We can't go back to the caves," Next-One-A-Boy said when they'd gotten halfway to the river, dizzy and bruised from hard riding. "We've betrayed the gallant fraternity."

"No!" said Flybait. "We saved our skins. It was not premeditated. It was a mishap."

"We panicked. The foreign devils were monstrous in battle, and we panicked."

"Yes, that's it! We were out of our minds!"

"And yet," Next-One-A-Boy noted, "we had the presence of mind to steal the horses."

"Aiya! The Cloud and Soil Society will never forgive us. Where will we go, then? I, a child of peddlers who are surely halfway to the Argosy Steppes by now. And you, a hen who crows."

Next-One-A-Boy folded her arms. "This hen who crows will give you good advice if you've the ears for it."

He paused, patted his ears as if worried he'd left one behind. "Okay. What?"

"We let the horses go."

"Oh! Yes, then the fraternity won't think we took them."

"No. Left to themselves they'll go back to the caves."

"Oh. Why, then?"

"*We* will be going somewhere else." She pulled out the magic scroll.

"Is that a map? Let me see it!" He grabbed.

"Wait!" she said, but it was too late. Flybait's expression changed from one of fear and greed to one of fear and wonder, as he turned transparent and vanished. His horse snorted, looked around, and whinnied.

"You idiot," she said, dismounting and taking both horses' reins. "Not you, horse. Well, at least now I'm sure it wasn't just a dream."

She heard a distant sound. It at first seemed an echo of her racing heart, but a dissonance revealed the sound of hoofbeats. She peered into the moonlit distance and glimpsed a white horse appearing and disappearing amid the shadows of tree trunks. It galloped as though the trees were giving way before an honored worthy.

Flybait re-emerged, toppling onto the ground. He was shivering, with a dusting of snow over him. "Hey! What was *that*?"

"Shh!" said Next-One-A-Boy. She shooed the horses into a run, and led Flybait in another direction. "We're being chased. We have to vanish now."

"I'm not going back in there! I was falling, and I didn't know who I was. I just knew I had to escape."

"You still have to escape. Someone's chasing us."

"Maybe they have a blanket?"

She dragged him low into the bushes. "Look," she said.

Caught in the moonlight, an Imperial official charged past on a huge horse with one extra rib. He raced on, following the bandits' horses.

"A dragon horse!" Flybait whispered, wonder shaking him out of his misery. "They are supposed to be the mightiest of steeds, from the lands where the Argosy Steppes meet the Ruby Waste. They can run tirelessly. Only a dozen exist in the Empire. Oh, to touch one!"

"You could touch one as it tramples you," she answered him. "That official must be working with the foreigners. Maybe he's bribed, or maybe they were Imperial agents all along. Either way, in a minute he'll catch the horses and start looking for us. Our only hope is to get this scroll hidden somewhere and disappear into it."

"Maybe you're right," he said. "The kind of official who'd have a dragon horse would be most formidable. But it's cold in there . . ."

"I know where there's shelter on the cold mountain. Hurry."

They heard the hoofbeats and whinnying begin, as they worked the scroll deep amid the roots of a bush. Next-One-A-Boy reached as far in as she could, and grasping Flybait's hand, she held the scroll and concentrated.

"He's coming!" Flybait hissed.

"Don't distract me . . ." she said. And the pair became like unto snowflakes, fluttering down to a white-dusted mountain.

Once again the experience was like a dream, or a tale. This time, however, they remembered their pasts. They settled down, hands linked, onto the white path. They stared at each other a moment, then let go.

"Where is this shelter of yours?" Flybait said, snow swirling about him. "I see nothing but wilderness."

"It is this way," Next-One-A-Boy said, gesturing downslope. "And you're welcome."

Snow crunched underfoot as they hastened down the path. From time to time neighboring mountain peaks loomed out of the mists like the fingers of giants. "Forgive me!" Flybait said. "I am a simple bandit with an eye for beautiful—valuables! I know nothing of strange magic. Where did you find this scroll?"

"The hollow in the Wall," she said, "where we met the New Year."

"You held out loot from me? Us? You cheated the gallant fraternity!"

"The same gallant fraternity we've betrayed together?"

"It's the principle of the thing!" Flybait said.

"I look after myself. I am Next-One-A-Boy. My very name proves the truth of my life, that I can count on nobody but myself. This scroll we're in represents power. Or wealth, if I can sell it. I might share such things with you, Flybait, if you prove yourself a considerate . . . business partner."

"You know, it's really time you stopped calling yourself Next-One-A-Boy," Flybait said, frowning. Apparently the word "partner" had flown right through his head like a bird through an empty cavern. "Maybe This-One-A-Girl."

"I don't need my name to tell anybody that."

"So true," Flybait said. He paused, shut his mouth, and pointedly stared at the mountains. She strode ahead of him.

"You know," Flybait said in a more sober tone, "in stories this is the sort of place to which holy men retire, to contemplate Emptiness and the flow of natural forces. Also, the sort of place to which bandits flee to contemplate empty purses and the flow of Imperial forces."

"It's also the sort of place where people freeze to death," Next-One-A-Boy said. "Let's hustle."

They descended. Mountains reared out of mist; rock piles reared out of snow; ideas reared out of her mind. What should be her new name?

Once upon a time a runaway arrived hungry in the village of Abundant Bamboo and a matron named Lightning Bug had offered a tray of delights— fish dumplings, fluffy bao, pork buns, shrimp rolls, shu mai, chicken's feet— and even though the girl's mouth watered and her stomach groaned she was paralyzed with indecision. What if something was too rich? Too spicy? Too rare, and a mark of presumption if she took it first? Too paltry, and a sign of ingratitude if she claimed that? Lightning Bug had smiled and claimed a bao, implicitly giving permission for Next-One-A-Boy to take its counterpart.

Next-One-A-Boy felt much the same in the matter of names. It was in some ways easier to have no choices. You could hate your life in a pure, uncomplicated way. You could take your meager pleasures with no guilt attached, and cheerfully kick others in the teeth, knowing they were better off than you.

But escape that purity, by way of running away from home, by befriending storytellers and bandits, by encountering the supernatural and surviving? That began to muddle things. Now there was better and worse. There was judgment and guilt. It was as though freedom led, not to happiness, but to a wilderness where happiness was just one of the many bizarre wild animals one might find. Some of the other creatures might be far worse than the demons of her past. Others might be preferable even to happiness. The possibilities left her feet frozen. But she had to go somewhere.

"Where to, Next One?" Flybait was saying. "Have you forgotten where this shelter is?"

"What did you call me?"

"Um, 'Next One?'" Flybait looked as if he expected to be punched in the face. She frowned. It insulted her to be treated like a maniac. At most she would have slapped him. He said, "I just was saving time talking because it's so cold." He shivered for emphasis. "And it's nicer than always calling you 'you.'"

"'Next One.'" It would do, perhaps. Until she chose her own name. "All right."

They found the hermit's cave. There was no fire now, but in the ashes they discovered a short poem inscribed by a stick.

Kids, listen up!
Flee your burning house
The wild horses wait
To take you to a greater dwelling.
Kids, keep calm!

It's all alike below the sky
Pick your trail it's all fine
The abyss is as good as the peak.
If you get my meaning
You can go anywhere you want.

"Yep," said Flybait, stirring the ashes with his foot. "Crazy hermit."

"Hey!" said Next One. "You've destroyed the poem."

"Well, if he wrote it in ashes, he can't have expected it to stick around. Like I said, crazy."

Next One scowled. "He didn't seem crazy. He seemed like . . . the other side of crazy."

Flybait laughed. "Have you ever been to the other side of crazy?"

"No," she answered seriously. "I always swim back. And you?"

He smirked. "I stay on shore where the shiny things are."

"They say there's treasure in shipwrecks."

"I like my treasures dry. Hey, where does this go?"

They followed the cave back into the depths of the mountain. It was not the vast, perforated sort of complex that provided homes for robbers, but rather a simple tunnel, its irregular floor swept, its indentations hung here and there with whittled wooden deities or painted mandalas or paper banners proclaiming such news as "This is a cave! How great is that?"

The snow-sheen behind them lit the way inside until in the dimness they found a bed of branches and an old blanket, baskets of dried berries and nuts, and a small collection of scrolls. Beyond lay an abyss leading into a vast darkness, steps spiraling narrowly around its perimeter. Next One nearly slipped into it.

Flybait helped her step back from the edge. "Why would anyone sleep beside a bottomless pit?" he said. "The answer is: because they're crazy."

Next One frowned into the abyss. "We don't know it's bottomless . . ."

Flybait walked back to the fire and returned with a short, char-edged stick. He dropped it into the darkness. They heard no impact.

"Bottomless enough for me," Next One conceded. "If you go down there, use the steps."

"After you," Flybait said.

She snorted. She turned to the scrolls. Maybe Wu's mockery still haunted her, because she opened one and read the title. "'The Jailer's Tale.' It's a story from long ago."

"A story?" Flybait curled up in one corner of the hermitage, watching her expectantly.

"How old *are* you again?" she asked.

"Everyone loves stories. It was only terror that made me reluctant at the Wall. I was raised on tales of derring-do and wonder, good morals and bloody blades, magic and practicality. My father himself was, in a sense, one rambling story of adventure and misadventure after another. And all I knew of him were his tales and the trinkets attached to them. My mother was also a tale, one that began with 'It was different when I was a girl,' and ended with 'now all the world is evil,' but with infinite variations between."

Next One sighed. "The world has always been evil. Grownups think the world becomes evil because they mistake their growing wisdom for a change in the land itself."

"You are a cheery one. How does this theory explain you?"

She strove for a blunt demeanor. "We who are tormented from birth gain the gift of understanding. We waste no time complaining."

"Well, unless this tale is a torment, read it!"

She considered punishing his boyish impudence. But reading aloud from the scroll would help her concentrate on it. And when she was not annoyed, he was a trifle charming.

THE JAILER'S TALE

Once when Qiangguo was young and the Walls as yet unmade, the First Emperor built his regime upon a foundation of bodies. So when he died, the pillars of the Empire slipped upon pools of blood. Warriors and princes vied for the realm's remnants. Meanwhile the Emperor's bureaucracy lumbered on like oxen, keeping their heads low, lest heads roll.

One such bureaucrat was nicknamed Youngster, a back-country jailer in his forties. In one scroll he bore his Imperial mandate; in another, a sample of

Living Calligraphy that manifested as a giant cobra when unrolled. He had never used the latter.

One morning while leading a chain-gang through the hills to the provincial capital, Youngster woke to discover half his prisoners gone.

The First Emperor's rule was harsh, and the bureaucracy retained that cruelty's shape, as a dead crab leaves behind armor and claws. Youngster knew that when he reported his failure, he would become a prisoner himself.

He chained the remaining thugs to a tree and went for a walk. It is said that he beheld a giant shoe standing alone in the forest. He pondered, and made choices.

When he returned, he told those who remained, "You are free—free in a land of fire and blood. If you would go, go now, and do not look back. But if you would be united, winning gold and glory with your own hands, I will lead you."

Most of the prisoners fled back down the path, toward Youngster's remote town. There they encountered the giant cobra Youngster had loosed from his Living Calligraphy.

They panicked and raced back to their jailer. Knowing the cobra's weak points, Youngster crept up and slew it, never revealing its origin. The prisoners acclaimed him a natural leader.

The band went on to a genteel sort of banditry, and in time Youngster gained the patronage of local nobles, who knew a useful protector when they saw one. There were other warlords more terrifying, more brutal. One might have assumed they would win the throne. But the people of the Empire had already known rule by terror, and they saw in Youngster something else: a man who could replace fear and force with generosity and guile.

Province by province, Youngster's realm became second-largest in the land, surpassed only by he who named himself Overlord of the Desert Margin. Youngster kept getting beaten by the Overlord, but more and more people flocked to his banner anyway. Some of those who defected were clever strategists. Youngster listened to their good advice and at last maneuvered the Overlord into an ambush.

As they advanced, Youngster bade his soldiers sing the folk songs of the Desert Margin. The Overlord heard these songs, and thought, "Surely those who sing are my own countrymen. If they now oppose me, what hope is left?"

At last the Overlord flung himself personally at the entrapping forces. He cut down scores before he fell.

Youngster gave the Overlord a stately burial, and humbly became the Second Emperor. He is remembered as wise and compassionate, adding to the Empire's strength a reverence for human life and a respect for cunning. As a result the Empire endures even now.

And it was he who, to protect his people, began a project to bind the dragons . . .

"What happens next?" Flybait demanded.

Next One frowned. "I don't know. The scroll looks torn, incomplete. I don't know what that last part about the dragons means."

Flybait looked disappointed, but he shrugged and smiled. "It makes sense the Second Emperor was a bandit, you know. Outdoor air, good exercise, clean living—all produce a superior man. Not like the decadent rulers of today."

"You sound like a wrinkled-up and toothless old man, pontificating between weiqi games at the tea house."

Flybait put a creak in his voice. He tottered toward her, shaking his fist in a meandering way. "How dare you mock your elders! You lack proper deference! I will educate you! You will now recite the three hundred major rules of ritual!"

She laughed. But her laughter ceased when she heard footsteps in the snow.

"It may be the hermit," she whispered to Flybait. "But I am not sure . . ."

"There's no harm in hiding . . ."

They crept backward into the deepest shadows.

In the soft light they beheld the strange Imperial official they'd glimpsed earlier in moonlit woods.

"How?" Flybait hissed.

"Sh," said Next One. Whatever his means of tracking them, he was here, and approaching. It seemed their choices were to fight, to surrender, or to explore the bottomless pit.

She rather admired that Flybait seemed to have reached the same conclusion. He was edging toward the abyss as well.

She groped her way down the spiraling stair around the pit, Flybait creeping behind her. The steps led deeper into gloom. Light disappeared altogether, but she kept moving by touch and the smooth shuffle of their bodies against stone.

Yet, minutes later, an unnatural hush fell upon the pit. So complete was the silence, not even Next One's own breathing reached her ears.

Now, only the sensation of movement and the cold touch of rock remained to guide her. She felt a warm hand upon her shoulder and she clutched it, grateful for the contact in this enchanted place. Warmth, comradeship, and shared fear—all were conveyed by Flybait's grip.

And all at once it vanished. She heard and felt nothing.

Now she was afraid. She sniffed, and found her nose still worked, bringing her the stink of her own sweat, the reek of fear within it. Flybait's own odor reached her too, and it reassured her that she was not alone, and even (*admit it, girl*) beside a man, of sorts . . .

But now all scents, too, were stolen away.

She had never taken much notice of the taste of her own mouth, but now she had this sense and no others. Because she expected this to leave her as well, she bit hard and tasted the blood of her lip, and sucked at this last evidence of life.

It faded.

It was intolerable to be thus senseless, here beside a bottomless pit.

Desperately she tried to shift her body, in hopes of sparking some response from the smothering dark. After an endless moment a surprising circle of light appeared—the top of the pit, its dim illumination now seemingly a blazing beacon.

A shadow appeared within that light, the blot of a man looking down. She tried to raise a hand in defiance—or surrender—but saw nothing. Could it be she was not so much insensible as nearly *nonexistent*, down here in the pit? A mote of consciousness, losing its connection to the world? For sound, too, drifted down to her, even though she could hear nothing of her surroundings.

"Welcome, young ones, to dissolution. You have reached the edges of the painting, and thus, I suspect, of existence. Your crimes are repaid. I must now attend to more urgent things, foreigners who could shake the Empire. I leave you with oblivion." The light faded. The voice was gone.

CHRIS WILLRICH

In the absence of everything but consciousness, what could she choose?

She recalled the words of a poem written in ash and rubbed out by a careless foot.

She tried to throw herself into the abyss. But she could not know if she had succeeded or not.

CHAPTER 7.

Morning came and made the mists appear blurred, like golden serpents coiling among the trees. Gaunt, Bone, Eshe, and the mysterious Walking Stick passed beyond the forest into a craggy region of jutting hills too rocky to admit cultivation. Here and there a shrine or temple teased free the light dwelling far above and between the clouds.

At last they descended to the steep valley of the Ochre River. There, in the shadow of the red-tinted Heavenwall, lay the village of Abundant Bamboo.

Bamboo was indeed abundant. Living bamboo fringed the town on the rocky far side of the river, and cut bamboo supported the multi-story buildings clustering there in a continuous maze. Some seemed to hug the Red Heavenwall itself. The ground levels were open-air gardens or tea houses or workshops or market stalls, surrounded by the stilts.

"If the Ochre River floods," Eshe said as Bone and Walking Stick helped Gaunt from the boat that brought them across, "the villagers lose these temporary constructions but not their homes."

"Do not the soldiers in the Wall offer sanctuary?" Bone asked.

"Not in living memory . . . Ah! There is my friend."

Eshe's friend was a sturdy Archaeopolitan named Tror, who dominated an open-air printing and calligraphy shop (it was a measure of Gaunt's exhaustion, Bone thought, that she barely noticed the scrolls, the ink, the marvelous machinery). Tror welcomed the travelers with big hands and a big voice. He wore a simple grey robe, but a swan medallion gleamed around his neck. His gaze was welcoming, but he narrowed his eyes upon seeing the Imperial official, and his bow was curt.

His wife Lightning Bug was a small, slender woman with strong arms and bright eyes. She was a striking beauty, and also a well-muscled one; Bone felt if she struck him in earnest, he would feel it for days. She moved quickly and deftly within a simple grey robe with a single yellow firefly embroidered at one shoulder, and soon she had the travelers safely settled and equipped with seats and tea (they declined the rice wine, which she swigged herself) watching the river boats bob past.

Bone noted that while Tror was abrupt with Walking Stick, Lightning Bug never even acknowledged him. Stranger still, the official seemed not to notice. Perhaps it was a distinction of gender?

Lightning Bug did acknowledge Bone, and immediately fussed at Gaunt. "You should not be traveling," she told the poet in Roil, the language of Swanisle and the Eldshore, touching her hand to Gaunt's middle.

Bone expected Gaunt to bristle, but his lover remained calm, even appreciative. For Lightning Bug conveyed nothing cloying nor predatory, as if born of a people too busy and practical for foolish privacy. "No, I should not," Gaunt agreed.

"Then stay," Lightning Bug said. "You too, Eshe."

"You honor me," the Swan priestess said.

Abruptly Lightning Bug fixed her attention on Walking Stick. "You may stay too, of course, man of the Garden."

"Does a woman of the Forest," Walking Stick replied, "invite me inside?"

Lightning Bug put a hand over her chest. "The Forest is within our hearts. Not our walls, Gardener."

"Then that is one Forest I will never wander." Walking Stick drew forth a scroll. Bone judged it to be very old, and likely valuable. Walking Stick handed it to Lightning Bug. "A gift, in return for this moment of hospitality."

Bone sensed caution from Lightning Bug, and controlled anger in Tror. There was history, there.

"A rich gift," Lightning Bug said, studying but not opening the scroll. "Is there a message here?"

"Sometimes a tree belongs to the forest, not the garden. I would plant it in this place, as a reminder that we both care for the growth of the Empire."

Lightning Bug nodded and tucked the scroll into the sash of her robe.

"Come, Gaunt, Eshe," Lightning Bug said, giving no more heed to Walking Stick and taking a traveler by each strong arm, "let me show you your rooms."

In the perplexing silence that followed, Tror coughed. "It is safe enough in Abundant Bamboo," he told Bone. "Whatever you are fleeing from, you are far from everything here, save a bored garrison in the Wall above. And from what Walking Stick tells me, you have diminished the bandit gang hereabouts."

"A refined thief should turn his attention to rich houses," Bone muttered, observing the villagers, "not poor peasants."

"Pardon me?"

"Thank you for the hospitality of your house." Bone bowed, and turned to bow to Walking Stick as well—but the official had already ridden away, his passage silent, his horse nearly lost in the thickets of bamboo.

"A strange man," Bone said.

"I have no choice but to respect him," Tror said, and paused as if ready to say more, but merely grunted and showed Bone the stairs.

The home was a six-story wooden affair, looming over its neighbors. Once it would have seemed modest, but not after the wilderness and the sea. From their cramped closet of a room, smelling of wood-dust and river-cooled air and distant pines, Gaunt and Bone looked out at an expanse of square roofs, and the dark curves of the river and hills beyond.

"I could readily cross the entire village," Bone whispered to Gaunt, studying the rooftops, "and never touch ground."

Gaunt patted his shoulder; then they looked down the stairs to find Tror and Lightning Bug and their three children all beaming and promising to assist Gaunt in the birth.

"We have three guests," Lightning Bug said matter-of-factly. "And soon enough, we will have four."

CHAPTER 8.

First, there was the taste of blood.

A scent of cold pine followed from the void, and on its heels blew the sting of frigid air.

Wind moaned among mountains, and light dawned to reveal them to her.

Her. A young woman. That was what she was, a human upon a mountain path, and her name was . . .

"Next One."

She turned and saw Flybait had also returned to reality. She laughed and hugged him.

"I *like* the afterlife," he said, pulling away with wide eyes. "It seems we've reached one of the lesser paradises. The divine judges are less severe than advertised. Good news for outlaws."

She cuffed him. "We're right back where we started. That official said we'd reached the edges of the painting. I think when we fell down the pit we left one edge. Now we've reappeared at another."

Flybait looked around, patting himself to measure his reality. "I recall my father telling of the sorcerer Hsuan Chieh, who could hide from his court duties by shrinking himself into a decorative landscape tray. I guess this place serves a similar function. But why then didn't we return to our world?"

"It may be that we have to wish it so. But I do not so wish it. The official believes us dead. I wish to explore. Perhaps the hermit will return. He did leave a clue with that poem about the pit and the sky."

"Let us try the sky, then," Flybait said. "It is warmer now. On other peaks I see pagodas. Maybe there's one here. Perhaps we can beg, borrow, or steal."

Thus emboldened, the youngsters made their chilly way up a mountain of fairytale. Trees spindled out into a misty vastness; waterfalls sliced vertical rivers through the rock; black birds flitted upon narrow wooden bridges that spanned jagged gorges.

Crossing a span, Next One said, "Who maintains such bridges?"

"Does such a question matter, in a world that was painted?"

"I want to know the why of things."

"Oh? Does not your ability to read grant you the wisdom of the ancients?"

"The ancients cared mostly for people and their ways. If you would know more about nature, or the composition of things, you must get your hands dirty and your feet wet." She thought a moment longer about Flybait's words. "Can you not read?"

He shrugged. "I am unencumbered by such matters."

"Spoken like a scholar. But you would play the part better if you could read."

"He who does, does. He who doesn't, documents."

"Spoken like one who failed the Imperial Examinations. But you could not even read the signs to get there. Well, I am stuck with you, so I may as well teach you."

"Ha! A girl teach me!"

"Old bearded men are in short supply."

"Hm. Well. It would be amusing to try. Some day."

"Oh—so you think I can say nothing of writing here, in the thick of nature? Not so." They rounded a pathway to the edge of the sky, and Next One swept her arm as she'd seen Lightning Bug do when speaking of forests, rivers, and mountains.

"The early sages divined classical writing from the symbols embedded in nature," she told him. "We start with high and low, bright summits and dark valleys, heaven and earth. And between them, humanity. That is the basic trigram: above, below, and us in the middle. Three lines." She swished her finger through a snowbank three times and slowly licked the melting slush upon her finger. (She had Flybait's attention.) "You can break a line—" here she clopped at "heaven" with the edge of her hand, "and make a new trigram. Break one of them, two of them, all three—you get the variations used in the fortune-telling sticks, as stipulated in the *Book of Jagged Lines*."

"So writing is fortune-telling?"

"No! But there's a connection. The sages taught that nature's deepest patterns can be represented in our arts. Thus the earliest characters of writing represent simple pictures. It is said that the Four-Eyed Sage of Antiquity divined the first characters by observing tortoise shells, rivers, birds, and stars—all the patterns of the world. The patterns lie at the back of everything. So, you can draw a few spiky lines for 'mountain,' or a kind of burst pattern for 'fire,' or a spindly one for 'tree.'" She swished out the patterns as she spoke.

"Okay. But come on, you know that most of the characters aren't really pictures. They're . . . squiggles. Squiggles upon squiggles upon squiggles."

"Well, people have had thousands of years to develop writing. It's gotten complicated. There's a lot to remember. But you can do it, Flybait." She echoed something Lightning Bug had said to her. "You're still young."

Now there appeared upon the heights a pagoda of cheerful-looking red brick, clouds winding above it and mists swirling beneath it, as though it performed a vaporous ribbon-dance.

Something about the movement of the clouds worried her. Two billowing, serpentine cloudbanks were moving toward each other, as if to battle or mate. It did not seem natural, even for this place.

"Hey, look at this," Flybait called. He pointed at a pine tree whose trunk was inscribed with knife-cut characters, a poem in the bark. She read it for him.

> *Trampling snow up the Peculiar Peaks,*
> *The mountain path meanders:*
> *The deep ravine clogged by an avalanche,*
> *The twisting creek, the fog-dimmed bushes.*
> *It hasn't rained, but we slip on the grass,*
> *It isn't windy, but the trees seem to breathe.*
> *Who can jump from the weight of the world*
> *And join me in the tumbling clouds?*

"Yep," Flybait said. "Crazy."

"No," Next One said, "it's as if he is anticipating us. Uh-oh . . ."

"Uh-oh what."

"Look at the clouds."

The pair of converging cloud masses had taken on the aspects of strange raptors, or dragons. Each flew sideways, such that Next One could see upon each only one eye, one mouth, one foreclaw, one hindclaw, one horn. Tails curved upward, framing the scene.

When the clouds came together, their forms merged to create one image. It was as though the world pivoted. The mouths conjoined, the eyes paired and seemed to gaze forward, the horns seemed as eyebrows and the claws as fur upon a hungry, monstrous face.

"Taotie!" Flybait screeched.

"What?"

"A devourer. A spirit monster shown on old bronze sacrificial urns. But now we're the sacrifices. Run!"

The two ran, and whenever Next One cast her gaze behind her, she saw the cloudy maw of the taotie bearing down on them. It grinned and blew, and strong winds appeared where none had been, bending and snapping trees. Rocks tumbled, and mists swirled all around.

"Where can we run?" Flybait yelled. "The cave's too far!"

Next One thought of something crazy. Or the other side of crazy. "The poem! The hermit was telling us something. 'Who can jump . . . and join me in the clouds?'"

"Jump over a cliff? That's a plan?"

"It worked in the pit!"

The taotie was almost upon them.

"Okay," Flybait said. "If it's that or be eaten . . ."

They held hands, took deep breaths, and jumped.

They spun within the void, the taotie following them down into endless mist. After a time all senses faded into a perception of bright emptiness. Next One's last thought was that this bright emptiness was the counterpoint of the dark emptiness of the pit, and if she could understand both sides at once, the light and the dark, she would understand what was beyond, the true empti—

CHAPTER 9.

Imago Bone heard the intruders the evening after settling in to Abundant Bamboo. Asleep beside the door (he had insisted, as it was after all their first night and who knew what could happen?) he roused to the sound of creaking two floors below, and of sharp whispers. He'd slept in his traveling clothes (again, it was the first night) and rose to a coiled crouch before he was fully awake.

Gaunt still slept upon the narrow bed, and he chose not to disturb her until he'd heard more. There. Another creak, and a bump, and some frantic whispering. This would not be their hosts, planning murder—such sounds would be closer. This was probably not their hosts' children—the voices sounded young, but not that young. House thieves.

Another bump. Amateur house thieves.

It occurred to Bone he could be useful to the family. The thought made him smile. He drew on his belt, the one with two sheathed daggers, and slipped out the door.

Tiptoeing down the stairs to the landing, he judged the intruders unaware, for their whispering continued unabated. They sounded confused, as though they'd gotten the wrong house. Bone considered whether to be lethal or merciful, and was considering the problem so carefully he nearly jumped when a hand came down upon his shoulder and another across his mouth.

It was the gentleness of the iron grip that made him relax and look into the eyes of Lightning Bug. She wore a dark outfit suitable for nighttime heists, with a hood not yet pulled up. He resisted speculation about her evening activities, whether criminal or carnal.

She released him and pointed downstairs. He nodded. In that moment he had no doubt she could defend her own home. But a guest had his obligations.

He proceeded down the stairs, she right behind him. He heard bickering in the language of Qiangguo. There were two shadowy forms in the moonlight cast by the sitting room window. One shadow examined a desk, the other a table.

Bone launched himself at the one at the desk, tackling him—no, her.

97

She squirmed and pounded and scratched and bit, and Bone found himself getting angry at her unwillingness to succumb to his superior thiefcraft. She grabbed at something on the desk and tried to club him with it. Luckily it was just a scroll. He shifted his weight and she fell. By this time Lightning Bug was there, and the second intruder already lay still.

Lightning Bug reached out and performed a rapid series of jabs upon the foe's head and chest.

The young woman stiffened and ceased to do anything but breathe.

"That," gasped Bone, "is quite a trick."

"Knowledge of the pressure points is very old," Lightning Bug said, "but the more exotic techniques are hard to master."

Bone nodded as if he understood.

Lightning Bug said, "Help me make them comfortable," and together they dragged the intruders to a couch and Bone stood over them, feeling superfluous, while Lightning Bug fetched a lamp.

Oil hissed and flame weaved, and the room awakened with flickering light. This was the scholarly nook of the house, draped with hanging scrolls of tumultuous mountains and serene lakes, banners of calligraphy like traces of dancing ink, and a hanging carpet dizzying in its unity of reds and yellows, squares and circles. A gnarled tree root in one corner served as the stand for peculiar artifacts of ceramic and wood and bronze, and a desk stood opposite with a pen and an ink block impressed with a tangle of dragons.

Previously Bone had only glanced at this room. He'd been distracted by Gaunt's needs, and the chamber's alienness baffled his appraiser's eye. Now he responded to the weight of knowledge and tradition as if he stood in the work-shop of a Western wizard. The presence of arts unguessed stirred his sense of wonder and his caution. He stood light on his feet.

Lightning Bug's voice pierced his mood, made the study seem less a somber encoding of culture, and more a record of a mind's pleasures. "I recognize them!" she said. "The girl has been my student, of sorts. A runaway; I taught her in return for labor. A project, really. The boy I have seen here and there. He is a bandit, or likes to think he is."

Bone realized he recognized them, too. "The ambush at the stone! These two were the wisest of the bandits, never having actually attacked us. How did they end up here?"

"A question to be asked over rice wine," said Lightning Bug.

Noises filled the upper stories, and as Lightning Bug filled in her husband and stilled the excited children in rapid-fire speech, the Western thieves checked on Eshe, who had not awakened despite all.

"She's just sleeping deeply," Gaunt said, after studying the enigmatic Kpalamaa woman, she who was sailor, cook, and Swan priestess. "As I wish I was."

"You could certainly return to bed."

"And miss how the local thieves surprised Imago Bone? I think not!"

He helped her downstairs and into a chair, which he crouched beside. Lightning Bug handed him a porcelain cup with a clear, warm liquor that burned in an unfamiliar but not altogether unpleasant way. "Not for you," Lightning Bug snapped at Gaunt's outstretched hand, in such a matter-of-fact way that Gaunt took no offense. "Tea is coming. *Tror*!"

With wine and tea, they contemplated the paralyzed prisoners.

"They will snap out of it soon," Lightning Bug said. "The technique is essentially harmless. They may feel a little drunk."

Bone felt a little drunk. It had hit him at last. Here he was, on the eastern fringe of the known world! He, a mere second-story man! And it was here Gaunt would bear their child. He took another sip.

The young man and woman on the couch stirred. *I was never such a pup*, Bone thought of the boy, and, *Odd, I feel protective of the girl. And a little afraid of her, too.*

The young bandits woke up, and were immediately caught in the volley of Lightning Bug's angry speech. Their eyes widened in shock—and in the girl's case, recognition. They lifted their hands and just as quickly made innocent-sounding objections. To a screech of a question, the girl knelt before Lightning Bug.

"This is," Tror whispered, "that girl. The one my wife takes in now and then. She has come on bad times."

"She has talent," Bone said.

"Oh?" Tror said.

"A quick mind," Gaunt put in. "The boy too."

"Hm," Tror said.

The interview was proceeding. The girl and boy were miming many strange things as they talked—a horse, falling leaves or snow, tumbling into a pit or off a cliff, dragons. And they pointed at the scroll upon the floor.

"I believe," Lightning Bug said in Roil, raising the scroll, "these particular trespassers can be released."

"What they have done is very serious," Tror said. "They are old enough to suffer consequences for their actions."

"I say the consequences should be these: they will do hard labor for this family, for a month. If they demur, we will call the authorities down upon them. For they were pursued by Walking Stick himself, and they will not want his wrath."

"Hm," Tror said. "So many guests . . ."

"These two, Flybait and Next-One-A-Boy, will sleep outside. They may come upstairs if the river floods. And Persimmon Gaunt and Imago Bone? I would like you to instruct them in your language, and for them to teach you ours."

CHAPTER 10.

And so it was that Next One found herself instructing not just a smelly bandit but two pale barbarians (for she taught them reading and writing all at once, and Flybait needed at least half of that). From the moment she'd tumbled out of the scroll-world and recognized Lightning Bug's home, Next One had concluded that the workings of the Way were somehow guiding her like the Ochre River's currents might sweep a carp. She decided she'd best not swim against them. And when Lightning Bug herself stood revealed as the Woman in Black, she could only kneel.

"Here is how it is," her mentor told her then, in the tone of an outlaw of the Rivers-and-Lakes. "You and bandit-boy arrived via the magic painting. You know it and I know it. The painting is mine now. That's half my price for not turning you in to the Empire. The other half is that you're going to help me bring down your gallant fraternity. They are becoming a nuisance. Oh, and the third half is that you're helping those ghost-faced lovebirds over there speak like civilized people."

"It is not our fault!" said Flybait, and, "Ten thousand abject pardons! We were not even there!" and many other things to this effect.

"Everything is your fault," Lightning Bug said. "Everything is my fault. Everything is everybody's fault. Therefore, everything is nobody's fault."

"Huh?" said Flybait.

"Hush," Next One hissed. "She's being mystical."

"Oh."

"You will learn to work together," Lightning Bug said, "like the opposites that bring forth the stuff of nature—light and darkness, rain and sun, man and woman."

"Hm," Flybait said. "Tea and beer?"

"It was an example of cosmic opposites!" Flybait protested after they were exiled to the stilts of the house, with naught but sleeping gear and a scroll of instructions. "Have you tried drinking one right after the other? It doesn't work. You get industrious and maudlin at the same time. You weep, twitching."

"I am going to weep twitching. Shut up and go to sleep."

"We could just escape, you know."

"From *her*? I now know her for the Woman in Black. We're not going to escape from her. And even if we did, the Cloud and Soil Society will still think we betrayed them. Our best chance is to stay right here."

"And *really* betray the Cloud and Soil Society? They weren't so bad to us, Next One."

"Chang wasn't too bad. Exceedingly Accurate Wu, now . . ."

"Wu . . . so the Woman in Black is going up against Wu."

"We're going up against Wu," Next One said.

"You have a grudge against her, huh?"

"We'll see if she calls me a child this time."

Sleeping outside wasn't really so bad, as long as there was warmth and some cover for the rain; she'd done it before, when her parents punished her for yelling at the Little Emperor after he punched and bit her. The night was chilly, but Lightning Bug and Tror had provided good bedrolls. River ripples, cricket trills, owl hoots, and fish splashes made peculiar music beside bamboo stilts and stars. Even Flybait amused her, rolling back and forth, sometimes emitting a snore, sometimes a muttered, "Ha-ha," or "Run away," or "I didn't do it." At last sleep came, and whether she dreamed of cold mountains or cold families, she remembered nothing.

Next One had to wait to satisfy her grudge against Wu, for the next weeks were chores, and language lessons, and more chores, and all of it involved more barbarians than she'd ever known before.

She knew not what to make of them. The only foreign devils she'd heard much about were monkey people from the lands across the eastern sea, and considering these were supposed to possess stone skeletons, prodigious magics, supernatural fighting arts, and the wisdom of two-year-olds, Next One suspected the stories were a trifle exaggerated. Rather than foils for the heroes of legend, these real barbarians seemed perplexities for the sages.

Imago Bone was pale and thin enough to be a hungry ghost, those emaciated specters who longed for burnt offerings of food and money, if they weren't after the very breath of the living. Certainly he gazed at potstickers and gold with enough longing to qualify. But in his leaping and climbing and skulking he might have been a monkey person indeed.

Persimmon Gaunt was even paler, but she was near to bursting with a barbarian baby-to-come. Her frame spoke of action and theft and generosity and narrow escapes. Her eyes spoke of tombs and flowers and elegies and inevitable decay. Her voice spoke of all these things and the glimmer of a silver thread that bound them.

Eshe of the Fallen Swan was dark like summer shadows in the mountains, and her smile was like the moon flung high in a winter sky. All seasons found their record on her face, which spun through springtime and autumn with the telling of one anecdote of Swanisle far away, or Kpalamaa, farther. If common wisdom was to know the dripping of years, then Eshe was wise with the torrent of moments.

"These are our companions," Flybait scoffed, "for storming the gallant fraternity?"

"Two only," Next One said, "for Gaunt will not join us. Rather she is writing a speech for what Bone calls our 'caper.'"

"I know that barbarian word now! It means to tumble and prance like a fool."

"I fear there may be some similarity," Next One said.

CHAPTER II.

It would be wrong to say that, for Gaunt and Bone, a month passed uneventfully. But in lives that had featured cruel sorcerers, murderous mermaids, and angels of death, the next weeks held a certain charm.

Gaunt swelled, and the life within her kicked and twisted. Bone made himself useful in lawful ways. He was clever at hunting and fearless in repairing roofs. He brought skins for the leatherworkers and closed leaks for the wood-workers. It was Lightning Bug who found him such clients, and Bone sensed there was a chain of favors being forged—but that was her own business.

He found able assistants in Flybait and Next One, and his language lessons often focused on such terms as *rope, handhold, balance, leap*, and *escape*. The town magistrate raised eyebrows at these nimble strangers, but Lightning Bug and Tror whispered to him about the fate of Five Finger Chang, about the involvement of certain barbarians in that event, and about the probability that the Cloud and Soil Society might have a second encounter.

The magistrate raised eyebrows again, but he nodded, and made no report of suspicious persons in Abundant Bamboo.

He had good reason, Bone saw. The bandits, as if freshly motivated with demonic intensity, had been waylaying travelers and shaking down farm-houses with near impunity, for the magistrate had just a handful of guardsmen. Worse, Bone gathered that there were so many kinship ties and kickbacks between the bandits and the villages hereabouts that it was hard to muster a militia. The villages endured the bandits the way a family might endure a violent drunk of an uncle. If the lout didn't press his luck too far, he could dare much. Thus Bone understood the seed of Lightning Bug's plan. This matter called not for honest Qiangguo folk, but for barbarians, ne'er-do-wells, and a vigilante in black. But first they had to work together.

"Shay-shay," Bone said.

There were smirks around the room.

"*Thank you*," Bone repeated in the Tongue of the Tortoise Shell.

The young people tittered.

"You sound as if you're sneezing," Lightning Bug said.

Bone tried again.

"You sound like a snake, my friend," Tror said.

"I've been called one," Bone said, and tried again.

"Now you sound like you're choking," Eshe said from where she lay bandaged on the couch. Now the youths and the children upstairs were all snorting.

Bone made another sound, under his breath.

"This time it sounds like you're shushing us," Lightning Bug said.

"I think he was," Gaunt said.

"No," Bone muttered, "it wasn't that polite . . ."

"Your characters are accurate," Lightning Bug said, "but they lack energy. Like sticks that happened to scatter in a particular way."

Bone snatched the pen and swished a character for "mountain" that stabbed the white paper sky.

"Violent energy has its uses, but we are looking for balance," Lightning Bug said. "Energy contained by purpose."

"Pretend you're robbing a mansion," Gaunt suggested.

"Show me the character for 'mansion,'" Bone said.

It reminded Bone of a spindly tree rising beside a three-story building, one busy with flanges and balconies and windows. Entry by way of the tree and the upper left window almost seemed too obvious, but a thief should not disparage what Nature and architecture provided. He copied the brush strokes, his mind upon speed, alertness, and light footwork. By the time he reached the ground floor and his escape to the right, he felt he'd escaped with a nobleman's fine paint brush and a clinking coin-chain.

"That is better," Lightning Bug said. "You may have some talent."

"Show me the character for 'treasury,'" Bone said.

"The lesson for today," Bone said, "is on going unseen." He stood leaning against a juniper near a slow-moving tributary of the Ochre River. Tror stood beside him, translating. Flybait and Next One had learned some Roil, but for this he needed to speak with flourish. This was serious. This was about craft.

"Let us say I'm a guard," Bone said pointing at the youngsters, "and I've just spotted you. How are you going to hide?"

Flybait knelt hunched, as though attempting to squeeze himself into a market basket.

"Wonderful," Bone said, "except that I've already seen you. I'll just assume you're surrendering or kindly giving me a slower target. What about you, Next One?"

Next One mimed throwing something. She accompanied the gesture with a torrent of syllables.

Bone's shaky grasp of the language was actually confusing him, more than if he'd been able to write everything off as babble. But Tror said, "She states that she has blinded you with a thrown dagger."

"I admire your active approach!" Bone replied. "However, we cannot assume that slaughtering the guard, with the usual accompanying screams and gurgles, will serve the cause of concealment. No, my point was that learning to sneak begins well *before* you stumble upon a guard. Nothing we do is direct. In this situation you've lost surprise, and your best recourse is to run away."

Next One said something and spat.

"She says all of your lessons are about running away," Tror explained.

Bone beamed, and twirled. "Yes! A flash of enlightenment through the branches!"

Now Flybait muttered something, and Tror said, "He wonders how we are to defeat twenty bandits without any fighting."

"You've answered your own question," Bone said, "if you phrase it a little differently. We are five against twenty. Any plan must employ methods other than fighting. Stealth. Trickery. Surprise. Superstition. Fast feet." He sought for old Master Sidewinder's phrasing. "Fights will surely occur, but these are coughs in a well-practiced chorus. It need not stop the show, but do not confuse it for the music."

Tror's voice trailed off. "I do not think I can translate that effectively."

"We run," Bone tried again, "so we can fight them where we want them."

Flybait and Next One soon wore identical fierce grins. They looked like a married couple. "Kids," he muttered.

They practiced walking over dry leaves.

Crunch, crunch, crunch, scatter, crunch, skitter, CRUNCH.

"You are the opposite of inconspicuous, Flybait," Bone said, tugging on his own hair. "You look suspicious even when you're standing around being saintly. When you give candy to children, guardsmen must stir from their sleep."

"Why would I waste good candy?" Flybait objected.

"You try, Next One."

Crunch-crunch-crunch-crunch-(whoosh)-Whump.

Bone fell, seeing the Aurora Borealis inside his dizzy head. He felt like an amateur. He simply hadn't anticipated her leaping and kicking him in the face.

"Are you all right?" Next One said as he cradled his leaking nose.

"Flybait, stop laughing," Bone said, rising. "Now, this is a teachable moment about blood. Not only do we need blood inside our bodies, but leaking wounds are a damned nuisance. Tror, a cloth please."

Bone bound up his nose with a long cloth tied around the back of his head. Soon he was smelling blood. Not being a Mandrake Marauder or a spider of Webness, he did not much like it.

"Now my mobements are somewhat inconbenienced. I must use aw my skiw. Awso, if I am not careful I wiw leabe a blood traiw behind me. Tror, try not to smirk."

Bone shifted around quickly, acting out combat and flight. It made him dizzy. "There is awso the danger of swipping in your own blood." He tee-tered—but he was Imago Bone! He had a reputation to maintain. Or rather, as these were the Starborn Lands, a reputation to establish. Where was he? He tried to focus his thought and speech.

"Not being seen. Not being heard. This is how you win against a greater foe. Show me how you'd crawl across dangerous ground!" He dropped low, and the youngsters joined him. "Consider how every leaf and twig can signal your approach. You are a puddle. You are a slime mold. Your progress is measured in inches. Your success is measured by silence. Until you leap!"

He sprang into action, scrambling up a tree, the blood rushing in his head. "Climb!" he called, and they did. There was something infectious in his mania, and their enthusiasm spurred him on further in turn. "Goblin book collectors are after you! Oblivion Knights are after you! Purple neurovores are after you, and they'll burp the offal of your dreams! Flee! Get altitude! Embrace our monkey lineage!"

They were in branches now and sunlight blazed in splatterbursts around the green knives of leaves, gossamer blazes webbing his sight.

A small golden burst hovered in front of his nose. Oddly, it did not disappear when he turned his head. There was a buzzing in his ears.

"Bone," Next One said, no translation needed.

Bone waved her off, and in the same moment slapped away the bug. He did not like bugs. Strange . . . more golden buzzing things were nearby . . .

Tror was shouting something. "What are you talking about?" Bone called. "Hide from what?"

"Not hide!" Tror bellowed. "Hive!"

Bone now noticed Flybait jabbing a finger at a brown blob upon the trunk.

"We see now the wisdom of running away!" Bone shouted. "You kids, move it! You're further away! I'll distract the bees!"

Bone launched toward the nearby stream and a branch dangling above. Unfortunately, more branches blocked the way down. He did not want to become entangled or battered.

He snatched off his long tourniquet, yelped a bit, and shimmied to the branch's end, where leaves dangled over leaping fish. He looped the fabric around the branch and jumped. The limb jerked, bent, and snapped, but the plunge was gentler that it might have been. He earned stings but no broken bones.

When they helped him escape the Ochre River ten minutes later, he sputtered and said, "Thank you." He wrote it too, with a stick on the muddy bank. The others thought him much improved on both counts. He beamed and sneezed blood.

"I have an idea for the bandits," Next One told him then, in excellent Roil.

"I listen," said Bone in the Tongue of the Tortoise Shell.

Dunked in the river of Qiangguo's language, Bone learned quickly, though not so fast as Gaunt. He began to think action against the bandits was not quite suicidal. He wondered if running a modest gang wasn't so terrible after all. They needed another fighter, however. They needed Eshe.

She healed, repaying their hosts with nightly tales of Kpalamaa and the surrounding lands. The children laughed at the story of the hat vendor whose wares were stolen by monkeys until only his own hat still remained upon his head, which he threw in a rage—and how the monkeys' imitative response prompted him to invent the discus. Eshe told of how the spider got the hippo and elephant to agree he was stronger, after they played tug-of-war with each other among obscuring webs, each believing the spider their foe. Bone learned of how a *Ghana*, a king of Kpalamaa, ventured into the wider world, bringing enough gold to topple the economy of Palmary. (That tale he knew by rumor, and he resolved again to someday visit Kpalamaa and the vaults of the Ghana.)

At last Lightning Bug called in favors, and leatherworkers and wood-workers and firepowder makers delivered wares.

"It is time," Lightning Bug said, "to prune the lands around Abundant Bamboo. We start by making you into a troupe of actors who will be playing dead. Except for you, Gaunt and Eshe, who have your own tasks, literary and mechanical." Both smiled. Lightning Bug thought a moment, and laughed. "And we must inform the magistrate that he will soon lose his office . . ."

CHAPTER 12.

The Cloud and Soil Society was in a restless mood. Life had been trying under Five Finger Chang, but it had been fun too. There had been laughter and song and drunkenness and storytelling and all the pleasures that a criminal life in the countryside ought to entail. Chang frequently reminded them all of the inherent duplicity of Imperial authority, and how honorable bandits were the necessary counterpoint. They would not have the blessing of the One-Shoed Immortal otherwise. They were not robbing the rich so much as lightening a corrupting load of unearned goods. They were not intimidating villagers so much as protecting them from mendacious tax collectors and debased marauders who lacked regular readings of *Romance of the Outlaw Kingdoms* to fortify their morals.

Exceedingly Accurate Wu would have none of that. They were *bandits*, she said, not heroes. They were not loved but feared. The outlaws of legend were lovable precisely because they were safely inside books, not at your doorstep shaking you down. No romances would be written about the Cloud and Soil Society. The Empire was as honest, and dishonest, as it had ever been. This was not an especially corrupt time, and it was useless to blame banditry on the government. There were big lies in life but the bandits who embraced the world of the Rivers-and-Lakes needed to be clear-eyed and cold-eyed.

"We are evil," Exceedingly Accurate Wu said on the evening of Lightning Bug's attack, yet another night of edifying speeches and small-group discussions, with no hope of song or alcohol or sex until the owls were hooting. "Do not be shocked. Evil is simply the flip side of good, and together the two sides are the coin of the world. Purity is all well and good, but it belongs to heaven. Man cannot live on virtue alone, for virtue is as a crusty bread. Evil is spice. Evil is meat. We evil folk are necessary. And not necessary because of some tiresome illusion of outlaw gallantry, no! Because we are part of the natural order. We toughen the society on which we prey. We make it better. And some day we may claim all of it as our own—evil bringing forth good."

A hand went up. "What do you mean? We're going to take over?"

"That is the natural trajectory of things. Did not the Second Emperor emerge from banditry? But if we are to claim a realm for ourselves we must be worthy of it. We're going to protect the ordinary people and improve their minds. If the peasantry of Qiangguo were to rise up, the rulership would crumple like a paper tiger. We must be patient as we arrange this, one village at a time."

Another hand. "Um, you want to be an emperor, ma'am?"

"I do not want to replace an old foolishness with a new one. You may speak of me as the Chair. I do not represent a change in dynasty, but a new power that expresses the will of the people. We will become a land that is Exceedingly Accurate. Those who cling to error will be isolated—or eliminated. Many monsters will be destroyed. Old superstitions will pass away."

A third voice. "Can we still be gallant? Just a little?"

"A certain style is expected," Wu conceded. "It is not what I would term 'gallantry.' 'Eliteness' perhaps. You are the elite. The vanguard."

A fourth voice. "Can we still have a good time?"

"Rewards are due the vanguard. But with rewards come responsibilities. You are an army now. You may not desert. Even if you are not currently having a 'good time.' Deserters will be punished."

There was a whistle from the sentries, and guards dragged someone in, and a whisper moved through the crowd, "Flybait! We've got Flybait!"

The boy was thrown at Wu's feet. Wu said, "The winds of history have blown you to me, boy. Why did you return? Where is your lover?"

"What?"

"The girl, you cretin. It is obvious you and she are a couple."

". . . Really?"

Wu planted her cane beside Flybait's gut. "You are due many beatings. Gather your wits, and I may leave your brains inside your skull."

"As you are exceedingly accurate, I have no doubt of your threat." Flybait sat up. "I am here with an offer of amnesty from the magistrate of Abundant Bamboo. If any bandit should appear to him, prostrate and weaponless, before the next full moon, that one shall be given pardon."

"If pardon means 'a quick death," Wu snorted.

"He is sincere. Look how weaponless and prostrate I am! I did not learn this bowing and scraping all at once, but practiced it in his office."

"Where then is Next-One-A-Boy," Wu scoffed. "Let us see *her* bow and scrape!"

"Alas!" wailed Flybait, hiding his face in his hands. "She would not! And the magistrate laughed and said she would regret her foolishness, for he had special friends."

Wu leaned on her staff, scowling. "Friends? That sniveling mouse?"

"He said his friends included a god with one shoe."

A hush fell upon the Cloud and Soil Society, and a murmuring.

But Exceedingly Accurate Wu said, "This young fool and the magistrate seek to frighten us! There is no such god, for there are no gods. Even those beings that seem magical are but the manifestation of congealed chi."

Flybait said, "Indeed, Next-One-A-Boy once spoke as you, for she confronted just such an entity, which had taken the form of the Nian! But when she scoffed at the magistrate, where he lectured us in the village, a shoe did drop."

And now the hubbub rose indeed. For there had by now reached the Cloud and Soil Society the word of a gigantic thunderclap in the magistrate's office, and word of deaths in its wake.

"Here is what remains of my dear friend!" howled Flybait, and he held up a strip of the bland grey cloth Next-One-A-Boy had been known to wear. A red smear soaked the fabric.

"Give me that!" said Exceedingly Accurate Wu, and she snatched the scrap away. She sniffed and licked. "Why, this is not human blood, but pig's blood. Do you think I am an amateur?"

But her words were drowned out by a thundering crash against the exterior of the hill. The bandits ran to and fro in fear. A sentry leapt down into the cave. "Mistress!" he shouted. "It is a shoe! A giant shoe!"

Not far away, in a secluded glade, Next One and Eshe of the Fallen Swan labored to reload the catapult which Eshe had constructed from a Kpalamaa design. This time the payload was a bee's hive, gathered with great care by Lightning Bug and wrapped in a cloth bundle secured with Imago Bone's ur-glue.

"Now!" yelled Lightning Bug from a treetop far above.

Next One swung a sword so heavy it made her arms feel ready to pop from their sockets. Once, twice . . . on the third cleave the rope split and the beehive took flight.

"Excellent!" called Lightning Bug. "It has landed in the midst of the sentries. Now the fire-buckets!"

Next One loaded a bucket of tar, while Eshe cranked. The strange Kpalamaa woman and her machine were a wonder to Next One, though Eshe assured her that catapults were well known to the generals of Qiangguo. She marveled at a woman who had learned so much and seemed, like Lightning Bug, to have acquired only an average measure of bitterness. She wondered if she too might be able to travel to Kpalamaa someday, or Swanisle, or any other place where women knew grace and light.

"Where will you go," Next One called, "when you are finished here? To Kpalamaa? To the court of the wise and terrible Ghana? We could come with you!"

Eshe laughed at some joke known only to herself. "No. To the capital of your land. You may indeed come. We have a more immediate task, however."

She grabbed tongs and lifted a burning piece of coal from a nearby bucket. The pitch blazed in a satisfying way.

"Now!" called Lightning Bug. Next One swung. Fire ascended and plunged.

"Continue in this manner!" called Lightning Bug. "I must take the path of treetops and meet Imago Bone. Persimmon Gaunt asked me to watch over him. Around a pregnant woman, even a wulin warrior must tread carefully!"

"Good luck!" answered Eshe.

Next One watched open-mouthed as Lightning Bug kicked off from atop her tree and arced gently to the next, and then the next, as easily as a girl leaping along a garden wall.

Eshe laughed. "You are amazed at my catapult? Qiangguo has machines even my folk do not . . . and as you see, its people are the most wondrous of all."

"How does she do it? Dance among the trees?"

"She has spoken of the 'ability of lightness,' in which the vital breath of her body is expanded, lofting the rest like a spark climbing the air. In truth, we of Kpalamaa are a materialistic bunch, and I do not really understand it. It is enough to marvel."

"To think . . . one such as she might have had her feet bound."

"Remember that," Eshe said, "when the rain falls cold and you are lonely and footsore and chewing on tasteless roots. Remember that at least you live free. Now—we have our own sparks to send high!"

The last time Imago Bone remembered challenging such odds as the Cloud and Soil Society, he'd been chased by maddened cannibals and quasi-sapient bears. That he and Gaunt had not been rent and devoured on that occasion he attributed more to luck than skill. Thus, as he slipped among the shadows of the karst cave, ears alert to the sounds of sentries near at hand and of commotion farther above, he took great care not to be seen. Fortunately the cave's topography was his friend. Stalactites and stalagmites made regular obstacles to his enemies' sight, and the underground river and waterfall made his movements a hush. Indeed, such was the range of concealment options that Bone thought the bandits somewhat cheeky for choosing this site. But then, they had reckoned on Imperial troops, not the greatest second-story man of the Spiral Sea.

Creeping close to the waterfall, he removed a pouch of chemicals supplied by Lightning Bug. Evidently she had contacts who knew alchemy. This "essence of the cinnabar heart" was supposed to have a sanguinary effect upon water. Bone shredded the pouch and poured the powdery contents into the waterfall's foam.

At once the underground stream flowed red. He listened as the already-nervous guards called out, "Blood! The waters flow red with blood! It is the war god indeed!" With a vast commotion the guards fled the lower section, the camp followers and hangers-on fleeing with them. Bone took the opportunity to take a dagger and stone and pound holes in the handful of riverboats the bandits maintained.

Now there remained only the bulk of the bandits proper.

Only!

Bone smirked, crept up a ladder, and listened to what had to be Exceedingly Accurate Wu, rallying her frightened force.

He understood enough of the Tongue of the Tortoise Shell to catch her gist. "It is only bees, you fools! Only fire! We are attacked by men only!"

"It is the Lord of Lost Causes! We saw the shoe!"

As Bone peeked out, Wu removed her own shoe and beat a bandit with it. "We are being tricked. Let us scare our foes for a change! Kill Flybait, and toss his body down the burning hill!"

"Um," said Flybait as he was held down by a man at each limb. "Aren't you guys my friends?"

"You gave up friendship when you betrayed us," Wu scoffed. "Such is never done. You are an outlaw among outlaws."

"Sorry, Flybait," said a big man with an axe.

"Hey, don't worry, Feng," said Flybait. "Mind if I scream and raise a fuss?"

"I don't mind," said the big man, "as long as you hold still."

Bone drew and threw a dagger, hitting Feng in the eye. The axeman screamed.

"I didn't do it!" Flybait yelled, flailing free of his startled guards. "I didn't do it!"

"There!" called Exceedingly Accurate Wu, drawing a dagger of her own. "A Western ghost! I knew it!"

"Boo," Bone said, and ducked just in time to avoid Wu's dagger, which hit the nearby rocks sharply enough to draw sparks. Wu was accurate indeed.

He felt a degree of kinship for Flybait, who despite his posture of self-centeredness was obviously risking his neck to impress a woman. Bone bellowed, "I am no ordinary ghost! I am a servant of the War God Guanti, he of the great clomping foot!"

There were fresh cries of alarm—but through all cut the voice of Wu: "That is pronounced Kuan Ti."

"That's what I said! Do you think I would get the Dread One's name wrong?"

"I think," Wu said, "that you and Flybait are cut from the same cloth. Funeral cloth. Kill them both!"

Bone threw a dagger her way and dove out of the opening. He hoped to sufficiently distract the bandits that Flybait would find a way to escape.

In fact, the bandits were all looking up.

Someone was cackling on high—someone dressed in black and clinging to a stalactite. "Rejoice!" came the voice of Lightning Bug. "Your fate is sealed! The war god has chosen you to be his shield bearers. Rejoice, as death initiates you into an eternity of service!" She continued in much this vein, plundering phrasing from the *Classic of Cardinal Directions*, the *Nine-Times-Nine Ruses*, and the *Romance of the Outlaw Kingdoms*. Persimmon Gaunt had researched Lightning Bug's speech well, drawing forth especially gruesome details as to the manner of this promotion—how the god's foot would squeeze out spirits like the guts from stomped crabs.

The upper waterfall, too, ran red.

Bandits were exiting at high speed. But Exceedingly Accurate Wu took aim at the shadowy form and threw her dagger.

Even Lightning Bug was not invulnerable, and the blade caught her arm.

"Look!" crowed Wu. "There is blood! True blood! Let outlaws of courage rally around me!"

Wu's confidence secured herself five champions even as their brethren hurried out of the cave. Fortunately Flybait's immediate captors were among the departed, the half-blind Feng of the axe included. Bone and Flybait took cover behind a stalagmite. Wu called to her men, "Give me daggers! I'll down this ill-omened bird."

Bone eyed the gigantic axe abandoned by Feng. "Two of us could lift that," he observed.

"You are crazy," Flybait said.

"Want to try it?"

"Sure."

Soon two screaming thieves were charging the bandits with an axe bigger than either of them. The weapon had not been designed as a pole arm, but it was in such a manner that Bone and Flybait rushed the knot of foes. Distracted by the wulin woman leaping from stalactite to stalactite, the outlaws were unprepared for an attack of such poetic stupidity. Two of them simply toppled as they leapt out of the way; a third managed to get himself impaled on a flange of the axe, more by his own misjudgment than any precision of the wielders.

At that moment Lightning Bug leapt. Wu threw a dagger with a victorious grin, but Lightning Bug plunged in a corkscrew spin and the dagger slashed her leg but did no worse. Wulin woman and bandit queen connected with a sprawl.

Bone saw that two bandits might readily pounce upon Lightning Bug, so he tackled one. Flybait tripped the other. While thus occupied, the man and the boy could not secure their advantage with the remaining three. Bone sensed their approach, and felt the scales tipping against him.

Now came a screech of fury and an ululating war cry. Next One and Eshe were here, and they carried a giant burning shoe between them. They toppled one bandit with the toe and brought another to heel. The remaining free bandit, clutching a gut wound from the huge axe, decided he hadn't the stomach for this fight. He ran, and the newcomers screamed inventive invectives from Qiangguo and Kpalamaa as he went. They proceeded to stomp the fallen bandits, who scrambled toward the sunlight after their companion.

Bone had his foe in a chokehold. Flybait gripped his own opponent's leg like an angry lap-dog.

"Get out of here, Muttering Chung!" Next One screamed in the man's face. "Wu's finished! It's over!"

". . ." said Muttering Chung, scrambling as fast as he could away from the crazy attackers.

"Ow-ow-ow-ow," said Flybait, before at last letting go of the departing Chung.

Wu stood alone, with a single dagger, backed up against a stalagmite. Lightning Bug crouched nearby, hands extended, poised to leap.

"I may be finished," Wu said, "but I will take one of you with me."

"We don't have to kill you," Next One said.

"We don't?" Flybait said, rising and checking himself for blood.

"She and I are alike in some ways," Next One said.

"After how she treated you?"

"I want her to be sorry," Next One said, "not dead."

Lightning Bug said, "This one will never be sorry. For this one is always right."

"Why, thank you," said Wu.

"It was not a compliment," said Lightning Bug.

"Can we let her go?" said Next One.

"What say you, Imago Bone?" said Lightning Bug, "Eshe?"

Bone studied Wu. He saw in her eyes the same gleam as certain operators and fanatics he had known, who regarded death and torment with much the same gaze they did the counting of coin. And yet, the paradox: the consideration of the monstrous in others stilled the beast in himself.

"Let her go," he said. "But since you're such a good leaper, Lightning Bug . . . drop her off on the far side of the Heavenwall. Give her an opportunity for fresh air, exercise, and a chance to reflect on her misdeeds before she can contrive to return to Abundant Bamboo."

"That is unwise," Eshe said. "She has killed and will kill again. Let the record show she has ended just one more life by her actions—her own."

Bone studied Eshe. "Since when does a house thief argue mercy, and a Swan priestess death?"

"It is a strange world," Eshe said. "And a dangerous one. I, who hear confessions, know this better than most."

"You want me dead on instinct, priestess," Exceedingly Accurate Wu taunted. "I am what you cannot tolerate. For I never lie, yet you are all about lies, are you not?"

"I urge you to finish her," Eshe said.

"Then what about you, Flybait?" Lightning Bug said.

Flybait looked from one grownup to another, seeking a better game than the one he was now forced to play. "I hate killing. I just want to get rich. If you can take Wu beyond the Wall, that works for me."

Wu laughed. "You just want to impress the girl. And she likes it, though she won't admit it."

"Do you want to die, bandit?" Bone said in wonder.

"I want to live," Wu said, "but only on my terms, barbarian. I have no patience for anything else. I like this offer. I will start again with nothing. I will again have my own kingdom in the wilds. I will not skulk in the alleys, or accept the limits placed on women, or indeed on any person of quality. In victory or defeat, I will never beg."

"Don't beg," Next One said. "I'd sooner hear a tiger weep. Please take her away, Lightning Bug."

"So I shall," Lightning Bug said. And she gestured most pointedly, and Wu let the daggers drop. The woman in black led the woman in grey to the cave entrance and they leapt like bats into the night.

Bone lost sight of their shadows beneath the stars, thinking of evils he'd known, evils he'd been. For a moment he thought he saw vast dark wings brush the River of Stars, but for most of the long walk back to Abundant Bamboo he convinced himself it had been his imagination.

Eshe took her leave the next day, claiming to seek employment downriver in the foreign settlement within the great city of Riverclaw. "I have decided to act on behalf of the Church of the Swan and take up Tror's mission," she said, "though perhaps my approach will be more subtle."

"Bellowing atop a crate was not subtle?" Gaunt said. Tror too had told stories. Eshe smiled.

Bone paid Eshe generously for her services as translator, enjoying the illusion that he was becoming some variety of honest man. The woman continued to puzzle him, however. "You spoke in a most grim manner, in the caves. And before, the night of the ambush . . . you had thoughts regarding the assassins who pursued us. In my preoccupation with bandits and babies I had forgotten."

"Idle thoughts only, Bone. I simply thought you might fetch a high bounty, as an example never to cross the kleptomancers of Palmary. But such speculation is beyond the experience of a mere priestess and cook."

"I am not so sure about that. It occurs to me that in Swanisle, Church serves Crown."

Eshe said, "Closer to the truth that Church and Crown are the left and right hand of Swanisle. What is your point?"

Bone shrugged. "My point is that you are an iceberg, Eshe of Kpalamaa."

"After all this time, you call me cold?"

"Not at all. Icebergs are beautiful things."

Eshe smiled, revealing bright white teeth. "Seek me in Riverclaw, Gaunt and Bone, if you wish mild free assistance, or serious expensive assistance. And blessings upon your offspring. I suspect it will be a lucky child. We will meet again."

Next One and Flybait surprised Bone by choosing to go with Eshe.

"We go to the big city," Next One said in careful Roil. "We will find a way to live."

"We will get rich," Flybait said, more directly.

"You will not stay here?" Gaunt said. "You are safe here."

"In some ways I am like Wu," Next One said in the Tongue of the Tortoise Shell, her fierce eyes steady. "I must be free. Here I would always be serving. Even if Lightning Bug is a kind teacher, I must be elsewhere."

"I am no teacher," Eshe said. "I will not direct them. I will merely preach at them."

"Take care of them, Eshe," Gaunt said, "whatever you call it."

Part of Bone wanted to go too, to see this metropolis and explore its rooftops . . . and to show these kids the best methods of access to a rich house. Ah, he was no longer young.

"Good luck," he said.

"Be careful," said Gaunt.

Bone rubbed Gaunt's shoulders as she sat beside the house-stilts, and they watched Eshe, Flybait, and Next One hire a riverboat and push off amid the fishermen and merchants drifting, rowing, and sailing down the wide, golden-brown river.

"I hope they will be all right," he said.

Gaunt said, "You still do not trust Eshe."

"Oh, I like her."

"That is not what I said."

"She is at home nowhere in the world."

"That describes someone else I know."

"I would not trust him either."

For a moment Bone saw Next One raise a bamboo cane she'd claimed from the cave as if stabbing at the sun, and in that moment of girlishness bursting like blue through stormclouds he finally saw her as a child, and wondered how many such unburdened moments under the sky she'd be allowed in the meander of time—she, and the new life within Gaunt too. But Gaunt shifted, and his hands moved to her face, and the thought, and the moment, and the girl, took a turn downriver and were gone.

PART TWO

LIGHTNING BUG AND WALKING STICK

CHAPTER 13.

"This is pointless, Father," said the man with the shard of magic mirror within his skull, the glass reflecting clouds writhing past on all sides, twisting into fabulous shapes which he did not heed.

"How so," rasped the man whose face was wrapped in bandages.

"Our quarry has clearly gone to ground. We do not know the language of this bizarre place. We cannot but terrify those who might aid us. And the soldiers on those curious walls are becoming more alert each time we pass."

The bandaged man looked down upon the dragon that bore them. A couple of crossbow bolts protruded from the majestic minerals of the creature's hide. "They are of little account."

"But Gaunt and Bone slip further away."

"No." The disfigured man raised up his lantern. Motes of fire writhed forth, lashing in every direction. "They are within the bounds of the horizon."

"I cannot foresee their capture."

"They are doom-ridden, those two. More so, the child Gaunt bears. The dragon senses it. It creates turbulence in time's pathways. A fog. But in time we will pierce it."

"I want to avenge the harm they did you! And . . . I don't wish to grow old here."

There was silence amid the clouds. A sunset commenced like burning roses beyond brown-blue mountains, fire-petals scratching away the blue twilight, leaving behind the night. Only the dragon took heed.

"Very well, my son. We will descend to the nearest village, and learn the language."

"They will not be eager to teach."

"Then we will find a learned man, a healer. I will unwrap my bandages, for I am sufficiently recovered. My face will stir his compassion. You will then emerge from shadows and gore him in the head. Your shard will extract the knowledge."

"Thank you, Father. I know you would prefer to wait."

"Such are the things I do out of love."

CHAPTER 14.

Bone was unused to the role of an honored citizen, albeit one most seen by night. He was unsure how to take tea with the magistrate, or calligraphy lessons with Lightning Bug, or the games of weiqi (something like the eccentric great-uncle of checkers) he played with Tror. He did know he was grateful not to be risking his neck in mansions or tombs while he waited on Gaunt, for the discomfort of pregnancy took an ever greater toll. And he was grateful the shadow of wings did not return.

Still, certain details of his coming to this haven nagged at Bone. He questioned Tror and Lightning Bug as he would have prodded an old scab. He and Gaunt continued to study the Tongue of the Tortoise Shell eagerly (Gaunt still progressing the fastest) and he pressed the citizens of the Empire for information.

Tror, as Eshe had said, was a follower of the Swan Goddess, and in his zealous youth he'd left the foreign settlement at the capital, bearing local costume and a case full of self-published tracts. He'd preached along the river before running afoul of the authorities in Abundant Bamboo. He convinced them his bookmaking skills would make better restitution than his head.

"My business grew, friend Bone. Now I am official printer—a publisher of such works as the province produces, a bookseller, a notary, and a peddler of pamphlets. Once a year I make my original pilgrimage in reverse, carrying my smaller wares down to Riverclaw."

As he spoke, Tror placed a white stone onto the weiqi board, a move that limited the options of Bone's black stones. The thief frowned. "Forgive me, but I am impressed such a business can succeed in this Empire, which seems so controlled."

"Knowledge is honored here, my friend, more so than in our homelands. They value warriors of course, and mystics. But scholars are the elite. Only the nobility rank higher. And so we hangers-on of scholarship can make a living."

Bone placed a black stone, on pure instinct, far across the board. "You do not miss your former calling? Nothing in you wanted to follow Eshe?"

Tror made a thoughtful smile, fingering a white stone in his reserve. "I still follow the Swan. I believe in honoring her example, and showing love to all thinking beings. I no longer believe, however, she calls me to convert a hundred million people. I think Eshe's desires are more modest than my own, and her chances of success correspondingly greater. She was always more worldly, that one. It is a survival trait in a priest." Tror's next stone was in the vicinity of Bone's far-flung scout. Bone knew he was losing, but he'd forced Tror to respond. That was something.

Tror laughed; whether at himself or the game, Bone did not know. "Devotion and arrogance are sometimes like palm and knuckle on the same hand," Tror said. "This I learned from Qiangguo. They understand balance here."

It happened that Lightning Bug overheard this exchange and alluded to it when she and Bone next spoke over calligraphy, adding with a smile, "Ah, Tror! He is still prideful enough to attempt to summarize us to foreigners. He knows enough to have an opinion about us. But not enough to know doubt. Now, try to make the stroke with your eyes closed, over the span of a single breath."

Bone raised the brush. "And how would you characterize your people?" He painted.

"You can't breathe while talking. Your character for 'harmony' looks like an earthquake hit it. And I would not characterize my people. There are too many of us. We are happy and despairing, free and imprisoned, passionate and cold. Beyond every garden you will find the forest."

Bone dipped the brush. "Garden and forest. You used those terms with Walking Stick, the day we arrived."

She nodded, with a faraway look. "Know this, Imago Bone, that below the surface of the Empire you will find many associations, formal and informal. A few have great strength. I belong to one such, called the Forest. Walking Stick belongs to another, the Garden. His society values connections in high places. Mine has its soul in the countryside. His honors women but keeps them subordinate. Mine celebrates the wildness of the female heart."

"Are you enemies?" Bone closed his eyes, took one breath, and painted.

"Ah, how Westerners seek to summarize! But if you must, call us opponents, as in a game of weiqi. You have made an excellent character. Alas, your mind has wandered, and you have not painted 'harmony' but 'haste.'"

"And how would you describe Westerners?" Bone asked, nettled.

"I would not presume." Lightning Bug smiled again. "Except, perhaps, that you are in haste to characterize."

CHAPTER 15.

A harvest moon found Gaunt's stomach distended and low, wrapped by the scarlet twistings of notional dragons, and she believed the baby might come within days. Certainly the way it kicked at her lungs and liver suggested it was feeling cramped. She lived as much as possible on the house's upper floors, finding it difficult to descend the long stairs.

Thus there was no possibility of hiding when, after moonrise, the official named Walking Stick reappeared. Bone was out scouting for any newcomer bandits, and Tror was peddling books in a nearby village. Gaunt was practicing calligraphy, and she heard Lightning Bug in the fore-room, arguing with Gaunt's former rescuer.

Gaunt could follow only snatches of their conversation, rapid as falling hailstones. From Lightning Bug's side there came an *outrageous request* and *she could not* and *of course I am loyal to the Empire*. From Walking Stick's side there was *apologize for the necessity* and *ten thousand regrets* and *your loyalty, once-beloved, will not be forgotten*.

Gaunt heard him shove past Lightning Bug. She knew something was wrong, and she imagined she should stand, grab her ink box as a weapon, or growl at least.

She was still struggling to rise as he entered.

Walking Stick looked much as before, clutching his fighting staff, wearing the black silk robe embroidered with a multitude of long-limbed white insects and one red firefly. He raised his staff and bowed to Gaunt and to the four directions. Then he advanced.

"State your business," Gaunt said, in the Tongue of the Tortoise Shell.

Walking Stick raised an eyebrow at her good diction. "It is the business of Empire, Persimmon Gaunt. Forgive me. The superior man must at times be harsh. You must be taken from here." He advanced.

Gaunt did not ask for an explanation. She took up her ink bottle and flung the contents at Walking Stick's eyes. The official ducked and blinked. Black liquid maimed the insects of his robe. Lightning Bug was shouting something. Gaunt could not easily rise, but she slumped from her chair and swung the little writing table against Walking Stick's chin. He sprawled backward in a flurry of paper.

There would be no time to escape down the stairs. Bone had sometimes lectured her on her unwillingness to kill. But she did not hesitate to stagger up, grab the chair, and bring it down upon him.

Yet Walking Stick was already rolling out of the way. He deflected the chair with his forearm, caught Gaunt's wrist, and swung her arm behind her in a way that blinded her with pain.

It was then she saw Lightning Bug, armed with a copy of the provincial census results, in hardback. She swung it as though attempting to convey the figures directly to Walking Stick's brain. He staggered and released Gaunt.

"Run, you fool," Lightning Bug said.

Running was not in Gaunt's vocabulary these days, but she was already partway down the stairs. She panted. She felt like vomiting. Somehow she reached the bottom and moved between and below buildings, bamboo stilts like bloody spears in the red moonlight. Crashes and thuds echoed within the house behind her.

She did not know how long she fled. Every door was closed, as if the inhabitants guessed her doom and wanted no part of it.

Out of the dark, someone hissed "Gaunt!"

It was Bone. Hope filled her veins like blood from her thundering heart. "Here. Where?"

"Up here." And there he was, upon the roof of one of the two-story houses. "I saw Walking Stick. Something worried me . . ." He dropped a rope. "Climb!"

"I'm too heavy," she said, feeling that her whole body surrounded that word, fattening the letters.

"Climb!" he repeated. He made his own emphasis, throwing gangly arms around the rope.

She tried, and he hauled. Both did better than she expected. Some desperate reserve of strength kept her scrambling up the rope, while somehow Bone kept it moving.

Indeed, soon Gaunt was startled at the strength Bone displayed.

She was about to gasp her gratitude when she took his hand, struggled over the top . . . and found Bone unconscious beside the rope.

The offered hand belonged to Walking Stick.

"The Garden requires you," the imperial official said. "It does not require Imago Bone. But the superior man should show compassion. Out of respect I will take him alive to the capital, if you submit."

"What do you want from me?" Gaunt asked, conscious of the empty air at her back.

"Your belly is a map of the realm."

"Beg pardon?"

"Crossing and recrossing the land are the Heavenwalls," Walking Stick said. "They are far more than gestures of defense or control. They channel chi to he who bears the Heavenwall Mandate. This power has chosen the life within you, and left its mark on that life's bearer. How would you like to be mother to an emperor, Persimmon Gaunt?"

"That is madness."

"That is power. Its ways often look mad."

"But," cut in a woman's voice, "they're not. Not *truly* mad. Accept no substitutes!"

And Lightning Bug was there, leaping up from behind Gaunt and tossing a flaming bottle of some high-grade alcohol at Walking Stick's head. He deflected it with his namesake staff and stumbled backward. Gaunt shifted out of the way.

Lightning Bug pursued, facing Walking Stick in a fighting stance while reaching into a sack. She tossed a scroll over her shoulder. The casual-looking throw landed it right in Gaunt's hands.

"Look, poet!" Lightning Bug said. "This is your vessel of escape. If I'd been sure of your peril I'd have given it over sooner."

Expecting a writ of Imperial amnesty or a treasure map or perhaps a piece of Living Calligraphy, Gaunt was nonplussed to unroll a sepia landscape painting of a spindly, cloud-entwined mountain, with a pagoda crouched near the peak.

"This?" Gaunt exclaimed, thinking, *What do I take away from this? That life is short and art is long?*

Walking Stick had recovered, and was preparing to leap at Lightning Bug.

"Wonder will out," Lightning Bug said, grabbing plum wine from the sack and leaping at her opponent like a shooting star. Ducking under his staff, she tumbled past and guzzled the wine.

"Typical Forest behavior," Walking Stick said, spinning. "Get drunk, then fight."

"Those actions need not be distinct." Lantern Bug broke the bottle and swung her arm, scattering glass and drops at Walking Stick's eyes. He deflected with his staff, which he spun to block Lightning Bug's stab. The remnant of the bottle shattered; she made a flying kick at his neck; he shifted back.

The flurry drew Gaunt's attention but she forced herself to focus on the painting and its red artist's seal . . . the seal of Meteor-Plum Long, sage painter and author of *Record of Brush Methods and Transspatial Dislocation*.

"Thank you," Gaunt whispered to the warrior woman who seemed to be in some indeterminate place between rooftop and sky, attacking and defending, defeated or victorious. Gaunt remembered Eshe's tales, and she knew the reputation of Meteor-Plum's paintings.

She stared at it, and it loomed large.

"Take care of Bone," she called out, in the last moment that she was a poet atop a roof, imagining she was upon an enchanted mountain.

Then she was upon an enchanted mountain, imagining she'd been a poet atop a roof.

CHAPTER 16.

"Bone," the voice said, and the thief knew it must be the Swan Goddess, or perhaps the Painter-of-Clouds, because he'd always known, somehow, he'd report to a deity sounding like a furious drunken Eastern woman.

"Bone, get your miserable ass up. You're not allowed to die. The painting has your lover inside it. Take it and run."

Bone's aching head convinced him he was alive. That, and how *The painting has your lover inside it* was exactly the kind of insanity life threw him regularly.

He took one long look at the scroll nearby, another long look at the four-armed, four-legged blur that was Lightning Bug and Walking Stick's battle, and he grabbed the first and fled the second.

He departed Abundant Bamboo by way of the rooftops and a meandering gorge funneling a tributary of the Ochre River. There he found Shadow Margin, the abandoned hideout of the Cloud and Soil Society.

Beside the shadowed waterfall he unfolded the painting and beheld a remarkable landscape seemingly far from the Wall: a foggy realm with rocky summits rising like fingers through the white. He squinted in a shaft of moonlight. Upon the nearest summit, Bone saw a tiny brush-stroked pilgrim speaking with a tiny brush-stroked woman. The woman resembled Persimmon Gaunt.

Vertigo was unsupportable in his line of work, but Bone felt it then.

Nor was this simply the effect of his disturbed guts; for now he had the sudden sense of rushing toward Gaunt from a high starting altitude. It was as though daylight burst overhead as he flew birdlike above a sea of cloud, dotted with tall, rocky islands wreathed in pines. The tallest one nearby bore Persimmon Gaunt and her mysterious companion. He wished to be nearer— and so it was, for he swooped toward her like a hawk.

At once she turned to him and shouted. He could not hear the words through the air, but they echoed in his mind. *Return to our world! One of us must keep watch!*

How do I back away, Bone tried to say, but the deed was done even as he considered it.

He returned to his senses in the cave, with his hands gripping the scroll so tight it twisted like a bow.

So. An enchantment spiriting one to the world of the painting. A place of sanctuary, perhaps. Unless the scroll was found and locked away . . . or buried . . . or burned . . .

Bone left that thought like a guard upon a wall, and set about repairing an escape boat he'd holed while chasing away the bandits. He gathered wood by moonlight, hammered by starlight, even assembled a decoy-Bone of straw in the clouded dark. He needed all his tricks, this time.

Always he kept the scroll close as a fragile lover, this greatest, un-stolen treasure.

CHAPTER 17.

Mist at her back, Gaunt had been deep in hushed conversation with the pilgrim of the painting when Bone's presence rippled the fog with the wind's cool kiss.

"Welcome," the pilgrim had said when first she manifested. "Welcome to *A Tumult of Trees on Peculiar Peaks*."

Looking around at white-wreathed precipices, Gaunt said, "That is certainly evocative. But not very specific. Where am I?"

"Good! You still have your wits. I'd hoped to ease the shock of transition somewhat, after the last set of visitors woke me from my long reverie."

"That is certainly interesting, but not very illuminating."

"As I said . . . this is Long's *Tumult*. A landscape painting dating from the First Autumn Dynasty." The speaker was shorter than Gaunt, as well as balder, and possessed of a wider smile. He was thick-built but hardy, and his patchy, dirt-spattered clothes hung loose upon him. He wore a hat of bark that tipped a little as he waved his strong arms.

"I remember now, the way of such paintings," the man said. "They invited gentlemen or ladies of quality to imagine strolling through the landscape, refreshed. Well, Long's genius lay in removing the need for 'imagination.'"

Gaunt raised her eyebrows. "Then accessing another reality is simpler than envisioning one?"

The ragged man clapped. "In this case, yes. He enjoyed the irony."

"You seem to know him well."

He bowed modestly. "I am an illustration."

"Beg pardon?"

"The painter left his self-portrait within his works. Thus the visitor might be guided. Thus too the self-portrait can keep an eye on things. I forget, sometimes . . . Sometimes I unleash dangers without meaning to . . . But such is my purpose on this cold mountain."

"Then I must speak to you, image of the artist. I am fleeing a hostile warrior. I am with child and need sanctuary."

The self-portrait of Meteor-Plum Long looked somber then, as though taking a splash of cold water in the face. "Garden or Forest?"

"Sorry?"

"Your foe. Is he Garden or Forest?"

It was *Which direction do you travel?* all over again.

If it's even odds, Gaunt decided, best roll with the truth. "Garden," she said. "I think."

The self-portrait relaxed, though sadness clung to his eyes. "Then be welcome. You would be welcome in any case, but this way it is easier. Though he sided with the Garden most of his life, my maker made peace with the Forest in the end. Come. There is shelter atop the mountain. The monks are chatterers but they're not so bad."

They ascended via a meandering path. Boulders and branches seemed to lurch out to brush them. Billows of fog crossed their path like unpainted canvas. Progress was difficult, and Gaunt had to inform her apologetic companion more than once that, yes indeed, a woman in late pregnancy was this slow. The summit was only rarely visible, its red pagoda rising like a banner. Other summits blazed in shocking sunlight above the cloud-waves, though Gaunt discerned webs of shadow on the paths beneath the exposed branches and stones. The quality of color stole her breath as much as the walk itself. It seemed to her such beauty, like a provocation, demanded reply. It would be a fine thing to learn landscape painting, she thought.

"The scroll was monochrome," Gaunt noted, pausing to rest. "This place is not."

"Indeed," said the self-portrait, leaning against a boulder. "It was ever the painter's task, to provide a fragmentary window suggesting an infinite universe beyond. To imply, with brush strokes, the full range of the artist's experience with nature, even as that experience was but a fragment implying the totality of a cosmos. Thus, for my prototype, ink and paper conveyed color, wind, mist, birdsong, fallen leaves."

All these things were present—as well as the sound of dripping to one side, the sound of dry crunching underfoot, creaking of wind-tugged branches, little darting shapes creasing the path as they shot between boulders.

"Is this place a sort of dream?" Gaunt asked. "Or am I truly in another universe?"

He laughed. "Every place is a sort of dream. But more to your point, this place is normal."

Now Gaunt laughed. "Having arrived via art appreciation, I question that view."

"Come, now. The term is borrowed from your own barbarian geometry. A 'normal' is a line dropped perpendicular onto another, or a plane inserted likewise. All your perceptual environment can be likened to shapes on a flat plane, like strokes upon a scroll. Within a higher-dimensional framework, your realm may contact others, as scrolls toppling from a poorly braced shelf may come to rest upon each other."

"And this painting intersects my world along a sort of perpendicular?"

"Quite. This mountaintop is sited at the 'seam.' In various spots here it becomes easy to move into and out of the painting, or even within the painting. Other tangents to your world are possible but are not as stable."

Gaunt looked around her. "Could the stability be upset?"

"Do not be concerned. While a catastrophe at this peak might—wait, someone new is intruding."

The wind had picked up. Moving by instinct, Gaunt crossed to a precipitous path-edge and looked out.

A churning filled the clouds and at their heart a misty human shape seemed paradoxically to be shrinking from giant to tiny proportions while simultaneously rushing toward her.

"Your enemy?" the self-portrait asked.

"My lover," Gaunt said.

"Beware. If he arrives here, and your enemy is still out there, who will protect the scroll?"

Suddenly frightened, Gaunt shouted at Bone to back away, for all that she yearned for him. A look of confusion crossed his misty face and he began backing like a swimmer, growing larger and less distinct. He said something but she heard only a slow, deep voice, blending with the wind.

Then she saw only cloud.

She lowered her head.

"The monks who dwell at the summit," the self-portrait said, "have great powers of perception. My progenitor specified them thus. With their aid you might contact your companion, should he still grasp the scroll."

"Let's walk," Gaunt said. "May I lean upon you, image of a sage painter?"

"You may," he said. Then, "The left arm, if you please. I practice my art with the right. I have to admit, I'm protective of it."

"What do you paint?"

"I don't." To Gaunt's smile he added, "I am a poet. Sometimes the apple rolls far from the tree."

"We have much to talk about," Gaunt said. "When I'm not so tired."

Up and up. Reaching the summit exhausted Gaunt, and she could barely speak to the monks in green robes who took her in. The red brick pagoda (how could all these stones have been hauled up here, when she could barely haul herself?) had five levels and a pointed roof like a chess piece. At first the place seemed dilapidated and ruined, because tree limbs had pierced the tower at several points. Then it grew clear that deliberate openings admitted the branches.

Sunlight thus speared past sandstone statues of saints, of gods, of artists, of drunks, the distinctions among them uncertain. One statue depicted a bald monk resting his head on a sleeping lion, another a sage staring out from a sculpted precipice like a sail in a strong wind, a third a plump scholar seated with one leg bent beside a wine bowl, as if his next act could be to either fight or sip. An elderly monk, bearded, grinning with golden teeth like an unfinished mosaic, seemed at first a fourth statue—until he spoke.

"You are in pain."

It was so, an ache coursing around the peculiar hollowness in her belly, from which kicks sometimes sprang. Gaunt had felt a similar pain further down the mountain path. She had learned enough from Eshe and Lightning Bug to know what this might mean.

"Have any of you delivered babies?" she said. "For one may arrive within days."

"There is one," said the monk, after a pause. His smile seemed frozen, and Gaunt could see that the gold leaf upon his teeth was decorated with the images of tree leaves. "A guest. I do not know if you would prefer her help . . ."

"Take me to her," snapped Gaunt. "Please," she added more gently.

"That is unnecessary," said a woman's brisk slap of a voice. A powerful-looking figure, not old, not young, stepped into view.

Even in a green robe, even with hair cropped even shorter than before, her presence commanded all attention. "I am willing to help, in return for news of the outside world. For I burn to know the fates of those who wronged me. You may call me Exceedingly Vengeful Wu."

CHAPTER 18.

In the moonlight, the woman Lightning Bug fluttered like a ghost at her own window. There was no point hiding now, and no time. She rapped upon it, and presently her husband answered.

Tror's beloved features revealed shock, and worry, and anger. He took her hand and brought her inside.

"You're hurt—" His fingers brushed blood from her lip.

"It is nothing, husband. I gave as good as I got."

"I have been worried. I returned to find the children hiding, and signs of battle. The magistrate's guards are searching. Did bandits—"

She shook her head. "Walking Stick."

"He dares!"

"Husband. Save your anger, for it helps no one."

"For years I have tolerated him, invited him into my home, not out of fear or respect for his station, but out of pure courtesy, such as Qiangguo believes barbarians incapable—"

"Peace, Tror."

"Peace! When he assaults my wife!"

"I assaulted him, Tror. Yes. He acts with official blessing, and it is in this capacity that he pursues Gaunt and Bone, and their child. When I lift a hand against him, I rebel against my emperor. Such is the spirit of the Forest, but—"

"Not only the Forest. The Swan is a fierce bird when its family is threatened."

"Yes! Family, Tror. I will not have the stain of my resistance spread to you or my children."

"I am your husband! Shall I not have satisfaction against your foe?"

"You are father of my children! Shall they be orphaned? For this is what we discuss, Tror. Forest and Garden may oppose each other, but there are customs to observe. Walking Stick and I are both of the wulin. Neither he nor I will make the conflict lethal if other means are available. But if you, an ordinary man—a foreigner!—raise your fist to an envoy of the government, your life is forfeit, and yes, those of our children. To make this point the emperor's men would slaughter a family even out to the tenth generation."

"So I must pace and fume. And you . . . you will be off again, into the world of the Rivers-and-Lakes?"

"The Rivers-and-Lakes is in my blood, Tror. I am sorry for the sorrow to you. But I must help Gaunt and Bone, and oppose Walking Stick. He must be checked. I will return when I can."

"It is exciting to you, isn't it? To battle him again?"

Lightning Bug looked away.

"You do not have to hide it, wife. He is your peer, as I am not. Even were there not old desire, there is the need to measure yourself."

"There is no desire."

"You need not say it."

"You accuse me of falsehood?"

"No. Only humanity."

"I must be away, before the children awaken. Tell them . . ."

"I will tell them their mother is brave."

CHAPTER 19.

Bone was preparing what he considered a most cunning device—a small hollow log in which he meant to conceal the scroll, plugging it at either end with fire-hardened clay—when Gaunt's voice came to him, a hushed sound emanating from the scroll beside his foot.

"Gaunt! Say again?"

"Imago. Listen. The baby's time is coming."

Bone stared. He had a mental image of a tiny scroll sliding out of the big one. "Is that possible? When you are transmogrified into silk and ink?"

"I feel all too much like flesh and blood. I'm persuaded you hold merely a gateway, not a whole world."

"Even so . . . I fret at the consequences. However, I fret more at Walking Stick and Night's Auditors."

"Yes. Otherwise I would flee this place. Bone, Wu is here."

"Wu! I thought she was beyond the Wall."

"Evidently Lightning Bug had other ideas. Yet . . . I feel safe enough for now. Wu has never seen me before, or heard my name. If she guesses my involvement in your attack she hasn't shown it. And the monks who dwell in this world are kind, if prone to lecture. I think they will protect me."

"I do not like this."

"Nor I. But we can do no better."

"Then I will bear the scroll downriver until we reach Riverclaw. Or . . ."

"Yes. You have some time, Bone. But one point of the monks' lecturing I must convey—although we can speak normally now, for me time is passing faster than for you. Two days have elapsed here."

"Two days! And the baby—"

"It could be today. It could be several days. Do not tarry, Imago. And protect the painting."

"At this moment, Persimmon, no one appreciates art more than I."

Bone had the notion, gleaned from a childhood in a fishing village, that all watercraft deserved names. He called his salvaged sampan *Cradle*. As he poled out into the still, lapping river and rode current and wind, Bone improvised a silly song beneath the cloud-spattered stars.

> *Tumble out, baby,*
> *In your treetops.*
> *When the wind blows*
> Cradle *will rock.*
> *When the bow breaks*
> *The river's rough foam*
> *Out will come baby*
> *And we'll share a home.*

He was, in a way, pleased Gaunt did not overhear his doggerel.

She checked in from time to time, using whatever mysterious power the scroll-monks possessed. She related days of fading energy and intensifying contractions. He related hours of whirling stars and gurgling waters. She did not seem as pleased with his descriptions as she had previously.

He did not relate how he had once glimpsed, far above the branches of an enormous dangling willow, a dark draconic silhouette.

Come morning, with dawn on the misting water like a volcanic slurry of gold slicing onyx shadows, pursuit had not materialized, nor had true labor commenced.

"This is taking some time," he observed to the scroll within the hollow log.

"This is . . . not uncommon, Wu says," Gaunt's voice emerged. "I do not think she would lie . . ."

"That I believe. Kill. Steal. Whip. But not lie."

"Imago, enough. I want you here."

"Persimmon, we are not safe. Riverclaw is another half day, I believe, in my timeframe."

"Forget Riverclaw, Imago . . . Conceal the painting in the wilderness. Come to me."

This was a rare thing, this speaking so urgently with their given names. Usually, *Persimmon* and *Imago* were names for campfire or bedroom, *Gaunt* and

Bone for dark alley or battleground. But now it was Persimmon and Imago who had the challenge to face; Gaunt and Bone were of little use.

"We might return to the world," he said, "to find ourselves buried alive."

"Hide it in the crook of a tree."

"Might it not become firewood?"

"I need you."

He studied the course of the Ochre. Ahead lay the dark curves and spikes of a pair of boats, like shadowy slices cut from the gleaming swirl of the morning river. At either hand the forest ebbed, and cultivated land stretched south, oxen-tilled fields and rice paddies nearly as wet and sparkling as the river.

The cover of the woodland was fading; the cover of the city was yet to come.

"Persimmon, I want to press on. I feel as I do when leaping widely separated rooftops. Sometimes I'm not sure I'll make it. But I rarely fall."

"Go. Do what you must . . . and don't be wrong. This is hard, Imago. Harder than I . . ."

"Yes. I know."

"You do not. Don't be wrong."

The murmur ended, and there was only the lap of water, the trill of distant voices and songs.

Bone passed beneath jutting karst ridges on the western shore, clouds wafting between as though a vast fanged maw sleepily blew smoke. Lanterns waved and blew out amongst the early laborers and the cormorant fishermen on their little plank boats. Bone watched a man release his noosed birds, and one of six returned with a fish wiggling in its bill. To the east the Red Heavenwall was a band of shadow with bloody highlights where the sun blazed jewel-like, a half-circle catching red flecks and veins within the stone. *I will be a father*, he thought.

It was not a notion attended by joy or fear, but a calm thing, certain as a plunging stone finding the river bottom. Everyday emotion was left behind like bubbles in its fall. Deep, hard-earned emotion would come later, like cloud of river mud rising on impact. Bone experienced then a love that seemed sharp and cold from the outside, because it kept its secrets. He knew then a deeper meaning to the phrase *heart of stone*.

The sun rose, and the towers of Riverclaw rose likewise in Bone's sight, crowned by the convergence of the Red and Blue Heavenwalls into the titanic fortress of the Purple Forbidden City, masses of curved roofs defining its twin draconic heads, far above the boxlike fortifications it sprouted like talons.

His gaze wandering, he spotted behind him the two-sailed profile of a large, oared river-junk.

It could be nothing but a merchant, thought his surface mind.

It is pursuit, thought his stony heart.

He made a calm estimate (and another part of him was amazed at this calm) and steered toward a knot of boats bobbing near the harbor wall.

Cradle must fall.

CHAPTER 20.

Through the first and second watches of the night, the man known as Walking Stick galloped upon his dragon-horse atop the Red Heavenwall, pausing only to wave an Imperial scroll in the face of any guard brash enough to question his presence there. His garments were tattered, for Lightning Bug had taken pains to tear off the embroidered firefly over his heart. So be it. She had long since chosen her destiny. He had his own.

When his horse's prodigious strength ebbed, he gave her into the care of a guard-tower, for though Walking Stick would kill coldly and efficiently for the Empire, he had yet to mistreat a horse. The soldiers were only just recovering from their astonishment when Walking Stick leapt into the air to continue his journey alone.

While night reigned and the River of Stars blazed overhead, he marshaled his chi to the task of haste. His legs frequently took him off the Wall, and when he descended he sometimes employed his staff to push off and fly further ahead. Long experience and the occasional watch-fire kept him from plunging off the fortification in the dark. He needed speed. Even with this Imperial highway and his skills, he might not catch Imago Bone.

He remembered Lightning Bug, dancing away from him atop a moonlit bamboo forest, taunting him with the fact of the barbarians' escape. And indeed, he deserved it, for letting old anger and jealousy and lust trick him into following her deep into the wilderness, away from his true duty. It had taken all the discipline of a Garden warrior to bow to her then, and to silently slip through the woodlands back to the Wall. There he commanded a contingent of troops to travel downriver, and before the breath was entirely out of his mouth, he was racing for Riverclaw.

Lightning Bug might think him in retreat, but he could anticipate Imago Bone's next move. Alone in a strange country, the urban thief would seek a friend. More, he would yearn for rooftops and alleyways. He would run to the city like a horse to its stable.

As the grey pre-dawn silvered the clouds and Riverclaw's towers rose ahead Walking Stick slowed, for though his talents were no secret, it would not be well to announce his coming to every tower and hovel and riverboat. He merely ran at a pace that would swiftly exhaust a lesser man. Now he was recognized, tattered or no, and soldiers bowed before him. The Blue Heavenwall was nearer at hand, and between it and the Red lay a region of cheap homes and iniquity, the inevitable refuse of cities. Ahead lay the mighty ramparts of the Purple Forbidden City, where the "heads" of the Walls converged, lofting the emperor's citadel skyward.

Soldiers waved him through iron gates and between stone guardian lions (every tenth of which bore an animating enchantment). He paused at the guard post beside the great stairway to inscribe a message upon a scroll—a single character, "Come." He instructed a soldier to seek the foreign district, and when the youth hesitated, his commander barked, "It is the will of the Garden, boy. You will be remembered now, one way or the other. Best make the memory a good one." Walking Stick bowed a little to the commander, a little less to the soldier, and leapt up the stairs.

Though the Forbidden City contained multitudes, it was nonetheless spacious, its huge buildings as separate as ships at anchor on a calm stone sea. This was by design of the Garden, which insisted on bringing some of nature's serenity to the heart of the Empire, to soothe the stormy hearts of rulers. It also made it possible for Walking Stick to avoid the prattle of the noble brats and servants and eunuchs who were an inevitable part of Imperial life, and a key reason why Walking Stick kept finding errands elsewhere. He strode past many such, who whispered and tittered at the state of his clothes. From time to time he rapped his staff on the white cobblestones, the echoes resounding through the complex, and enjoyed the silence that fell.

He might have seen to his appearance, but that would be a concession to triviality. And something in him wished to display what Lightning Bug had done to his heart.

His steps brought him to the Windwater Garden, a place near the palace with an inconspicuous high wall of the same rock as the cobblestones. There were greater gardens in the Forbidden City, the Earthly Paradise of the nobles and the Meditation Pools of the officialdom. Those gardens invited observation, but this one was invisible save from a high balcony of the palace visited only by the emperor and his inner circle. Access was only via the palace or through a back gate guarded by wulin masters who were also master gardeners. They recognized Walking Stick as he passed through, giving him no acknowledgment. Had they not recognized him, he would have been assaulted by rake and pruning shears, in a fighting style he had helped develop himself.

Once within the garden it was as though he retraced his journey, for there was a path mimicking the Red Heavenwall, and another imitating the Blue. Forests appeared beside them as miniature trees. The Ochre River was a gurgling stream. Cities were stone pagodas, and Riverclaw was a rocky platform with a chair for the Emperor, a pond at its back for the sea.

The Windwater Garden was a map of the Empire, and Walking Stick stepped lightly upon it. He sat cross-legged at the right foot of the Emperor's seat, and waited.

A breeze blew past, and clouds sped swiftly overhead. He noted the passage of a red-winged hummingbird to and fro in the vicinity of "Riverclaw." To his knowledge, such a hummingbird had never been seen in the garden. He watched it carefully.

After a time the gardeners brought the woman to him. He did not turn his gaze. The hummingbird flew above the nearby stream, as if searching for something. He said, "You have been instructed, as to the singular honor done you?"

"I know of this place," said Eshe of Kpalamaa. "I will not so much as sneeze."

"Please sit." The gardeners faded into the garden. The barbarian sat.

"Betrayal, even for a good cause," Walking Stick said, "forever marks the betrayer. Do you understand?"

"Is the superior man loyal to people?" said Eshe. "Or is he loyal to the Way?"

"Very good, very good. But for the Garden, the Way and the people are inseparable. The Way does not ignore the truth of conflict among individuals. I may be loyal to one master and you to another, and our conduct may be impeccable, yet if our masters are enemies, so we are enemies."

"Yet if your master brings down my master's house, and betrayal offers me a chance to preserve what remains, where lies the Way? A similar problem I confronted when I beheld dragons on Persimmon Gaunt's belly."

"You speak glibly of the Way, yet you are the product of foreign lands and foreign ideas. I do not blame you for this but it also impedes my trust."

"Bluntly, then, Walking Stick. To my eye, your Way seems like law bereft of love. Talk of betrayal and conduct and loyalty is all very well, but without love it is a dry riverbed—structure without life. And like water in a riverbed, love's passage makes changes. The law cannot be the same thing season after season. At times the law breaks hearts, and at times the river must flood. Out of love for them do I betray Gaunt and Bone."

"Barbarian gibberish. What you call 'love,' and insist upon as an axiom, can just as easily be whim. Immaturity. Rash animal impulse."

"If you think me no better than a beast, then why am I here? I can go elsewhere to snort and stomp."

"I have lost Persimmon Gaunt. She has failed to understand the honor the Empire's chi has bestowed upon her. I believe she or Imago Bone may come to you seeking protection."

Eshe's eyebrows rose. "Indeed."

"Her child may or may not have been born, and it is the child that most concerns me. Ensure its passage into the Forbidden City and you will be well rewarded."

"I seek no reward for myself."

"The Empire will look favorably upon your superiors."

She hesitated. "And Gaunt and Bone?"

"I cannot promise their safety, for they are barbarian rogues. I can promise forbearance. This means more than any assurance of protection from a lesser man."

"I believe you. When do you expect Bone?"

He had lost the hummingbird, but now he noted a pale ant riding a leaf downstream.

"Perhaps very soon. You must excuse me. Remember our words."

He left the shocked Eshe behind and departed the garden with two steps and the crack of his staff.

A small tremor shook the city, and he would have to answer for it later, but haste was indicated.

Just as he cleared the garden wall the hummingbird circled him once, but he had no time to consider the portent, nor who might witness his leaping passage toward the Ochre River.

CHAPTER 21.

"I have seen too many barbarians of late," Exceedingly Vengeful Wu told Gaunt while preparing buckets of water, rags, and slim blades carved with rough but ornate handles suggesting tigers and carp and horses. Gaunt tried not to look at these. She lay upon a cot, propped by pillows and wracked by periodic pains through her middle. She gazed out through an oval window graced by a leaf-whispering branch growing through the skylight. Wu continued, "I do not mean to complain about you personally, Persimmon Gaunt. But the Emperor is allowing too much outside trade. It brings strange folk and strange ways."

"You are a traditionalist?"

"Indeed. Organized crime is sometimes the last bulwark of decency. I don't suppose you came on the same ship as a pale, mongoose-like man, and a very dark and powerful woman?"

"I have seen people matching that description," Gaunt answered. "You must understand, that where I come from very dark people are not so odd, and pale people crowd the land like trees."

She pointedly studied the forest. Outside, sun-lit blobs of cloud crossed a thick mass of blue-grey storm front, looking like ice islands sliding through a dark sea. Below, the pine trees of neighboring peaks speared up against the featureless canvas of nimbus, as though the mountains guarded the edge of this world. And who knew, perhaps they did.

"Wu," she said, as if simply following her own trail of thought and not trying to divert Wu's, "who lives on the other mountains?" For she had glimpsed other pagodas and even other travelers on the paths of the other peaks.

Wu grunted. "A vexing mystery. Even to the artist's self-portrait. No one from this peak has ever reached another and returned to tell of it. The paths proceed downward through wreathing mists as far as anyone here has traveled. I myself once descended for three months, living off berries and honey, and neither reached nor sighted flat land. If there is commerce between peaks it must be by way of the cloud-dragons we sometimes sight, but such we cannot tame. Indeed, they can be a menace."

"Dragons . . ." Gaunt mused, thinking of the one that had savaged the

Passport/Punishment. Thinking of it made her shiver, but that was better than thinking only of her fears and pains. A new contraction seized her, and she breathed long, slow breaths until it passed. The true labor, Wu had said, hadn't commenced, and might not for some time. Gaunt needed distraction. Even conversation with Wu would do.

"Do you know something about dragons?" Wu asked her. "One had been sighted now and again shortly before my downfall, out there in the world. A dragon unlike any seen in living memory. Might you know of it?"

"It?" Gaunt said. "I couldn't say. I do know something of dragons, however. At least, the Western kind. They are articulated, brassy. With guts of fire like the volcanic mountains. Hatched from shooting stars, they are in immature form like embers spat from a bonfire, floating on the breeze. Later they bore into this world of Earthe, leaving fires in their wake, seeking and enriching the world's heat as *candlewyrms*. Emerging from volcanoes with an encrustation of metals, they become *arkendrakes*, and settle in various places around the land. Often they nest among the carcasses of their ancestors, sleeping among jeweled hides and bones. For this reason folk imagine them hoarders of ill-gotten gain when in fact the only human loot they claim is from dragon-hunters."

"You are surprisingly well-informed. Yet you have seen no specific dragon of late?"

"No. But I would say something more of them generally. It's said they have two fates, if not slain: to grow in solidity and immensity until they take on the characteristics of a mountain, rumbling occasionally in their mineral sleep . . . or to mate. For it is little known that all Western dragons are male. In search of females, some go East. And I have heard that those who find a mate never return."

"Ah, there your sources are correct, Persimmon Gaunt. Know then, that even as your dragons are linked to fire, earth, and metal, so ours are allied with water, earth, and air. They are yin to the others' yang. They hatch when meteors plunge into the sea, and the calls of their elder sisters bring them to our shores. As youths they are currents, then spring skyward as forks of lightning, and in their full majesty they are serpents of cloud. In maturity they are cloud-shouldered forests . . . unless they mate. For mating with their male counterparts brings storms of mad ferocity, in which eggs of cloud are quickened by sperm of fire and shot into the encircling night, whence they become the nearer stars."

Gaunt thought of what disadvantages came of mating, as a contraction came over her. She winced and breathed, and when the latest pain passed, said, "Are these storms dangerous to humans?"

"Indeed. In antiquity these storms wracked our shores, breeding typhoons and raising volcanoes. For the mating of dragons, the *Dragonheat*, destroys the lovers."

"You of the East know much that we don't."

"Flattery. Interesting. But it is perhaps merely by proximity that we know more of dragons. They were ever in our thoughts. We represented our emperor with a dragon, basing our astrology on the encircling dragon-eggs (as yours is based on stars farther afield). We know, too, the effect of dragons upon the growth of the world. Its structure is enriched by the male dragons, whose life is enhanced by the females. It is even perhaps a side effect of their chosen haunts that our continents now have differing characters: our fertile, river-washed land is largely unified by one Empire; your land is broken into rocky peninsulas and divided into squabbling states."

"There may be more to it than that," Gaunt said, who had heard many one-note theories of history.

"Even so," said Wu. "Yet it is sure enough that the Dragonheat once caused great harm to our land . . ."

"But no more?"

"In the days of the Sage Emperor the dragon mating ground changed. Know you the Ruby Waste? That desert between East and West so heat-blasted one can only skirt its edges? There the dragons now go to mate."

"That—that is . . ."

"That is a great mystery, yes. Why did it change? What did the Sage Emperor do?"

But Gaunt had not responded to Wu. "That is . . . my baby," she said, wincing, breathing fast. "I think it is time . . ."

"I will summon assistance."

"First I must speak to Leaftooth."

"Certainly. He can serve me as well as any monk."

"No, there is a tea ceremony he must perform."

"Most interesting. I was not informed of this ceremony. I look forward to witnessing it."

CHAPTER 22.

The Phoenix Kite teahouse topped a hill near the flank of the Blue Heavenwall, in sight of both rich merchants' homes and commoners' hovels. True to its name, it offered kites to its customers, who staged aerial battles for the amusement of the teahouse's other patrons. Even now a flying lion chased a fluttering sea serpent. The winner would fight the proprietor's phoenix kite, now undefeated in twenty engagements.

The hooded woman watched the proceedings while setting out a game of weiqi, sipping yak-milk tea from the Argosy Steppes. A girl, also hooded, walked up to her table.

"May I join you?"

"Only if you play."

The girl's weiqi game was lackluster, and the older woman carefully built entrapping nets across the board. The goal was not to crush her opponent, nor indeed to win, but to prolong the game just as long as needed.

"I have heard report of friends," said the older woman.

"Oh?"

"Gaunt and Bone are coming. They will arrive soon, I think."

"Oh! Are they coming for you, Eshe? Or for us?"

"It could be either, Next One. Or neither. They are hunted, and may simply be using the city to hide."

Outside, the sea serpent fell to the lion, plummeting earthward.

The girl paused, finally setting down a stone. The placement was rash, Eshe decided. Next One said, "Things have changed quickly since we came here, Eshe, since you got us settled. I have a new gang, new responsibilities. The kids we found in the streets, they need me. Nightsoil keeps challenging Flybait, and Stinkblossom takes on too many risks, and Goatbreath only talks to that crazy mutt of his . . . They need guidance."

"Bone guided you, for a time."

"I'm grateful for that. But I got to know him, Eshe. He's mad for thieving. He's even worse than a man just crazed for gold, because nothing will satisfy him but the next challenge. Only Gaunt can calm that in him. I'm no Gaunt."

Eshe smiled. "Nor I." She placed a stone, secure in her strategy.

"I'll give reports to you, as we agreed. But I won't shelter Gaunt and Bone. They'd bring disaster on us. I can't do that to the kids. And Flybait . . . gods know, he needs someone halfway sensible to keep him from dancing on cliffs."

"I am not asking you to shelter them. I want you to watch for them. And I suspect the place to do so is the riverside wharf."

"All right. We'll start looking tomorrow."

"Today. As soon as we're done here."

"All right, today. But the game is young . . ."

Eshe placed a single new stone. Outside, the lion fled the phoenix, and hit the ground.

"Oh."

"Now," Eshe said.

CHAPTER 23.

As the pursuit drew near, Bone drove *Cradle* behind a fishing boat, propped up his fake Imago Bone of straw, lashed the rudder, and leapt across to a family houseboat.

Curses surrounded him—*crazy, ghost-man, grab him*—and Bone danced his way past men, women, children, and dogs (a truly astonishing number of denizens) with an apologetic smile on his face and his improvised scroll case in his hand. Reaching the far side he dove and swam, holding upon the surface the small log, whose ends he'd plugged with clay. The painting was protected, or so he hoped.

Moreover, an entirely separate hole through the width of the log admitted a reed, which he now used for breathing.

Where once there had been Imago Bone, now there was a floating log drifting cityward—and a decoy sailing downriver.

Swimming, breathing, swimming, Bone neared the harbor gate. He dared a peek into the air. Hundreds of yards away the large river-junk loomed beside the abandoned *Cradle*.

In the other direction lay a vast harbor wall with a dragon-maw gateway, soldiers and passers-by crowding a crenellated road that creased the dragon's eyebrows. Beyond that, Bone could see the land rise like a billowing carpet of foot-crowded streets, banner-speckled markets, rectangular peak-roofed houses, and slender pagodas. There was even a clock tower, hands pointing to characters in the Tongue of the Tortoise Shell. All roads converged upon the high purple wall at the feet of dragon-fortress of the Forbidden City, staring down with glowing eyes crowded with scores of paper lanterns.

Bone forced his gaze downward, for ahead lay the harbor gate and a conundrum. The gate admitted boats; but iron-barred side grills admitted water and smaller detritus.

Bone could slip through the gate, but his log might alert the guards above. On the other hand . . .

If he dared, he could allow the log bearing the painting to slip through the grill. He would swim like a seal through the gate, deep under the soldiers' noses, and reclaim the log on the far side.

All this would require was a long breath, some exertion, a little luck and a cold willingness to risk never seeing Persimmon again.

At that moment the log hummed.

"I am busy," he began, voice low.

Imago! I need you! I can't do this!

He saw the crew of the pursuing junk toss his straw dummy overboard.

"You can do this, Persimmon Gaunt," he said, swimming, risking all by staying in air and speaking. "You did not break with your bards, leave Swanisle, face angels of death and sorcerers and cannibals to falter now. *You will get through*. This will be a memory. And together we'll hold our child."

He dove. He shoved the log bearing A *Tumult of Trees on Peculiar Peaks* through the grill.

When he resurfaced he saw the wharf-side ahead, piers spearing out from artificial islands linked to the city by arching bridges. He also noted a commotion at the harbor gate, with bellows echoing between the guards and Bone's pursuit. Not much time.

He searched and saw the log spinning near a dilapidated pier to one side of the islands and bridges, in the shadow of the city wall. A quartet of rumpled, dirty-looking youngsters lurked nearby.

A yapping arose, and a boy released a dog, a patchy-looking grey mutt who seemed all snout and legs. It splashed into the water with evident joy and nosed directly for Bone's log.

Bone swam. He dared not lose speed, so he stayed on the surface, kicking and stroking until his whole being seemed an aching wave that surged toward shore.

But he was too late. The dog snatched the log in its mouth and dragged it toward the pier. Bone pursued.

Sound could sometimes travel swift and clear over water, and Bone heard snatches of conversation as he swam.

"Hey, Goatbreath!" called a boy. "Control your dog, willya? We're supposed to watch for barbarians, not play in the water . . ."

"Dog does what Dog does, Nightsoil!" came the voice of a younger boy. "I do not control him. He is wiser than we . . ."

"Leave Goatbreath alone, Nightsoil." A female voice now. "He and I had few friends since we escaped the orphanage, except this dog . . ."

"Sorry, Quickcloud," said the first voice. "I guess I get bossy. I used to be solo, and it's weird working in a team, especially with you-know-who riding us all the time . . ."

"Flybait's not so bad, Nightsoil . . ." said a new male voice.

"Stinkblossom," said the one who must be Nightsoil, "you're just like Flybait. You both lack a survival instinct . . ."

Flybait? Bone sputtered in the water, tried to call out.

"Hey!" said the youngest boy. "There's someone coming after Dog!"

"There must be something valuable inside that log!" said the girl.

He saw the child-gang take the dog's prize and run with it to a nearby alleyway, the dog an amiable wet cloud behind them.

Now Bone recognized the young man and woman who met the quartet at the mouth of the alley, even as they turned away: a lanky, cocksure boy with tangled hair and a slim girl with straight hair and a direct gaze. "Next One!" Bone gasped. "Flybait!"

But he was exhausted, and his shout emerged as a rasp. He staggered from the water, but before he could take more than a few steps a dozen Imperial soldiers in lacquered, dragon-ornamented armor barred his path. They raised gently curved broadswords with expressions lacking in gentleness altogether.

From the harbor behind Bone came the voice of Walking Stick.

"Respected devil Imago Bone!" the official called from the soldier-filled junk. "You have given a good chase! But I mean only honor to you and yours! Where is Persimmon Gaunt?"

Bone, heart like a stone, was ready to tell Walking Stick the answer.

As he opened his mouth, dripping and downcast, he saw a huge shadow absorb his own and those of all the soldiers—and he heard the booming of wings.

Flame burst from the skies.

Night's Auditors had come to Riverclaw.

Warriors scattered, warehouses caught flame, citizens screamed, but Walking Stick leapt upon a pier and raced toward Bone.

The dragon of the West plunged then, and wrapped itself around the wharf-side where Bone now stood alone. Its tail slapped a boat, which flipped against the harbor wall and splintered. Its wings stretched and windows shattered. Its snout casually immolated the pier upon which Walking Stick ran, before its body closed in a circle and blocked Bone's view, trapping him within a ring of metal- and jewel-encrusted dragon-flesh.

The dragon had two riders. The first concentrated upon the serrated shard of magic mirror embedded in his skull. Images of a leaping Walking Stick appeared within. Hackwroth hissed a command, and the dragon's tail whipped through the air. Bone heard a *crack!* torment the air, and saw the Garden warrior tumbling head over heels back toward the harbor like a child's doll.

The second rider, a hulking figure bearing a lantern upon a chain around one arm, extended the other arm toward Bone. "Imago Bone!" cried Lampblack. "Surrender, and we offer rescue. Fight, and we offer death."

There seemed little choice. A few more minutes of life might provide a few more opportunities. Bone raised his hands. "I can surrender myself only."

"So we see," said Hackwroth, as Lampblack leapt off the dragon to secure the thief. Bone was transfixed by the livid bright scarring of the auditor's face, the dull hatred of the auditor's stare.

Bone complied, and at Lampblack's direction grabbed the lacing of ropes that wrapped around the dragon's upper neck. Up he went, considering the merits of simply scrambling down the far side. The odds of stabbing or immolation seemed unacceptably high. *Wait*, he told himself. The dragon rose, and the staring, shouting citizens became the apparent size of cats, then squirrels, then ants. Buildings and ships whirled below.

"A long chase you gave us," Lampblack said, "from the Sanctuary of the Fallen Feather to this land of strange minds."

"I've surrendered myself to you," Bone said, "because of your reputation as honest workmen."

"We have earned that reputation," Hackwroth said, and Lampblack added, "Sometimes to our cost."

"Then hear me out. I assume your task is to audit myself and Persimmon Gaunt."

"Indeed," Hackwroth said. "Your minds will be pulped, the juice of knowledge extracted."

"Which the kleptomancers of Palmary will sip," said Lampblack.

Riverclaw spun below like the appendage it was named for, following the delta of the Ochre. From here Bone could clearly see the Red and Blue Heavenwalls merging at their heads like mating dragons, their nuzzling resulting in the Forbidden City. Their claws made divisions of the wards facing the river and the sea, while their gigantic backs framed a shadowy district inland. Seeing their stone embrace, Bone ached for his lover. "Is this," he said, "what I have bought with my surrender?"

"For your wisdom," Lampblack said, "we will make your auditing more graceful. There may be enough of you left to perform simple repetitive tasks. You might be a farm hand, a stone-hauler, a gravedigger. The opportunities are endless."

"So is my gratitude."

"You killed two kleptomancers, Imago Bone. Persimmon Gaunt was an accessory. You were both unwise to return to their realm."

Bone nodded. "I had assumed they would let sleeping bygones lie."

"They are patient, and forget little."

As Lampblack spoke, Hackwroth guided the dragon into the clouds. Bone shivered in the misty chill, though he could sense the supernatural fire coursing within the creature beneath. A hush came upon the world, and Bone felt light-headed. He gripped the ropes tighter, though he suspected falling was an easy death he'd not be allowed. He recalled Eshe's words the night of the bandits: *What if you are not simply a threat, but an opportunity?*

"So be it," Bone said. "And no others are included in the contract?"

"You refer, I assume, to your unborn child," Hackwroth said, "whom I have glimpsed in the shard." (Here the auditor's eyes crossed and consulted the fragment of magic mirror.) "Of course he will need to be cared for. The kleptomancers will claim him."

"Him?" Bone said. "You know the gender?"

"Indeed. As I know his three most probable names. It is a burden, my knowledge."

Bone could not resist. "What are the names?"

Hackwroth studied him. "Do you not understand your position, thief?"

"Please. The names."

"*Innocence*, if his parents name him. *Kuang Nu You*, if named by the folk of Qiangguo. *Lamprey*, if named by the kleptomancers."

"Innocence," Bone said. Then, "I'm surprised we'd name him that."

"You haven't," Hackwroth snapped, images swirling in the mirror in his head. "All is in flux. Now is the time of decision."

"I'd prefer Imago Junior."

"Enough," Lampblack said. "You would bargain? Bargain. Else we'll disassemble you here and now."

"A guaranteed catch of me, if you recover Gaunt from her current fate, and let her go."

"You hope by this to save mother and child," Hackwroth said. "But the cost is too high. It is the child the kleptomancers want most."

"You have revealed something, then. You would doom an innocent?"

Lampblack said, "No one is innocent."

Bone laughed bitterly. "That's a lie I'm familiar with, having used it in my own profession."

Hackwroth said, "You think us unacquainted with familial love? It is my own father here, whom you doused in boiling water."

Lampblack said, "And it is my own son, who suffered from my experiment that shattered a scrying mirror. It is greater comfort than I deserve, that he chose to stay with me, and learn my work."

"I saw the futures where I turned to bitterness," Hackwroth said. "And saw that staying with my father would bring me to a glorious bright fate, though the details escape me."

"Yet knowing love of family," Bone said, "you'd destroy mine."

"Come now," Lampblack said. "Hypocrites speak of 'love of family' as if that were all one thing, and all families united. You and we know, however, that all clans compete. It is biological necessity. We wish our own spawn to cover the earth, and tolerate other bloodlines only to the degree that they serve or strengthen our own."

"Not so!" Bone said, thinking of many strangers who'd become friends on the road. "Not so."

"The vehemence of your denial suggests my father may have struck a nerve," Hackwroth said. "How often have you stolen from others, for the benefit of yourself and Gaunt?"

"Those others could well afford it," Bone said. "I steal, with rare exceptions, from the wealthiest, such as those who employ you."

"Irrelevant," Lampblack said. "You select rich targets with whom you lack affinity. That is strategy, not idealism."

"It is natural you defend those whom you serve," Bone said. "Those who keep you comfortable in your assassin's trade. The best defenders of the rich are always those beholden to the rich."

Hackwroth laughed. "He taunts you, father! You call him ignorant of biology; he calls you ignorant of poverty. And meanwhile Persimmon Gaunt gets further away."

"Let us follow her, then," Lampblack said. "Very well, Bone, you have bought Gaunt's eventual freedom. We will let her bear the child, then take it and its drooling father back to our masters."

"Your generosity overwhelms me," Bone said.

"Descend, Kindlekarn," Hackwroth snapped.

Bone was surprised to recognize the dragon's name, though from where he did not know. But he had no time to consider the question as the creature plunged and Bone gripped the ropes, perhaps as surrounded by enemies as he'd ever been in his life, studying the intricacies of Riverclaw for any sign of the miscreants who held his hopes.

CHAPTER 24.

Time within *A Tumult of Trees on Peculiar Peaks* moved differently than time in the world that spawned it, and this relationship was a fluid, twisting thing; and so Gaunt and Bone never knew that the moment the dog snatched the painting from the waters was also the moment of their son's birth.

There was a time during the delivery when Gaunt hated Imago for leaving her, while simultaneously clinging to his words: *You will get through.* The idiotic monks and the daft self-portrait of the Sage Painter said foolish things about how well it was all going, when she knew perfectly well the baby's passage through her loins was going to snap her pelvis like a wishbone.

Wu at least understood. "I have heard it said," the outlaw confided, "that outside of a mortal wound, this pain is the greatest that one may experience."

"Thanks so much," Gaunt snapped.

"It is also said that a blessed veil falls over the memory afterward, so that the thought of agony torments you no more. Otherwise no woman would ever have a second child."

"No chance of that," Gaunt moaned.

"Indeed," said Wu, leaning close and whispering, "for I know now who you are, consort of Imago Bone. I knew you were no innocent. Do not fear. I will be an honest midwife. But you will lead me to him one day."

Gaunt could not even focus on this new peril. At last she gave herself over to life as a cripple and bore down. Leaftooth babbled something about the baby crowning and the self-portrait was beaming (and writing a poem about it, for Swan's sake!) and then she found energy from some unknown source, prayer or love or raw spite, and the baby was out. The blades had only been needed for one thing, the cutting of the umbilical. Wu placed the little one upon her chest. The wrinkled-red-damp-perfect boy cried in a resigned, irritable sort of way, like a mad genius surrounded by fools, quieting as he shared her skin-warmth. He did not suckle at first, nor look at her. He just breathed in, out, in, out, staring at the light beyond the window. She admired her son's priorities, and imitated him. Wu had the gall to ask for more pushing, and she wanted to kick the bandit in the face, but she obeyed and got the placenta out, too. Meanwhile the baby snuffled around for her breast, and after some fumbling Gaunt fed him, an act somehow both painful and satisfying. In time the latter would eclipse the former.

She was not crippled. She ached as though she'd been folded inside out and back again and wondered why, if this process were necessary to procreation, humanity was not extinct. But she was not crippled. She found the strength to stroke the baby's little cap of tiny brown hairs. "Then this was all worth it," she whispered. "In a sense." She looked again at the diffuse grey light gently filling the Peculiar Peaks, and despite everything she smiled. "In a sense. Innocence."

In Swanisle unmarried women gave their names to their children, whether the father was scoundrel or king. So began the life of Innocence Gaunt.

The name was duly recorded in the annals of the Peculiar Peaks, transcripted into the Tongue of the Tortoise Shell. Thus the baby gained a second name, via the meaning of characters vaguely echoing his name in Roil: "Nu You Kuang," or in the Qiangguo manner with surname first, "Kuang Nu You." Gaunt gathered "Nu" meant something along the lines of "skilled striving," and "You" meant "friendship." "Kuang" had no particular meaning, sounding reminiscent of "Gaunt."

"You are an innocent striver for friendship," Gaunt told the baby, aware how peculiar cooing sounded, coming from her. "Yes, you are."

Gaunt was never ignorant of the dangers around her, or the implications of Bone's silence in the following days. It rained and thundered for a time. The air cleared later in the week, but the wind mimicked the distant barking of dogs and the laughter of naughty children. The monks readied themselves for another communication with the outside world, preparing a mysterious tea from purple leaves of the misty slopes. Meanwhile, however, Gaunt felt an unaccountable joy grow upon her. The feeling was highly suspect, as Gaunt's days were filled with rocking, nursing, patting, burping—and cleaning waste with a bizarre resemblance to mustard—and her nights were as bereft of sleep as any time she'd spent on the run from guardsmen or monsters.

No doubt her body had ambushed her, demanding she perform the animal duty of motherhood, and repaying her with mere bliss. Torn from Bone, her future unknown, she did not argue. Innocence grew.

"He is smiling!" she announced to her companions.

"The facial muscles assume many random positions at this time," Wu said, "including that of mirth. The time will come when he smiles in truth, and knows you as more than a cloud of color and comfort. Until that time—"

"He is *smiling*," Gaunt repeated, less amicably.

"As you wish."

Without a break in her nursing, or a hint of modesty, Gaunt added, "You still have no sense of what is happening out there?"

Leaftooth sighed. "I fear *Tumult* has changed hands. Soon the tea will be ready, we will be able to communicate with the outside again, and we will see. Your Imago Bone sounds like a resourceful one, however. So perhaps this situation will change."

"If our enemies found the scroll," Gaunt said, "would they be able to force entry?"

The image of the Sage Painter said, "I am afraid my prototype meant the painting for the enjoyment of all. I can keep an individual in the Peaks . . ." —Wu scowled as he spoke— ". . . but I can only protest, not prevent, an arrival. I can, however, deflect an approach, so that newcomers will have a considerably longer journey to the mountain crest."

"I would ask you to do so," Gaunt said, "if the visitor is not Bone."

"It shall be so. Now tell me again of this city of Palmary, that I might write poems about it. The squalor and majesty of such a place intrigues me . . ."

Innocence fell asleep, and fell off the breast. Gaunt lifted him, head draped over her shoulder, and thought, *Ah, now I can—*

Her desires crowded together, jostling for approval.

—*sleep!*

—*ransack the archives!*

—*sleep!*

—*question the monks!*

—*sleep!*

—*explore the Peculiar Peaks!*

—*sleep!*

—question the self-portrait!
—sleep!
—write a poem, to ground my racing head!
—sleep . . .

"Persimmon Gaunt," said Leaftooth.

She shuddered, jerking her head. The light was different, dimmer. Leaftooth was the only visitor. The wind was howling outside. A heavy blanket was over her, and there was no pressure on her shoulder and chest.

"The baby . . . where's the baby . . ."

"Asleep in the basket yonder. As you were asleep, until moments ago."

"I . . . I shouldn't be weak . . ."

"Cherish weakness. Flow to the lowest level, and all will come to you."

She shook her head, yawned. "The better I learn your language, Leaftooth, the less I understand you."

Leaftooth smiled as well. "We have a visitor. A boy. He has a story that will interest you."

Gaunt was surprised to recognize the gangly, tangle-haired Flybait. He was shivering from his long journey up the mountain, and obviously frightened, but his gaze was defiant as he addressed the gathered monks, the self-portrait of the Sage Painter, Wu, and Gaunt. "My gang has the scroll."

"Beg pardon," said Gaunt, "but the Cloud and Soil Society was destroyed."

"Yes," Wu said, staring at the lad.

Flybait sucked in his stomach, straightened his shoulders, and aimed his nose skyward. "You refer to my old outfit. I have come into my own as a man to be reckoned with."

Wu laughed. Ordinary laughter was to Wu's laughter as embraces were to head-locks. "You, Flybait, are an ignorant fool."

"Would it be better to be a knowledgeable fool? I am a man of action, with my own operation now. Your whole universe is in my hands."

"That is a large claim," Leaftooth said. "This realm extends far beyond the scene depicted in the scroll. It has its own peculiar reality."

Flybait gave an evil grin. (Gaunt noted the distinction: a truly evil man would have smiled in the ordinary fashion.) "Shall we test that premise," he said, "by burning the scroll?"

"You cannot threaten us, young man," Leaftooth answered, "standing there wrapped in our blankets, sipping our tea. Even the self-portrait of the Sage Painter knows not what will happen if you burn the scroll. What of it?"

Flybait sneered. "Would you try to stop me, old man?"

Leaftooth said, "Perhaps, less-old man. We are not all-passive, we monks. The Way of the Forest does not forbid action—for it forbids nothing. But we cannot guess what outcome your destruction, or our response, might engender."

Flybait began to look confused. "That's a threat, right?"

"It is reality. Suppose you throw a rock at a window. You may have done so at one point. That is bad, surely?"

"You're a little late to lecture me about that."

"Yet say the window is as yet unrepaired when a fire breaks out in the house, and a family escapes more easily through that empty frame. That is good, surely? Yet as the survivors huddle together on the street, a sick member of that family spreads the illness throughout the crowd and then the entire city. That is bad, surely? Yet the suffering of the city causes the Emperor to pass it by when his armies need swelling. That is good, surely? Yet the Emperor's mercy means he has not quite the soldiers to defend against an invading horde. That is—"

"Okay, okay!" The boy held up his hands. "I get it. You're too mystical to threaten. No need to torture me with philosophy. Just send me back and we'll sell you off to a pawnbroker. Gaunt. You're a friend, sort of."

"Why, thank you," Gaunt said.

"You can come with me . . . is that the baby?"

"That is the baby."

"He's cute . . ."

"Thank you. These people have sheltered me. You will not harm them."

The self-portrait of Meteor-Plum coughed. "I could prevent you from leaving, Flybait, but I will not. It already pains me to imprison one life here." Wu glared at him, but he continued. "But I can advise against your departure. Persimmon Gaunt has spoken of those pursuing her, and they are formidable."

Flybait looked uncomfortable. "We saw lots of troops, sure. And that stick guy. And that freak dragon. It looked different from the ones in all the rich people's fancy tapestries and clothes, but even I know enough to be scared of the thing."

"You do have a talent for self-preservation," Wu said grudgingly. "What about that girlfriend of yours?"

Flybait looked wistful. "Next One's not my girlfriend. She's waiting outside the scroll. We got away from the dragon, from the troops, everyone. We've brought in smart kids—they know all the alleys and sewers and tunnels. We'll be all right."

Gaunt said, "Idiot. Even my lover, Bone, greatest second-story man of the Spiral Sea, is never so cocky. That dragon is commanded by Night's Auditors, assassins of the mind. If they don't know the tunnels, they'll ransack every brain in Riverclaw to learn. They will find you. Or Walking Stick and his Garden will."

"Their vision of the Way is a harsh one, the Garden," Leaftooth said. "But none can deny their devotion, or the skill they bring to their misguided willfulness. A Garden master might defeat any ten ordinary warriors, on open ground."

Flybait sneered and spat, but he looked nervous now.

"You're not a bad sort, Flybait," Gaunt said, "a little loose with property rights, but I'm a pot, you're a kettle." To his blank look she added, "I'm not leaving, but I have another idea. The monks might shelter and feed your gang for a time. Rotate your crew through the scroll, while you find a buyer. Let me venture out to assist you. I have some experience moving valuable hauls."

"And how does that help you?"

"The right buyer might be able to protect the scroll from the auditors and the Garden. I'm told the most powerful figures of the Empire live in Riverclaw. If anyone can protect us, we'll find them there."

Flybait put his hands to his head. "All right, all right. I'll trust you. I'm tired. A bed sounds nice. I'll think about it."

But in the morning the boy had left his room, his tracks passing through muddy ground, back down the mountain road. Wu spat down it after him. The self-portrait said that by noon he would have no choice but to send Flybait back to the Empire of Walls.

Innocence slept fitfully that day. He seemed not to have quite mastered the art of releasing gas, and Gaunt's existence seemed to consist of jiggling him gently so he would get it out one end or the other. When he stopped wailing and finally slept, it was in her arms. When her arms ached and her eyelids fluttered, she would place him in the basket, but within minutes he screamed his outrage, and it was back to jiggling. All was motion. She wondered if that had something to do with the Way the monks spoke of. Yet the Way sounded much more restful than what she was doing.

Flow down to the lowest point, baby, she thought. *Like water. No, wait—you don't have to flow down your water just yet. Sleep . . .*

The day grew hot, hotter than at any time since she'd arrived. The clouds burned away and a searing sun, perhaps a bit larger than the one back home, beat down upon the gleaming emeralds of the Peculiar Peaks. Gaunt took her jiggling routine outside. Innocence was finally asleep on her sweaty shoulder when Flybait returned at a run, a terrified-looking girl with long black hair and a bamboo cane panting beside him. Gaunt recognized Flybait's serious-eyed friend. She opened her mouth to ask Next One what was the matter, but was startled by the girl's wail.

"They're dead! They're all dead!"

CHAPTER 25.

The poorest region of Riverclaw was its Shadow Ward, inland from the Purple Forbidden City. Hemmed by that citadel and the high barriers of the Heavenwalls, it suffered long shadows except at midday. The roughest district of the Shadow Ward was the Neck, where the Heavenwalls bent close, marking the boundary of the Ward before winding separately across the land, and where the rival garrisons of the Red and Blue Walls snarled and sported, with Riverclaw's poor as pawns and hangers-on. And the bleakest section of the Neck was the Necropolis Wall, an afterthought of a barrier running between the Heavenwalls, guarding the city from an ancient burial ground infested with hopping vampires and hungry ghosts.

The dragon Kindlekarn, guided by the visions in Hackwroth's skull, dove over the Shadow Ward and flapped toward the Necropolis Wall. *Of course Flybait and Next One would make their base here*, thought Imago Bone, who had heard tales of Riverclaw from Tror and Lightning Bug. *Death, to young toughs, is less terrifying than humiliation.*

Bone's musing on terror was interrupted by the panic of the people below. Citizens screamed and fled through squalid streets, sometimes to be trampled by a rush of Imperial soldiers or city guardsmen. At times those warriors took aim at Kindlekarn, and crossbow bolts clanged off the metal and jewels in the dragon's hide. Occasionally, by luck, a bolt found a seam between encrustations and stuck. Kindlekarn grumbled as if stirred from a reverie. He spat fire. Men burned, but Bone thought more damage was done to the surrounding neighborhood than to the combatants. Yet even this attack might be kinder than the auditors' methods.

Lampblack swung his lantern. The fiery entity called Flick, evidently recovered from the sea, twisted and spun in the lantern's vicinity. Its burning tendrils coiled toward the Necropolis Wall. Bone's gaze followed the gesture, and he squinted at tiny figures disappearing through the fortification's old stone. "There!" he told Night's Auditors. "Those look like our urchins."

"I apprehend," Hackwroth said, "that this old wall has many fissures, natural and hewn, allowing communication with the graveyards beyond."

"Yes," said Lampblack, "And I sense Persimmon Gaunt's presence, though it is strangely remote. It is as if she were thousands of miles away, even though Flick points to the wall, not the horizon."

"She is remote," Bone said. "I will explain the manner of it shortly."

"No need," said Hackworth. "I perceive now . . . she is a prisoner of an artifact, a gateway to another world. Interesting. Kindlekarn, proceed into the necropolis. We will cut them off."

"Best drop me off on this side," Bone objected. "We will block their retreat."

"A worthy suggestion," Lampblack said, "so long as I accompany you."

"It should be me, father," Hackworth objected. "Your injuries—"

"You have the mastery of this dragon, not I. No, I shall keep watch on Bone. Set us down before the wall."

Hackworth grunted, Kindlekarn descended, and Bone leapt onto a narrow rooftop. Lampblack alighted less steadily. With a look of warning at Bone, Hackworth urged Kindlekarn over the wall into the city of the dead. The morning air cooled notably with the dragon's passing. The sky overhead was soft blue, but the early sun cast a long shadow from the sharp ramparts of the Forbidden City. That was good. Bone preferred darkness.

He considered fleeing, but feared Lampblack's power, and his footsteps would in any event converge with the auditors' at the painting. Best to ride the coattails of chaos, and see what opportunities came.

Thus he helped the auditor down with as much grace as he could manage.

"Thank you," muttered Lampblack after they slid together off the hovel roof.

"Mention it not—"

Bone was interrupted by a scream from the rickety dwelling they'd descended. A thin woman and two young boys, all dusty and dressed in rags, burst from the house and fled from Bone and Lampblack, their departure guarded by a short, shuffling man with many missing teeth and a rusty knife that looked ready to snap in the breeze.

Bone held up his hands and began to speak reassuring blather, such as he'd uttered to hundreds of surprised householders.

But Lampblack spat and waved his lantern, and the fiery apparition of Flick dashed out and burned through the ears of all four people, not unlike a knitter threading a diamond pattern. It returned, a notch brighter, to its master's lantern.

Bone's fevered excuses became as ashes on his tongue. The family shuddered as one, before becoming as still as the doomed crewmen of the *Passport/ Punishment*.

"Accompany us," the auditor told them. "Throw yourselves upon all who threaten us."

They nodded with gaping mouths, and lurched toward Lampblack.

Bone lowered his hands. "There is a hell reserved for you," he said to Lampblack. "I say this not from my brain but from my sinew, which knows it must be so."

"You speak as a primitive," Lampblack said. "There are no ultimate punishments or rewards. Only processes, which the skilled can exploit."

Bone shuddered, feeling then that Lampblack had had a point about the struggle among bloodlines. For despite the fate of this family, he would not risk killing them and ending their enslavement, knowing their thralldom temporarily served his goals.

He imagined Brother Clement's gaze upon him. He felt more self-disgust than at any robbery.

"I will lead," Bone managed to say, gesturing toward the Necropolis Wall. "Rude streets and tunnels are, after all, my element."

Lampblack agreed. "This allows me to watch you."

Watchfires flared around the Shadow Ward. The Necropolis Wall, a four-story affair slumped between the titanic Heavenwalls, was roused to action. Soldiers in cheap armor rushed along it, bearing spears. Ambling and creeping as instinct bade him, Bone reached a muddy track that ran before the wall. From a crumbling temple nearby he hefted a chunk of masonry and hurled it far; it clattered and distracted the soldiers even as he skipped in a peculiar dancing motion through the shadows toward the wall, pausing just once, to scratch twin converging lines in the mud. For this was the one moment in which Lampblack could not fully see him.

Even as Bone reached the wall, Lampblack crouched and hurried afterward. At the same time the auditor pointed his mindless thralls toward the stone Bone had thrown.

Soon the doomed family caught the eyes of the nervous guards upon the wall. They were promptly gutted by thrown spears.

Bone shuddered as he found what he believed the gang's tunnel: a fissure in the wall, covered by thick netting painted stone-grey. He pushed the camouflage aside and slipped within, taking little stock of Lampblack or of the sounds of the better-armed Imperial troops converging on the wall.

Bone found himself within a hot, dusty and winding little passage, cramped even for a youth. The confinement strained his composure as he slithered along. The words of Lampblack at his heels made it worse: "You interest me, Imago Bone. You obviously suffer at the hurts of children. You felt lost as a child yourself." A light flared behind Bone, and the burning blob of Flick rushed past Bone's ear to light the tunnel before him. Bone forced himself to breathe evenly. Lampblack continued, "You felt bereft of the love of your parents, perhaps? Many thieves substitute shiny trinkets for paternal affection."

Bone willed himself to press on, Flick bobbing before his eyes. "You will not steal the minds of these children," Bone said. "There is no need. I will convince them or overcome them."

"Your solicitude amuses me," Lampblack said. "Succeed, and their minds will remain intact."

The passage continued for what seemed half an hour's crawl, with frequent descents. Bone suspected the Necropolis Wall lay well behind.

His suspicions were confirmed when the path ascended. Flick burned past his nose on its return to its master, and Bone emerged within the shattered frame of a mausoleum.

Whomever the tomb once sheltered had been of some importance. It had the dimensions of a small manor, hewn from cracked grey stone, threaded with green vines and worn calligraphy. Faded murals depicted men in dark robes and women in colorful gowns. Bas-reliefs of dragons amid trees and mountains glowered dustily, with chipped tails and noses. The ceiling was mostly gone, and blocks of masonry testified to its undignified fall. Above glowed the morning sky; all around lay shadows and whispers. He crept forward, keeping his movements to two mouses on his personal scale of sound.

The crack Bone ascended from lay partly under a vast block of stone swarming with characters in the Tongue of the Tortoise Shell, and judging by the whispers, the block's far side was swarming with characters of a different sort.

"It was Goatbreath's dog who snatched it, Flybait!"

"And who leads the dog's pack, Nightsoil? Even the mutt understands the ranking around here. Give me that scroll before I mark you with my scent!"

There were hoots and catcalls.

"But you are not the brains around here," the boy called Nightsoil countered. "You'd be no one without Next One. She's our expert appraiser!"

"The one who can read, you mean," Next One replied. "I should refuse. We were supposed to watch for a barbarian, not run off with treasure."

"There's always an exemption for treasure," Flybait protested. "Everyone knows that."

"Give it here," Next One snapped.

It sounded as though the scroll were passed over, for without further argument Bone heard it unrolled.

There was a gasp. "The seal of Meteor-Plum Long," Next One said. "I know this scroll."

Bone thought it would be a good time to step forward, but he could not resist eavesdropping.

"That thing!" Flybait said. "The one with the taotie and the bottomless pit!"

"Should that mean something to me?" Nightsoil said.

"This artist made paintings into which one might disappear," Next One said wonderingly. "There's a whole world inside here."

"Like a trap?"

"Like a gift." There was a wistful sound in Next One's voice. "This will secure our fortunes, if we can sell it in the right place."

There was a chorus of indrawn breaths, a medley of murmurs.

"Let me test it," Flybait said, and by the sounds, took the scroll. "I want to make sure. I just concentrate . . ."

"He's gone!" one urchin shouted.

Bone sensed the appearance of Lampblack in the crack near his feet. He was out of time. He stepped forward.

"Next One," he said. "I—"

"A spy," someone said, and "Get him!" said someone else.

His opponents numbered five: three boys, a girl, and a dog. Next One herself held back, the scroll at her feet, evidently shocked by the return of Bone.

The dog leaped. Bone had considerable experience with guard dogs, and did not expect to talk it down. He sprawled it with a savage kick.

"Next One!" Bone said, "Call them off!"

"No," she said, raising the cane that once belonged to Exceedingly Accurate Wu. "I know you, Bone. You want this prize for yourself."

"That's true in a sense, but—"

He tried getting another word in, but the third boy, the smallest of the bunch, ran screaming at the thief. Bone elbowed the boy's gut, grabbed him, and slammed him face-first into the stone block. The boy whimpered and did not rise.

Bone could not pause for breath or regret. Lampblack was peering around the corner.

Now he had to mangle the kids to save them.

He drew a dagger and advanced on the nearest opponent, this one a teen-aged girl with clipped hair who bore a dagger of her own. She snarled and lunged. He saw it coming, and took advantage of his height by tripping her. Before she could rise he stomped upon her weapon arm. She screamed and dropped her dagger.

He rolled away from a simultaneous attack from the two older boys— the one he'd temporarily blinded and the one he'd kicked. He rose again in a corner, sizing things up at last. Three foes down for now. Two advancing with daggers. He estimated he could kill them, but as he wished to be less lethal, his odds were less sure.

Beyond them, Next One was opening the scroll of Meteor-Plum Long and calling out for Flybait.

"Listen!" Bone said to them all. "I can sell the thing for you. At the foreign district, where you needn't fear the crime lords getting a cut."

"Why should we trust you?" sneered a boy.

"Hear me out! I could have killed your friends but didn't. I only want the scroll so I can free someone from it."

"Wait . . ." Next One said, as though listening to faraway music. "Bone tells the truth . . . this foreign thief tells the truth. I'm sorry, Bone. Flybait is trying to leave, and he's met Persimmon Gaunt."

"How is she?" Bone could not help crying out.

"She's well, he says. And she has a baby boy."

There was a snarl from Lampblack then, and a sound of armored figures climbing into the tomb. Shadows sharpened as Flick blazed. There came the distinct sound of armored figures falling.

For better or worse, the Imperial troops had found Bone's arrow in the mud.

"Kids," Bone said, "you don't have to like me, but listen. You're in over your heads. I have no quarrel with you getting rich off the scroll. I salute you. But help me get my lover and my son out of there."

"I can't reach them directly," Next One said. "Time passes differently there . . ."

"I know." The clatter of battle continued. Bone took a chance, leaning closer and saying as quietly as he could, "Take the scroll with you. Keep them all inside. We'll get out of here first."

The three kids still standing met each other's gazes and, after a moment, nodded. Bone helped the youngest boy to his feet, wiped his bloody face as he cried and sneered. The older girl nursed her arm and watched Bone with hate. The dog limped. But the gang followed him to the mausoleum doorway.

Though the sounds of battle were fading behind him, Bone paused to study the landscape. A series of crumbled ruins in this gloomy canyon formed by the great Walls, jabbing at the narrow sky like the fingers of skeletal hands, could offer some running cover. "We need a different path back to the city."

Next One crept up beside him. "There, where the Necropolis Wall meets the Red Heavenwall, is a tunnel—"

A draconic snout, encrusted with jewels, filled the space ahead.

Heat like a king's oven blazed into the mausoleum.

Bone slammed Next One and himself against the wall, out of the direct path of the blast of coiling flames that exploded through the entrance.

The fury seared Bone's back even through his clothes. Then it was gone.

The smell of burned meat and new death hung thick about the tomb. Bone and Next One turned, and saw the charred remains of children and a dog.

"No," the girl said. "No, no, no."

Vast claws supported by monstrous arms tore at the doorway, and rubble fell all around. Bone shielded the girl and the scroll, battered by stones and clouds of dust. At last the sounds of collapse subsided and the air cleared. The ruin lay open to a sky choked with dust reddening the ascending sun.

And that sky was filled with the dragon Kindlekarn.

From this angle, at least, Bone reflected, Hackwroth would withhold a blast of fire, for fear of killing the nearby Lampblack, still engaged with Imperial troops. Probably.

"Girl," Bone hissed. "Leave the scroll. Run far, far away from here."

"No," the girl repeated. "No, no, no."

Bone snatched the scroll, unrolled it, and pushed it against her nose. "Then Flybait needs you," he began, and before he finished she had turned transparent. When he drew breath again she was gone.

"You cannot escape, Bone!" Hackwroth called from Kindlekarn's back. "Should you enter the scroll, who will defend it?"

Bone shifted toward Lampblack's melee, and its dubious cover.

"The shard perceives no allies for you," Hackwroth said, as images swirled within the glass in his head. "You have no hope."

"Those statements aren't equal," Bone muttered.

Then he saw something resembling hope.

A shadowy shape leapt from the tallest remaining spur of the ruin, and onto Kindlekarn's back. It was Walking Stick.

Hackwroth spun upon the dragon's neck, clutching the tangle of ropes, but beside the Garden warrior the auditor's movements were clumsy, oafish. Walking Stick seemed to dance to Hackwroth's position, swinging his staff like a thunderbolt. Hackwroth dodged, his eyes less upon his foe than upon his embedded magic mirror.

As Bone watched his enemies battle, he heard them fence with words.

"Magic is an inefficient and corrupting use of chi! The superior man does not employ it save at great need!"

"One who names himself 'superior' must secretly believe himself deficient! Now that I see you clearly, I see old age and decay upon you and your Empire!"

"Age is honor! But indeed the West knows nothing of this!"

As they sized each other up, seeking weakness, the dragon Kindlekarn ceased his exertions, as though unwilling to rend and burn without specific instruction. Bone edged along the ruin's walls, then glimpsed the lantern-flame of Flick shooting up to circle around Walking Stick's head. Glancing toward Lampblack, Bone noted that no sounds of battle could now be heard, and many fallen soldiers covered Lampblack's side of the tomb.

The words of old Master Sidewinder came unbidden to Bone, *The enemy of my enemy is a pain in the ass*, as he crept around a pillar encircled (appropriately enough) with a carved stone dragon. He saw Lampblack's fingers perched like the legs of a spider upon the forehead of the last of Walking Stick's entourage. The soldier's eyes had rolled backward in his head and spittle twisted like a little egg sac at his mouth. Bone remembered Brother Tadros, and the lost family at the Necropolis Wall, and the roasted gang here in the tomb, and the voice of Gaunt.

He tumbled up behind the auditor, rose, grappled, and slashed the man's throat.

"Murderer . . ." gasped the auditor as he fell, gurgling, and Bone found the little flame of Flick was now circling his own head. It flitted toward his right ear.

Bone dropped low and stuck the blade between the ribs, finding the heart. "Assassin," he named the auditor.

Such was the last conversation of Lampblack.

Now the little flame bore into Bone's ear, and he felt a burning and something worse than a burning, an immolation of his thoughts, a conversion of his mind to a fine haze, the easier for extraction. Striving and rage, love and adventure were soon to be equalized, mere fuel for the thing of the lamp.

And then the thing itself buzzed and burned its way back the way it came, for its master was dead. It skittered like a firework across the stone squares of the tomb and descended through a crack into the mysteries of the deep Earthe, from whence it had been summoned years gone.

Bone reeled beneath the scream of "Father!" and the weapon-cracks above, the shadow of the wings and snout and tail of the great beast and the flicker of battle above it. He could not recall his own name, nor the names of the combatants; he only recalled he should flee with his prize. Taking the scroll he escaped the tomb and ran through the necropolis, past fallen pagodas and fractured arches and cracked stone soldiers and the vestiges of a sacred gate, all the way to the place where the city wall met the Red Heavenwall, and a tunnel a few feet overhead that led through the Necropolis Wall to Riverclaw.

He was climbing into the tunnel when a blow like a boulder sprawled him upon the stony ground.

The shock freed him of the effects of Flick. He recovered his wits, taking stock of a battered body full of complaining cuts and bruises, and saw a trio of silvery claws snatch up the scroll with great care.

Bone looked up to behold Kindlekarn, riderless, glaring down at him. The reptilian snout, gleaming with rubies, filled the sky.

Bone snarled and leapt for the scroll. Kindlekarn swatted at him, but he leapt upon the other leg. The dragon rose into the air, flapping its wings.

"Dragon!" Bone screamed. "Master of sky and fire! Why do you serve human scum?"

There was a vast shaking of a head. Kindlekarn rushed into the air over the city of Riverclaw. Behind, in the necropolis, Bone glimpsed Walking Stick and Hackwroth atop the mausoleum's central slab, still fighting.

The dragon tried to scrape Bone off with its claws, but the thief scrambled further up the leg, finding ample handholds in the encrustations of jewels that marked Kindlekarn's body. Also, the need to preserve the scroll kept Kindlekarn from scratching with the other foreclaws, and the rear claws were difficult to bring to bear.

"Dragon! I remember now, where I heard your name! A wizard of the West once told me you'd come East to mate! What has happened, that you enslave yourself to men?"

The dragon roared and shot back over the Shadow Ward, over hovels and streets and taverns and guardhouses and then the flared dragon-heads where the Red and Blue Heavenwalls met, where the Forbidden City lofted from the interface of the draconic flanges like a fanciful hat shared by both creatures, gardens and pagodas and palaces gleaming in the sun. Shouts of alarm and weary men with crossbows greeted Kindlekarn's passing, but the dragon was now diving toward the cavernous maw of the Red dragon, who loomed over the Foreign District and its warehouses thick with merchants from many lands.

Bone was even then managing to crawl, inch by terrifying inch, across the chest of Kindlekarn. Here he gripped a wartish diamond, there a lump of silver, and afterward a wrinkle of iron. Wealth to astonish came and went beneath his fingers (or above and sideways of his fingers, if one considered the actual pull of gravity at any given moment). He focused only on movement, straining closer and closer to the painting of Meteor-Plum.

Kindlekarn dropped low, just over the foreign warehouses, swinging back around toward the lower fangs of the vast stone dragon.

Bone looked up in time to roll a little with the blow as the five-story stone tooth knocked him off Kindlekarn's hide.

The tooth was smoothly sloped, and Bone spun, tumbling instinctively with the blow, to spill through the air and splash into a garden pool. Breaking the surface he gasped and screamed, "No!"

FOOL, boomed the voice of the dragon, in Roil. I WOULD PRESERVE YOU. The echoes of the words reverberated in ripples across the water. Kindlekarn spun in the air and began flying toward the Shadow Ward, the scroll still in its claw.

"Not without her!" Bone shouted, coughing water. "Not without her!"

But the dragon was gone, returning to its master.

Almost, Bone stopped moving, let the waters close overhead. From the harbor to the tomb to here, he had never, in a long and bloodcurdling career, fought so hard and so well. He'd felt dim amazement at his own passion and skill. And all for nothing. Innocents were dead. Gaunt was captive. Bone was alone.

He saw a squad of Forbidden City soldiers, a dragon-banner writhing before them, emerge from a gateway between the tonsils of the stone dragon's mouth. Bone considered bobbing and waving, allowing them to kill him.

But no, there was still a thin chance to preserve Gaunt and their son. And if that failed there was vengeance. He knew also that revenge would be on Hackwroth's mind as the auditor considered Gaunt's fate.

Anger rose within him like bubbles from the bottom of the pond, and with them came the memory of Eshe, she of Kpalamaa and Swanisle, and a notion entered his mind, red-fringed. With battered body, he swam from the pool and fled through ornate rocks and bushes toward the foreign district and the dubious sanctuary Kindlekarn, in his perverse mercy, had offered.

CHAPTER 26.

Just as Kindlekarn disappeared from Imago Bone's sight, Persimmon Gaunt manifested from the painting.

She discovered herself perched upon the claw of a dragon, winging above the Purple Forbidden City. She gasped, clutched at a section of gem-studded hide, and vomited all over a glorious brass talon.

SPARE SOME PUKE FOR THE HUMANS BELOW, DOOMBEARER, rumbled a voice, in Roil.

"I—" Gaunt said. "I— I— I—" She looked down at peaked orange roofs embellished with mythical beasts, stone balconies guarded by grinning sculpted lions, swarms of elegant robed servants screaming at the flesh-and-blood monstrosity overhead. That unnerved her, so she looked up, into the sardonic vast gaze of the dragon who'd spared her life beside the sea. She had been prepared for Western assassins and Eastern martial artists, not this. "What?"

THEY BIND MY KIND, the dragon said. THE HEAVENWALLS CONSTRAIN OUR MATING. I PISS MOLTEN GOLD UPON THEM!

Gaunt heard a spattering, and distant screams.

"I did not know," Gaunt whispered, thinking it was impossible for her to be heard. "Perhaps that was wrong of Qiangguo."

I BLAME ALL HUMANITY, the dragon replied.

"Oh."

BUT MY WRATH EBBS. FOR NOW. BEFORE THEY LOOSE GHOSTROCK WARRIORS AND LIVING CALLIGRAPHY, I WILL DEPOSIT YOU UPON A ROOF.

"You will?"

I WAS LAST COMMANDED TO ACQUIRE THIS TRIFLE, NOT YOU AND YOUR MATE. I CHOOSE TO BE LITERAL AND SPARE YOU, DOOMBEARER.

"My mate! Where is he?"

CLOSER TO THE SEA. BUT I WILL NOT RETURN THERE. I WILL SET YOU DOWN.

They hovered above a palatial purple roof, with a gentle slope.

"My baby! Let me go back for my baby!"

NO, YOU MAY NOT BRING THAT DOOM BACK INTO THE WORLD.

"Doom? He is an infant!"

I HAVE NO TIME FOR ARGUMENT. GO!

"Time flows faster there! I can be there and back in moments."

I DO NOT HAVE MOMENTS. ALREADY AN ATTACKER COMES.

Gaunt looked, and was shocked to behold Lightning Bug, racing across the Forbidden City's rooftops in her grey robe with the golden firefly woven at the shoulder, even now sprinting to begin a leap toward them, palace guards chasing her all the while.

"Gaunt!" called Lightning Bug. "At last I've found you!"

"She's a friend!" Gaunt told the dragon.

SHE IS HUMAN.

Flame lit the sky above the Purple Forbidden City as it receded below them. Gaunt lost sight of Lightning Bug, and of freedom. But she had some of her wits back, and some of her physique; she could leap now, and perhaps live.

She clutched the end of the imprisoned scroll to her chest. "Take me back," she whispered to it, and was gone.

CHAPTER 27.

The hungry ones smelled the fallen man's chi, and one by one they shuffled, hopped, or glided to where he lay upon the old spirit way leading to long-unvisited royal tombs. Some were green corpses with long white hair, and they leapt upon the stone dogs and lions to better regard their unconscious prey. Some were contorted spirits writhing their way through the air, and they pointed and hissed like spittle upon a fire. Some were majestic even in death, and clad in fine billowing silks that might have blended with a noble's wedding feast; these came along the spirit way as though they owned it.

The hungry ones rarely came out by day, but the shadows of the Walls were long, and the prize was rich. The hungry ones were discriminating. They had ignored the youths who frequented the mausoleum, for the living sometimes lost their senses when their children were taken, and a foray by the Emperor's army would be disruptive of the dead community. Besides, children made small morsels. The strange dragon, too, they had avoided, for its power might unmake even them. Most found a vile existence better than no existence. Those who objected to devouring chi, or who were incautious in its pursuit, did not last.

But the man who had battled the wizard with the magic glass in his head—he was a rarity. Even senseless, his staff fallen from his limp fingers, he fairly crackled with chi.

The hungry ones began whispering to each other, a chorus of rustling and wheezing and hissing, every one of them uttering the same word.

"Mine."

"Mine."

"Mine."

Their horde was hundreds strong now, yet they advanced in spurts. Each one feared the warrior would awaken and destroy the nearest. At the same time, each one feared to lose its chance for a morsel of delectable life-force. The struggle between fears was written in the mob's trembling advance.

"Mine."

"Mine."

"Mine."

All their eerie senses were focused upon the warrior, and thus they were entirely unprepared for the woman who leapt upon the nose of a lion statue, the head of a dog statue, and the shoulders of three hopping vampires to land beside the man. She snatched up his staff and swept it in a circle, staring down all the dead horde.

It paused in a complete silence unthinkable for a living mob.

"Mine," she said.

She whacked the staff upon the road beside the man's ears. The echo filled the necropolis.

Walking Stick was on his feet in one motion, his hand grasping the staff. Lightning Bug did not relinquish it.

Their eyes met.

"You came for me," he said.

"I had questions for you," she said.

"I am somewhat busy."

"A shared task may go more quickly."

"Indeed. It is . . . good to see you."

"I confess I feel that as well."

There was a quickening of their breath. A hungry sigh emerged from the ranks of the dead, for they sensed an enlivening of the matched warriors' chi. The dead surged toward the pair, who shared a single look of guilty understanding.

The wulin could hide the strength of their feelings, from others, from themselves. But the dead did not lie.

Lightning Bug removed her hand from the staff.

The hungry ones surged forward with a howl of desire.

Lightning Bug and Walking Stick moved back to back. He flourished his staff. She downed a flask of wine.

A vampire hissed in her face and she kicked its head half off its body. Another leapt at Walking Stick and found itself whacked into the crowd. Maddened, the hungry ones tore their compatriots to pieces.

"There is no holding back," he said.

"No," she said. "Not in this." And she smiled.

CHAPTER 28.

The foreign district was like a separate city, or several separate cities, compressed into a small space. Here the Empire tolerated the presence of foreign merchants, each delegation housed somewhere within thirteen vast converted brick warehouses, baking in the sun. Bone knew to expect some of the far-traveled traders of Mirabad and the other minaret-studded cities near the Sandkiss Sea, devout men in turbans and robes, honorable and urbane, who followed the Testifier and his revelation of the Law of the All. He also noted without surprise a few tunica-clad Amberhornish, still imperious despite ruling a remnant realm smaller than any province of Qiangguo. His eyes widened at the tall black mariners of mysterious Kpalamaa of the jungle and savanna, whose technical skill and sleek galleons surpassed that of every land Bone knew, including this.

But here at Riverclaw were also peoples unguessed-at. He saw men clad in beautiful white robes seemingly made for leisure, but bearing also elegant curved blades and gazes stern as stone or ice. He saw men and women with tangles of tropical bird feathers in their hair, the women wearing garlands of flowers, the men sporting intricate maze-like tattoos on their faces, and the delegation otherwise naked but for skirts of tightly woven beige reeds. He saw another group still more lightly garbed, wearing only grass loincloths and white face-paint, yet bearing themselves with an alert sophistication to rival the Kpalamaa delegation.

Some groups Bone could scarcely believe: long-eared, leaping, furred beings wearing Imperial silks and carrying their wide-eyed young in natural stomach-pouches; dapper looking black-and-white bird-creatures draped in water-skins and bearing umbrellas; huge crabs the color of sunset with pastel-painted barnacles on their shells and pouches with quill and ink hanging from their fore-shells.

Bone blundered into a line of those crabs. Silently, but for a troubling clicking and a gasp from nearby humans, they encircled him, dipped their brushes and painted black calligraphy upon their red shells. OFFENSE, Bone read in the Tongue of the Tortoise Shell, repeated eightfold.

He bowed to the crab-folk and leapt back into the crowd, but now the foreign district constabulary supplemented the Imperial troops . . .

Bone scaled a warehouse and ran among the crenellations and sculpted beasts as though intending to leap to the west. Dropping low, he crawled north instead.

Reaching the edge he slid down into an alley, grabbed a Mirabad gurkha from a clothesline and threw the robe around himself, rushing quickly west, as far from the Mirabad habitation as he could get.

He needed sanctuary. Unfortunately, those most likely to feel kinship with him might know his reputation. That left his options meager: beg for help among people (or non-people!) he understood less than the folk of Qiangguo, or dash into the armada of merchant craft circulating through the nearby waterways and seek safety elsewhere.

Or find sanctuary with his quarry. Eshe.

As he thought this, he glimpsed beyond the warehouses and the little shops—crowded with locals offering foreigners food or handiwork or medicine or palanquin travel or puppet shows—a little white shrine capped with a silver swan.

Bone hustled as fast as he dared through the throng, barely more than a persistent shuffle. Finally he made it to the temple doorway and scurried inside.

Two Amberhornish acolytes gasped at this son of Mirabad, but Eshe, looming in flowing white robes, drifted across the little temple as smoothly as a ghost, her eyes suggesting she beheld one.

"You are most welcome, brother. The Swan's love is for everyone."

"The Testifier," Bone said, aiming for a Mirabad accent, but only hitting a bad one, "bade us respect the creeds that came before ours, O priestess."

He earned stares, however, for his strained, overwrought impression. And Eshe cocked her head. Coming closer, she murmured, "Are you in haste for consultation, brother?"

Bone whispered, "A full conversion might be in order."

"I am good at my work." She led him toward the back and said loudly, "It might be best if you return for the sunset service. Let me show you a pamphlet and the back door." They stepped among the pews and past the Swan altar to a vestry filled with robes, candlesticks, censers, and other accouterments of the faith. Bone was looking with interest at a golden swan figurehead upon a stave when Eshe opened an adjoining back door, loudly. Suddenly she pulled Bone through another passage, into a tiny office no bigger than a closet, and gently shut the door.

She pried up a floorboard. "This hiding place has never been tested."

"That may change," Bone said, descending a narrow ladder.

"This service will come at a fee."

He searched her eyes, and imagined icebergs. "The fee will be paid."

"Through honest means."

Bone composed a face of shock, and Eshe dropped the trapdoor nearly on his head.

The space was a narrow one, wood-walled, with only the ladder for company.

If his suspicions about Eshe were correct, this might be a poor place to have delivered himself.

He set about establishing if all the walls were simply that.

Judicious tapping and listening revealed that one wall could slide to reveal an earthen passage. It led beneath the thick of the foreign district.

As one could hardly expect a thief to ignore a hidden passage, Bone slipped inside, closed the panel, and began crawling. He proceeded through the darkness for many minutes. It was a cramped excursion, but far more pleasant, he reflected, than his trip beneath the Necropolis Wall.

The recollection froze him there, and the cold wind of his recent memories bore down upon him. Unseen by any eyes, even his own, he shuddered, curled upon himself, and wept.

Not far ahead, voices sliced the silence.

Bone went silent himself, and dared to creep forward, probing the darkness with his fingertips. Not more than two feet away there was another wooden panel. Beyond it lay the voices.

Bone could not understand the language, but he believed he recognized it, for he had heard Eshe sing in the tongue of Kpalamaa. More, he heard the words "Eshe," and "Qiangguo," and "Kindlekarn."

He backed up slowly. There was a fury in him, which he envisioned dropping deep into the soil and stone below, where he might find it again at need. He could no more afford rage now than tears. He returned to the space beneath the Swan church, slid back the panel and waited.

Feet filed in, above. The chants of a Swan service hummed through the floorboards. Bone found it beautiful and unintelligible. But some of the hymns had a sound he recalled from the Sanctuary of the Fallen Feather. The litany of the Swan's sacrifice by quenching the Sun, much brighter in the mythical days of the story, was identifiable though he could make out no words. He knew also when prayers were said.

He made a few of his own.

Old remnant gods of the West, dead or sleeping—Swan Goddess beneath your Isle, Walrus God of the Contrariwise Coast, Arthane Stormeye, Rakwhille Dreamer of Lightnings, even you, bloody-minded Nettilleer Kinbinder . . .

He heard the ritual drinking of rainwater and eating of fish, but his own prayers continued.

Gods remote—Painter of Clouds, and the All-Now, and Eye of the Mosaic . . .

The benediction came, the farewells, the filing out.

Gods of the East—the Million Deities or One, the Oddsgod, the Lord of All Kitchens, the Dust on the Mirror . . .

And the last of the regulars, talking with Eshe overhead, easy and pleasant banter, but in its own way yet another ritual.

I am a lover of heights and I am walled all around. You gods, you who knock aside all human things, help me now. Break the walls that trap my family. Shed light.

The trapdoor opened.

Eshe descended with dry fish and water. Bone ate like a savage.

When he could think again, Eshe said, "You cannot stay."

"How long until you turn me out?"

"It seems you found your own way out." She paused. "That did make it easier to hide you from the Imperial guards. They were thorough. I will have to lodge a complaint."

Bone smiled. Smiling thieves were less likely to be killed as inconvenient. He hoped. "How long have you served the Ghana of Kpalamaa, Eshe? Or did you never stop?"

"Ah." Eshe sat cross-legged and leaned back against the wall. "Who says I do? A traveling priestess might like to visit her countrymen every so often . . ."

"A traveling priestess, speaker of many languages, friends in many lands, skilled combatant . . ."

Eshe smiled. "You and Gaunt wander. There is nothing peculiar about that."

"Indeed?"

The smile left. "Where is she, Bone?"

He needed Eshe. He forced himself to chew through the truth.

"She is lost to you then," Eshe said when she'd heard enough.

Bone shook his head. "Lost to the world perhaps. Not to me. She is trapped in an item of art, and I am a thief. I will find it."

Eshe shook her head. "You are an item of art yourself, Imago Bone. But Walking Stick, or Hackwroth . . . one or the other will have prevailed to claim it."

"If it is Walking Stick, he wants it for the Forbidden City. If it is the other, Kindlekarn will bear it. Palaces and dragons are difficult to hide. I will find her."

"You cannot even leave this district."

"Is that a threat?"

She frowned, waved a hand theatrically. "A fact. The danger is quite high. Consider an alternative. Gainful employment."

"With you?"

She blinked. "Let us say my people value travelers' tales. I am a storyteller, a *Jelimuso*. That is my first training and calling. The fact that I am voluntarily exiled from my homeland has not changed that. But the stories I tell are no longer those of Kpalamaa's exploits and lineages. Now my stories come from all the Earthe."

"Stories," Bone said. "The kind of stories a ruler would want to hear? Especially late at night, in a secret room, with maps on hand?"

She nodded. "Understand, Bone. Ours is a world where peculiar portents and enchanted evils can arise from anywhere. Doppelvolk dragging people into mirrors. Scumbloods rising from the sewers. Necroconomists plotting financial doom. These ills can be challenged by random heroes. But they are best quelled by *directed* heroes—guided by those who keep our ears to the wall."

Bone smirked. "You speak of 'heroes.' I don't see what business that word is of mine."

"It is everyone's business. Bone, generations ago there were two moons in the sky. The Archmage Sarcopia Vorre dragged the Blue Moon underground, where she chains it and slowly devours its power. If nobody prevents her, will she one day claim the Silver Moon?"

"Darkness benefits thieves."

"Thirty years ago, the Archon of Night arose in the taiga beyond the Argosy Steppes. He and his Man-Wolves sought to conquer the world. Countries convulsed to bring him down. Champions arose and died. Some claim it was the end of an Age."

"I was strictly a local criminal at the time."

"Five years ago the Dauphin General of Aquitania seized and excavated a pyramid in Northern Ma'at, setting his sorcerer-scribes to translating the inscriptions within. Within a month he had become a mummified sorcerer, his Dead Fleet terrorizing the Spiral Sea before an alliance of nations and pirates brought him down."

"I do recall much activity in the harbor. Much loot, too."

"Last year the mercenary Lord Runestock located Fangthrone, seat of dread powers of prior Ages. He meant only to loot the fortress, but he learned to his cost why so many grim lords set up shop in that location. For it was the literal Fangthrone itself, a toothsome iron chair, that was the evil mastermind of that place. It took the combined sacrifice of Eldshore's Dusk Knights and Amberhorn's Whisperguard to slay Runestock and melt down the throne. The world shook."

"I recall some crockery falling, in our cave."

"That you lost no more than pots is in part because I and others like me roam the Earthe, listening for prophecies and portents, omens and dooms, so that the proper forces can be in the right place at the right time. To shape events, for the world's sake."

"And you think I could be one of those listeners."

"You have the skills. You could accomplish much good."

Bone looked at the dirt below his feet. "I have never sought to do *good*. The prospect has little luster for me. But I have *known* good. What life I have now, I owe to Persimmon Gaunt. She has rescued me more than once. Sometimes from myself. At last it's my turn. And her child . . . our son . . . that is my responsibility as well."

"But if there is no hope, Bone?"

"If there is no hope, it is because too many people saw Gaunt's pregnancy as a thing to control." Bone rose. "You alluded to this before, Eshe. Palmary sent Night's Auditors, not just to punish us, though that is a fringe benefit. They wanted our child, who is somehow touched by this land."

"Bone—"

"But you did more than allude, didn't you, storyteller? You speculated to Walking Stick about the nature of the child. You had glimpsed the suggestive stretch-marks on Gaunt's belly, and knew what they implied. Perhaps in your own way you sought to help us. But it may be that, for all Kpalamaa's good intentions, it has a stake in helping install a friendly Emperor of Qiangguo, and earning the gratitude of the Garden."

Eshe looked to the floor. "Bone. You must understand . . ."

"I understand that empires, even empires devoted to good, have ways mere thieves cannot grasp. Oh, I do not condemn, storyteller, priestess, wanderer—agent. Only do not pretend to be like me, or like Gaunt. Do not pretend to be free. And do not presume to tell me when to surrender hope."

Eshe was silent. Then: "A Western dragon was seen flying southeast, not so long ago. Boatmen more recently arrived report it was spotted winging toward the haunted tropical islands of Penglai, where none dare go."

"Then I have my direction."

"I will find a way, to let you leave. My kinsmen can help. We can disguise you, take you aboard a galleon, bear you southeast."

Bone nodded. "Thank you. That is generous." He kept the anger from his voice. Angry thieves were less likely to be indulged. And more, there was still in Eshe and her dark freckles something girlish and joyful, something he would like to believe still lit the woman's life.

Even if it was merely a glint of sun upon the ice.

She sighed. "If you say so. At night we can smuggle you to the galleon. We can leave midmorning."

He paced. "It should be dawn."

"We can't arouse too much suspicion, and there is always paperwork, and some bribery."

"Very well."

"But . . . forgive me, Bone. Even if the dragon is at Penglai, how can you hope to catch it, or its master? And will not Gaunt and your child be doomed by then? It is a very long journey."

"I do not think either is a problem," he lied, or hoped. "Hackwroth will want me. And my family will be the bait."

CHAPTER 29.

Near the maw of the Forbidden City's great Red Dragon lay a public park. This was not the precisely fashioned miniature world of the Windwater Garden, nor the immaculate visions of nature found in the other gardens of the high city. This was a place made for commoners and ordinary tradesmen, and while it aspired to the heights of those other locales, the trees ever needed pruning, the rock gardens demanded weeding, the ponds bordered on brackish, and litter needed removing. It was not an unkempt place, simply large and modestly budgeted. It had sounds never heard in the high gardens—barking dogs, crying children, chattering lovers.

Recently it had even had a swimming thief.

Lightning Bug thought it a controlled place, but tolerable for a city. Walking Stick found it an eyesore, but better than wandering in the wastes.

The two leaned on each other as they ascended the bridge, battered from their battle with vampires and ghosts. It seemed to Lightning Bug they passed ghosts once again, though of a very different kind. These specters were of the mind's eye. There was a giggly young woman leaning on a dashing young man, both dressed in the plain grey robes of Garden acolytes. They were fresh from sparring and weeding, and while carnal pleasures were forbidden them, the air around them seemed to crackle with the tension of breath, sweat, contact, heartbeat. They stared at the pond and its carp, listened to the trees rustle and echo with birdsong, and stole glances at each other as though separated by the length of the park.

"Oh, kiss him, you fool," murmured the Lightning Bug of now, as she passed the spot.

"Eh?" said the old Walking Stick beside her. He did not see her ghosts. She wondered if he saw anything but rules, precepts, strictures. But she remembered the fight at the necropolis, how her drunken fire complemented his icy calm, how he cleared the path for her with his flashing staff even as she watched for ambush from all sides, and she knew that young man was still within him, trembling with pride and desire. The young woman within her kicked and raged at being trapped inside this future moment, because all the might of her middle-aged body could not tear time asunder.

They reached the top of the bridge and sagged against its stone railing. "No birdsong," he said.

"What?"

"No birds, no frogs. There are dogs, of course, but humans brought them. The wildlife of the Empire ebbs. Do you not remember, the day of our sparring, when we knew . . . ? It seemed a full opera of life attended us."

"The Garden does not speak of this," Lightning Bug said in wonder. "We have been warning . . ."

Walking Stick said, "Year by year, it was easy to discount the changes. And sadly, your warnings themselves discredited the idea. For it is human nature to mistrust a message when it is delivered by an opponent. But I have been away from the cities, searching for signs of a new Emperor. The feeling has grown in me, that the land is weakening. Yet only now, when I remember that day . . ."

"That day is with me too."

Even in what now seemed a bleak silence, the park was beautiful. Clouds blew in from the sea. Kites bobbed. Children tackled their parents, all laughing. A fish surfaced, as if to say, "Here, here, still here."

Lightning Bug said, "Is it true, then, that the Walls . . . ?"

"I will answer with a story."

THE TALE OF METEOR-PLUM

The Master Architect of the Second Emperor, the man charged with planning the Walls, was a careful planner in other ways as well.

In the proper time his son married into the extended Imperial family, reaching a station not too high, not too low. The Walls expanded, and in successive generations there was always one woman of the Master Architect's line who in pregnancy bore the belly marks echoing the Walls' ultimate shape.

The firstborn of such women proved to have a great communion with the chi of the land, as it billowed through the tracks of the Walls. Such children prospered, yet the family kept this power secret. Until the time of Meteor-Plum.

Meteor-Plum was born to one of the then-Emperor's prized concubines, she who in time was elevated to Empress. As was sometimes the case, the eldest son of the favorite became crown prince.

Yet the boy's father was remote. Concubine Long Ting, mindful of the family secret, was ambitious on her son's behalf. Although she recognized that a future emperor of such promise should have a thorough education, she berated him for showing too much interest in art, literature, science, magic, and the welfare of peasants. Meanwhile she praised him for wearing proper clothes, showing proper decorum, and crushing his enemies.

Meteor-Plum Long was a kindly man by nature, and thus was torn in two. His virtuous impulses brought him shame.

Yet to be his own man, he must at times defy his mother, and the nature of his rebellion took the forms of poetry, painting, philosophical inquiry, magical experimentation, and charitable works. He proved cunning at all these tasks.

The more the common people praised him, the sharper his mother's words.

"You let them control you like a puppet," she sneered once. "I see I have erred by allowing you too much leisure. Starting tomorrow your days will be meticulously planned, your current laziness supplanted by readings of the military classics, tutoring in etiquette, swordplay, and supervision of punishment."

"Supervision of punishment?" Meteor-Plum asked.

"You possess too much compassion. You are out of balance. I would have you preside over a spate of state executions. This will serve two ends: to sharpen the blade of your heart, and to temper the people's love of you with fear."

Meteor-Plum wrote a poem the next day that alluded artfully to a desire to kill himself.

The date coincided with one of Long Ting's routine searches of his rooms. Long Ting found the poem and mentioned casually over tea, "Should any child of mine be so weak as to desire suicide, I will personally hand him the knife."

Meteor-Plum would have appealed to his father, but the Emperor was far away in the Ruby Waste, supervising aspects of the Walls' construction and the monitoring of the cat-eyed denizens of that land.

Meteor-Plum needed to escape. He bent all his knowledge and skill toward an exit that would occur under the court's nose. Thus he created his scrolls of transspatial dislocation.

In other realities, bereft of human beings, Meteor-Plum found the freedom he needed. Arranging the flow of time to suit himself, at first he simply caught up on lost sleep. Back in the court he displayed a new calm, born of a rested body. He marveled at how much of his despair was founded in fatigue.

Once recovered, he set about exploring his worlds in earnest. Having great skill in landscape painting, his scrolls reached worlds with a rich range of natural forms. He hiked, climbed, and sketched. He learned to swim unharmed in the torrent of a waterfall, making his body flow with the chi of the water. At other times he got drunk and composed poetry. He painted upon the edges of cliffs.

Undistracted by the bafflement of human speech, Meteor-Plum considered the Way that lies beyond all words, the word *Way* included. When he painted, or wrote, or swam, or climbed, in a manner unencumbered by words or formal thought, his skills soared. More, he learned to sense that flow of chi within him which was his birthright. And he came to understand something about his homeland.

The Walls of Qiangguo were not merely channeling chi from the people and land in order to trap the mating dragons. The Walls funneled chi from the dragons' very death-throes back to the Forbidden City, and most especially to *him*. The process was young yet, but it would intensify over the generations until the Emperors would be like unto gods.

Meteor-Plum believed (humbly) he might absorb such power without becoming mad. But what of men like his father? Worse, what of men like those his mother wanted him to be?

Meteor-Plum resolved that future emperors be bound with legalism and tradition, so that they would not treat the people as a child treats his playthings. Scouring the records of the ancients, he extracted what he considered the best of their wisdom, and founded a tradition of scholars to study these teachings. He called his school the Garden.

Affected by the scrolls' strange time-flow, Meteor-Plum seemed to have grown up overnight. Because he had not wasted his time, he conveyed the aspect of a sage who followed the Way. People heeded his teachings, and the Garden's.

Order based on punishment produces scoundrels who obey its letter, not its spirit.

Order based not only on punishment, but on excellence through example and imitation of excellence through ritual, will produce people of good character.

Show respect for the magical world, then stay as far away from it as you can.

Harmony depends upon good relations throughout the hierarchy. If there is discord in the family, there will be discord in the Empire.

To rule others, one must first rule one's self.

What few but Meteor-Plum understood was that his primary hope was to bind the powerful, not the weak. Meteor-Plum now returned his mother's scorn with impeccable courtesy, though minimal obedience. Consort Ting did not understand this combination, and baffled by it she at last withdrew to her narrow circle.

When his father perished in battle with the grass-sailors of the Argosy Steppes, Meteor-Plum ascended to the throne. He oversaw the completion of Riverclaw and spread the Garden's influence throughout Qiangguo. The land prospered. All seemed well, and his number three wife in time bore the stretch marks proclaiming the approach of the next chosen one. She was elevated to empress, and the child was born.

The child was a girl. And Meteor-Plum was dismayed.

 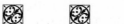

"Ah," Lightning Bug said. "Here we come to the part that I know."

"Tell it to me, then. It is well, I think, that at this moment Forest and Garden tell each other their stories. We have been too long silent."

"Our superiors might not agree."

"We are off dry land at this point, don't you think?"

"That is for you, me, and the fish to know."

THE TALE OF SNOW PINE

Perhaps from unthinking transmission of tradition, perhaps because of dislike of his mother, Meteor-Plum had constructed a scheme of ritual that gave women a secondary role. There had been female rulers in Qiangguo but they had been exceptions—widows, or firstborns in families with no sons. One reason for the system of multiple wives and concubines was to improve the odds of a male heir. Even if the Son of Heaven had trouble siring a boy, he could be given many opportunities to try. Yet Meteor-Plum had always assumed that the Wall-marks on the mother's belly would unerringly signify the new ruler.

It simply had not occurred to him the new ruler might be a girl.

In the end, though he knew the private truth of the girl's power, he could not go against tradition and the very amplification of tradition that he'd authored himself. He believed it would cut his own legs out from under him. And so, weeping, he conspired to have the girl killed, and the story put out that she'd died in childbirth.

Some of the sages of his own Garden were aghast at this decision. They secretly broke with Meteor-Plum. With their help, the concubine escaped the Forbidden City and fled to the wild woods of the provinces, taking the girl with her.

That day was born the secret society of the Forest.

Human order had failed—so believed the Forest. Only meditation on natural order, and on the Way that lay behind it, could bring humans to their proper state. Thus the Forest sages lived in the wilderness, as Meteor-Plum had once done. And his daughter Snow Pine climbed her namesakes, raced animals, fished with her hands, and seemed at times a wild animal, at times a cultivated maiden. She learned fighting arts and the mysteries of chi. She dared to put some of the Forest's beliefs into words.

The Way that can be walked on foot is not what we call the eternal Way. Even the name "Way" is far removed from the eternal Way.

The spokes of a wheel all yearn toward its center, yet the true center of the wheel is but the emptiness reserved for the axle. Thus nothingness is the most important part of the wheel. Nothingness and being are intimately acquainted.

Consider water. It benefits all, yet does not strive for the high places but flows toward the low. It moves aside if pierced, yet in time carves holes through the mountains. Likewise, to forego high station for anonymity is in accord with the Way. To move in accord with the flow of the world brings success.

Those who have the greatest skill should not be employed in the workings of the

State, for they will engender envy. Let them live anonymously in the woods, and let word of their deeds trickle to humankind like water flowing downhill.

Honesty is stone, rhetoric is silk. Those knowledgeable in the Way have no need to preach it, for they have withdrawn and are anonymous. Thus, if one speaks fine rhetoric to sway the mass of people, one is far from the Way.

Snow Pine learned and grew strong, and her words were stone and not silk.

Yet, striving not, she felt her path drawing inevitably toward her father's. And the day came she went to see the Emperor.

Meteor-Plum was old then, having often retreated to his scrolls to ponder the endless cares of empire. And when he saw Snow Pine approaching along the highway of the Red Heavenwall toward his position above a bamboo forest, he sighed, dismissed his retinue, and ordered the nearby garrison to march east.

"I know you," he said as he met her beside the empty battlements, for he sensed the pattern of her chi.

"I am here," she said.

"What would you say to me?"

"Words are not needed, Father. I wish simply to stand here and breathe the same air as you."

"You may not have the Empire."

"I have sufficient Empire already, having nothing."

"You speak like one of the Forest. I have heard of those rebels."

"The Forest rebels against nothing. We seek only accord with the Way."

"So you admit it! They know nothing of the Way, child. The Way is to be sincere and fair, nothing more."

"Benevolence and righteousness are but echoes of the Way, Father. They arise as a counter-force to villainy when the true Way is neglected. But best never to forget the Way in the first place."

"I think we are two people divided by the same word. The Way is simply the path of human affairs."

"Human affairs are simply one product of the Way, which gives rise to all of nature."

"Hm. We are perhaps reading different classics, daughter. That bodes ill. Again, you cannot have come to me just wanting to breathe the same air— though you are welcome to it!"

"I do just want to breathe the same air."

They stood thus, she leaning on a battlement, he standing in a relaxed, yet attentive pose.

"You needn't posture on my account, father."

"I am quite comfortable. Yet an Emperor must have a degree of pomp about him, or he will fail to inspire awe. That is the Way. You, by contrast, seem slovenly and thoughtless."

"If I seem dull and unkempt, it is because I travel with the Way, letting it take me where it will, rather than using it as a tool."

"And it has taken you here. To breathe the same air, you say."

"Yes. If you would be silent, you might understand why."

"You command your Emperor to silence?"

"I command nothing. Do as you will."

The Emperor went silent. Meteor-Plum stood with Snow Pine, breathing. His awareness began taking in things he normally missed, the play of light upon the Wall's stones, the chirping of birds in the distance, the vibrations underfoot . . .

Vibrations. Yes, something in the Wall was shaking, as though an earthquake had begun. He might have spoken, but an intuition told him to continue stretching his awareness, taking in the flow of chi.

And he understood. The chi currents coursing through the Wall were beginning to eddy here, where two of the Walls' chosen stood side-by-side. The Walls could not sustain the presence of them both. Soon the flow would build to a destructive level.

"Ah," he said.

"You cannot flee far enough, Father."

"This will kill us both."

"It is better thus, than to have such power so concentrated."

"You claim to follow a Way. I say your way is revenge."

"Then kill me, Father. That is the only way you can prevent the calamity. You cannot flee far enough, fast enough, even by descending the Wall."

He smiled. "You are incorrect, daughter." He took her hand, and ceased smiling. "I am sorry." He let go and leaped from the Wall.

"Father!" Snow Pine jumped after him.

Did she mean to save him? If so, had she repented her actions, or did she merely mean to keep him alive until the detonation of chi could disrupt the

Wall? Had his self-sacrifice changed, in an instant, something between them?

In any event, she who could defy gravity by application of chi could also assist gravity by propelling herself more rapidly downward. Her father, however, was her equal in this, and he too hastened to his doom.

Both perished upon the hard ground, even as she got her arms around him, even as the eddy of chi built to its catastrophe.

Snow Pine had meant by this meeting to shatter the Wall, but this would not now occur. The Wall was deeply cracked but remained intact. Even so, the excess of chi burned off in a manner that shook the land, and it had an effect unforeseen.

The life essence of Meteor-Plum and Snow Pine roared across the world like a thunderclap, and the gift or curse of the Wall-marked went likewise. From that day forward, a new Wall-marked child could be born in any province of the Empire . . . or indeed in any part of the world.

Sometimes the Garden seeks these children. And always the Forest is there to prevent such a finding. To date, no Emperor of the Wall-mark has risen since the great Meteor-Plum.

The clouds beyond the treetops had grown darker, and the air cold.

"You were wrong," Walking Stick said at last, "to break with the Garden and join the Forest. Yet you were right, too. Part of me always thought you would return. Abandon your ideals. Abandon your barbarian mate and children. What I fool I was."

"I can admit, now," Lightning Bug said, "that I broke with the Garden in part because I was angry. Angry with you for obeying the rules so strictly. Who would have cared if we indulged our desire in secret? It had happened before. In a few years we would be initiated as full Gardeners and have the right to marry, so who would mind?"

"Indeed. A few years only. Not so long for us to wait . . ."

"Here we are again! The difference. Perhaps we are cursed to incompatible perceptions of time. I have always yearned for the Now, you for the Later." She laughed. "And in the end I settled with Tror, lover of books, who cherishes the Bygone."

CHRIS WILLRICH

Walking Stick gave a dry chuckle. "It is amusing. We call him barbarian, you and I, yet we fight and rage, while he studies and publishes."

"And cares for my children. While I leap at another mad adventure."

"He is a good man . . ."

She looked away. "You are a good man . . ."

"I have longed to hear you say it. Allow me to prove it."

He walked a pace away from her, standing straight, staring eastward.

She nodded, eyes wet, imitating his stance.

"I have a proposition for you," he said.

"Yes."

"A barbarian madman has captured the mother of the Emperor-to-be. This seems to me intolerable. This seems to me a concern of both the Garden and the Forest."

"I concur."

"Perhaps, until this problem is rectified, we might forgo our usual arguments."

"Perhaps. And perhaps, given a certain . . . agitation . . . between us two, we might direct those frustrated energies toward kicking an evil sorcerer's hindquarters."

Walking Stick bowed. "I concur."

Rain fell. It would be an inauspicious day to travel. Good, Lightning Bug thought. That would be something else to fight.

CHAPTER 30.

Once every week, regardless of exhaustion, Persimmon Gaunt had sat at the topmost room of the temple and taken her tea with the sunrise in the manner the monks had shown, reaching out to the world beyond the scroll.

Each time she had perceived the presence of Hackwroth.

Each time she withdrew in haste, wondering why the Night's Auditors did not follow her into *A Tumult of Trees on Peculiar Peaks*. Perhaps they were concerned about what resistance she might muster, what allies she'd found. Yet surely those factors could only strengthen with time. Why delay?

The reason had to be Bone. If Bone did not endure, there would be no reason to wait.

So she clung to hope, and spoke every day to Innocence of the boy's father.

At first such speech was mainly a patter Gaunt maintained to keep herself company, for the baby understood only the texture of her voice, not the meaning.

She invented stories that might have been cruel had Innocence understood. As the boy cried himself awake for perhaps the three hundred and fiftieth time, Gaunt said, "What's that? What happened since I saw you last? You were kidnapped by underlurks and wrapped as a pastry? You escaped by boring to the surface with a dull weepfruit spoon? But balloon-pirates stole the spoon and you chased them riding in the mouth of a roc? And the bird swallowed you up and if it hadn't belched you right back into the tower you'd be in its belly now? Oh, baby, poor baby!"

This whimsy did not calm the crying but did console Gaunt.

She was informed by Next One, who had attached herself to Gaunt as the closest thing to a confidante in this place, that Innocence had the "night crying." This was, Gaunt suspected, a shortened version of "inconsolable anguished night crying that might also occur in the morning or noon or afternoon but whenever it happens surely drives hot steel daggers into a mother's heart." However, "night crying" was easier to say.

"You can't cure night crying," Next One said. "You can change their position. You can wrap them tightly. You can give them warm baths. You can stop taking milk, or avoid eating those vegetables that resemble trees. You can make whooshing noises as if you were a windstorm or a river. You can jiggle them gently against your chest—but resist the urge to shake them. Mostly these efforts just keep you busy, so you don't notice the crying as much."

"You know a great deal. Um . . ."

"Yes?"

"*Was* the next child in your family actually a boy?"

Next One pursed her lips. "A little prince, and I his servant. Heir to the pig farm. Long may he reign, far away from me." She sighed, touching Innocence's head. "That was another world. May your little emperor be a delight."

Gaunt's chosen form of delight was jiggling. She took long walks, because staring fish-eyed at the mountainside scenery kept her sane. Bouncing and strolling helped both child and mother, a little. During this period Gaunt learned to treasure sleep episodes of an hour, or half that, or ten minutes. Whenever relieved by Next One or Flybait or Leaftooth, she collapsed. Such sleep did not fully restore her, however, and she lived in a twilight world full of stumbles and drops and misspoken words. At least there were others around to catch her and clean up after her and guess her mumbled meanings. Gaunt learned that the usual Eastern reserve melted like old snow in the presence of a baby. She tried to help with meals, but was at best a camp cook. She tried to help with mending, but had difficulty focusing.

The others shooed her away from chores and encouraged her to hover over the baby, so she did. She nursed, she sang, she drew pictures on her wax tablet, she brought in leaves and stones for him to hold.

One day she found a copper coin of Qiangguo on a path, a pair of dragons on one side, the name of the prior Emperor on the other. She had no idea where it could have come from, so she pocketed it for luck, as it was too small to be safe with the baby.

She thought back to her and Bone's original plan to raise the baby in a cave near Palmary, he taking dangerous jobs now and then to supplement their supply of stolen coin. She now considered this notion like an account of bizarre gods and heroes written in hieroglyphs and dug up from ancient sands. They had been idiots. This work was hard even with a small army of monks at her back.

"When we get out of this," she told Innocence, "we will find a real place to settle. I suppose it cannot be in Qiangguo after all. We do not want to be hounded by scowling old men with sticks. We will have to travel, you and your father and I. Perhaps one of the strange islands of the Starborn Sea. Perhaps the meandering Eldshore, or my old home of Swanisle. Maybe we'll go to a village guarded by a wizard in an upside-down tower, or a town crouched beside a crater, where they salvage stones from the sky. But we cannot do everything on our own, Innocence."

That night Innocence slept for five hours. Gaunt woke to his cries, feeling more lucid than she had in weeks. It was as though solidity and color had been restored to the world. She nursed him, actually enjoying the sensation, dozing and thinking idly about pleasant nothings—doomed pale princes and shambling dead armies and moldering catacomb-laced castles and fainting damsels who learned how to fight and better regulate their breathing. When feeding was done, she burped and bounced the baby and went directly to Leaftooth.

"I want to know everything," she said.

Slowly, with the monks' help, she worked through the temple's records over the weeks and months. She unrolled scrolls of legend, history, science, magic, philosophy.

"You apply yourself," said Exceedingly Vengeful Wu one day. "You slump over from your fatigue, yet you keep studying. You do not allow yourself to wallow in misery. I am impressed."

"Are you in love, Wu?" Next One said.

"Next One," Wu said, "is exactly what I am talking about. She has nothing better to do than to gossip, stroll the mountain, look after the baby, and cavort with her bandit boy."

"What is wrong with that?" said Next One. "That is life. I am living. Each moment is a gift, not a stepping stone to the foundation of the Empire of Wu."

"The young cannot understand. You have never tried to build anything."

"You are a criminal!"

"Hey," Flybait called from the next room. "Can you all keep quiet? The baby is sleeping."

Wu said, "The time will come, when you must choose to join my new order or continue with your meaningless, aimless life. Gaunt has promised that in return for my help she will plead my case with Lightning Bug, to let me escape."

"Is that true?" asked Next One.

Gaunt nodded, trying to study a scroll about the building of the Walls.

Wu said, "The self-portrait of the sage painter does favors for Lightning Bug, for reasons I cannot fathom. I think he is infatuated. For her he was willing to agree to keep me locked within this painting. As such I must forgo my vengeance upon Lightning Bug, and upon Gaunt, who will plead my case, and, because it was Gaunt's price, upon Imago Bone, and Eshe of Kpalamaa . . . and you, Next One, and on that worthless lunatic you love."

"Hey, thanks!" Flybait called.

"Bereft of vengeance, I can only vent my anger upon one individual: the Imperial official named Walking Stick, who began the killing of my old gang, and who by all accounts is a worthy foe."

Next One said, "I too, have lost a gang, Wu. In this one thing, I know how you feel."

Wu scoffed. "Again you claim an affinity you have not earned. What was your gang, but mutts and strays? I had at my command a gallant fraternity of the Rivers-and-Lakes! You had gutter trash."

Next One was in tears, shaking her fist at Wu. "They were people! They were my friends!"

"This is why you remain a child. You give friendship, and love, too easily. You pretend to be stone. But you are grass."

"Hey!" called Flybait. "That's my girlfriend you're talking about."

"You are even worse," Wu said. "You are a weed among the grass."

"Grass bends, Wu," Next One said. "Stone breaks."

"You have spent too much time in this temple. You absorb its platitudes uncritically. Gaunt, by contrast, takes what she needs and will apply it to her own larcenous pursuits."

"Aiya!" Next One said. "You are like the fussy old grandmother of crime! You complain that the younger generation is being crooked *in the wrong way*!"

"It's enough to make me honest," Flybait agreed.

"Where is respect for the old?" Wu snarled.

"Where is respect for the young?" Next One shouted.

"Where is respect for a sleeping baby?" Flybait said.

"*Shut up!*" Gaunt screamed.

In the silence that followed, Innocence began crying.

"Leave us alone!" Gaunt bellowed, stomping toward the next room, Flybait rushing through the door to get out of her way.

As she yanked back her robe to feed the boy into submission, she heard the three whisper knowing remarks about barbarians and their inexplicable rages.

One day, fireworks crackled and boomed outside, and colored lights blazed in the nighttime, for it was New Year in the reckoning of the Peculiar Peaks. Gaunt read about explosives, and began making a list of items to pack for the return to her Earthe.

She read works on childcare as well, albeit diffidently. She found it more calming to read about bloodshed than breastfeeding.

Although Innocence was sleeping longer, concentration remained as ticklish as a watery mirror. If he cried in his sleep, it was like a foot stomping upon the puddle of her mind. Just as an image started to clear, down came the foot. And if Innocence was silent, it was not long before she'd run to check if he were breathing. Still, she learned things. And she told Innocence, innocent of the meaning, what she learned. She made stories out of it, and out of her and Bone's wanderings, and out of the light and mist outside. She told of the Jailer who became Emperor, and how he planned the Walls. She told of the Master Architect's son and the fox-girl. She told of mermaids who built sandcastles, and bears which hunted men. She told him poems she'd written in alleys, and poems she'd seen scratched on the rocks of this mountain.

> Since I painted the Peculiar Peaks
> How many centuries have drifted past?
> Acquiescing to destiny I fled into wilderness
> To live and experience strange liberty.
> Few ever visit these heights
> Concealed among the clouds.

CHRIS WILLRICH

Gentle grass can be a bed
The indigo sky a blanket.
Let a stone be a pillow;
Let all the worlds crumble and renew.

As she finished reciting this particular poem, bouncing Innocence in the foyer of the many-holed, mist-shrouded temple, Next One came up to her and said something every bit as surprising as *the temple is flying* or *the moon is knocking at the door.*

"Flybait and I are getting married."

Gaunt just stared. "Oo," said Innocence.

"You disapprove," snapped Next One. "I can tell."

"No, no . . ." said Gaunt, finding her voice. "No! I . . . well, clearly you are fond of each other."

"Not everyone wants to raise a child without a husband."

"I—you are pregnant."

"Yes. Probably. My bloody time did not come. Even if I am not pregnant, I . . ." Next One touched Innocence's hand. He ensnared her finger.

"It is wonderful," Gaunt said. "Foolish and mad, perhaps, but wonderful."

"I do not want to be like Wu, Gaunt—all anger and purpose. I want to be anger and purpose but also laughter. Does that make sense?"

"No. Yes. I do not know. But I am glad for you." She thought of Bone—not her husband, but longed for like a soldier-groom gone to war. "When will this happen?"

"Well, there is no need for marriage negotiations, because we have no family and own nothing. So that saves time. Indeed, no one here has possessions to speak of, so there need be no wedding gifts. I am supposed to seclude myself in a special bedroom, but there is no place for that in the temple and you need help with the baby. So really there is no reason not to do it tomorrow."

"May I help in any way?"

"I am supposed to have a good luck woman attend me. She has some minor duties."

"I don't feel lucky."

"Would you have me use Wu?"

"I see your point."

"Besides, for our purposes, 'lucky' means fertile, and you are definitely that. There are also things for Innocence to do—as the only child here it is lucky for him to be around. Do you think he could flop around on the marriage bed?"

"You have a bed?" The monastery's rooms were somewhat spare.

"We have a bedroll," Next One said.

"He might drool."

"That would probably be lucky too. He can drool anywhere in the marriage house."

"You have a house?"

"Well, a cave. The sage painter said we could use it. He says it's been too long since he lived in the monastery and heckled the monks. I think that was the first time I've seen Leaftooth look grumpy."

"This I must see. You have our services as lucky woman and lucky baby." She thought for a moment and frowned. "I do advise you to find a place for Wu. I recall stories where overlooked wedding guests pronounced curses. Wu may not be able to curse anyone, but her stare comes close."

"Do not worry. She has a role she's well suited for."

"Who dares claim this woman?" snarled Wu, her bamboo cane restored to her.

"Um, me," said Flybait. He had been carried from his "family home" to Next One's "family home" on the shoulders of a troop of monks led by Leaftooth, who for luck bore the bewildered Innocence in his arms. This really meant they had gone out the kitchen door, made a perambulation around the temple, and returned through the main door.

"Have you any riches?"

"Are you kidding?"

"Then you must fight for her."

"You know, this is really supposed to be symbolic . . ."

"Fight!" Wu cracked her cane upon the stone floor. The monks lowered Flybait, who, from Gaunt's vantage behind a huge statue of a drunken sage, wore a betrayed look.

She knew how he felt.

"Hold steady," Next One complained. "I can't see."

Gaunt huffed and tried to better balance the girl on her shoulders. "'Some minor duties,'" Gaunt muttered.

"I have no weapon!" Flybait was yelling.

"That is not the concern of the bridal guardian!" Wu swung the cane in front of Flybait's nose.

"You are just using this occasion to get back at me."

"The bridal guardian has no idea what you are talking about. Fight!" Wu chased Flybait around the foyer to the hoots of the monks, whacks resounding through the temple.

"Perhaps you should stop this?" Gaunt said, back aching.

"This is fun," Next One said, peeking through the red scarf over her head. "Besides, Wu needs to work out her anger."

"I think the baby is crying," Gaunt said.

"He is in good hands."

"Ow!" yelled Flybait.

"Ha!" crowed Wu. "And this one you will take in place of Imago Bone! And this one for Eshe! And this one . . ."

Eventually honor was satisfied, though it took a degree of pleading. Gaunt brought out the bride, literally, and traded her for the baby. Gaunt led the procession as both Next One, shrouded by the red scarf, and Flybait, bandaged around the head, were carried back around the temple to the sound of firecrackers. They returned through the kitchen door. The monks set down Flybait and waved Next One over a lit oven, to burn away any evil influences around her. The sage painter lay down a red carpet, and the monks deposited her there. "Welcome to the 'groom's house,'" the portrait said, and gave back to her a string of copper coins she'd loaned him for the purpose.

Flybait stepped forward and raised the red scarf from Next One's face, revealing an impish smile.

"You enjoyed that," he said.

"Thank you for fighting for me," she said, and Gaunt saw how he was overcome by that grin and by the notion of being gallant. She thought of her own thief and held her baby tight as the lovers kissed.

Because the Lord of All Kitchens was important to weddings, the couple bowed first to his statue by the window before returning to the foyer and honoring the gathered immortals, sages, and images of the Million or One. They spoke the names of ancestors, even ones hated, even ones little known.

The couple bowed to each other, and the gathering cheered.

Wu surprised everyone by saying, "Lightning Bug sent me on my way with a flask of rice wine. Let it be my gift to you, for it is sometimes the custom for the newlyweds to drink from the same cup."

The couple thanked her (Flybait somewhat sullenly) and drank the wine in turn.

Leaftooth came forward. He gave them a scroll. "This is from our library. A gift from the assembled monks."

"This doesn't take us anywhere, does it?" Next One said warily.

"Only in a manner of speaking. *The Ninety-Nine Passionate Positions* has been known to distract the young from their surroundings."

Flybait seemed quite ready to exit for the nuptial chamber, but there were other gifts.

"I tried to compose a poem in the manner of the sage," said Gaunt. She handed them the scroll of characters she'd inked that morning, and recited:

> *Upon a cold mountain, I found a coin shed by snow*
> *Treasure of realms far beyond or below*
> *And in its icy faces, back-to-back*
> *I glimpsed the warm riches I now lack.*
> *Not of wealth—for that spreads out high*
> *In the trees and waterfalls, peaks and sky.*
> *Not of glory—for that I have*
> *In a gurgling voice that learns to laugh.*
> *But of bodies back-to-back that brace to fight*
> *Or turn about to frame delight.*

"Here is the coin," Gaunt said, holding it out.

Next One reached out to take it, but paused and withdrew. "No, the poem is our gift. Keep the coin, and think of Imago Bone."

"I am glad Persimmon Gaunt wrote a poem," the sage painter's portrait said, "for I have been taking up painting. My gift is something else. You will see."

Gaunt was surprised to find that all were invited to the nuptial cave, though any potential voyeurism was dispelled by the jokes of the crowd and the drool of the baby. That was as well; Gaunt still felt such rawness from giving birth that her only desire for that part of herself was rest. At last the party left the newly-weds to their sport or their exhaustion, however it would be.

Gaunt's only clue as to the sage painter's gift came when Next One and Flybait slipped into the monastery, naked and laughing and covered in dirt and twigs, babbling about a taotie blowing them into a bottomless pit at an artistically mischievous moment. She did not understand it, but took note of the sage's smirk.

Innocence became mobile. Before he learned to crawl, he learned to roll and skitter and twist like a windblown leaf. He loved to moan into jars, making an echo like the wind. He laughed when Gaunt dropped one thing into another—tea leaves into water, oranges into a bowl, a handful of coins into a jar.

"This," she said, running her hands among the coins, mementos of Palmary, Amberhorn, Maratrace and other unreachable places, "is all Mama has to remember Papa by." The other coin, the one from Qiangguo, she kept on a cord around her neck.

"Mmmaaa . . ." he said, thinking hard. "Ma . . . ma . . ."

It was his first word. It was apt, that Bone's son learn to speak beside the jingle of mismatched coins.

After an endless short time, Innocence was a year old, and Bone was still not there.

Innocence still could not understand her stories, but she kept telling them, and he paid keen attention to her voice.

He heard many tales, of emperors and thieves, and made new ones of his own.

CHAPTER 31.

The four-masted Kpalamaa galleon was called the *Anansi*, which Eshe said meant Spider-Storyteller, or something like that. "A figure from legend," she had explained. "The trickster who cajoled the first stories from the Creator's hands."

It might take a spider, Bone reflected, to scale the high cliffs of Penglai.

Months had passed, months in which the Kpalamaa mariners had found gainful employment for the thief, much to his relief. His hands proved cunning at the endless knot-tying, his body limber amongst the complex rigging, his camp recipes a novelty for the galley, his voice enthusiastic (if not sonorous) in the *Spider-Storyteller's* shanties. A few were even in Roil:

> *The Starborn Sea is deep and wide*
> *We'll meet the lost on the other side*
> *(Away, haul away, we'll haul away, Ojo!)*
> *The Starborn Sea is dark and cold*
> *Chills the flesh but not the soul*
> *(Away, haul away, we'll haul away, Ojo!)*
> *My father sought the Starborn Lands*
> *To eat the fruit and walk the sands*
> *(Away, haul away, we'll haul away, Ojo!)*
> *And so I journeyed out to sea*
> *Where the lost and found may be*
> *(Away, haul away, we'll haul away, Ojo!)*
> *Captain, row the gig ashore*
> *Then you'll hear the ocean roar*
> *(Away, haul away, we'll haul away, Ojo!)*
> *Ocean, sound a jubilee*
> *For the lost and you and me*
> *(Away, haul away, we'll haul away, Ojo!)*

"This shanty sounds somewhat familiar," Bone commented once.

"We adapt songs as we find them," the shantyman said, resplendent in a hat of interwoven blue, green, silver, and black. "A good line can be made from many fibers."

A *good line* was what Bone needed, he thought, at last getting a close look at the steaming isles, soaring mountainous and forested from the foam like the green-bloodied fragments of some titanic splintered insect. The islands were intricate with cliffs and spires, emerald jungle clinging to any place remotely flat. Such places were far above the sea. He would have to climb well above the normal haunts of a second-story man.

"Our fleet scholars," Eshe said, stepping beside him at the prow, "believe this archipelago a limestone remnant of a larger landmass. Legend, however, says this is an abode of sleeping dragons."

"Which do you believe?" Bone asked.

"Both, of course. The sleeping dragons are the forests, the limestone their bed."

Bone looked up and down the great ship. It was not so large as *Passport/ Punishment*, but with its bewildering pattern of rigging, its cheery brown-and-brass decks, its bustling, professional, laughing crew, it too seemed the work of keen minds, considerably in advance of his own people's. "Your folk are rather dedicated to the rational arts," he said. "I feel like a superstitious primitive among you."

"We love you anyway."

Bone chuckled, looking upwards again toward his objective. There was something light in his step, these recent days. Despite everything, to accept his likely doom and still strive for something worth the striving—that made an unnaturally old man feel young again. Just a little.

"In any event," Eshe said, "I am not much better in their eyes. I 'went native,' so to speak, in Swanisle."

"Your conversion was a sincere one?"

"Indeed. And ever since I have had the privilege of being regarded as a freak by both my own people and by the Swan Church hierarchy, neither of which quite knew what to do with me. Thus I wander the Earthe. Few can tolerate me for long."

"That surprises me."

She studied him. He kept himself studying the cliffs. "No irony? Imago Bone, are you distracted by my wiles?"

"I am as loyal to Gaunt as moss to a rock," Bone said with a smile, "though I occasionally notice others, not being dead." The smile faded. "I intend to marry her yet."

"I am yet a priestess. I'd be honored to perform the deed."

"I'll give you your chance."

One island loomed taller than the rest, poised like the neck of a colossal decapitated mantis, rearing up defiantly. Rugged cliffs surrounded the island, rising perhaps six hundred feet before the jungle began.

"The dragon will be there," Bone mused, "and Hackwroth with him, I feel sure. I wonder how Kindlekarn feels, surrounded by elder females of his kind?"

"He will notice," Eshe said, "not being dead."

"Hm. This place has a liveliness to the land, that I did not see in Qiangguo."

"Yes," Eshe said. "Interesting, that a realm that so honors dragons has so few of them."

"Perhaps I will ask Kindlekarn about that, when I meet him. Could your crew take me alongside?"

In the end, the Kpalamaa crew let Bone approach by gig. Eshe accompanied him, as he strapped on climbing gear purchased in haste at the foreign district of Riverclaw. The sunrise cast a trembling golden path upon the rippling sea, but at least this spot was sheltered. Bone need only concern himself with rock and gravity, not wind.

The Kpalamaa crew called out something in their own tongue. Bone had learned enough of their speech to understand they were saying *ship!* or something of the sort. Eshe pointed at a fleck of white on the horizon, and bade Bone use her cheetah-marked spyglass.

As their own small boat surged up and down, Bone struggled to pin the distant sail in his sight. At last he caught a view of a small brown-and-black junk, two-masted, bobbing with the blue swell, bow aimed toward Penglai. He noted two figures scrambling about but could not glean any details.

"Qiangguo pursues," Bone said. "Though with a rather small force."

"If it is Walking Stick," Eshe said, "he does not need a large force."

"It is time," Bone said.

"I would accompany you," Eshe said, "but . . ."

"But you are not insane."

"Good luck."

Bone nodded, leapt, and grabbed an outcropping largely free of barnacles. From there he caught the bundles of gear Eshe threw at him. He had no intention of dying on this climb. At the very least, Hackwroth or Kindlekarn would have to do the honors.

Looking up, he saw a variegated, mist-threaded mass of rock that seemed to beg for climbing. It would be tempting never to secure a rope, but if time were of the essence then Gaunt and his son were already doomed. Likewise, if Hackwroth knew of his presence he was as good as audited.

To be of any use, he had to take care.

He waved to the Kpalamaa crew in a wan attempt at cockiness, and ascended.

The handholds proved more generous than he'd hoped, though he stopped at times to thread his rope into cracks or hammer in a piton. He did acquire a number of nasty cuts, however, for the rock edges were sharp, and at times would fracture in unpredictable ways. When he rested on ledges, he found it necessary to bandage his hands, arms, and legs. By the time he cleared the top, his hands carried a ghastly looking assemblage of chalk, bandages, and blood. Yet he grinned, for despite everything the technical challenge had been bracing, and for all that he worried pursuit would follow, he took pride in the trail of pitons he left behind. Imago Bone was here.

Seabirds screeched, and insects chittered, as the sun set with a momentary green flash over the turquoise horizon. Bone could see no ships, either from Kpalamaa or Qiangguo. He might as well be alone upon the Earthe. He looked to the forest.

Bone perched at one edge of a shallow bowl of rock a quarter-mile across, filled with a jungly canopy. At the far side, the summit reared, and within the rock bulged the mouth of a limestone cavern. Kindlekarn could fit inside with ease. As the dragon failed to soar and rage and burn anywhere else in his view, Bone began hiking.

He picked his way among twisty trees, spindly trees, trees arcing and flaring with fan-like leaves, trees so bristling with branches as to appear like monstrous skeletons picked clean. Little brown lizards studied him, big rainbow birds squawked at him, still bigger snakes flicked tongues in stately acknowledgment. Mist obscured his path, and leaves dripped a delicate chorus all around. He saw a white, five-petaled flower drift by on a stream, almost regal, like a beheaded monarch.

He knew he was not alone.

He crouched, searching with eyes and ears for a glimpse of movement or a telltale rustle, but nothing stirred but trees and beasts. Then he realized this was the very source of his unease: an expectancy had come to the forest, formed of the regard of animals and a stillness in the plants. Madness to think of it, but the forest kept him company.

Or not madness? Eshe had spoken of the rain-aspected dragons of the East, the females of their kind, who if eschewing mating settled down to become mist-swept forests, even as the males of the West became mountains.

Was this wood the resting place of a dragon? Was she aware of him?

"Dragon," he whispered, and he bowed. "If my guess is correct, there is a male of your kind nearby. You may sense him. You may also sense the power of his companion, and the power of the paper relic they carry."

The sky overhead had darkened to the cobalt hues in blue-and-white porcelain, with dark clouds drifting by like stains.

Bone sat cross-legged on the ground.

"In the past few months I have already prayed more," he said, "and to more gods, than in my whole adult life. It is not in me to pray again to you, dragon. It is not in me to beg. But, oddly, it is in me to give."

Time was passing in the world, and more of it in the land of the scroll. Bone's being tugged at him to move. He stayed, however, and sought for the art of description Gaunt had coaxed.

"I give you the Shimmerwork Range . . . threading from Eldshore's north down to its capital, their snowy sides glinting in the sun, rock-pierced, dappled grey and white like . . . vast palominos. I give you the Sunderlights that dominate the southwest . . . sharp sentinels slicing the day. I give you the Homonculous Mountains that divide Eldshore from the Wheelgreen . . . grey cliffs forever casting suggestive shadowy shapes. I give you the Heavenwalks . . . that seem like hallucinations of mountains as seen from the desert near Palmary . . .

"I give you all the mountains that I have known and loved, and even scaled for a time. I give you these because I know that some must be your kin, and many more must be places your kin have loved. And I give you words in honor of she who taught me better to use them . . .

"I give you these images, I who have nothing else to give, because I must find her, and win her back . . . and our child. And there is no possibility of help in this place, save from you . . .

"Yet if you cannot help, know that I speak also for her, Persimmon Gaunt, and say . . . I am honored to walk your quiet and gentle shadows, and if that is all the boon you may grant, I welcome it."

It seemed to him he heard creaking here and there. As he rose, butterflies flittered past his nose.

Bone rose, bowed to the four directions.

"That was lovely."

Bone spun, and confronted Lightning Bug, whom he'd last encountered in Abundant Bamboo, when she harangued him to rise and run. She was a shadowy figure sitting on a tree branch, the dimming sky beyond. She wore a subdued grey traveling robe, her hair bound back tight in a bun, and looked almost sane up there. Bone had seen her in battle, however, and knew the lunatic that lay behind that calm stare. Not that he minded.

"That was you," Bone said. "On the junk following us."

She nodded. "You were difficult to catch, but a deep knowledge of the Way, and the manipulation of chi, made it possible for us to coax the winds."

"Us?"

"That is why I am in haste to speak to you, Imago Bone. I am traveling with Walking Stick."

Bone looked around, spying nothing but deepening shadows. "Your enemy?"

She smiled, though Bone saw sadness in her gaze. "He is no one's enemy . . . and no one's friend. But once he was much more to me than either, and I flatter myself that I was more to him. That was before Tror, of course, long before . . ."

Bone nodded. "But there is something, in a lover who shares danger with you."

"We are both of the wulin, those who master fighting skills to protect others. Alas, in our youth it was easier to agree upon a shared Way. For me the Way is a dance of life and love, of change and acceptance. For him the Way is a straight road from the Imperial Palace into the future. Let none object to the paving, and all will be well."

"My family will not be paved."

"No. I would have your child, who may yet become our Emperor, be as free, and as wild, as you and Gaunt. That would be a good thing for Qiangguo, the cracking of our control. It is not good for the land to have its chi so tightly channeled." She looked up toward the first star of evening. "But that is a matter for later. Walking Stick and I have agreed that whether Garden or Forest prevails, it is better that than have your family destroyed by this mind-assassin."

"I appreciate the point. Are you asking for my consent?"

"That, and one other thing. If you see things my way, then allow the boy to dwell in Qiangguo. The Forest will hide him. Let him know this land, that he may in time assist it."

Bone thought of the long roads he'd walked, the gold of the tundra, the opal swell of the Western sea, the emerald hills of Swanisle. Qiangguo was wide, yes, but . . . "Why must this be his fate? Why does the Empire call to him?"

"For better or worse the chi of the Heavenwalls seeks a master. It may be that it conceives Qiangguo as too isolated, and so seeks an Emperor farther afield. This has happened now and then. We cannot fully know its motives. But the boy has been chosen."

"Indeed," came the voice of Walking Stick. "And that is why, despite this treacherous attempt to manipulate the father, the boy must be raised properly."

Bone looked up at a tree opposite Lightning Bug's. There stood Walking Stick, a stiff shadow in the dusk, clutching his wooden namesake upon a thin branch that surely could not support him.

Bone muttered, "There is perfectly good ground down here, you know."

Lightning Bug did not seem to hear. "You would stuff the child into a starchy robe and have him reading the classics dawn to dusk!"

Walking Stick said, "I'm glad you acknowledge my superior pedagogy."

"Insufferable. Let him contemplate the carp and dream of the butterflies! Let him swim beside waterfalls and compose drunken poetry in the mountains! That is education for an Emperor!"

"I will consider that. When I am ready for the barbarian hordes to trample the frontier and drink wine from our skulls."

Lightning Bug laughed. "Aha! The usual refrain. Let one child's calligraphy be off by a stroke, the whole Empire goes down in flames. Honestly, the sheer constipation of it should have ruptured your bowels by now."

Walking Stick, who had shown such composure fighting Hackwroth on a dragon's back, now bellowed, "It is well, woman, that we never had children!"

"Ha! As if you'd stay undignified long enough to sire one!"

"Um," Bone said, "if I may . . ."

"Enough!" snapped Walking Stick. "It is clear you cannot be trusted. We settle this now."

"Gladly."

There was a vast gulf, Bone observed, between the mundane spark of the spat and the heavenly conflagration of its execution. The wulin leapt off their branches and fell sideways, careening into each other with soft, quick snaps of fist, foot, and staff. They separated like dancers seeking new partners, each tumbling into treetops with a crackling rustle, spinning into new positions like fish, kicking off into the air again as though a mere leaf was sufficient brace.

This time they met with more force. Walking Stick shoved his weapon horizontally toward Lightning Bug's head, but she ducked and gripped the staff, swinging herself into a kick directed at the man's face. He rolled backward in the air, swung his staff one-handed, catching the tumbling Lightning Bug at the ankle. She grunted and shoved into the sky by way of a kick to Walking Stick's nose. Blood seeped down his face, but this seemed only to annoy him. He fell toward the ground but one tap of his staff served to reverse the plunge, send him shooting after Lightning Bug.

Bone beheld the once-lovers intersecting like dark birds in the sky. He, for all his many years of tumbling, climbing, sneaking, and filching, felt in comparison like an oafish dolt.

The sort of dolt who might keep his head low. And slip through the underbrush toward his objective while his betters fought. Yes. Quite.

Whether his plea to the spirit of this place had succeeded, or whether his senses had been invigorated by the aerial battle, Bone found his way largely free of stumbling and entanglement, and although the spare sunlight vanished and stars and moon ruled the sky, he kept his orientation. At times he thought he heard a distant cry, whether of beast or wulin he could not say.

At last beneath a descending moon he found the entrance to the cavern. He crouched beside it until his eyes adjusted, and beheld glistening in the moonlight an eerie mass of toadstool-like, upward-thrusting stalagmites, and tapering sharp descending stalactites, and terraced columns like broken and crudely set bones, and an undulating stone surface shaped across many years by mineral-rich water. The bandit caves had been bland hovels by comparison. The whole mass put him in mind of maws and stomachs and fungi and parasites and other things disconcertingly organic, for all that the mineral caves-cape betrayed no actual sign of life.

If the dragon was here, he was further within.

The auditor, however, could be anywhere.

Bone slid into the cavern and maneuvered around the perimeter as well as he could. He slithered through narrow crevices and clefts. The temperature dropped within the cave. Damp as he was from sweat and sea spray and jungle mist, he shivered. Already he feared growing disoriented within the intricate pitches of the stone floor. But he was Imago Bone, greatest second-story man of the Spiral Sea, and his sense of direction was strong. He could retrace his steps blindfolded.

Indeed, so attuned was he to the way out, that he nearly stumbled into Kindlekarn's teeth.

His warning was a sudden wave of heat.

Bone jumped back a good five feet, and promptly stumbled, shuffling and shifting to a degree he measured at four mouses, in his personal scale of sound. To his mind this was like hauling out pot and spoon and sounding a march.

The dragon seemed to agree.

FOOL, hissed a voice through rows of shut teeth, rubies tall as lances, wide as corpses. YOU SEEK DEATH.

"I seek Gaunt," he whispered.

SHE ABANDONED HER CHANCE AT FREEDOM. YOU WILL NOT RECEIVE ONE. HE WILL AWAKEN.

"Hackwroth? He sleeps, then."

BUT LIGHTLY. HE AWAITS YOU, NESTLED WITHIN THE COIL OF MY TAIL. IN HIS GRASP IS WHAT YOU SEEK. I INFLUENCE HIM NOW, SUBTLY, TO KEEP HIM SLEEPING. WE MAY SPEAK.

"Good! Keep him that way. I will be swift."

CHRIS WILLRICH   223

NO.

"You cannot want to serve him."

HE IS LIFE TO ME.

"Explain."

I WISH SURVIVAL. BUT I CANNOT OVERCOME THE DUAL DRIVES OF SEX AND TRANSMOGRIFICATION.

"Explain in human terms?"

IF I MATE, I WILL PERISH IN FIRE. IF I DO NOT MATE, I WILL BECOME INANIMATE. SUCH IS THE LOT OF DRAGONS. HACKWROTH WILL SELECTIVELY AUDIT MY MIND, MAKE IT POSSIBLE FOR ME TO EVADE BOTH DRIVES.

Bone considered. "I sympathize with your goal," he admitted. "Mortality may be inevitable, but for that very reason, why rush? Yet it is possible to give up too much in the quest for longevity. You serve a murderer, dragon."

HAVE YOU NOT MURDERED, THIEF?

"I dislike killing," Bone conceded, recalling the bandits in the woods. "But I've killed to survive. At times I may have killed when I did not need to. At other times, people have died because of me." The faces of the gang at the mausoleum returned to him. Then there returned to him what remained of their faces after Kindlekarn's flame. "It is tempting to say that anyone who enters the game of aggressive self-advancement deserves their fate. It is also tempting to say that no one is innocent." He thought of Lampblack's cut throat. "I think both statements are convenient lies, however—means of evading guilt. So I'd say that I am guilty of much, and possibly murder besides." He sighed. "I deserve little consideration, Kindlekarn. Persimmon Gaunt deserves more, however. And our child deserves most of all."

I SEEK NOT YOUR FAMILY'S DOOM. BUT MY LIFE CLAIMS PRECEDENCE.

Bone considered. "It is the shard of magic mirror in Hackwroth's brain, that gives him the confidence of knowing minds, and altering them."

IT SEEMS LIKELY.

"This implies a way, gruesome as it seems, to impart that knowledge to you directly."

AH, I FOLLOW YOU. IF YOU CAN ARRANGE THIS, YOU WILL HAVE MY AID.

"I need your aid to arrange this."

TO THIS DEGREE ONLY. I WILL NOT INTERFERE, UNTIL COMMANDED.

"Generous."

DO NOT MOCK ME, LITTLE THING.

"Oh, I speak gently to dragons."

Bone crept past the vast beast, scrambling over the mineral-laden hide in places, for Kindlekarn had neatly slithered into the depths of the cave. Bone approached the sleeping form of Hackwroth—nestled around a heavy pack and encircled by a coiling tail gleaming with tempting gems—steadily fixing his gaze on the assassin's head and its jagged shard of glass.

The shard flared with light. Images danced within. One image was of Bone attaching a rope to the shard with three drops of ur-glue.

Hackwroth opened his eyes.

At once the auditor leapt to his feet, raising a hand.

Bone felt a pain in his skull, as the shard showed tiny scenes of his life in Palmary, women loved, jewels taken, rivals outwitted, lawmen outrun. At first he felt a keen edge to the memories; then he felt nothing for them, for they stirred nothing in his mind, as though they happened to another man with his face.

At last the images faded, and he knew many days of his life were gone from his memory forever.

"Thief," Bone said.

"I will take more," Hackwroth answered. "Murderer."

Bone threw a dagger, but not before the image of that act flashed within the mirror, and Hackwroth dodged aside. Bone rolled to trip the auditor, but again Hackwroth danced out of the way.

Bone made a crazy series of leaps, acting on intuition only, striving to think as an animal, but Hackwroth sensed him coming, and Bone thudded on his tailbone upon the rocky floor within the dragon's tail.

Once again he had a profound sense of recollection—at loving a woman atop the citadel of the Black Thumb Banking Concern, scarlet sunset clouds threading the skies above the desert like the blood humming through their veins—then he wondered what the memory of waking up alone on a roof was all about.

"I will take it all," Hackwroth said, "clipping the wings of your mind, until you are but a larva of immediate sensation. And then your only sensations will be pain."

"Killing your father was regrettable," Bone lied, more or less. "I only wanted to shake your pursuit."

"It is too late to repent."

It seemed too late for much of anything. *Nothing we do is direct*, old Master Sidewinder had taught, and yet for Hackwroth nothing was circumspect. The shard could anticipate even moves Bone was hardly conscious of. And yet— here on impulse Bone rose and scrambled upon the dragon's back, shuffling out of eyeshot—while Hackwroth had displayed similar insight in their brief melee in the West, he had shown none such at the city of the dead, nor upon the *Passport/Punishment*. It might be the case that the fractured seeing-glass's subjects had to be in close proximity.

Bone pulled forth a vial and placed three drops of ur-glue upon a glove. Replacing the vial, he donned the glove. He threw his hooked rope around a stalactite and it caught. From Kindlekarn's shoulder he leapt.

"Kindlekarn!" he called. "Choose heads or tails!"

EH? HEADS—

Hackwroth had sprung into a defensive stance. But Bone's final target had not been chosen until Kindlekarn spoke. An uncertainty had been introduced—and Bone glimpsed his form blurring within the magic mirror.

"Tails" had been the shard. Bone instead aimed for the thing he'd assigned to "Heads," the scroll bearing *A Tumult of Trees on Peculiar Peaks*, leaning beside Hackwroth's pack.

He grabbed it, rolled with it, leapt over the dragon's tail, and fled deeper into the cave.

YOU BREAK YOUR TRUST, Kindlekarn boomed after him.

"No," Bone muttered, "I improvise."

The space around him narrowed. He slipped down a pitch, lost his footing, landed painfully on a sharp outcropping and rolled. He held fast to *Tumult*, slid into a deep passageway. Bone trusted his instincts for dark places to save him from cul-de-sacs.

Hackwroth would pursue, but here Kindlekarn could not follow. This compensated somewhat for darkness and confusion and pain. He knew his way around castle tunnels and secret passages in manors, trusted his footwork in sewers and web-strewn ruins. He'd never been a caver, however. The constant irregularity of the floor seemed at times a deliberate affront. Twice he simply plunged into shallow pits, lacerating himself on the rocks to the intensity of ten *mouses*. At least there were echoes to confuse Hackwroth. He did not dare spare a moment to attempt to contact the world beyond the scroll . . .

A plan then occurred to him—a plan madder than the one he currently pursued.

The trouble was implementation. Somehow, in the dark, he must evade Hackwroth long enough to find a very deep drop. And then jump into it.

Deep enough, and Bone might throw himself into the world of the painting before hitting bottom. Deep enough, and Hackwroth would never find the scroll. No one would.

If he did this thing, he'd indeed be breaking his word to Kindlekarn, just as he'd essentially broken his promise to Brother Clement. Justifiable, certainly. Still. It rankled. He was a thief, not a cheat.

So he searched for a drop, or a steep pitch, with intent to set ambush. His other plan would be there, waiting in the dark.

He groped carefully, listening for any clues in the reverberations around him, any variations of temperature or breeze. It was harder because the scroll was glued to his glove. Bone's gait resembled more a centipede's than a rabbit's. Hours seemed to pass. He grunted over sharp little peaks and scooted through narrow shallows. Once he chanced nosing into a tunnel requiring a slow crawl toward a fresh breeze; he got blocked when the passage narrowed to the size of a melon, sucked in a deep breath of cool moist air and backed out, expecting Hackwroth at his feet at any moment.

He escaped the predicament and found an alternate route, picking his way among a rough patch with numerous stalagmites, drawn by moisture and the sound of dripping water. And now there was something else: a hallucination of light.

No, he decided . . . true light, but exceedingly dim, and in the direction of the water.

Nearer that light, and still uncertain as to its source, Bone beheld natural wonders fit for kingly hoards. He threaded a barricade of titanic crystals stabbing everywhere like the splintered teeth of giants. Further was an irregular archway of glittering stalactites resembling white feathers or snow-wrapped branches or the tendrils of medusae. Whatever the metaphor, Bone hesitated to touch them, ducking beneath these mineral formations seemingly so alive.

Beyond, his metaphors became shrines, temples, cathedrals.

This cavern was immense, more so even than Kindlekarn's above. Bone knew this because shafts of light speared from roof to floor like ghostly, hundred-foot pillars. Water trickled from crowded stalactites, feeding a vast shallow pool. Further on, the pool dribbled rivulets down an immense pit yawning beneath the illumination, darkness slurping light.

Bone crept forward, skirting the great pool, feeling as though he intruded upon a ceremony as devout as the one in Eshe's temple, though no one was about. When he reached the pit, more details glowed into view. Above, among the stalactites, massive roots crisscrossed like the work of a giant, drunken weaver. Wood merged with stone, such that there could be no untangling the two. At the apex, gaps in the ceiling admitted sunlight. The light was pale, and Bone judged it was now early dawn. If he could climb out of here, there was a chance of escape. Yet a mishap would plunge him down into the pit. Fifty feet wide, it filled half the cavern and the sunlight could not fathom its depths. Down there in the dark the trickling waters plunged, and he heard no stream announcing the bottom.

There was a place one might get a better view, however. An outcropping of rock split the curtain of gentle waterfalls, and upon it rose a most peculiar formation.

A white column the size of a temple altar stood there gleaming in the light, its smooth surface reminiscent of a turban or a cocoon. Rocks in the pool led irregularly, yet inexorably, to the outcropping.

"Did it form by accident," Bone mused aloud, "or intent? But who would ever visit here?"

There was no answer but the dripping.

"It might be against my better judgment . . ." he murmured. He walked out across the stones.

Within the altar was a clear pool, nodules of white stone set within like a clutch of pearls. Bone looked into the water, perceiving his own face. He had a moment of disorientation.

Who is this? he wondered.

Once upon a time an angry boy had fled home to seek his fortune.

He would not have recognized himself now, nor the fortune.

As he thought this, he saw his face give way to the boy's. The lad leapt upon driftwood on the sands of the Contrariwise Coast. He saw his brothers, fishermen, laughing in those days before, one by one, they were claimed by the sea. He saw his scowling parents, determined to make him fish, when he longed to see the world. He saw the grim adolescent highwayman he became.

"Stop . . ." he whispered, but the images rippled on.

The highwayman wandered to Palmary of the Towers, where he learned the trade of a city-thief. All was well enough until he fell for a kleptomancer, Vine, and was entangled in the schemes of Vine and her lover Remora. That ended badly for them, and so they set upon him two angels of death.

"So long . . ." he gasped.

Yet the two deaths checked each other, paradoxically extending his life by decades, until the spell was broken by the words of Persimmon Gaunt, and what began with a foolish infatuation at last ended with a wise one.

"Gaunt . . ."

Together they wandered, doing deeds larcenous and heroic, crushing the stuff of life to their mouths like wet fruit. There was the sand castle of the mermaids and the misty citadel of Rainjoy. There rose the golden Vault of Heaven and the pustulous Tower of the Contemplators. There was warm rain on the southern ocean and pale snow upon the tundra. And through all of it they were together.

"Oh, my . . ."

Gaunt had said that the stare of a dragon tore away pretense, revealing a naked soul. Bone knew that in this pool, he saw himself as a dragon would. He saw that he was but a bright, irrelevant fluttering thing, a torn feather on the wind, lacking as he did the weight of Gaunt's hand.

The images faded. He lowered his head. He raised the scroll, saw its reflection in the water. "Dragon," he whispered.

Gusts swept into the cavern from the gaps above, rippling the pool upon the altar. And the gusts and ripples became words.

I know you, little thing who speaks of mountains.

Bone dropped to his knees. It couldn't hurt. And he was tired. "All I love is in this thing. Might you guard it?"

Birds nest in my trees, ants crowd my roots, salamanders swim my streams. What is it to me if you leave your scroll?

"But will you protect it?"

A man pursues you, man. Your business with him is your own.

"My . . . mate, and my child, are in this scroll. I know that might be hard to believe . . ."

A triviality. I understand your scroll, man.

"It is not trivial to me."

The frenzy of mating and birthing is of great importance to little things. I have larger concerns.

Bone slumped. He was exhausted, hounded by forces far greater than he. It would be better to flee, scramble, climb. The animal in him understood that. He had to think instead.

Animal. The tone of the dragon's conversation reminded him of his talks with Lightning Bug. It occurred to him that some of the East's philosophy might have its origins in the female dragons. He tried to recall those conversations.

"A mouse sees grass, roots, and seeds," Bone ventured. "A bird sees a green expanse, a canopy of leaves, and bright dots of flowers. Neither sees quite what the other sees. Yet each sees truly."

The rippling had the quality of laughter. *You may be a mouse, but to you I am no bird. Think of clouds, rather, or the sky.*

"Fine," Bone said. "This mouse would ask a boon of the sky. You were not always in this form. Once you darted hither and yon like us smaller creatures. Once you were an egg, then a juvenile, then an arkendrake like the one who nestles in a cave far above here."

Not like him. I was like clouds then, truly. A wistfulness, perhaps, to the ripples.

"Male and female are different," Bone said, speaking from intuition, imagining he were Lightning Bug. "Mountain and valley are different. Being and non-being are different. They are unlike—yet kin. From their interaction arises the world, ungoverned yet organized."

You speak of the Way, human? Anger, now. *The Way that can be spoken of is not the true way. Human speech is unequal to it. Human schemes can only impede it, like your Walls.*

"Why do you speak of the Walls?"

They bind us, requiring us to mate only in the Ruby Waste. By this strategy they confine the energies of mating to one place, so as to preserve their cities and farms.

"Is that wrong?"

The presence of so many dragons in one place is confusing, and breeds conflict among us. And the eggs that result from such matings follow narrower paths than once they did. They are more likely to collide and be destroyed. They fall in a narrower range of places. Dragons suffer, but so too does the world. Over time, the eggs fall in fewer places, and the structure of the world becomes deficient.

Bone made himself shrug. "Who can say what is good or bad?"

I can!

"Then perhaps we have something in common. For I can say that the loss of my family is bad as well."

There was silence, then a trill of laughter sketched in wind and water.

There is another reason, little one, I do not wish to guard your scroll. I sense within it the next Emperor, he who would command the energies of the Walls.

"If you keep it," Bone said, "someone will come looking for it."

Yes.

"It is my desire to escape with my mate and child, and run far from this place. But if I cannot do that, I would hide within the scroll, if it is well-protected."

The arkendrake could bear you away. Yet I cannot coerce him. Were I to stir, I would rouse his lust, and he mine . . .

"Then help me against the one who pursues."

Fight him here, then, little one.

"He can anticipate . . ."

"Indeed I can," came the voice of Hackwroth. The auditor stood at the edge of the path of stones leading to the altar. He was removing a peculiar vessel from the pack at his foot. "You, Bone, are about to slip the scroll into a nook within that altar, hoping the she-dragon will guard it. Go on. It's probably a good idea."

Bone could see no better option, and he did so. He stuffed the scroll into a pocket that seemed made for it, and extricated his hand from the glove that still held it, twisting a bit like a peculiar flower on a wide stem.

Did the altar stone constrict a little at that moment? He hoped so.

"Have you seen your own death?" Bone asked conversationally, stepping backward along the further path, coming close to the plunge.

"Many times," Hackwroth said, raising a peculiar bottle whose top coiled and merged with its base. "All different. But each instance seems like a story that happened to someone else."

"Have you seen mine?"

Hackwroth smiled. "That would be telling." Light began swirling like a dust devil within the bottle. "But I am more interested in the other end of your life." A boy appeared within the bottle, bent over a toy sailing ship hand-made from driftwood twigs. As Bone watched, transfixed, a foot appeared and crushed it. The boy sobbed and thrashed.

"I had forgotten . . ." Bone said.

"What we forget still may whip us on. You are still that boy, hounded by powers greater than you, grasping at fetishes of freedom."

Bone took a hesitant step toward the bottle, despite himself. The image of the boy blurred like a ship in the rain. "You could use your gifts to heal, Hackwroth. How many of us are a little mad, raging against weathered old hurts?"

"Healing doesn't pay," Hackwroth said. "But I will heal you, Imago Bone. Step closer, and you will have peace."

Bone wavered. More images formed: stick-fights with his brothers, which degenerated into stick-ball with little Imago as the ball; his mother slapping him for using good wool for his sea-explorer's hat; hiding on the roof from a father angry that Imago had painted classical-style eyes on the front of the fishing boat. He found himself stumbling toward Hackwroth like a moth flitting toward a cruel torch-waving boy.

He passed beside the dragon-altar and chanced to look within.

Images shifted in the waters. They were cool drops upon hot wounds. His brothers declared him King of the Seas and let him command them as they rowed and sang shanties hither and yon across the bay, blue moonlight in the sky. His mother introduced him, a giggling toddler, to the tickling surf. His father and he stick-fought like duelists of Aquitania, and somehow Imago got to win two times out of three.

The wounds were still there. But they were never the whole. He stopped. Something groaned under Hackwroth's weight. The auditor leapt as a stone slipped from its socket and rolled across his path, smashing his vessel before rolling into the pit.

"Dragon!" Hackwroth called. "Immense though you are, you're a creature within time, and I can anticipate you!"

The ceiling groaned.

"A bluff," Hackwroth said.

Flakes of stone fell.

"I would not mock a dragon," Bone observed. "Especially from inside one."

"I have no quarrel with you, old one!" Hackwroth boomed. "I mean to take the child you fear far away from here!"

The groaning subsided.

Bone's dim hopes faded further. Or was the dragon's change of heart another bluff?

Gaunt's words returned to him. *Even childless in the heart of Archaeopolis we would sometimes depend on others.*

He turned and raced along the path, reached the far side of the cavern, and climbed, trusting the walls not to betray him.

"Such a coward!" Hackwroth called.

I've never claimed courage, Bone replied silently. *Stubbornness, rather . . .*

He ascended as quickly as he could, grasping rocks and roots. For a long interval he was simply a thing that climbed, until he hung from a bundle of roots beside a shaft of light.

Hackwroth stood below, beside the dragon's altar. "Bone," he called, "I believe there is nothing preventing me from grasping this scroll and shifting to the world inside. You will have to follow."

"Are you certain? You just called me a coward."

"A coward," Hackwroth said, "not an abandoner of family."

"But you cannot be sure, Hackwroth," Bone called from a hundred feet above. "I believe I'm far enough away that you cannot be sure."

Hackwroth grunted, hesitated, then reached for the scroll. He found that it had slipped deeper into the altar. He stretched his fingers . . .

Bone took the opportunity to remove his vial of ur-glue, and empty it on the end of a rope. That was the last of the valuable stuff. He dropped the vial into the pool atop the white altar.

Hackwroth heard the sound, and gazed into the pool. As the ripples steadied, he stared at whatever scenes of Hackwroth's life the dragon's perspective revealed. *Your foresight can't protect you*, Bone thought, *if you are fixed upon the past.*

He threw the glue-stained rope. It hit the edge of Hackwroth's shard of magic mirror. Bone waited a moment for the ur-glue to settle.

He yanked.

Hackwroth's head snapped to the side. He snarled. Blood seeped from the edges of the mirror. Bone glimpsed baleful red light within the shard, as though the future held a lifetime of crimson.

"You . . ."

"I will protect my family."

Hackwroth screamed, "*Kindlekarn!* Aid me! Kindlekarn!"

Hackwroth stepped directly under Bone, creating slack. Bone kept pulling. "Kindlekarn!" he shouted too. "I have a gift . . ."

Bone yanked again. Blood seeped, but the shard remained in place.

Then the crimson within the shard flared bright with reflected flame.

Dragon-fire belched down from overhead, through one of the shafts of light.

Flame roared across Bone's arm, down his hand, onto the rope. He struggled to keep his grip, but his agonized nerves had already betrayed him. The rope fell. Bone nearly fell as well. He gripped the hanging roots.

"*Now* I perceive your fate!" Hackwroth snarled, hand upon the shard of magic mirror. He used the mirror's edge to sever the end of the now slackened rope. "Limited man! All of you time-blind creatures are as worms to me. Burn him, Kindlekarn!"

More flame cut the cavern air. The chamber trembled as the arkendrake's weight settled upon it, rocks and clods of earth flicking into the pond. Or was there more to the disturbance?

Hackwroth said, "*You* are worms as well, agents of the Garden and the Forest."

What? Bone thought.

Bone looked down and beheld Lightning Bug and Walking Stick, advancing together along the stones toward Hackwroth. He saw them pause and turn to each other.

"We are agreed, then?" Walking Stick said.

"Yes," said Lightning Bug.

"You two are enemies," Hackwroth objected.

"We are citizens of the Empire," Walking Stick said.

"You would destroy what should be preserved," Lightning Bug said.

The two wulin flanked the Western assassin.

"You are my superiors in every respect," Hackwroth said. "Save that I know all you will do."

Bone shouted, "Listen! In the interplay between two beings lies uncertainty. You fight in different styles . . . play off each other. Let the other choose your moves."

Lightning Bug grinned. "The Way is larger than each of us, my old love," she told Walking Stick.

Walking Stick smiled thinly, and tossed her his staff. "When we seek to embody the whole Way, we merely become more useful pieces of it. Our love has served its purpose."

Lightning Bug laughed. "Perhaps its destiny was this."

"Fight me!" Hackwroth snarled.

And so they did. But Imago Bone did not linger to see Lightning Bug's elegant staff-play or Walking Stick's erratic leaps and lunges, nor Hackwroth's ducking, rolling, and savage head butts with the serrated shard. Rather, he grasped roots and shifted painfully across the roof. From time to time rocks fell and flame gouted, but he kept moving and reached his goal, a spot precisely above the altar of the Eastern dragon. He tied a rope around a massive root and descended.

He crouched by the altar and wiggled his fingers into crevices beneath his abandoned glove. At last he touched paper. "Gaunt . . . Gaunt . . . hear me."

After a moment, "Father," came a voice.

PART THREE

GAUNT AND BONE

CHAPTER 32.

Time passed strangely, and whether this was the influence of the Peculiar Peaks or simply the strangeness of motherhood Persimmon Gaunt could not know. But it seemed to her that suddenly she looked up and Innocence was three years old, a sober splasher in puddles and investigator of bugs, wise mentor to two-year-old A-Girl-Is-A-Joy, she who worshipped him in between tussles.

And Bone was not there.

More, Gaunt turned to a mirror and saw a single grey hair, and traces of wrinkles at her mouth and eyes. Nothing of import. Marks of character. But it came to her then that three years of her child's life was three more years of hers.

For the boy, each year was a titanic passage, a personal aeon. It was not so for her, and yet it was as if some of that small immensity was transmitted by the blood-tie, so that those three years weighed upon her like five, or eight, or eleven.

Gaunt was hardly old, but no longer young.

And Bone was not there.

Even should he come, a long chapter in her life was done. Grey bore down upon her mind even when the sun blazed above the Peculiar Peaks. *What have I done?* she thought more than once. To raise a child seemed now more doom-fraught than seeking the World's Edge.

Yet even in the worst days there were moments when a light seemed to pierce her worry like sun-shafts through thunderheads. Once Gaunt stopped with Innocence for a quick game of hide-and-seek in the courtyard, and the serious puddle-splasher was suddenly her gleeful and giggly Innocence. It would not last, of course. She had to give up thinking of him as a baby. He patted his hair, then reached out to pat Gaunt's, suddenly enthralled by the idea that they both had hair on their heads. His was coming out red like hers, and he had her eyes; but his chin and frame were his father's.

When he tired of this game, and pounced upon her, she said, "Your father would be proud of you."

"Where is my father?" said Innocence, for what might have been the hundredth time, and the serious boy was back. He was a skilled talker for a three-year-old, and all the pagoda commented on it. He badgered the monks and the self-portrait and Wu, who gave him confusing answers. He preferred chattering to Flybait and Next One, but those two were thoroughly occupied with the business of family, and after eight or thirteen or twenty-one questions they would shoo him away.

So he used his skills to vex Gaunt with difficult subjects. Living in a place of monks and exiles, Innocence knew little of ordinary life. He knew his father only through stories, only slightly embellished, of the greatest second-story man of the Spiral Sea.

"Your father is in another world," Gaunt said.

"Can we go there?"

"Some day," Gaunt said, "either he will come here, or we will go there." She hoped it was true.

"Is there a pagoda in the other world?"

"There are many pagodas in that world, and castles, and mausoleums, and aqueducts, and cathedrals, and coliseums, and treasuries. Your father could tell you stories of the most wondrous architecture and its weak points."

"Will I be a thief when I'm bigger?"

She pictured Innocence falling from the top of the pagoda. "You must understand, things were difficult for your father and me. Also, one tends to apply the skills one knows to any situation . . ."

"I will be a thief. I will steal things!" Innocence ran in circles.

"That outcome would not surprise me," Gaunt murmured.

Innocence kept circling. Soon he said, "I'm a horse! Look, Mommy, I'm a horse."

"That outcome *would* surprise me. However, it is a strange world. Come, Innocence. I will show you something of your father's world."

In the library, she opened scrolls filled with twisting calligraphy framing paintings of emperors and courtiers and sages, gowns all flowing.

Innocence studied the pictures. "Those are humans."

Gaunt asked, "Humans?"

"Yeah."

"What do you think of humans?"

"They scare us."

"But we're humans."

"We're horses too."

Innocence commenced to galloping around the small room. Gaunt searched for another scroll. "I have a story to find for you."

Innocence ran up. "I have a story!"

"Yes?"

"Yes! It goes like this. Once. Upon. A. Time."

ONCE UPON A TIME, NUMBER 12

A boy and his family, his mother and his father, they went to a pagoda. It was a pagoda in a strange world. They were horses. The father climbed up to the top. There was a book there. He wanted it. He was a thief. He started to fall. The boy jumped up REALLY HIGH and catched the father. They fell into the pond. The mommy got them out. They all had dumplings. Dumplings are good, but I don't like the meat inside. I think that's the end.

Gaunt clapped. "I am proud of you. You are telling real stories. Would you like to hear another one? There is an important story I have been meaning to tell you."

"What is it?"

She told him about Meteor-Plum the artist and Emperor, as she had learned it from the hints of the monks, and the scrolls of their library. She told him how Meteor-Plum had discovered his child, his blessed child filled with the Heavenwalls' chi, had been a girl—to his dismay.

"Are there lots of girls in the other world?" Innocence said.

"There are."

"What are they like? Are they all like A-Girl-Is-A-Joy?"

"Girls are much like you," Gaunt said, "except when they are not."

"What is dismayed?"

"Upset. Mad. Ready to run around and hit things."

"Like this?" Innocence gallivanted and gleefully struck the earth, the trees, the grass.

"Yes. But for grownups, especially grownups from Qiangguo, the running around and hitting things mostly happens inside their heads."

"Like this?" Innocence stood perfectly still, arms folded, as he'd seen the monks do every day of his life.

"Quite. So Meteor-Plum might have looked on the day he met his baby girl."

"Why was he . . . dismayed?"

"That is complicated. As I said, girls are much like boys, but as they grow up, they become a little more different. I believe the world makes far too much of the difference, but it is real. Girls often grow up to be mothers, Innocence. In some places, that earns women great honor. In others, it earns them barely concealed scorn."

"I don't understand."

"I hope your understanding of the scorn is always incomplete, Innocence. Just know that Meteor-Plum had wanted a boy so much, he never even imagined having a girl."

"That's dumb."

"It was the grownup kind of dumb. We might call it a tragic flaw."

"Dumb. Mom?"

"Yes."

"There's a Meteor-Plum who lives here. The one who paints."

"I know. Shall I go on?"

"Yes."

She told him the story of the girl Snow Pine, and how she began the society of the Forest, and how she confronted her father atop a Wall, bringing about both their downfalls.

"Why?" Innocence said.

"Why did they fall? Why did the power of the mark travel so far? Why did they have such different ideas of the Way?"

"Why were they mad at each other?"

Gaunt hugged him. "Alas, sometimes a parent is very cruel to a child, because the child does not fit into the world the parent has made. Often a world built of very hard work indeed."

"Mommy? Where is your mommy?"

"She is somewhere in the world your father is in, far away in Swanisle." *If she and my father are still alive*, Gaunt thought.

"Why do you not see her?"

"She gave me away to Swanisle's bards. I suppose I am angry about that."

"Maybe if she said she was sorry, you would be friends again."

Gaunt laughed. "How simple! How impossible! And yet, Innocence, for you, I might make that journey, if only so that I can show her her grandson and let her see her own eyes in his face."

"When will we go?"

"I do not know, Innocence. There is so much I don't know."

He hugged her back now. "Well. That's okay, Mommy. That's okay."

"Thank you."

"I'm hungry."

Before she could respond, there was a scampering of feet outside, and Next One and Flybait burst into the chamber. "The self-portrait says Imago Bone is coming!" they said in a combined hubbub.

Gaunt's feet were taking her outside before her brain had truly absorbed the words. They echoed with each footfall, until finally when she reached the clearing where the monks had already assembled, she thought she understood. *Bone is coming.*

The self-portrait of Meteor-Plum was already speaking.

"I have made it possible for him to manifest here atop the mountain . . ." he said. "Wait . . ."

A-Girl-Is-A-Joy was sitting on Wu's shoulders, studying the sky.

Innocence ran up to the self-portrait, hunger forgotten. The boy stared at the man, having recently seen his image on a scroll. Innocence looked as though he would speak, but then turned his face toward the clouds.

"Look!" A-Girl-Is-A-Joy said.

The face of Imago was forming, sketched in vapor and light.

"Hello," she whispered.

"Father!" Innocence shouted.

CHRIS WILLRICH   243

CHAPTER 33.

Imago Bone had the sense of awakening from a dream in which life had gone rather differently from reality, as if he'd experienced a life as an bureaucratic Underseer, managing the Eldshore's crumbling metropolises; or had sailed the pirate vessel *Sea-Glare*, acquiring swag and prosthetics; or had been a barbarian of the Bladed Isles, wearing body parts as jewelry. He shook himself, for seeing his three-year-old boy within the world of the scroll, leaning on Persimmon Gaunt's leg, was every bit as disorienting.

"*Bone!*" called Gaunt. "*Imago! Are you coming through?*"

"We are in danger yet," Bone said. She seemed different as well: not so thin, not so fierce, yet strangely more determined-looking for all that. Sadder? Happier? Both, neither . . . He told her, "Lampblack has fallen, but Hackwroth is mad for our *auditing*. Hello . . . boy."

The boy hid behind Gaunt's legs. "*He is called Innocence, or Kuang Nu You.*"

"As long as it is not Lamprey," Bone said, and quickly added, "Hello, Innocence. You're right, I'm your father. Sorry I haven't been around. Gaunt—can you fight?"

She grinned. "*I've been waiting.*" She turned to one of the robed men nearby. "*May I?*"

"*Simply wish it,*" Meteor-Plum said. "*You may transit from this spot.*" He nodded to a monk, who dropped a heavy backpack beside her. "*Here is your gear, as you long ago requested.*"

"Our location is precarious," Bone began, and suddenly he was holding Gaunt's hand, keeping her with her heavy pack from toppling into the void.

"Isn't it always?" She settled into position beside the altar. She took in the battle of Hackwroth and Lightning Bug and Walking Stick, the eerie cavern, the gouts of fire spurting through the ceiling.

"Life is so much more interesting with you," she said.

"Wait—I feel someone else coming . . ." Suddenly Bone held Flybait's hand, and helped him find his footing, and then Next One was there too.

"We could not abandon Gaunt," Next One said, and Flybait added, "And we will have satisfaction for our dead friends." The child-thieves looked like adults now, with less ferocity but more will. The hint of partnership between them was now more than a hint. Bone nodded. He could not deny their right to this battle, even if he wanted to.

But then . . . another hand grasped Bone's, and Exceedingly Accurate Wu was there, and grasping her hand was the boy Innocence.

"Father?"

Bone had not expected the additional weight and imbalance. He briefly lost his grip and Wu and Innocence tumbled toward the dark pit. Wu grabbed the edge of the natural altar, but Innocence was slipping from her fingers.

Bone swore and splashed down stomach-first at the edge, his arm flashing forward and grabbing Innocence's hand.

Innocence screamed. So did Gaunt, or maybe that was Bone himself, he wasn't sure.

"Father! Want to help! Want to *help!*"

"Don't thrash, damn it! If you want to help, don't thrash!"

It was too wet and slippery here; his grip was not tight enough, his own position unsure.

"Bone, I'll grab you . . ." Gaunt said.

"No—Gaunt! Help Lightning Bug! Only you can do that. The others can grab me, keep me from falling."

"Don't *lose* him . . ." she said as she moved off, and he knew this was perhaps the hardest thing she'd ever done, trusting Innocence with him, after all this time. Disorientation whipped his mind, but already he felt the grip of Flybait and Next One, anchoring him. Wu was successfully climbing over the edge, and they had no time for her.

I won't, he told Gaunt silently, knowing that losing Innocence could mean losing her. And perhaps himself. He shimmied forward, got another hand around the wide-eyed boy and pulled.

CHAPTER 34.

Gaunt reached the fight just as Lightning Bug fell.

Hackwroth, battered but grinning, butted the wulin woman with his head, gutting her upon the jagged shard of magic mirror.

She slid back, dropping a staff, clutching her belly, falling into the shallows beneath one of the ceiling's openings. Light fell upon her, and its rippling weave upon the waters grew red as a bloody fishnet.

Upon Hackwroth's shard, images of Lightning Bug's life shone behind a crimson sheen. She knelt beside various children, finding a Way amidst yelling, laughing, weeping, leaky-nosed chaos. She embraced Tror beside the bamboo supports of their home. She stood beside Walking Stick on a bridge. She burned in a cavern underground, Walking Stick screaming nearby . . .

Gaunt shoved Lightning Bug through the water just before the dragon-fire gouted down into the spot where they'd been.

"Thank you," Lightning Bug gasped, even as more blood flowed onto her hands.

"I'll bind you," Gaunt said, flinging down the pack she'd had three years to prepare.

Hackwroth was hurt, Gaunt saw in snatches as she worked—exhausted from the assault of the Forest and Garden warriors. Yet still he fought. And Walking Stick, seemingly now an ally, was unable to lay a hand upon him.

"Your gambit required a partner," Hackwroth said.

"I am not defeated," Walking Stick said, and danced his foe toward the pit. Away from Gaunt.

"He is . . . out of range of his fortune-telling trick," Lightning Bug said, her belly now covered in a mass of bandages thick as a stand of bamboo. "Have you a throwing dagger? A crossbow?"

"Something better," Gaunt said.

"You will need to aim it," said a new voice.

Gaunt turned to see Wu, reaching out her hands in a gesture halfway between "peace" and "gimme."

"What is she doing here . . . ?" Lightning Bug said.

"I have wronged you, Persimmon Gaunt," Wu said. "I convinced the self-portrait it was time to plead my case. I brought your child, thinking he would be leverage for my escape. I did not mean to put him in such danger. Let me help. I am Exceedingly Accurate yet."

CHAPTER 35.

Bone raised Innocence carefully up. Closer . . . closer . . .

"Don't want to be like the girl and the emp'rer," Innocence told him urgently.

"Very well," Bone said, having no idea what the boy meant. "You won't be."

Then Bone felt the sinking sensation that he'd just forgotten this conversation. He had felt this way before.

Hackwroth . . . Hackwroth is near . . .

Why was Innocence dangling into the pit? He'd just seen the boy within the scroll!

Hackwroth . . . Hackwroth was beside him, fighting off Walking Stick of the Garden, laughing, face covered in blood and laughing.

"What?" cried Flybait.

"Huh?" shouted Next One.

For the thieves of Qiangguo had lost their immediate memories as well.

Imago Bone's reflexes were up to the task of a cliffside rescue, even having forgotten how exactly he'd gotten to that cliff in the first place. His life was like that.

But the youngsters holding his legs flinched. They let go, and Bone tumbled into the pit.

And Hackwroth laughed . . .

Bone grabbed a ledge (*bless the irregularity of limestone*) which crumbled (*curse the fragility of limestone*), slid and gripped another, whose collapse bought time to seize another, which held.

Somehow he still grasped, in his other hand, the boy.

"Help the barbarian!" Walking Stick snapped at the kids, and they of the Rivers-and-Lakes remembered they were of Qiangguo first, and they obeyed their elder. They strained to reach Bone, both leaning over the brink to grab his arm.

"You are all beaten," Hackwroth said. "I have foreseen it. Bone and Gaunt I will sift, for such is my contract and my revenge. I may or may not spare the boy. He has been much trouble. Perhaps I will be just too late to save him. The rest of you I may kill or not, as suits my mood. I would withdraw were I you."

"Imago Bone," called Walking Stick. "This creature offends me, yet I may not be able to defeat him. What I might be able to do, is preserve your son. He who is more precious to Qiangguo than any jewel."

"My son?" Bone gasped. From his memory-robbed perspective he'd been walking on the ceiling but a moment ago. "This is my son?"

Bone shifted in the thieves' grasp. Rocks careened into the abyss.

"Father!" cried Innocence.

"He is your son, and he may yet be the future Emperor. But I swear on the blood of Lightning Bug that I will consider his welfare first, the Empire's second. I, a Garden warrior, pledge my honor in this."

"Do it!" Bone cried. "But take the two kids with you. They've done enough."

"No such luck," Hackwroth said, leaping and landing with a dreadful thud, one foot each upon the backs of Flybait and Next One. Their cries echoed around the cavern and seemed to have no end. What did end was their grip upon Bone.

Bone grabbed furiously at the moist rock, but began an inexorable slide. He saw the two lovers share a look. He had been half of such looks before.

At that moment a firework rocket shot across the cavern and detonated against Hackwroth's head.

The auditor howled, clutching his burned face. As firecrackers erupted around him, Flybait and Next One struggled to restrain him while still holding Bone, shoving their bodies against Hackwroth's legs.

Now Walking Stick connected with a series of savage blows to Hackwroth's middle.

Hackwroth moaned like a beast, and crouched like one. Like a lion with downed prey, his head lunged and grunted, until the shard of magic mirror was thick with Flybait's blood.

"No!" Next One screamed, distraught and bloodied herself, and she released Bone to clutch at Flybait.

Bone, still gripping Innocence's hand, toppled into the void.

But Walking Stick saw. The wulin grabbed the scroll from the altar, called, "Farewell, my love," and leapt.

Unaccountably, the Garden warrior fell faster than Bone, as if propelled by some unseen force. He grabbed Innocence's left hand, while the right hand was yet upon Bone's.

"Join me," Walking Stick said, as they plunged through a dark that seemed endless.

"Take Innocence—" Bone said.

"Father . . ."

"Go!" Bone gasped. "I will take the scroll."

Walking Stick nodded and the Garden agent and Innocence faded from reality. With a last effort, Walking Stick passed the scroll to Bone. The thief grabbed it even as he plunged into deep water.

Quick as an eel, a current snagged him and pulled him under.

CHAPTER 36.

Gaunt saw Bone and Walking Stick fall . . . even as Hackwroth rose.

"Gaunt," Lightning Bug said, "if the mirror meets the altar—"

She did not truly understand. She did not need to. She needed to act. There was a world of despair, rage, desperation within Persimmon Gaunt, and in that moment it was as though all of it became a searing lump which she swallowed, absorbed, pressed into the muscles of one foot.

Gaunt ran, leaped, and kicked.

Hackwroth—burned, battered, enraged, distracted, shard of magic mirror drenched in blood—sensed her attack, and turned away from Next One to face Gaunt. But whether it was from the exhaustion of battle or the crimson stains upon the mirror, he responded sluggishly. He no longer had the resources to evade her.

His face slammed into the waters of the natural altar.

Blood filled the basin. Images shifted within.

Hackwroth staggered backward, dripping, head washed clean of blood. It occurred to Gaunt that with Hackwroth's enhanced perceptions, he of all men had now best perceived a dragon's thoughts. His eyes bulged, and he sank to his knees.

"What can be gridded, accounted, controlled," he whispered, "is a paucity. The regular and linear is but a simplified example of the churning tumult that is the whole. The future is not one of clean lines but of chaos . . ."

The cavern shook, much harder than before. The images within the pool now showed a thing that filled Gaunt with terror and wonder.

Within the waters she saw the island crumble and a green, winged form rise from within it, a shape composed of branches and leaves and soil, dark wings like a forest's shade. She saw the Eastern dragon embrace a fire-breathing Western dragon far smaller than itself. She saw the red dragon explode from within, a burst of incandescent energies; and the green dragon roar into flame and collapse upon the ruin of her isle. And then she saw the explosion that flung skyward a luminous dragon egg like the inverse of a falling star, and a volcano rising from where its parents had been.

"Dragon," she said, "this will kill us . . ." She looked into the dark depths where she dared hope Bone and Innocence still lived.

I must answer the call, whispered a voice from all around. *For within the mind of Hackwroth I perceived the converging worldliness of three sets of lovers, Flybait and Next One, Lightning Bug and Walking Stick, Persimmon Gaunt and Imago Bone. I cannot but echo such love, even I, a dragon. I will not be denied. Flee now.*

"Not without—!"

The pit below leads to waters flowing to the ocean. Soon my substance will splinter, and there will be great gaps leading to the sea. I will see to it, while I have mind to spare. Go!

Lightning Bug was beside her then, staggering, but standing, leaning against Wu. "I have skills. I can guide you . . ."

Wu screamed and dropped Lightning Bug.

Hackwroth had leapt up and stabbed his mirror-shard into the back of Wu's neck, embracing her like a lover.

"No . . ." he gasped. "Even if all is chaos, you will not escape me. I will know satisfaction before the bright ending promised me . . ."

"Go!" Wu snarled, blood filling her mouth. "I, an evil, will prevent a greater evil. I will keep the barbarian here. Go!"

She drove herself backward into the shallow waters of the cavern, where the pair sprawled and splashed, Hackwroth raging, Wu screaming and laughing.

Gaunt helped Lightning Bug to her feet, looked at the struggling pair, and turned her eyes to where Next One cradled the unmoving Flybait. "So young," she whispered, feeling so old. She felt no hate for Wu for endangering her child, nor anything for Hackwroth at all. She took Next One's hand, and tugged the bereaved girl gently up.

"Live," Gaunt told her.

Next One stared as though from ten thousand leagues away. She nodded, a movement like a settling stone.

Gaunt heard a gasp far below, thought it contained the word *Gaunt*.

"Bone?"

"You must find him," Next One said.

"I will take you to him," Lightning Bug said. She took Gaunt and Next One's hands, and together they leapt.

CHAPTER 37.

Bone fought the current, but battered and dragged in the dark, he knew soon enough that he could either let go the scroll, or drown. He could choose to enter the scroll, and perhaps enchanted as it was it would endure, for it did not lose its resilience in the water. But he would be lost to Gaunt.

There came a great booming, as of rock shattering. The waters rushed with renewed force. He clutched at the scroll and went under. He was a feather tossed on the waters, and the scroll was not the anchor he needed. But his child was there. His son. He did not remember anything about the boy, but he projected his words into the world of the scroll.

I am sorry. I am so sorry. But I cannot go with you. I must be with your mother. It is who I am. But never forget that I am also your father.

He thought he heard an answer: *Help mama.* A blessing? Or a call for help? He could not know.

He let go the scroll.

He struggled to the surface, a surface filled with sounds like concussions and roars. He gasped out, "Gaunt!"

Then he toppled back into the water, was dragged along into the dark. Somewhere in that endless time he thought he felt hands upon him, but that seemed a warm and distant dream.

CHAPTER 38.

He felt like a horse was kicking him, and a water snake strangling him. He coughed up water onto a wooden deck.

Eshe of the Fallen Swan was staring down at him, spitting out a little water of her own. "There, it's done," she said, regarding him a moment longer. "He'll live."

"Gaunt . . . Persimmon . . ."

"She will live too, you great fool, as will Next One. Thanks to Lightning Bug. Chi power or no chi power, I cannot imagine the strength it took to get the three of you away from *that*."

Bone looked up and saw smoke rising from the sea in a vast cloud. It billowed westward like a grey pillar toppling under the weight of fuming fungus.

He lay there a long time, aching and breathing, watching the smoke carry away the dreams of dragons and outlaws. *So I did betray you, Kindlekarn*, he thought. *As I've betrayed so much else.*

He crawled toward Gaunt. She looked exhausted, her eyes wide. She sat next to Lightning Bug, who moved little, her complexion pale, her midsection covered with bandages that seeped blood.

"Lightning Bug," he said.

"I am glad . . . you are alive . . . I go to rejoin the world's breath."

"Lightning Bug," he said again. "I can't . . . how can I . . ."

"Bone," Gaunt said. "Innocence. Our son."

Bone felt as though all his long life until this point was one chapter. The next would not be happy. The page must be turned.

"He is back inside the scroll," Bone said. "And Walking Stick went with him, to guard him. And the scroll is . . ." He looked up at the smoke plume, back at his knees.

"No," Gaunt said. "No."

"Do not despair . . ." Lightning Bug said, and Bone could see much how the effort cost her. "The scroll is not so easily destroyed. It was Meteor-Plum's last work, you see . . . And Walking Stick is not quite the man he was. He showed me I was right to marry my husband. And yet he showed me he still had a good heart, deep under that fine robe. All may yet be well. Who can tell what is good or bad. Who . . ."

She fell silent, as if marshaling her strength. If so, in the next moment she spent it, or it deserted her. Bone had been staring for minutes at the wulin woman, Gaunt silent beside him, before Eshe appeared to close Lightning Bug's eyes.

"Wherever you would go," Eshe said at last, "I can promise you we will take you there, if it be a sane destination."

"I have no sane destinations," Bone muttered.

Gaunt studied him a long time. "To Qiangguo, and the coast. In Abundant Bamboo there are children who need to know their mother is not coming home."

Eshe nodded, lingered, then departed.

"Persimmon . . ." Bone said.

Gaunt said nothing. She stood and strode toward the ship's bow.

Bone stayed with Lightning Bug. What else was there to do? He would guard her body before the sailors committed her to the churn of the sea. Perhaps he would come along.

He looked toward the bow and saw Gaunt stand beside Next One. The two were talking, their arms jabbing, their backs stiff, their forms comprising some unknown character representing grief.

He saw Gaunt raise a coin, contemplate it, and flip it. She regarded the result, and tossed the coin into the waters. Back she came, down the deck, toward the fallen warrior and the kneeling thief. He waited.

"You let him take Innocence," she said, and the lack of emotion in her voice cut deeper than any scream. "You let Walking Stick have our son."

Bone could have protested. He had no heart to. The essence was true enough. "I had to do it. To stay with you."

"I do not know if I would have made the same choice, Imago. I think I would have done the opposite. I am sorry."

Bone nodded. "I also. It has been so long . . ."

"Imago Bone. I think I may hate you now. And yet the hate, too, is in the service of love." She knelt and took his hand, stiffly, yet he, stupid animal that he was, thrilled at the touch of her. "I will not be parted again without calling you *husband*, for that is what you are, have long been, for better or for worse. For you came back to me when you could have had a clean escape beside your son. I hate you for that decision, yet the hate is a small, gridded part of the chaos we call love. Call for Eshe of the Fallen Swan, Imago. Do it now before I change my mind and hurl you into the sea."

Bone obeyed, for all was as she said, and he experienced that strange, chill calm in the midst of wind, of a lover new-forgiven. He hoped it would last.

I am your father, he thought to someone toward the smoke plume. *I swear I will find you again.*

CHAPTER 39.

Winter had come to Abundant Bamboo. Snow fell from veiled skies like flecks of white silence and muffled the hubbub of all but the children and the river. Since the passing away of the bandits it had become a safer, steadier place, and the printer Tror felt a lightness in the steps of all feet but his own. Even his children, for all that they yearned for their mother, were engrossed in their snowball fight, and he repeatedly shooed them away from his machinery so no official proclamations would be spattered in the crossfire.

He needed his work. For all that Lightning Bug could be a mystery to him, he liked her as a close mystery. He missed her snores and her tendency to battle invisible monsters in her sleep, for all that this sometimes left him dizzied on the floor. For that matter, their lovemaking had at times the same effect. He missed planning his days and waiting to see exactly how she would upend those plans. Things were getting far too reasonable and predictable. She would say he was getting too fat, and then make a pot of fried rice far richer than anything he'd had in months. She would say he was letting the children run around like wild animals, before joining the snowball fight herself. He would sigh and bemoan his fate. All would be well.

He watched a few brave boats bobbing up and down the river. One sturdy travel barge was tying up even now. He wondered what places the travelers had come from. Wondering made him consider making something up. Even now at the teahouses they were telling stories of Devil Bone and the Dagger Poet, the students of the Woman in Black, and their endless battles against the Staff Sage and Exceedingly Sorcerous Wu. Tror figured he could do better than most in promoting that myth. And he had a printing press. Perhaps he could slip a little covert Swan scripture in, just around the edges . . .

A knot of four travelers was headed his way, and Tror's daydreams ceased. Through the snow he could not make out the three cloaked travelers who paused on the street of cold, crunching mud, but he knew the girl who came forward and removed her hood—no, not a girl, not anymore. But he knew her.

"Next One," Tror said. "What . . . ?"

"I have things to tell you," she said, and in her voice he knew already what the first thing would be, and gripped a bamboo post for support. "And help to offer you and your children. But please . . . call me Snow Pine."

THE TALE OF INNOCENCE

In the temple in the Peculiar Peaks, Innocence Gaunt studied his classics and practiced calligraphy beneath the paintings that were the gifts of the self-portrait of Meteor-Plum—the landscapes of Swanisle and Palmary, Penultima Thule and the Contrariwise Coast, and many another land, as described to the artist by the woman in the portrait by the window. She was a thick-boned farmer-turned-poet-turned-thief, bearing a rose-and-spiderweb tattoo, and she seemed sad and kindly and motherly and mischievous, like one who has seen much but refuses to surrender anything, even laughter. She had also described the man in the portrait opposite, the thin rogue with a flame-scar on one side, the blade-scar on the other, bearing a look implying even the end of the world had its amusing aspects.

Outside coughed the stern man who paced beside the outbuilding so methodically, the grim-faced man with the staff, who said the boy had a destiny, out in his parents' world.

Above the land, the sky had a thick, grey countenance, almost like paper that had sopped too much water. It rained often. Monks venturing from the temple down the mountain paths reported a great lake making islands of the peaks. Every year the level of the lake was a little higher.

"How then can I fulfill this destiny, O shade of the emperor?" Innocence asked once of the self-portrait. "How can I escape into my parents' world? And even if I could, with the power you speak of, what ill deeds might I commit there? Would I enslave the world, be it in the manner of the East or West, garden or grid?"

"You cannot know these things," said the image of Meteor-Plum. "You can lay plans, but you can never control the future. Only, learn from my maker's folly, and seek not to command what you love."

Innocence left off his studies for a time, and gazed out at the window. Soon he would return to painting intertwined dragons, but for now he was hoping against hope to see the sad-eyed and wise and beautiful A-Girl-Is-A-Joy, the orphan who was his best friend, and yet whom Walking Stick increasingly tried to keep him away from, muttering things about "distraction" and "vital energy" and "youth." Sometimes he had a dim memory, of his mother telling him a story of a boy in a similar predicament. He could not quite remember. Something about a fox.

I am your son, he sent his thoughts toward the grey sky. *I will know the storied seas and lands of your world, where the stars rise and more. I swear this.*

Though almost every day the rain fell, the boy did not stop wishing, or laughing. His work was too serious for that.

Here is the first Gaunt and Bone adventure, reprinted from The Maga-zine of Fantasy & Science Fiction, *June 2000, in which the poet and the thief clash with the kleptomancers of Palmary, and in so doing find their fates entangled forever.*

THE THIEF WITH TWO DEATHS

Once in the ramshackle avenues where Palmary meets the sea, a poet loved a thief with two deaths. It might have been the May-December match of a hundred poor songs and a thousand worse jokes, save for two points which balanced the scales: owing to his odd condition the old thief more resembled a man of nineteen than of ninety-nine; and the young poet had a taste for graveyards.

It was in a graveyard that they sealed their fates.

Fanned by moonlit palm trees, chaperoned by star-aimed white obelisks slicing the surf's roar into baffled echoes, Persimmon Gaunt stroked the thief's dark hair and smiled. "Now I will ask the third time, and you will answer. How did you earn your name?" Her face betrayed her origin on a farm upon distant Swanisle: sturdy shoulders caught her merry cascade of red hair. Yet her cheeks were pale, and one bore the tattoo of a black spider tickling a web-snagged rose.

Imago Bone smiled back. A short burn scarred his left cheek, and a long cut spanned the neck to below the right eye. "I do not properly remember."

"You are not senile, Bone. You may forget which palmgreaser's house you looted last, but surely you recall your fame."

As befitted his profession Imago Bone's frame was slight, though it captured all the coiled energy of a hungry ferret. He uncoiled to draw Persimmon Gaunt to the hallowed earth.

Smiling, she pushed him away. "That's a better ploy, but it too will fail."

"A better way to while one's time," he said, "than unearthing what's buried."

"What better ground to unearth it from? Where better to explain these 'Two Deaths?' Have you died twice, Bone, and returned?"

He smirked. "Nothing so familiar."

"Or are you a sorcerer, with two night angels bound in your service?"

He snorted. "Service? Now that's amusing."

"You laugh at 'service,' not 'sorcerer'? Why?"

Bone rolled and leapt, attaining an obelisk's highest seam (an action as natural to him as stretching the quill-arm was to Gaunt). He surveyed the shore. Owing to ancient regulations the desert city kept the shape of a human hand, and only the coastal Sleeve spilled away in the random manner common to living, growing towns, dangling warehouses and tenements and commoners' graveyards like loose threads. This tryst was far up the northern strand and hidden from living eyes.

Moonlight sketched his sigh. "I'm no sorcerer, thank the night. Now, then: I've already pledged to recover your manuscript from whomever stole it; surely I owe you no more."

She rose, shivering with pleasure at the wind. "'Owe'? You believe I sold my charms?"

"I did not say that. But I am not a curiosity for your morbid lyrics, Persimmon Gaunt."

"Nor did I say that."

"At ninety-nine I am entitled to privacy." Though Bone strutted overhead, his voice checked her laughter. He said, "Now then, from whom must I pluck your *Alley Flowers*?"

Now Gaunt sighed. "To business? Very well, if you cannot trust me with your story. It was the goblins of Hangnail Tower."

Persimmon Gaunt studied his reaction. It was as she feared.

Imago Bone stared at her, then the stars, scratching his chin so his hand cradled the two wounds of his face. Few in Palmary knew why Imago Bone was called the Thief With Two Deaths; but all understood the Goblin Library of Hangnail Tower was no place for borrowing books.

First she feared he would refuse. Then the crimson light surrounded her, and her fears became altogether different.

Bone was lost in a time eighty years gone, a journey that lasted one long heartbeat. Then his heart skipped into the present, and his skin thrilled at the nearness of doom. It was too familiar a doom, after so long, to surprise him. Indeed, he could almost welcome it as a friend. Nonetheless, he had to challenge it.

Bone leapt to earth, tumbled to his jerkin, rose with a knife.

"Release the woman, Joyblood, or I will strike."

He pricked his own chest.

"Ah, Bone." The lips were Persimmon Gaunt's, but the voice was not.

It more resembled a choir of perfectly tuned, cackling madchildren. This was not so distracting as Gaunt's stance, for she levitated a foot above ground, cloaked in a ruby glow like sunset glinting off scarlet pools at a battlefield. She twitched like a marionette, and mocking fires danced in her eyes. "Do not struggle. Your end has come. The seeds of love have rooted in two stony hearts."

"Seeds?" Bone chuckled. "Harbinger of death at a lover's hands! And you are satisfied with *seeds?*"

Gaunt's eyebrows drooped in vexation. "What else have I to work with? Eh? Anonymous tavern wenches wooed in disguise? Bored palmgreasers' wives who wouldn't know love from caviar indigestion?"

"Concede," Bone demanded, twisting the dagger and wincing. "This poet is a devotee of nightmares, a student of decadence, and would no sooner *love* me than write poems about pretty ponies."

"You are a decadent nightmare in your own fashion," the death persisted. "Ah, be reasonable, Bone! The future romance of Bone and Gaunt is flickering in your eyes. Accept your destiny. Do not wriggle with technicalities."

"*I* wriggle?"

Then a cold wind arose seaward, stirring pebbles and earth. A vortex of dust and spiderwebs swirled and compressed, making the sketch of a tall, hooded figure. One hand terminated in cruel pincers, the other in a sweeping scythe.

"You are late," said Bone.

"Late?" The word was like a dry breeze rustling a heap of old leaves and bones. "Three lives still twitched in the balance from your last barfight. After eighty years my fate still astounds. I am a death, yet I spend my nights protecting life. To wit—"

And here the death sighed its way between obelisks, scythe cutting air.

"Curse you, Severstrand," said one death.

"Redundant, Joyblood," said the other.

"Be mindful of Gaunt," cried Imago Bone, and the dark angels shot him such a glance as mortals send slow-witted children.

Joyblood waved a hand; flame licked the air like burning cat-o-nine tails. Severstrand dodged waist-deep into the ground. The scythe shimmered upward into Persimmon Gaunt's belly, but Severstrand checked his blow at the last. Joyblood's essence billowed forth from the poet with a screech, like a smoke-cloud cradling its own fire-source. Gaunt slumped to the earth.

Bone crouched beside her. She still breathed. Her fingernails curved out an inch from her hands, her hair spilled to her waist, but she breathed. "You're precise as ever, Severstrand. Thank you."

"I do not want your thanks. I want your end. I want you to perish, friendless, loveless, in cold despair."

"I do not take it personally, Severstrand."

"I am glad, for I do respect you, Bone. Though you must die."

The scythe twitched a little; but Joyblood shimmered into new solidity, all smoke and flame, eyes and mouth shining like rubies beside a prince's fireplace. "He is not for you, decrepit one. That woman will love him."

Severstrand proffered a thin, spiderwebbed smile. "Indeed? As he's loved by the courtesans of the Pinky Palisade? The whores of Thumbbottom?"

"Those are sparks beside the bonfire. Ah, why do you never relent, Severstrand? I offer Bone a death of wild romance!"

Severstrand shrugged. "I offer an end. Nasty, brutish, short. Anything else is sugarcoating."

Bone coughed. "Let me register again my desire to expire peacefully in bed, surrounded by adoring women and an ill-gotten hoard."

Both deaths turned in scorn.

"But if the matter is buried for now," Bone said, "I would like my privacy."

Joyblood bowed. "Ah, very well. Passion will out. Shall we adjourn to a mortuary, decrepit foe, and debate over games of chance?"

Severstrand nodded. "Very well, mad opponent, if the odds are long. Enjoy your dalliance, Bone. I will destroy you later."

"Happy dicing." The two deaths faded from the air like morning mist.

Bone reviewed Gaunt's sleeping form, and uncharacteristically he did not linger upon her physicality but tried to divine something of her heart. Here was a pale woman who idolized the grave; yet a brush with death gave flush to her cheeks, left her chest pulsing steadily with the ancient greed for air. And here was Imago Bone, dancing between two headstones marked with his name, as though the liveliness of his feet defied the narrowness of the ground. Gaunt thought she understood death, but truly, it was life she embraced.

Bone caressed the spiderweb tattoo of her cheek, and her eyelids fluttered. "That was . . ." she said, "that was . . ."

"That was," Bone said with a smirk, "you might say, my family. And the reason I will take your commission, and storm the Goblin Library. As I should have done eighty years gone."

At sunset next day, poet and thief crossed from the Sleeve through the Bracelet Wall and onto Via Viva toward the Fingers, threading the shadows of the towers.

All the Spiral Sea knew the towers of Palmary, nine, ten, eleven story monstrosities of brick, adobe, granite. They were monuments to the hubris of rich palmgreasers, but more to the point, they were an outgrowth of zoning laws. To secure certain magical advantages, Palmary proper took the form of a human hand. Roads mirrored lifelines; hills mimicked the mounds of the palm; canals irrigated digit-like boulevards, with the spaces between surrendered to the sands. Violators lost fingers, so the city clawed enthusiastically skyward, and it was said that birds scorned the palm branches for belfries, and that bats and squirrels outnumbered their cousins the rats, and that true cat burglars the world over died and went to Palmary.

But there was one tower unstained, untouched by burglar or squirrel. Certain bats flew there only, a rare breed that alighted in silence.

The Hangnail Tower was hardly Palmary's tallest, but it stood alone. It rose nine stories in the sharp lines of a graveyard obelisk, and all its stone was tarnished gray. Near the top, scores of severed fingers dangled from their tips upon irregularly spaced iron spikes. Rearing in the sunset where the desert lapped the end of Index Road, the tower attained a hue of scabrous blood.

From their vantage in a narrow lane between manor houses, Gaunt said, "I've never been so close to the home of the kleptomancers."

"And you'll get no closer," Bone said. He wore a signature costume of black leather studded with various tools and weapons. Fully half of these were balsa wood fakes, to intimidate anyone he came across. He would never carry so much real weight. "You'll await me at the assigned place, until I return with my prizes."

"Prizes? There is something beside my manuscript?"

Bone laughed. "There are many things beside your manuscript. But there is one thing in particular that I will need for my salvation, and yours. The most terrible of tomes. Nothing else will do."

Gaunt looked doubtful. "Bone, I wonder now if it was right to steer you this way. The tower will be riddled with traps, and now this book . . ."

"You are a wise woman," Bone said, wrestling free a sewer grate from the cobblestones, "but still a young one, though you wish otherwise. You do not see that sometimes even we old folk must toss the dice. I may die, but it is a reasonable risk. Much more reasonable than another eighty years with my friends Joyblood and Severstrand."

"I still do not understand about them . . ."

"Pray you never do. Now wait one hour, then make for the location I showed you."

He slipped down into darkness.

Gaunt replaced the grate. She shivered as the sky purpled and blossomed with stars.

A whisper came to her. "I will teach you, Persimmon Gaunt, what you wish to know."

Hangnail Tower was divided in three parts.

The lowest level (which Imago Bone trod, light as a famished ant) housed the bureaucrats who ran the city in the kleptomancers' name. It also sheltered vaults bursting with coins, gems, tapestries—all the wealth the kleptomancers seized from the palmgreaser elite. The kleptomancers did not prize such things; but their vassals did, and that was all that mattered.

The topmost level formed the sanctum of these sorcerers of theft, from which they regarded their strange instrument, the city. For Palmary itself was like the hand of a thief, stealing the magical energies of the surrounding land and sea.

And all the space between held the Goblin Library, sheltering the only treasure the kleptomancers loved for itself.

At the Library doorstep Imago Bone drew a dagger he'd nicked from a kleptomancer eighty years ago, and which he had employed only once. It was slender and silver, its hilt took the shape of a slender tome, and the blade glinted with intricate notches as Bone waved it before the door.

The Library possessed but three portals. One led to the kleptomancers' sanctum. Another opened from the Goblin Reading Room onto empty air. The door Bone pondered in flickering light was a huge brass panel proclaiming *Ex Nihilo* in the style of a bookplate. A sculpted goblin face, three-eyed, with bat ears and a single nostril, grinned a brassy grin. Its third eye cradled a torch.

Sweating, Bone slid the blade into the goblin-nostril. He twisted.

There was no reassuring click. Instead, there was a thin whistle.

His sweating redoubled, and he sheathed the dagger and covered his face with a mesh woven of sweetair leaves. With one hand he flicked open a metal case bearing six customized, notched daggers.

As he worked the lock, Bone's neck tingled in the accustomed way. Was Joyblood nearby, *tsking* at the passionless nature of death by gas? Severstrand, displeased it might be painless?

The second dagger worked.

Bone advanced, welcoming cool, moldy air.

The Library filled seven stories. Or would have, had there been stories to speak of.

Instead it was one vast chamber, festooned with balconies which were linked by a mad arrangement of rising and falling staircases. The stairway railings shimmered with hundreds of glass spheres, each aglow from dozens of trapped, luminescent insects. But the balconies had no railings; that would have meant less room for the bookshelves.

The shelves' hollows clutched motley volumes sheathed in cracked bindings and cobwebs; while their frames scowled with goblin calligraphy, proclaiming each balcony a branch of knowledge in the goblin bibliographic system.

Thus Imago Bone knew he crept through the Alcove of Martyrs (whose urns cradled the ashes of incinerated books) and thence to the Vault of the Vanished (whose squarish marble statues honored books lost to time). Beyond these he arrived at a major fork dividing the Library into halves: books written by the left-handed and the right-handed. Bone's forehead wrinkled, and he jogged left.

The directions in the memoirs of Dolman the Charmed were tantalizing

CHRIS WILLRICH　　271

but unspecific; and Bone himself had been here but once. So he pattered cautiously through the balconies: Cynical Stories by Innocents; Innocent Stories by Cynics; Polite Arguments for Cracking Heads; Coming-of-Age-Tales-cum-Cruelty-Manuals; Vast Philosophical Systems Proving Why Mommy Was Wrong; Books Proudly Shocking the Sensibilities of a Generation Already Dead; Books with Excessive Use of Semicolons.

"You risk much, old companion," came a disembodied whisper, and Bone knew it drifted to his ears alone.

"Really, Severstrand?"

"The librarians are admirably bloody-minded."

Bone allowed a smile. "Would that satisfy you? Bloody or not, it wouldn't be by your hand."

He leapt silently past bookshelves contrived to sprout blades and sandwich idle browsers. The sepulchral voice followed him. "That is a point." Severstrand sighed. "I have fallen somewhat, Bone. Once I would not have hounded my prey so."

"Once it was merely a duty, killing people."

"Quite. Personal attendance was unnecessary. A true night angel is an arranger. Somewhat like a mortal florist. I needed only a touch of fever, a few old worries, some slippery cobblestones, and a frightened horse team. I no more needed to manifest than the florist needs to kiss the young lady personally. Nevertheless . . ."

"Nevertheless, you and Joyblood have hounded me for eighty years. Is that not enough?" Here Bone avoided the attractive "fallen" book sculpted of everlasting glue.

"I confess I sometimes tire of the matter, Bone. And yet. If I quit the field, Joyblood triumphs. Death at the hands of a lover—utter melodrama! It dishonors you and the cold eye you've turned upon life."

"Why, thank you."

"Of course. However, death by the fury of goblin librarians—that might do. I regret the end of our conversations, Imago Bone."

"They have been diverting," Bone agreed, ducking under the invisible wire rigged to topple an upper stack brimming with bricks in leather covers. "But I am not finished yet."

"Soon," Severstrand said. "And then I may destroy my foe."

Bone stopped. "You would attack Joyblood? Even with me gone?"

"Of course. Joyblood feels the same. Our feud has lingered too long, Bone. It demands satisfaction. But that—and all else—is beyond your concern. Farewell."

There came a gentle *swoosh* from far overhead; and a few seconds later an oversized bat with human hands for claws tumbled dead at Bone's feet.

As the bookbat's *thud* echoed among the balconies, there rose an excited murmuring from all around, as the goblin librarians looked up from their shelving and straightening, cataloging and indexing, and scampered hissing toward the sound.

Persimmon Gaunt brandished a dagger, mainly to salve her pride before Joyblood possessed her anew. But the crimson apparition merely sighed. "Ah, have no fear, mortal! Although you would love Imago Bone in time, I concede you are unripe for my purposes."

"I'm no romantic," Gaunt said, lowering the blade. "In fact your little speech just slew any spark I might have felt."

"Please tell yourself that; you will fall all the harder. Not that it matters, anymore."

"Whatever do you mean?"

"The wheel has turned. Imago Bone has gone home."

"Home? The Hangnail Tower?"

"Where Bone, as he is now, was born. Where he has returned to die. And in a gruesome fashion that will no doubt please my rival."

Persimmon Gaunt felt something graveyard poets are not supposed to feel. "Does he seek his own destruction there? And did I push him in?"

"I believe the answer to both is Yes—but do not blame yourself! The Tower has haunted him for eight decades. He had to return."

"Tell me why."

"As you wish." The red miasma's eyes flickered. "When Imago Bone was truly nineteen his heart was like a torch fanned by a gale, and the windstorm was a woman. She was a kleptomancer of Hangnail Tower, and he was a street thief, down from the Contrariwise Coast seeking fortune, beckoned by the

CHRIS WILLRICH   273

hand of Palmary. The kleptomancer Vine stole the young man's gaze, but she loved and abandoned him, as the kleptomancers are wont. Worse, she berated him for weakness, never elaborating on the theme.

"Like many men before, Bone was flogged to madness by this word 'weak.' He pursued her. He hunted all talk of her. Of late, he learned, she dallied with many men from the poorer creases of the great hand . . . but primarily she shared the bed of the kleptomancer Remora. Now, as this rival treated Vine with imperious contempt, Bone supposed there was a chance—nay, a duty— to replace him. And yet Vine spurned Bone's advances and clung to Remora, for that alliance brought power to both."

"A sad tale," said Gaunt. "It seems to me Bone was better off without love."

"Without love?" jeered the death. "It is the brightest light of existence."

"But not the only. Can not the sun share sky with the stars, the moon?"

"The sun banishes the rest."

"Perhaps because it is jealous, and craves all eyes. And does it not blind?"

"Feh . . . I will not argue with poets. Remember: the end of all arguments is silence."

"Do not be silent yet. How does the story end?"

"With a beginning. For at last Bone's passion whipped him toward the Hangnail Tower. He purchased—not stole—one perfect violet. No roses for him! So armed, Bone sought to fling himself at his lady's feet. Luck and stealth, but mainly the first, bore him through the Goblin Library. At last he attained Vine's chambers—but she was not alone."

"Remora was there, taking his pleasure."

"Not in the sense you mean," said the death. "The two stood amidst a dozen bound and gagged citizens of Palmary, six women and six men. Gore streaked the room, as Remora and Vine fed, into a burning brazier, the first victim's heart."

"No," Gaunt whispered. The grave, skeletons, decay—these things stirred Persimmon Gaunt's soul; but cruelty was something else.

"It was then," Joyblood said, "that Imago Bone understood why Vine the kleptomancer called him weak. She meant that he was weak in magic, and thus an undesirable sacrifice. That is the way of kleptomancy, for its power turns on theft. And to metaphorically *and* physically steal hearts, well, that is quite a path to power. Vine and Remora meant to become immortal."

"Ah, Bone," Gaunt said, and her heart contracted in sympathy.

And at that moment Joyblood the death looked into her soul and nodded with satisfaction. Then he was gone.

After Severstrand dropped his noisy parting gift, Bone flung a rope and ascended from Kitchen Sink Narratives to Thin Painful Volumes. From there he scampered this way and that, until he spotted the rumored blue volume that triggered a spinning shelf, leading to Non-Sentient Cookery. There he listened, cold sweat glistening in the dim, flickering light.

The goblin librarians were notorious lovers of tales and infamous collectors of tomes. Their bookbats scoured the city for both. But these obsessions were distinct.

Goblins believed a living tale was a spoken tale, and in the writing was slain, lying still and unchanging. Therefore the Library was a mausoleum, and the most a visitor might do was offer complimentary bookmarks of pressed flowers, which the librarians placed in the honored tome. Browsing was forbidden, borrowing unheard of—unless you were one of the goblins' patrons, the kleptomancers. Such privileges were tolerated as sad necessity.

The presence of any other browser could make a goblin librarian chartreuse with rage.

Bone heard more scampering from nearby, and excited *glurpings*. He squeezed between shelves, then leapt to the alcove for Simple Things Made Obtuse.

Skidding, he bumped a stack. Three flights below, a goblin troop shrieked and clambered upward. Bone caught a glimpse of their variable shapes: jutting noses, gray pockmarked skin, glowing yellow eyes (one to three apiece). Each bore a long catalog-card file strapped to its back.

Bone smirked and snapped one of his balsa daggers; within was a glass bead. He tossed the bead and it shattered among the goblins, bathing the area with noxious fog. Bone turned and ran—but two flights up he encountered another troop, squeaking in fury.

They unsheathed the copper rods of their card files, each one slender and honed to a point, scored with old ink and blood.

Bone jumped sideways, wriggled himself into a crack, and toppled a collection of scholarly offerings, smiling thinly at the cries of outrage and pain. He threw another rope to an upper alcove, and climbed.

As he ascended he glanced up to spot a huge goblin grinning furiously (beneath the shelf for Tales That Could Not Have Been Written By Their Dead Narrators). The goblin clutched an enormous tome, the very *Anthro-Goblin Cataloging Rules, Thirteenth Edition.*

"Curse you for requiring this," said the goblin. It dropped the book.

Bone had an instant to admire its binding, its stately solidity, its weight.

After Joyblood vanished, Persimmon Gaunt hurried to a haycart stashed in an alley up Index Road. She suspected Joyblood, despite all denials, hoped to employ her in slaying Bone. Of course, she thought, her heart did not truly belong to Bone—but if the death believed it, the thief was still endangered. If she fled across the city, Joyblood could not use her.

Yet if she were not at Hangnail Tower, according to plan, Bone might die anyway. A nasty, brutish death, satisfying Severstrand.

She gripped the reins, but could not decide where to go.

"Horns of a dilemma, my dear?"

She shivered: the shadowy death himself appeared, sketched in old soot and moonlight. Ghostly spiders crawled upon his non-substance. Yet this apparition suited her better than Joyblood's flames. Gaunt found her voice. "You can read my thoughts?"

"No. Better to say I sense their tenor, when I am their subject."

"I've just spoken with Joyblood."

"That is why I appeared."

"He believes Bone's race is run."

"It may be so. It would be fitting if he died at Hangnail Tower, home of his tormentors."

She frowned. "You're not speaking of you and Joyblood, are you? You refer to the kleptomancers, Remora and Vine."

"Indeed. Please do not think ill of us, Persimmon Gaunt. Though we two deaths are antagonists, we share a respect for Imago Bone. We often speak of him while he sleeps. (Death in sleep would satisfy neither, you understand.) We wish him a poetic ending, after our own fashion, no worse."

"I fear I must think ill of you, Severstrand."

"I am sad."

"But I may think worse of others. You are an instrument, I would guess. Vine and Remora's?"

"Remora's. Joyblood is Vine's doing."

Gaunt frowned. "But you work at cross purposes."

"Quite. And rather than ending Bone's life we have stretched it unnaturally—all because of two enraged and careless kleptomancers."

"Enraged because he interrupted their ceremony?"

"Worse." Severstrand paced about the cart. The horses shivered as if scoured by hail. "We deaths sense the circumstances of our summonings, as you recall a fading dream. So I still taste the bile in Imago Bone's throat as he beheld the butchery. It was not that Bone was a good man. Rather, he saw what he might have become, had his own greed been augmented by magic. And a small, pathetic portion of him still ached at Vine's dismissal, and wished to stand by her side."

"What did he do?"

"He acted quickly. In that a common thief may best a kleptomancer. He kicked open the shutters, so those within other towers might witness the crime, and those upon Index Road might hear. Then—in the most unseemly romantic fashion—he swung by the rope of a tapestry into the fray. He had no plan, only anger, and he tossed upon the fire the blossom he'd carried for Vine.

"You are unversed in kleptomancy, Persimmon Gaunt. Understand that this violet was in no sense stolen, and represented as honest a love as Imago Bone could muster. It was the antithesis of the spell. The flames died and the ceremony was lost."

Gaunt's mind thrilled with the image. "He fought them then?"

Severstrand chuckled, and across the alley a cloud of moonlit gnats tumbled to earth. "He might say so. But in truth he fled the tower. After the initial fury he knew fear and shame: though he now despised his paramour, her contempt still stung."

"How like a man, swayed by beauty though a monster wears it."

"The pair swore to punish Bone for his infatuation with Vine; but the senior kleptomancers locked them away for a month. Such was their sentence for murdering gutter trash. But in their separate cells, Remora and Vine pronounced frightful curses, tapping the power of their one stolen heart. Though they could not become immortal, they each had enough strength to raise a death for Imago Bone. Yet their arrogance betrayed them. For each believed the opposite sex to be simple, easy to predict. Thus they assumed they could anticipate each other's curse, doubling its strength. In fact, all they understood of each other was a shared lust for power.

"Remora cursed Bone to die in despair, never again knowing love. While Vine swore the next woman to love him would doom him."

Gaunt said, "And so Bone survived."

The specter nodded. "And in his own way, prospered. When Joyblood and I emerged from the vaults of the night we embraced as kin. Then we fought. Evenly matched, we settled into a long game of waiting and watching. I will never forget Bone's laughter when he understood."

"What a strange life." Gaunt patted the horses, more to reassure herself than the team. "Bone, protected for eighty years by a stalemate of deaths. Neither can allow the other to claim him. Neither can allow age to touch him. Meanwhile, Joyblood must keep thrusting women into his path, while you must . . . kill them?"

"Frighten. Even were I inclined otherwise, Bone has charged us to protect all sentients near him, or he shall end his life. Such self-sacrifice would thwart us both." The death shook his cowled head. "His barfights are particularly vexing."

"He must be lonely."

Severstrand's eyes took on an eerie, moonlit glow. "One would suppose he would despair. But he has not."

"He has you for company, I suppose."

The death shook his head, his thin voice wavering oddly. "I must away. Joyblood will undo my latest attempt."

"Why did you come at all, Severstrand?" Gaunt demanded. "If you think me Joyblood's tool you have not frightened me, much."

The death shrugged, turned his back, and vanished.

"Did you need to explain yourself?" Gaunt asked the air. "Be forgiven?"

She thought a long moment, watching a few hardy gnats buzz about the alley.

"Be careful, Bone," she said, "for I do feel something for you, after all."

She stirred the horses toward the tower. They were eager to depart, unaware they followed the source of their fear.

Bone's bones complained in seven places, but at least the chair was comfortable.

Chair?

Opening his eyes, Bone decided he sat in the Reading Room: tomes sprawled upon chairs, desks, and pedestals, awash in multihued light from stained-glass windows depicting goblin storytellers regaling goblin crowds. And besides, there was a goblin crowd surrounding him now.

They prodded him with cardfile-rods. "See, O Rex Libris," said one. "See! It is the Imago Bone, he who recently trespassed."

"Eighty years ago," Bone clarified.

The massive goblin bearing the *Cataloging Rules* laughed and sneezed through his single nostril. He was the very model of the brass face of the lower doorway. "I *do* remember you, Imago Bone. I know the stories; some of them found final rest here. As have you. I am honored."

All assembled looked at the Rex Libris in surprise.

"Do not stare! Are we not goblins? Do we not love stories? Look around you, Bone, behold our vice. Bookbats return each morning, clutching tomes to inter." The Rex Libris nodded at an oaken door between stained-glass panels, a door that led to empty air.

"Can you not forgive our temptation to learn the books' secrets, to speak, as it were, with the dead? So we read each acquisition, savor it—then shelve it forever and speak of it no more. Can we condemn those who would share such pleasure? No, we can merely kill them. So I must admire your attempt. Please satisfy my curiosity. Which book?"

"Will the answer prolong my life?"

"For a time."

"Then for a time I will answer. I seek not one, but two volumes."

"The nerve!" shrieked some goblins, and "The courage!" squeaked others.

"The first," Bone said, "is a thin volume of poetry even now, I suspect, on loan to your landlords. For the sake of this *Alley Flowers* I am merely traversing your domain to their sanctum. It is for the sake of friendship, and a nominal fee."

The Rex Libris chuckled. "For this, I might release you with a maiming. The kleptomancers have grown thoughtless in their borrowing. Only half of us had the opportunity to read this brooding verse. Such funereal splendor! But what of the other book?"

"Ah. That. It is a cursed tome, O bibliophiles, and most rare. Even connoisseurs of such material whisper its name, if they know it at all."

"Ah," said the Rex Libris with cheerful interest, "a student of blasphemous power. You seek the *Nominus Umbra*."

"Nothing so grand."

"The dread *Geisthammer* then."

"No."

The goblin frowned and scratched its chin. *"Dead Richard's Almanac?"*

"No. This book's fame is rather circumscribed. Even among scholars willing to risk being whisked off to the stars by amorphous things with shadowy wings — even among such sturdy folk, few will speak of it."

"You mock me. I would know of such a book."

"I think not. *Mashed Rags Bound in Dead Cow* is not a book that inspires bibliography."

The gauntlet was thrown. The room filled with the susurrant flipping of thousands of pages.

"No such title!" meeped a goblin.

"He lies!" gurgled another.

"Take him to the bindery!" chirped a third.

"No," rumbled the Rex Libris. "For his insolence we shall brand him with hot accession stamps."

Then the Rex Libris shuddered in a cocoon of crimson light.

"Hello, Joyblood."

"This one admires you, Bone, despite his outrage. It is almost love."

"You wouldn't."

"Fear not. I have other plans." Joyblood raised the Rex Libris's voice. "Friends! Lovers of books! Read elsewhere, please."

The goblins waved their cardfile rods.

"Do not—" Bone said.

"Do not kill them, I know," sighed Joyblood.

Joyblood spat red fire, singeing the carpet. Sparks fell near a pile of books. The goblins dropped their rods and backed away, hands raised.

Joyblood said, "You would save even these creatures! Ah, you've grown soft, foolish, sentimental. I am pleased. Soon you'll earn your death by romance." He scratched the nose of the Rex Libris. "May I ask why this *Mashed Rags Bound in Dead Cow* is so important?"

Bone rose and stretched. "Sometimes the best weapon is one the enemy already owns."

Joyblood said, "It is a weapon, not a book?"

"In a sense all books are weapons, but this more than most."

Joyblood laughed, the Rex Libris's chest heaving. "Ah, keep your secrets, Bone. You always plan fascinating thefts. I shall miss you."

Bone lowered his head. "I'll miss you too, O romantic."

"Ah, so you sense I'll succeed!"

Bone sighed. "I simply buckle under life's despair."

"Despair . . . You do not intend to give yourself to that boor Severstrand?"

Bone smiled, shrugged, and left the room.

"Severstrand?" Joyblood cried. "Show yourself!"

Bone waited around the corner until Severstrand's whispers answered Joyblood's wail. Good: they would argue for a time.

Unhindered, Bone stalked the alcoves. At last he came to Stories About Rich And Beautiful People Stupider Than Ourselves. There on a low shelf stood *Mashed Rags Bound in Dead Cow*, caked in a thin layer of dust.

There is no better way to hide a book than to misfile it in a library.

It had taken twenty years to trace the hints to the whispers to the legends; to bribe witnesses under moonglow and scour testaments by candlelight. The thing's compiler was long dead, the various authors in worse states. All the owners had met bizarre accidents. But rash scholars had skimmed its pages and scribbled warnings in the margins of their journals. One, Dolman the Charmed, sorcerer and thief, unearthed the thing itself. He read a page and burned a year of his notorious luck in one day. It was the horrified Dolman who slipped into the Goblin Library forty years past—not to steal books, but to bury one. Yet Dolman had his pride, and coded the location into his memoirs.

Imago Bone lifted the book. It did not bite. He blew dust from its uninscribed cover.

Then he was off, vaulting up the stairs, as energetic as the day he turned sixty.

The topmost landing was empty of books. Overhead loomed a dark opening fragrant with guano, beyond which bookbats chittered of titles and covers. Bone hurried across the landing and opened a palmwood door.

Outsiders imagined the kleptomancers lived among silk and jewels, for the sorcerers wore such things outside. But among themselves they dropped pretensions. The high chambers had all the elegance of a well-ventilated dungeon.

The only decorations were baubles glinting under glass covers in the torchlit stairway Bone ascended: here a wooden pony missing one leg; there a stone block with a half-sculpted face; and now a circle of human skin, caressed by the tattoo of a woman's name. He saw nothing he would steal, and arrived at the uppermost chamber.

"Imago Bone," said a woman who seemed fifty, standing upon a carpet of drab, woven rope. "It has been so long."

"So long," echoed a man of perhaps sixty, perched upon a wooden stool behind a vast granite desk, "to find the nerve to return?"

Vine and Remora had aged at a crawl, but aged nonetheless. And they had not aged well: she seemed a skin garment cinched across sharp bones, while sagging, glistening flesh embellished his frown.

"Nerve?" Holding the tome behind him, Bone edged nearer the desk and its one feature, a battered manuscript below a glass cover. "Nerve is for youth. I should never have survived Hangnail Tower. Yet your two deaths—" he raised his face and the burn and scar framing it "—showed me I had years to hone my skills. At thirty I contemplated return. At forty I itched to try. But to what end? Your own lives are a better revenge than any I could devise."

"You deny your weakness," said Vine. "Weak in magic, weak in courage. How you disappointed me." She adjusted herself as if he must still find her attractive.

"You have aged," chuckled Remora, "but learned nothing. Do you even know what you want? We cannot lift your curse."

"No, but you can lift that glass."

They blinked in confusion. "This?" Remora raised the glass, fingered the stack of pages. "A minor poet's spew? I just acquired this trifle and meant to mock its innocent evocations of despair. It is nothing."

"It is everything, to the one who lost it."

Remora smiled. "You *have* learned something. Yes, the passion of the former owner, that does matter, if you've learned to taste it, devour it. But you are deficient in magic, and cannot join us. Even if you could, this book is but a token."

"Nothing like stealing a dozen hearts."

Vine smirked. "Nothing at all."

Bone said, "Nevertheless. It is Persimmon Gaunt's sweat and toil. I would have it back."

Vine smiled. "You love her."

Bone shrugged.

"Come," chuckled Remora, "we are both old men. We know what young smiles conjure."

"I still have my lechery, kleptomancer, thank the gods. But I am not here for that. I like Gaunt. She reminds me what I've lost."

"You are in love," Vine said, "vulnerable to my curse."

"No, Vine," said her companion. "Mine awaits. Abnegation. Despair. Why should we give you this book?"

"Why not?" Bone said.

"Because it would please you. Even now we steal that thwarted pleasure."

Bone sighed. "Very well. I did come prepared to bargain. I carry a rare tome."

Vine's eyes narrowed. "Let us see."

Bone slid the volume across the table. Vine gingerly opened it.

"'I tell you truly,'" she read, "'death is neither romantic nor grim. It merely is, and what it is most, is humiliating. My own last words were, 'Fools! The longbow is a child's weapon . . .'"

Vine frowned, passed the book to Remora, who flipped to the middle.

Vine said, "What in the five corners is this, Bone?"

"The testimony of one thousand ghosts, one per page, all of whom died in foolish or freakish ways."

"'So I told my brothers,'" read Remora, "'see, candleflames don't hurt. But as I waved my finger I knocked the whole candle over, whence it spun into the face of Father's mastiff, who promptly mauled my groin . . .'" Remora looked up in disgust. "This is a significant tome? Even Gaunt's poetry has more merit."

"Its merit is not literary."

"Certainly not," Remora said. "Such anecdotes should be forgotten; they steal all meaning from life."

He slammed the cover so fiercely that an old flaw in a stool-leg fractured, pitching him forward into a crunching impact with the corner of the stone desk. He slumped dead to the floor.

"Eh? Remora?" Vine appeared more irritated at Remora's stupidity than concerned for his safety. As she imperiously approached, she tripped over a loose rope of the carpet. Her head shattered the glass dome upon the table, and by freak happenstance, several large glass wedges impaled her face and throat. She gurgled and expired.

CHRIS WILLRICH   283

"It is neither romantic nor tragic," Bone said, nipping both books from the table. "But it will do."

The Reading Room was empty of speaking things. The deaths had vanished and the goblins still hid in the twistings of the library. So Bone had a clear path to the door of the bookbats.

He fell seven stories. But he'd read no story in *Mashed Rags Bound in Dead Cow*, so he had a chance.

And Persimmon Gaunt waited below, with a horsecart full of hay.

As he groaned, she drove them back to the alley, calling repeatedly, "You have it? You have it, Bone? Are you all right?"

"Yes, yes, quieter please."

When they were quite alone she leapt into the hay and kissed him. "I will copy my *Alley Flowers* now, I think. Thank you, Imago Bone. You've returned my life to me."

"You had more poems in you. Better poems."

"But not these poems. You risked all for my children, here. Yet I would not have asked this of you, had I known what I know now. At least, that is what I wish to believe."

"Eh? Know what?"

Ruddy light flared above them, as Joyblood cried, "I have succeeded! This woman loves you, Bone, just enough."

"Just enough," Gaunt whispered.

"And yet I must ask a question before I whip her into murderous, jealous rage."

"A question I share," whispered a cold voice from the flickering shadows. "How is it," Severstrand asked, "that two such as Remora and Vine could perish so suddenly, without even a night angel to claim them?"

"Behold, gentledeaths," said Bone, rising and lifting the answer. "The accursed tome that slew them."

"I am versed in accursed tomes," hissed Severstrand. "I recognize it not."

"You mock us," wailed Joyblood.

"Not at all. This tome distills the essence of perverse and pointless deaths. It pronounces existence meaningless and absurd."

Joyblood said, "Foolishness! Life screams with meaning!"

Severstrand said, "Joyblood may fear such a work. But it would suit me well."

The shadowy death approached, as the crimson death hesitated.

Imago Bone raised the tome higher, and Severstrand grew hazy, like half-glimpsed midnight smoke. Hissing thinly, he backed away and grew more substantial, gasping as if for breath.

"Old companion," said Bone sadly, "you represent despair. But despair, like passion, is a meaning. This book embodies meaninglessness. Not a cosmos cold and cruel, but one like a blank page, adorned in one corner by a smeared insect. No poetry, not even graveyard verse. And without poetry, even you cannot endure."

"Joyblood," Severstrand wheezed. "You allowed this."

"I? You interfered at every step. Persimmon Gaunt is but my latest success. Had you stepped aside . . ."

"I could not! I was his death!"

"Bah. I shall be yours."

Scythe met fire. Stray sparks lit the hay.

The inhabitants of Index Road would have nightmares for days, but only Bone and Gaunt would understand the cause, and they but dimly.

Joyblood's fire-whips blazed the light of love denied, and bits of burning cobweb rose on the wind. But Severstrand's scythe-hand hissed the promise of final darkness, and the wave of pure morbidity parted the primal fires: and Joyblood screamed. But the fires rejoined, and the scream became a crackling, a cackling.

All along Index Road people shuddered as the fires of obsession cast the shadows of despair, and they fled, or fell to their knees and awaited world's end. Imago Bone and Persimmon Gaunt felt their souls tremble in their bodies, buffeted by hot and cold winds they felt beneath the skin.

Had the deaths been equal, they might have struggled until the city dissolved, its reality torn by opposite dooms. But Severstrand had been damaged by the accursed book, and at last his substance smoldered from Joyblood's fire, and he collapsed against a refuse heap, harried by gnats. His scythe and snippers twitched, but could not ward Joyblood. The other death, shrunken but burning bright, laughed in triumph and raised the arm of fiery whips.

"Stop!"

The two deaths stared. So did Imago Bone.

Persimmon Gaunt stood before the two deaths, palms raised. "No," shouted Bone, rushing to her side.

She pushed him away. "How can you allow this?" she asked him.

"Allow? They are deaths!"

"They are *your* deaths. How can you let them perish?"

Bone stared in bewilderment; and the deaths were too startled to move.

Gaunt said, "The night angels embody poetic endings, yes? Well, I am a poet, you fools. I wrote my *Alley Flowers* in a place such as this. I cannot stand here and watch one poem slay another."

She walked between the deaths.

"Leave us," Severstrand whispered.

"Go!" Joyblood raged.

Bone watched for a heartbeat that seemed eight decades long. Then he raised *Mashed Rags Bound in Dead Cow.*

"Joyblood. Hold your anger. Or I will read from the book."

Joyblood said, "I would regret your death, Bone, but it is no longer my obsession."

Desperate, Bone said, "But consider! If I, the Thief With Two Deaths, die of freak happenstance in an alley, what would the tales say about the angels of the night?"

"They would say you are irrelevant," Gaunt declared. "There would be no fear, no awe."

Joyblood hesitated.

Bone jumped to the cobblestones. "But if not that, consider this. For eighty years, who have been my companions? Not my dalliances, not my clients or rivals or marks. You. We have not been friends. But who has bandied philosophy beneath eclipses and beside battlefields? Who has championed maximum-casualty chess? Who has lit scores of birthday candles, and who has snuffed them?

"We have walked together O deaths, and your shadows have comforted me." Bone regarded his tome. "I fear my ending, but even more I fear the world as revealed in this book. Should one of you vanish, we come closer to that reality."

Silently, the deaths regarded him.

At last Joyblood said, "We are not friends, we three."

Severstrand said, "Do not mock us, Bone, at the end."

"I do not mock, and we are not friends. Do as you will."

He flung the book into the burning hay. It would not be damaged, but for now it would be difficult to touch.

Joyblood lowered his blazing head and edged backward. With his shears Severstrand scratched his cobwebbed chin. They regarded one another.

Then moldy death and blazing death each gave a nod as fleeting as rose petals upon a grave.

They walked toward opposite ends of the alley, but never reached the streets. They dwindled as they went, like birds, then bees, then fireflies, then like the memory of fireflies. And Bone and Gaunt were alone.

She took his hand. "I've spent lifetimes stealing," he said, watching the fire, "but today you have given me something new."

"What will you do now, Thief With One Life?"

He smirked. "To begin, I have an accursed book on my conscience, and no place to hide it. I must find one. It may be a long journey. And, Gaunt, I've forgotten how to live, without the company of deaths."

"There are ways," she said, drawing him closer. "I do not know if Joyblood was correct about me, Bone, but if I swear not to slay you in a fit of passion, perhaps we can learn. For they say the nearness of death awakens certain appetites, and I would like to see for myself."

ABOUT THE AUTHOR

Chris Willrich grew up in Olympia, Washington, where Mount Rainier could seem to materialize out of nowhere on the horizon, where one of the local television stations showed old science fiction movies every Saturday, and where you could bicycle to a drugstore that sold milkshakes, comic books, and issues of *Galaxy* magazine. It's possible he was doomed to want to write fantasy and science fiction.

His first published story, "Little Death," appeared in *Asimov's Science Fiction* in 1994, and after six years and many rejections, his second paid publication, "The Thief with Two Deaths," appeared in *The Magazine of Fantasy & Science Fiction*. For a while he was worried he could only sell stories with the word "death" in the title. Luckily Gaunt and Bone went on from "Thief" to appear in "King Rainjoy's Tears" (*F&SF* July 2002) and many other non-morbidly titled adventures.

He's had a number of interesting jobs, particularly as a copy editor in Guam and a harbor cruise deckhand in Seattle, but his best jobs have been in libraries, especially as a children's librarian in Campbell, California, where he got to indulge his inner ham actor while reading picture books at storytime. He lives in the San Francisco Bay Area with his family and is now writing full time. *The Scroll of Years* is his first novel. Visit him online at www.chris willrich.com.